"The longer we wai[t the further] away the kidnapper gets. I love my son even if you don't."

He dragged her against him, crushing her chest into his. "I love Jake more than life itself. He's my reason for living."

His move left her breathless, the feel of his body against hers more shocking than his accusations.

"Okay, so you love him. What next?"

"We find him."

"Then what are you doing now?"

"Making a mistake," he said, staring down at her, his smoldering black eyes burning into hers. "But for some damned reason, I can't help myself."

"Then don't." She leaned up, pressing her lips to his, which started an avalanche of repercussions neither expected.

Dear Reader,

We hope you enjoy the Western stories
Bundle of Trouble and *Hostage to Thunder Horse*,
written by bestselling Harlequin Intrigue author
Elle James.

Harlequin Intrigue books deal in serious romantic
suspense, keeping you on the edge of your seat
as resourceful, true-to-life women and strong,
fearless men fight for survival.

And don't miss an excerpt of Elle James's
Bodyguard Under Fire at the back of this volume.
Look for *Bodyguard Under Fire,* available
September 2013.

Happy reading,

The Harlequin Intrigue Editors

BUNDLE OF TROUBLE
&
HOSTAGE TO THUNDER HORSE

—

Elle James

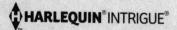

HARLEQUIN® INTRIGUE®

ISBN-13: 978-0-373-68920-0

BUNDLE OF TROUBLE
& HOSTAGE TO THUNDER HORSE

Copyright © 2013 by Harlequin Books S.A.

The publisher acknowledges the copyright holder of the individual works as follows:

BUNDLE OF TROUBLE
Copyright © 2010 by Mary Jernigan

HOSTAGE TO THUNDER HORSE
Copyright © 2010 by Mary Jernigan

Recycling programs for this product may not exist in your area.

This edition published by arrangement with Harlequin Books S.A.

For questions and comments about the quality of this book, please contact us at CustomerService@Harlequin.com.

Printed in U.S.A.

CONTENTS

ABOUT THE AUTHOR

A Golden Heart Award winner for Best Paranormal Romance in 2004, Elle James started writing when her sister issued a Y2K challenge to write a romance novel. She has managed a full-time job and raised three wonderful children, and she and her husband even tried their hands at ranching exotic birds (ostriches, emus and rheas) in the Texas Hill Country. Ask her, and she'll tell you what it's like to go toe-to-toe with an angry 350-pound bird! After leaving her successful career in information technology management, Elle is now pursuing her writing full-time. Elle loves to hear from fans. You can contact her at ellejames@earthlink.net or visit her website at www.ellejames.com.

BUNDLE OF TROUBLE

This book is dedicated to my wonderful editor, Denise Zaza, for having faith in my writing and helping me to grow as a Harlequin author.

Chapter One

Sylvia Michaels balanced tenuously on one long strand of barbed wire as she slung her leg over the fence. So far so good. Sweat dripped from her hairline, running down her forehead toward her eyes. No chance of brushing it away, not when she needed both hands to hold on.

Bowing her legs around the jagged barbs, she perched one foot on the wire and swung her other leg over. As she dropped to the ground, her jeans snagged on a sharp barb, ripping open the denim and tearing into her flesh. She screamed and fell the rest of the way, landing facedown on the ground, coughing up dust, bleeding and wishing this nightmare would end.

Overheated, tired and scared, she worried that this was just one more wild-goose chase she'd rack up on her quest to find her child. Adding to her stress, someone had been following her for the past couple days since she'd left the coroner's office in San Antonio. She choked not only on the fine Texas dirt, but on a sob welling in her throat, despair threatening to take control.

Six months. She'd given up six months of her life to find the son stolen from her in Monterrey, Mexico, last March. He'd be ten months old now. She'd missed seeing him sit up for the first time, missed watching him learn to crawl. Possibly even missed his first word.

Damn it! She pushed to her feet, wiping the tears and dust from her eyes with her dirty hand. She hadn't come this far to fail. She hadn't risked her life investigating a potential baby-theft ring terrorizing mothers from Mexico to Texas. She'd been the only one to come forward and give a detailed description of the person who'd stolen her child. None of the other witnesses in Monterrey had seen the man's face or had the guts to identify the perpetrator if they had. She'd gone to the U.S. Embassy in Monterrey when the Mexican police had done nothing.

She should never have brought Jacob to visit her ex-husband. So what if his work made it impossible for him to travel to the States for his scheduled visit? She should have insisted he come to the States. And he'd blamed *her* when a man had knocked her down and taken Jacob from his stroller in broad daylight in a crowded marketplace.

After six months, a half dozen dead ends and completely draining her savings, she'd reached her limit, her last hope—the Vincent Ranch in Texas hill country. She'd followed every lead imaginable from a frightened Mexican woman who barely spoke English to an adoption agency in San Antonio. A child matching her son's description was adopted by Texas multimillionaire Tate Vincent two weeks after her son was abducted. When she'd tracked down the woman who'd signed over the child, she'd found she'd died in a hit-and-run the day before.

Sylvia had tried to get an appointment with Tate Vincent, but his personal assistant made excuses every time and flat-out told her to buzz off. It didn't help that she couldn't be openly honest with his assistant. What chance did she stand against a millionaire in claiming the son he'd adopted was in fact her son? She didn't have money left to fight a lengthy court battle to request an opportunity to even get close to the boy. All she had was the cash left in her wallet, beneath her car seat.

After all this time, Sylvia wanted desperately to see Jacob, to hold him in her arms, to hear his baby voice.

Sylvia had hidden her car a mile away behind brush, near a creek along the highway. She moved among the shadows to avoid detection, keeping close to a stand of dwarfed live oaks. A large field stretched in front of her, rising up a hillside with only scattered clumps of cedar and live oak. She hurried from shade patch to shade patch, sweat oozing from every pore.

When she'd left her car, her temperature gauge read ninety-eight. It felt more like well over one hundred. Her gaze darted from side to side, and she listened for sounds of people, horses or motor vehicles. As she topped the rise in the terrain, the Vincent ranch house came into view, a large, sprawling, white limestone one-story with a wraparound deck.

Her gaze panned the exterior, searching for movement. Careful to stay out of sight, she made a wide circle around the homestead until she rounded the front of the house. She paused in the shade of a tree, leaning against the gnarly trunk and squinting in the haze of dust and heat. Then she gasped, exhaustion, dehydration and hope bringing her to her knees.

There in the shadow of a large red oak stood a playpen. Leaning against one side was a baby tossing toys onto the grass. The wind ruffled the leaves on the shade tree, and a ray of sunlight found its way through the branches to the baby, gleaming off his head.

Sylvia clapped a hand to her mouth to keep from crying out. The baby had a cap of pale blond hair, highlighted by the sun's beam. It had to be Jacob. Her baby had spun-gold hair just like hers.

She staggered to her feet and pushed away from the tree, stumbling down the hillside toward the ranch house.

TATE VINCENT SLIPPED his right foot out of the stirrup and slid from the back of Diablo, his black quarterhorse stallion, one of the many horses he'd raised from a colt, since they could afford quality horses on the ranch. When his boots hit the dry Texas soil, a cloud of dust puffed up around him. "Need rain."

His foreman, C. W. Middleton, snorted. "Needed rain a month ago." He reached for Tate's reins, his own gelding tugging to get into the barn. "Let me take Diablo. I thought I heard Jake out in the yard. You go on—I'll manage the horses."

Tate grinned. "I'll take you up on that as soon as I get Diablo's saddle off. And remind me I owe you one."

"You don't owe me nothin'. You're the boss. I'm just hired help."

"Bull. We both know who runs this place." Tate followed C.W. into the cool shadows of the barn, tying Diablo to the outside of his stall. "You've been more than hired help since Dad died." He pulled at the thick leather strap, loosening the girth around Diablo's belly. When the strap dangled free, he lifted the saddle off the beast. The saddle blanket was drenched in sweat and coated in a heavy layer of fine Texas dust from their ride along the northern fence line. "Jake was asleep when we left this morning. I would like to see him again before he goes down for the night."

"Go on. Get out of here." Brush in hand, C.W. took over the care and grooming of Diablo, urging Tate out the door. "That boy thinks the sun rises and sets on you. 'Bout time you spent a little more daylight with him."

C.W. had been his friend since they'd met as army recruits. They'd gone on to Special Forces training and Afghanistan where they'd tracked down the al Qaeda rebels in the desert hills. Ranching in Texas seemed tame in comparison. But C.W. had fit right in, learning all the responsibilities of a good ranch hand. He'd learned how to ride, rope, brand and mend fences in a matter of weeks, too stubborn to admit defeat. Just like the boss. When the foreman had passed on, C.W. stepped up to the plate, assuming the role like he'd been born to do it.

Tate crossed the hard-packed ground between the barn and the Vincent homestead established by his great-great-grandfather in the mid-eighteen hundreds. He had to remind himself that he could hire people to do the work he did out in the field. The ranch wasn't what made him the money. His investments had taken him from struggling rancher to multimillionaire in just five years. Too bad his father hadn't lived longer to enjoy his son's success.

Richard Vincent had passed on five months earlier, his presence still missed by his son and the ranch staff. He hadn't gotten to know Jake a little better and Jake wouldn't know his grandfather.

Tate flexed his muscles, rolling the tension and weariness from his shoulders. Sure, he had the money to hire more ranch hands, but he liked the hard work. It kept him humble. At one point in his struggle to rise from rags to riches, he thought for sure he'd lose the ranch. He'd lost nearly everything else, including his wife.

Tate's mouth pressed into a thin line. Laura didn't have the stomach for the hard times. When cattle prices had plummeted and the creditors came knocking on their door, she'd packed up and left, stating that she'd only married him because she thought he was a wealthy landowner. Not that he was sad to see her go. He was more upset at having wasted two years of his life on chasing her dreams instead of his own.

When he rounded the corner of the house, he spied a bright blue playpen situated in the shade with his son standing up against the inside of the pen. The child pushed a plush toy over the edge and watched it drop to the ground. Pickles, the black-and-white border collie, barely waited for it to leave Jake's hand before she grabbed it and shook it. Jake giggled and tried to get a leg up over the side of the pen. He liked playing with Pickles.

A swell of love and pride filled Tate's chest. Jake was his reason for living. He would never have thought he'd become so completely besotted over a kid. At the urging of his dying father, he'd arranged to adopt a baby boy. He'd paid big bucks to skip over the usual routine of social services snooping around his home, going directly to an adoption agency his executive assistant had located, one that specialized in quick adoptions. Pricey, but quick.

Now he couldn't put a price tag on what Jake brought to the Vincent household. Disappointed that Tate hadn't remarried and had a dozen grandchildren for him to spoil, Richard Vincent's dying wish was to hold his grandchild in his arms.

Tate stopped in front of the playpen.

When Jake saw him, his smile widened and he gurgled, reaching up with one hand.

"*Por favor,* don't pick him up, Señor Vincent." Rosa Garcia hurried forward, a frown on her pretty dark face. "*Usted está muy sucio.* Dirty. You are dirty."

"A little dirt never hurt a kid." Despite her admonishment, Tate lifted his son from the playpen and tossed him in the air.

Jake screamed and giggled, drool slipping from the side of his mouth to plop against Tate's shirt.

"Poor baby is still teething." Rosa reached out with a burp cloth to wipe up the drool.

Tate didn't care. He loved Jake more than anyone on God's green earth. Besides, a little spit was an improvement to his dust-caked clothing. "Hey, buddy. Have you and Pickles been playing fetch?"

"Da, da, da," Jake said.

Tate's eyes widened and a grin spread across his face. "Did you hear that? He just called me Dad."

Rosa's dark brown eyes rolled skyward. "He says that to me and *mi madré.*"

Tate frowned. "Give a guy a break, will ya?" He tossed Jake into the air again, making the boy squeal with delight.

"*Madré de Dios.*" Rosa hurried forward, reaching for Jake. "He just had a bottle of juice. Unless you want to wear the juice, don't shake him up so much."

Tate held Jake away from Rosa. "It's a little hot for him outside, isn't it?"

"We've only been out for *quince minutos*. Mama is cooking supper, Señorita Kacee drove to town to drop off papers at FedEx. *Por favor,* let me have Jake. You should shower before dinner is served."

Tate handed the child over to his caregiver, chucking him beneath his chin. "Okay, for now. I guess I am a little dirty."

Rosa plugged her nose, shaking her head. "Understatement." She balanced Jake on her hip and headed for the porch steps.

"Wait!" A shout from the field behind him made Tate turn.

A woman wearing jeans and a smudged white shirt—her hair flying out in long, blond strands—ran across the field, yelling, "Wait!"

Tate's brows dipped low. The fences along his property were posted with no trespassing signs. Only people with legitimate business were allowed access past the gate with clearance from his security service.

The woman's face was red and streaked with dirt and sweat. Her jeans were torn with blood staining the ragged edges, and she had a wild look in her eyes.

Tate shot a glance at Rosa. "Take Jake inside."

"Who do you think she is?" Rosa asked, clutching the baby to her chest.

"Do as I say," Tate bit out.

"*Sí,* Señor Vincent."

Rosa had been his buddy since childhood, having grown up on the Vincent Ranch alongside him. Why she insisted on calling him Señor Vincent was beyond him. With a wild woman crossing the field toward them, now wasn't the time to argue the point.

Rosa climbed the steps and hurried inside the house,

Jake reaching over her shoulders, a wail rising from his little mouth.

"No! Please! Don't take him away!" The woman came to a halt at the wooden fence surrounding the yard. She grabbed the top rail and hauled herself up.

"Stop where you are." Tate didn't want her anywhere close to the house and his son. A crazy man who'd gotten past security had ultimately been the cause of his father's death five months ago. He refused to take any intrusion onto his property lightly. Without waiting for the woman to cross the fence, Tate marched across the manicured lawn.

Perched precariously on the top rail, the blonde swayed and fell over the fence, landing with a crash, her head hitting the post with a sharp crack.

When Tate reached her, she lay on the ground, her eyes staring up at the sky, blinking.

For a moment, Tate forgot to be angry with her.

Dirty and sweat soaked, she was still a beautiful woman beneath the layer of smeared dust. When fat tears rolled out of the corners of her pale blue eyes, Tate couldn't help a sudden swell of protectiveness. He chalked it up to the fact that her eyes were the same pale blue as Jake's.

He dropped down beside her, forcing his voice to sound stern and distant when his instincts urged him to pick her up and carry her into his house. "Who the hell are you, and what are you doing on private property?"

She raised a hand to her head, and scraped it over her eyes. "Please. I only want to see him."

Tate's brows furrowed. "See who?"

"My son," she said, her voice wavering, dropping

down to a whisper. Her eyes closed, and the woman had the nerve to pass out.

"Damned woman." His gut knotted and Tate swore. What did she mean by "my son"? He reached down and shook her. "Wake up."

She didn't budge.

He bent low, pressing his head to her chest to listen for breathing.

Although shallow, her breaths came regularly. Impatience gnawed at him. He couldn't shake her awake to answer his questions, and he couldn't really leave her out in the full force of the Texas sun. With his luck, her fall might have given her a concussion.

"Whatcha got there, boss?" C.W. trotted up beside him. When he got close enough to see the woman on the ground, he whistled. "Another stray?"

Tate glared at his foreman. "Looks like it."

"Want me to call the sheriff?"

"No." Why he didn't do just that, he couldn't explain. Something about the way she'd looked up at him, her gaze pleading with his, made him want to question her before he turned her over to the sheriff. Maybe she'd been mistaken, gotten the wrong place, hallucinated due to dehydration. She couldn't mean Jake. Jake couldn't be her son. He'd met Jake's mother. She'd signed the papers allowing him to adopt the boy. This woman was a stranger.

"If you're not going to call the sheriff, do you want me to call an ambulance?" C.W. rocked back on his boot heels. "Looks like she hit her head, and she's got a gash in her leg."

Tate's frown deepened. "No."

"Can't just leave her in the sun. She'll die of heat-stroke."

He knew that, still he hesitated. "She's trespassing."

"Maybe so, but she is another human being. If you leave her here, you could be up on charges of negligent homicide."

If he took her into his house and she threatened his son, he'd be up on charges of murder, anyway.

C.W. bent and reached for the woman.

"Don't." Tate held out his hand, blocking the man's attempt to lift her. "I'll get her." With all the trepidation of a man cornering a poisonous snake, Tate lifted the woman into his arms. Thin, light and limp, she had curves in all the right places and a soft pink mouth much too close to his own for him to think straight. What did she want? And why did he have this feeling that he wouldn't like what she had to say?

Morbid curiosity made him carry her into the cool air-conditioned interior of his home. He'd force-feed fluid into her and get her back on her feet, hear what she had to say and then send her packing. If that didn't work, then he'd call the sheriff and have her forcibly removed.

Rosa stood in the living room, Jake propped on her hip. "Who is she?"

"I don't know." Tate shot a pointed look at Jake's caregiver, a woman he'd hired not only for her skills with a child, but also for her skills as a bodyguard. A former Austin police officer, she had a proven track record taking out bad guys. "Take Jake to the nursery."

"But it's dinnertime."

"Feed him dinner in his room."

"Sí, señor."

He laid the woman on the brown leather sofa in the living room.

Maria, Rosa's mother and also the housekeeper, entered through the doorway leading to the kitchen, carrying a damp rag and a glass of ice water.

Tate took the damp rag and laid it across the woman's forehead, mopping away a layer of dust and sweat. "Wake up, lady," he muttered, willing her eyes to open.

"Get her to drink," Maria urged.

Tate lifted the woman in one arm and touched the cool glass to her lips, letting the liquid slide down her throat.

At first the liquid filled her mouth and trickled out the sides. Then she swallowed and coughed, her eyes blinking open.

"What…" she said, her voice hoarse, her gaze blurred. "Are you—" she coughed again "—Tate Vincent?"

He frowned. She knew who he was, which meant she'd found her way to his place on purpose. Was she just another gold digger out to get money from him? "Yes," he answered, his tone clipped. "Who are you?"

Her eyes closed for a moment and then opened again. "I think you have my baby." After delivering that punch in the gut, the woman had the audacity to pass out again.

Chapter Two

Something blessedly cool stroked across Sylvia's fore-head as she swam through the murkiness inside her head. A deep baritone hummed in the back of her mind, pulling her closer to the light. When the strokes moved to her cheek, she turned her face into the coolness and surfaced, her mind inching toward clarity. "Ummm, that feels good."

"Glad you think so. I'd appreciate it if you'd wake up before the sheriff arrives."

Sylvia's eyes popped open and she stared up into intense, brown eyes, so dark they could be considered black. A man with midnight-black hair and thick dark brows drawn into a frown glared down at her.

Fear and something else shot through her veins, pushing her to a sitting position. As soon as she sat up, her head swam and her world turned fuzzy around the edges. When she would have toppled over onto the floor, strong arms circled her shoulders and cased her back to cool leather.

"Who are you?" she asked as she edged one eye open and attempted a look around. All she could see was the broad chest and intimidating glare of the incredibly sexy man in front of her. He smelled of dust, sweat and leather. Very earthy and tremendously appealing.

"We'd already established the fact that I'm Tate Vincent. You're trespassing on my property." The man's countenance didn't change, except the glare deepened until his black eyes shot sparks. "Who the hell are you?"

She sighed, draping an arm over her brow to block out her unwanted attraction to the grouchy man. "Sylvia Michaels." As her vision cleared, so too did her memory. After a moment, she dropped her arm, her eyes widening. "You're Tate Vincent?" She sighed. "Oh, thank God."

"Don't be thanking Him yet. Give me one good reason why I shouldn't have you hauled off to jail for trespassing."

"I'm sorry. I tried to get an appointment to see you, but your assistant wouldn't give me one."

"That's why I have an assistant." His frown deepened, his face fierce. "Now that you have my attention, what exactly do you want?"

She stared up at him, her determination wavering briefly under his angry countenance. "I'm here because there's a good possibility that you have my child."

For a moment he said nothing. The only sign he had heard her was the muscle ticking dangerously in his jaw. "How much do you want?"

Sylvia's brow furrowed. "Want? What do you mean?"

"Most people who trespass or sneak onto my property want something, usually money. What's your price?"

Anger and indignation shot into her veins, stiffening her spine and forcing her back into an upright position. This time her vision didn't waver. "I don't want anything from you. I only want my child."

"And what makes you think I have him?"

Her eyes widened and a gasp whooshed from her lips. "The baby I saw outside is a boy?" Joy filled her chest. "I knew it," she said, her happiness stealing breath from her lungs. "How is he? Where is he?" She leaned to the side to look around Tate.

Strong fingers gripped her arms, forcing her to look at him. "I don't know what kind of game you're playing, but I don't have your son."

She took a deep, steadying breath. "Did you adopt a child about six months ago?"

"Anyone who follows the gossip columns would know the answer to that." The muscle ticked in his jaw again. "Besides, it's none of your business."

If she wasn't mistaken, she'd scored a hit and she wasn't backing off until she got answers. She stared up at him, her mouth firming into a determined line. "It is my business if that child was stolen from me."

"You're wrong. I met the mother of my son. She signed the papers in front of an attorney swearing the child was hers and that she was giving away all legal rights to him."

"Was her name Beth Kirksey?"

Tate's eyes narrowed. "And if it was?"

"She wasn't the mother of the baby you adopted. The birth certificate was forged. She'd given up her real baby for adoption four months earlier. The baby she gave you was mine."

"I don't believe you." He reached for the cell phone in his back pocket. "A quick call will confirm."

"Don't bother. Ms. Kirksey won't be answering."

"Why?"

"She's dead." Sylvia swallowed hard. "She was killed in a hit-and-run 'accident' a week ago."

"I'm calling the sheriff." He stood, towering above her.

If he'd intimidated her before, he terrified her now. Well over six feet tall, his massive presence and his ferocious scowl could stop an angry bull in its tracks.

But Sylvia hadn't come this far or risked this much to give up now. "Just let me see him. Please."

"No way. For all I know, you're crazy and might hurt my son. You'd do well to get the hell out of my house now while I'm feeling generous enough to let you go without a police escort."

Sylvia crossed her arms over her chest. "I'm not leaving until I see my son."

"We'll see about that." He nodded to the man standing in the doorway. "C.W., call the sheriff."

"Will do, boss."

"Wait." Sylvia couldn't afford to waste time in jail. She had to see her son. "I can prove he's my son."

"Yeah, and I'm the King of Hearts." Tate turned away. "I don't have time for this nonsense. Keep an eye on her, will you, C.W.?"

Sylvia rose from the couch, swaying but determined, and reached for his arm before he could walk away. "He has blond hair and blue eyes just like mine, doesn't he?"

"So what if he does? His mother had blond hair and blue eyes."

"Does your son have a star-shaped strawberry birthmark on his right hip?"

About to take a step, the man stopped in midstride, his back to her, his body rigid. "That proves nothing."

Her hand tightened on his arm, her nails digging in. Then she let go, her fingers going to her waistband. She loosened the button of her jeans and unzipped the fly. Then with a deep breath, she shoved the jeans down low enough to expose her right hip. "Does it look like this?"

The man Tate had called C.W. stopped in the doorway and let out a long, low wolf whistle.

Tate's chest expanded and contracted before he finally stared down at the mark on her hip. "How do I know that's real?"

"Touch it," she said, her voice catching in her throat. The thought of the big cowboy touching her made her tingle all over, but she held steady. She had to do this to get her son back.

His hand came out and he rubbed a work-roughened thumb across the birthmark. "It could be a tattoo."

Sylvia's breath caught in her chest and she held it for a moment before replying, electric current tingling throughout her body from where his fingers touched her. "You know it's not. It's as real as the one on my son's hip." She pulled her jeans up and zipped. "Can I see him now?"

His mouth drew into a tight, forbidding line. Then he caught her by her arms and shook her. "Get it through your head, he's not your son! Now, get out of my house." He practically flung her away from him.

Steadying herself against the back of the couch, Sylvia struggled to remain calm. Even with Tate breathing fire down on her, she refused to give up. "Not without my son."

"You won't see him without a court order. I'll be contacting my lawyer. I suggest you contact yours."

Sylvia's heart dropped to her stomach. She didn't

have a nickel left in her account and she'd been living on credit cards for the past month until they had maxed out. A long court battle would be way out of her league. She flung her long hair back and stood with her shoulders squared, her feet wide, hands propped on her hips. All she had left was false bravado and her conviction that she'd really found her son. "If you want me to leave, you'll have to call the sheriff. I'm not going anywhere until I see my son."

"Let me remind you who is trespassing and who is within legal rights to shoot you."

"Wouldn't be the first time I've been shot at trying to find my son. Go ahead." Inside she shook, but she refused to show him an ounce of fear. "I want to see the son stolen from me in Mexico six months ago."

"What's it going to take to convince you that he's not your son?"

"Show me his right hip. If the birthmark isn't there, I'll leave, no argument." Sylvia held her chin high and when her mouth threatened to tremble, she bit down hard on her lower lip.

Tate sucked in a deep breath and let it out. It did nothing to calm the racing beat of his heart. He sucked in another breath and tried again. But as long as the woman who claimed to be his son's mother stood in his living room, he couldn't get enough air into his lungs.

After all the years he'd begged Laura for children… then she'd left and his father had died. Tate refused to give up the only family he had left. Ever since he'd adopted Jake, he'd had that niggling worry in the back of his mind that someone would someday come and claim him. Hadn't he seen court cases where the mother came back and claimed she'd been wrong to let her child go? Never afraid of anything in his life, Tate feared losing Jake. He stiffened.

No way in hell.

"C.W., help me load this woman into the truck so we can kick her off the ranch."

C.W.'s lips curled upward. "Gladly." As he walked toward Sylvia, his grin widened. "If you don't mind me saying, I wish it had been me touching that birthmark, ma'am."

Sylvia raised her fists to a fighting position and squared off with C.W. "Touch me, and I'll break every one of your fingers. I won't leave until I see my son."

Tate shook his head. "Lady, I don't know what happened to *your* son, but since you're not going to see *my* son, you might as well shove off."

The front door to the house slammed open. "Tate?" Kacee LeBlanc's heels clicked across the hardwood floors in double time. "What's with the fire down by the creek?" She jerked to a halt when she spied Sylvia with her fists up. "Who the hell's she?"

Tate nodded toward Sylvia. "This woman claims to be Jake's mother."

"That's just bull. I was there when the real birth mother signed over the child. She didn't look anything like this woman. Other than the blond hair." Kacee whipped out her cell phone. "Have you called the sheriff?"

"We were just about to do that." Tate stared pointedly at Sylvia. "Care to leave before he gets here?"

"You call him Jake?" Sylvia smiled. "My son's name is Jacob."

"I don't care what *your* son's name is. He's *my* son."

"I'm not budging until I see the baby."

"Oh, you'll be budging, all right." Tate nodded to Kacee. "Make that call."

She punched a button on her cell phone. While she waited for an answer, she frowned. "There's a fire down by the creek. You might want to get some of the ranch hands on it before it spreads."

"Fire?" C.W.'s brows rose. "Damn. As dry as it is, it'll spread fast." He nodded at Tate. "You can handle her on your own?"

"Go. We can't afford a range fire. Take Dalton, Cody and anyone else who's back from the south range."

"Will do." C.W. ran out of the room.

"Yes, we have an emergency. This is Kacee LeBlanc out at the Vincent Ranch. We have a fire by the highway near Rocky Creek. We also have a trespasser at the ranch house." Kacee's steel-gray gaze scraped Sylvia from head to toe. "Send the sheriff. The woman claims to be Jake's mother and refuses to leave. Thirty? That's the best he can do? Okay. Thank you." She flipped her cell phone shut and tilted her head to the side. "The sheriff will be here soon." She crossed the room to Tate and touched his arm. "Want me to get a gun, Tate? You know you can shoot trespassers, especially if they're threatening you or a loved one." Her voice was hard, her words menacing. She meant to scare the woman across the room, dressed in a dirty shirt and jeans, looking like she'd been run through the wringer of his grandmother's old-timey washing machine.

Despite her threat to his son, Tate didn't like where Kacee was going. "No. I reckon she's harmless."

Kacee leaned in to whisper, her breath warm on his ear. "That's what you thought about that homeless man who stabbed your father."

A band tightened around Tate's chest. "That's enough, Kacee." But he wasn't taking any chances. He walked to the desk in the far corner of the room, removed a gun from the drawer and dropped the clip from the chamber. From another drawer he retrieved bullets, sliding them into the clip. "But it doesn't hurt to be cautious."

"Good grief. I'm not here to hurt anyone. I only want my son." Sylvia Michaels, eyes wide and face pale, backed toward the door, her hands raised.

"Take one more step, and I'll shoot," Tate warned.

She paused for only a moment, her gaze connecting with his, determination hardening her chin. Then she spun around, throwing her parting comment over her shoulder. "Then just shoot me."

Chapter Three

With a gun pointed at her back, Sylvia's skin crawled, but she pushed forward, headed for a hallway and the sound of a baby squealing happily.

"Damned woman." The cowboy cursed behind her, his boots clattering against the wooden flooring.

"Give me the gun, Tate. I'll shoot her," the woman Sylvia assumed was the assistant called out.

If Sylvia had any chance at all of seeing Jacob, she'd have to move faster than the two people behind her. She shot away from the man holding the gun, her heart pounding in her chest. Several doors opened off the hallway, only one remained closed and the joyous sounds of a baby could be heard through the wood paneling. Without slowing, she grabbed the handle and opened the door.

A large hand clamped down so hard on her shoulder she jerked to a halt, unable to move another step.

She caught a glimpse of a baby boy sitting in a high chair, a cracker clutched in his fist. All she got was that little peek before Tate Vincent flung her around and shoved her against the hallway wall. "You hurt one hair on my son's head and I'll kill you."

With the door wide open, the sounds of the baby's

cooing reached her, warmth spreading throughout her body, filling all the cold, empty places she'd endured since Jacob had been stolen away from her in Mexico. Tears welled in her eyes, blurring her vision. "Please." She sniffed, unashamed of begging for a chance to see her son. "Please. I want to see him. If he's not mine, I'll leave."

For a long moment, the man glared down at her, his heavy hand never leaving her shoulder. Based on his size, he'd probably be ten times stronger than her. More than Sylvia could hope to fight off, but she would do anything to see Jacob again.

"You say your son was abducted six months ago. How will you recognize him besides the birthmark? Babies change a lot in six months."

"I'll know," she said. Didn't mothers always know the cries of their own babies? After six months of searching, she'd almost given up hope. Could this cowboy be right? Would she recognize her son? Her shoulders pushed back and she wiped the tears from her eyes with an angry hand. "I'll know."

Another long moment passed, Tate's eyes narrowing into slits. "How do I know you're not here to hurt him?"

"Oh, God." A nervous, almost hysterical laugh escaped her lips. "I wouldn't hurt my own son. I've spent the past six months looking for him, hoping no one has hurt him. I just want to see him. That's all I ask." She'd work on custody once she was satisfied the baby truly was Jacob. "Don't you see? You could be just as much a victim as I am. My baby was stolen. Your baby could have been signed over to you illegally."

"I met the mother, she signed the papers, I adopted

him. My lawyer went over the paperwork at least a dozen times."

"Still, you could have been duped. The baby may not have been that woman's to give."

He smacked the hand holding the gun flat against the wall. "The contract was ironclad. You're a liar!"

Sylvia winced, but stared up at him, meeting his glare with a level stare. "I don't lie."

"And if my son has this birthmark, that doesn't prove anything."

"Maybe not. If the birthmark is there, then we do a DNA test." How she'd come up with the money, she didn't know, but she'd get her baby back if she had to sell her soul to the devil himself.

The baby giggled in the next room, so joyous and innocent.

All the motherly longing she'd buried deep inside surged into her chest, squeezing her lungs so hard she couldn't breathe. "Just let me see him."

The man's eyes narrowed even more. "I don't trust you."

"Search me. I'm not carrying any weapons. I only want to see if he has the birthmark. I won't try to take him away. I won't hurt him." Her voice caught on a sob, rising up to choke her. "I need to know."

"You're not buying this crap, are you?" The woman in the business suit stood with her hands held out in front of her, a small pistol clutched between her fingers.

Tate Vincent shot a stern look at her. "Put the gun down, Kacee."

The beautiful assistant pouted. "You take away all my fun."

"Put it down." Tate stared at Sylvia, his words directed at Kacee. "I can handle this. I don't want my son injured by a stray bullet."

The other woman's hand lowered. "Good point. Besides, the sheriff should be here any moment."

"Why don't you go watch for him."

Kacee frowned. "But, what if…"

"Just go," Tate bit out. "I can handle this." He stared down at Sylvia, his steely brown-eyed gaze boring into her. When Kacee rounded the corner, he growled, "Why should I believe any of this?"

Tired, dizzy and beyond her endurance, Sylvia stared back at the millionaire who could have had her physically removed by now, but for some unknown reason hadn't. "If you had your child stolen from you, would you just let him go?"

The man holding her arm continued to glare, the silence lengthening between them. When Sylvia thought he wouldn't respond to her question, the man sighed, his grip loosening. "No. I would never stop looking."

"Exactly." Hope blossomed in her chest, a smile trembling on her lips. "Then you'll let me see him?"

His hold stiffened. "I didn't say that."

She raised her hand to peel his fingers loose from her arm. "Please. I've been searching for so long. If there is any chance the baby in there is mine…"

For a brief moment, Tate's face grew haggard, then his mouth tightened, the expression returning to the cold hard mask of a harsh businessman. "Are you prepared if the boy isn't yours?"

"If he has the birthmark—"

"I repeat, the birthmark proves nothing." Tate's hand squeezed tighter. She'd have a bruise there by morning.

"If he has the birthmark, will you agree to a DNA

test?" To be this close was killing her. "Look, I know this can't be easy for you, either. You've had Jacob for the past six months. I only had him for four." She gave a watery smile. "But I remember what a good baby he was, always laughing and happy. If he's like he was back then, anyone would fall in love with the little guy. His smile could light up a room."

"I'm going to let you go. Don't try anything." Tate's hand loosened and dropped to his side.

Sylvia closed her eyes and sent a silent prayer to the heavens. Then she opened them again. "Then, you'll let me see him?"

"On one condition."

"Name it."

"You can't touch him. I don't want you anywhere close to my son."

Sylvia dragged in a deep breath and let it go. Her arms ached with the need to hold her son, but she could wait a little bit longer. She swallowed hard. "Okay."

Tate sensed that by showing the woman his son, everything would change. But the look in her eyes, the desperate plea to see the boy tugged at Tate's heart. This dusty woman who'd defied his "no trespassing" signs, crossed long distances, chased leads and finally made it to his home showed a courage he hadn't seen in the women he'd known. *If* everything she said was true. Not that he believed any of it, yet.

The thought of having Jake stolen from him made his stomach clench into a bigger knot than he could have imagined.

"Señor Vincent?" Rosa, clutching Jake against her chest, peered around the door. "Is everything okay?"

The golden-haired child spied him, squealed and

reached out for Tate. Instinctively, he held out his arms for his son. Jake fell into them, giggling.

Over the top of his son's golden head, Tate could see the trespasser's eyes fill with tears, spilling over and running down her cheeks. Her hand rose as if to touch Jake.

Tate stepped back, out of reach.

Her hand fell to her side. "Will you look?" she whispered.

He told himself it didn't matter if his son had the star-shaped birthmark. Nothing short of a DNA test would convince him. But the pale blue of his son's gaze reflected through the sheen of tears in the woman's eyes. The bright gold cap of silky smooth hair resembled that of the woman with the long, straight, blond locks.

"Please," she said, her voice a quiet entreaty in the hallway.

His heart heavy, Tate pulled the tape tab from the right side of Jake's disposable diaper and pushed the plastic and cotton aside.

There on his right hip was a light red birthmark in the shape of a star.

Sylvia gasped. "Oh, God, oh, God…I've found him." Then she sank to the floor, burying her head in her hands, silent sobs shaking her narrow frame.

"Tate, the sheriff's here." Kacee's heels clicked a sharp staccato on the smooth, Mexican terra-cotta tiles. "He wants to talk to you. I told him about her." His assistant's brows rose as her gaze found Sylvia on the floor. "Good Lord, did she pass out again?"

"Rosa, take Jake to the kitchen and let him finish his meal there." Tate handed his son to his caregiver and squatted beside the overcome interloper. "You come with me." He held out his hand.

When she placed her hand in his, he couldn't ignore the spark of electricity, the flare of desire he'd felt. She was just a crazy woman out to take his son away from him. Most likely, she was after more. Maybe she wanted to blackmail him.

But the watery blue eyes staring up at him were just like Jake's and had a similar melting quality that affected him more than he'd likely admit. Angry with himself for feeling anything for this person who claimed Jake was hers, who threatened to take away the only family Tate had left, he jerked her up off the floor.

Sylvia came up so fast, she slammed into his chest. His arm came up around her narrow waist, steadying her against him.

Her breath caught on a gasp, her fingers laying flat against his shirt, her eyes wide. "I...I can stand on my own." She gave a light push to free herself.

"Sure you can." For some reason he couldn't let go, his arm slipping around her waist. Mistake, his brain warned. "You've already fainted once. I refuse to give you another opportunity to bring a lawsuit against me." The lawsuit of his life loomed like a dark cloud of doom. If Jake truly was her child, he'd be in a hellacious court fight like no other.

He steered her toward the living room. Her gaze darted toward the kitchen doorway as they passed, Jake's giggles carrying through. "I've found him," she whispered, a smile curving her lips.

"Don't count your chickens, lady," Tate grumbled. "You're trespassing on private property."

Sheriff Thompson stood in the living room, his hat in his hand. "Mr. Vincent." He nodded.

"Sheriff." Tate guided Sylvia to a seat and pressed her into it.

"Ms. LeBlanc tells me you have a trespasser." He tipped his head toward Sylvia. "This the one?"

Tate didn't look at Sylvia. "Yes."

The woman in question gasped. "I only wanted to see my child. How can that be a crime?"

"You want to file charges, Mr. Vincent?" Sheriff Thompson crossed the living room and stood in front of Sylvia, his feet parted, his hands fiddling with the case containing the handcuffs attached to his utility belt.

The blonde stared across at Tate, that same desperation in her eyes gnawing away at the knot in his gut. Damn it! He didn't need this. "No," he said.

"Are you crazy?" Kacee marched over to him and laid a hand on his arm. "Remember what happened to your father? Are you willing to let something like that happen to Jake?"

Tate finally turned and stared into Sylvia's eyes. "I really don't think she'll hurt Jake."

"You willing to bet Jake's life on that?" Kacee planted hands on her hips. When Tate refused to meet her eyes, his gaze still on Sylvia, Kacee threw her hands in the air. "Don't get mad when I tell you I told you so."

Sylvia stood, her mouth pressed into a thin line. "If you don't feel comfortable with my being around Jacob, I'll leave with the sheriff. But I promise I'll be back for my son."

Tate's gaze nailed hers. "For the moment, she can stay."

Sheriff Thompson shrugged. "Okay, then maybe you

can tell me whose car it is burned up in the creek outside your property?"

Sylvia's gaze shifted to the sheriff. "A car in the creek? Was it a Ford Escort?"

The sheriff's eyes narrowed. "Yes, ma'am."

"That's my car!" Sylvia's hand rose to her mouth.

"Sorry, lady. It's totaled. Looks like someone didn't like where you parked."

"What do you mean?"

The sheriff shook his head, his mouth a thin line. "Someone lit a rag and stuffed it in the gas tank. By the time we got to it, it was already history."

Chapter Four

Sylvia sank onto the couch, suddenly light-headed. "That's all had left," she whispered. Worse, it confirmed her worst fears. Someone had been following her since she'd left San Antonio. Burning her car had been a message.

Dear God, the car had been her home for the past few weeks. She'd let her apartment go, sold her furniture and everything else to allow her to continue her search. Now that she'd found Jacob…what next?

How could she start over when she didn't have enough money in her bank account for a cup of coffee and all her credit cards were maxed out? She didn't have enough money to hire a cab to take her back to town, much less hire a lawyer to sue for custody. Despair, fear, joy—the emotions drained every last bit of fight left in her.

No car and no money meant she'd never get her child back. Even if she did, would she provide a safe home for him? Who was after her? What did he want? Why burn her car? Her head spun with the unending barrage of questions.

Then she heard a child's happy squeal echoing against the walls. Her back stiffened and she forced herself to a standing position, facing the sheriff. "That was my car, Sheriff."

"Since it appears to be arson, we have to have it towed to the impound lot for a thorough investigation. I'll need a statement from both you and Mr. Vincent, seeing as how the car was found in the creek, which is part of Mr. Vincent's property."

"Were there any tracks or clues as to who might have done it?" Tate asked.

Sheriff Thompson shook his head. "I arrived just minutes before the pump truck. They sucked every last drop of their tank dry putting out the fire and tamping down the dry brush around the site. Nothing left but mud and ashes." He turned to Sylvia. "Why did you park in the creek anyway, Ms…?"

"Michaels, Sylvia Michaels." Sylvia swallowed and looked down at her dirty hands. "I needed to see Mr. Vincent." She glanced up, her gaze clashing with Tate's.

His brown eyes narrowed and he shook his head slightly, almost imperceptibly.

Sylvia turned toward the sheriff. "On a personal matter."

"So you trespassed." Sheriff Thompson's brows rose. "You sure you didn't light the fire in the car yourself?"

"No, sir." Nor could she tell either of the men that she thought she was in danger. What court in the land would give her custody of any child if they thought her unfit to provide a safe haven for him?

"Really, Tate, you trust this woman in your home? She just admitted to hiding her car so that she could get in to see you." Kacee rolled her eyes. "If that isn't crazy, I don't know what is."

"It's up to you, Mr. Vincent. I'm headed back to town. I can take her with me. Just say the word."

Tate Vincent stared at Sylvia for a long, drawn-out moment.

Her heart hammered blood through her veins, pounding against her eardrums, but she refused to look away from his intense gaze. She pushed her shoulders back and her chin tipped upward just slightly. If she had to, she'd beg to stay. But for now, he needed to know she wasn't backing down.

"She can stay." His eyes narrowed even more. "For now."

Kacee snorted. "Tate, be reasonable."

"Thank you, Sheriff Thompson. Let us know what you find out about the car." Tate walked toward the front entrance, opened the door and held it for the sheriff.

The sheriff gave Sylvia one last look, plunked his hat on his head and took the hint. "I'll be in touch."

Once the sheriff had descended the stairs and climbed into his SUV with the word "Sheriff" marked in bold letters on both sides, Tate let the screen door swing shut.

Sylvia braced herself for the storm to come.

"What are you going to do with her now?" Kacee asked, her high-heeled foot tapping against the wooden floor.

"On your way home, contact Dr. Richards. Tell him I want a DNA sampling kit out here ASAP."

Kacee flipped her phone open. "I'll just call him now."

Tate glared at her. "Do it on your way out, Kacee. I don't need your services for the rest of the afternoon."

"But—"

The man stopped her next words with the look on his face.

Sylvia almost felt sorry for the woman, except for the fact she would have happily shot her for trespassing. Once the millionaire's assistant left, Sylvia would be alone with Tate Vincent. In his current mood, the meeting wouldn't be pleasant. But at least she could speak plainly when they were alone.

She'd let him know she'd fight with every last breath to get her son back. But she wouldn't tell him her breath and the clothes on her back were all she had left to her name.

Tate stood at the door, holding it open much as he'd done for the sheriff. Kacee pouted, her brows drawing together as she gathered her briefcase and car keys. "We haven't gone over the figures on the purchase of the Double Diamond Ranch."

"Tomorrow." He held the door and waved his hand, inviting her through.

Kacee sucked in a deep breath and blew it out, crossing the threshold as directed. When she passed by Tate, she leaned close to him. "She's nothing but trouble, I tell you."

"I can handle it."

"I know…without me." She glared over her shoulder at Sylvia.

Tate shut the door behind Kacee and stared after her as she climbed into her car and drove away. Not until her dust trail cleared the driveway did he drag in a deep breath and turn to Sylvia standing quietly behind him.

"You know I'm telling the truth, don't you?" Sylvia whispered. "You know Jacob is my son."

Anger bolted through him. "No, I don't know anything." But that niggle of doubt made him more afraid than any other time in his life. Losing Jake ranked right up there with losing his father. Jake was family. He couldn't lose him. "What other proof do you have that you ever had a child?"

Sylvia reached into the back pocket of her jeans and pulled out a crumpled piece of paper and a tattered photograph. "His birth certificate and a photograph of him when he was four months old." Her lips twisted in a semblance of a smile and she shook her head. "They are the only things I have left of Jacob. Everything else was in my car." Tears filled her eyes, making them a shimmering blue, so like Jake's when he didn't want to lie down for his nap.

Rosa always told Tate to let Jake cry himself to sleep, let him learn to soothe himself. But Tate couldn't, not when the child looked up at him through those liquid blue eyes. He wanted to hold him, make the fear go away, make him know that nothing on the earth would take this child away from him.

Tate's fists tightened and he resisted the draw of Sylvia's blue, watery eyes. He snatched the paper and the photograph from her hands. Prolonging the inevitable, he bent to read the words on the document, etched in permanent ink with the state seal of Texas embossing the corner.

Mother's Maiden Name: Sylvia Leigh Michaels. Father: Miguel Tikas. Baby's Name: Jacob Paul Michaels. The birth date indicated ten months ago.

Ignoring the knot twisting in his gut, Tate handed the paper back to Sylvia, telling himself it was just a piece of paper. It didn't prove anything. Then he stared down at the picture of a baby with golden hair and bright blue eyes. The baby could be Jake six months ago. He had the same smile, the same halo of golden hair. Damn it! Jake was his son!

He clutched the photograph in his hand, his gaze rising to lock with the woman in front of him. "How do I know you really are Sylvia Michaels? That you aren't lying and that you didn't steal this document?"

The dusty blonde fished in her back pocket, pulled out a card and handed it to him. He stared down at the hard plastic of a Texas driver's license. An image of a blonde woman smiled up at him. Less gaunt, her hair neatly combed into long, straight lengths, she looked happy, healthy and different than the woman standing in his living room. But the resemblance was there. On the license, the name read Sylvia Leigh Michaels, just like on the birth certificate. The address was in San Antonio, Texas.

Again, Tate forced himself to remain calm. This was all just a bad dream. He inhaled a full, deep breath and let it out slowly, handing the card back to Sylvia, his hand still curled around the photograph. "What do you want from me?"

She folded the driver's license into the birth certificate and shoved them into her back pocket. "I only want my son." She held out her palm. "May I have my picture back? It's the only one I have left."

Strangely reluctant, he handed her the photo, their fingers touching briefly, the impact sending a jolt of something he couldn't describe through his veins.

"So what now?" she asked.

"I won't let Jake go without a fight."

"Then you admit there might be truth in what I say?"

"You present a good argument, but anyone can forge

documents. You could have had a child. There's no guarantee my son is the son you had stolen."

"But you agree that there is a possibility that someone might have forged the birth certificate you have?"

"I'm not agreeing to anything until I have my lawyer check into it."

Sylvia nodded, her shoulders rising and falling on a sigh. "I didn't expect you'd give up without a fight. But I'm not, either."

"Please leave. My lawyer will be in touch with yours." He moved toward the front door, holding it open. "And I need to know where you will be staying."

Sylvia stared across at him, her lower lip caught between her teeth. That little display of uncertainty doing funny things to him. She didn't answer.

"I'll need an address to forward any documents from my legal staff."

"I don't have an address."

Tate shook his head. "What do you mean you don't have an address? Don't you live in San Antonio?"

"I did. I don't. Oh, hell." She threw her hands in the air. "I haven't lived anywhere but hotels and my car since Jacob was stolen. I let my apartment go."

"I'll have my foreman drop you at the hotel in Canyon Springs."

"Wouldn't do much good," she muttered, refusing to meet his gaze.

"What did you say?" Tate asked.

"Nothing. Never mind. I'll accept that ride since my car is toast."

"Answer me first. What did you say?"

When she stood in stony silence, refusing to answer him, Tate grabbed her shoulders. "You try my patience, woman. You've barged into my life, threatening to take my son from me… The least you can do is answer my question."

Sylvia threw off his hands, dull red spreading up her neck into her cheeks, her eyes flashing. "I don't have anywhere to go. Everything I owned went up in flames in my car. What little money I had left with it. I'm broke, I'm homeless and I'm tired of you yelling at me! All I want is my son back."

Her hand lifted to her mouth, her eyes widening. "Don't think lack of money will stop me from getting Jacob back. I can provide him a good stable home. I can. No judge or jury in the state of Texas will deny my right to Jacob. He's my son!"

She stood trembling, her fists clenched at her sides, her blue eyes turning stormy.

If Tate wasn't facing losing Jake, he'd find her defiance attractive, her flashing blue eyes beautiful and the tilt of her breasts appealing. But damn it, she wanted to take his son away from him. "You'll stay here for now."

Sylvia gasped. "What did you say?"

"You heard me. Now don't make me change my mind."

"I can't stay here."

"Take it or leave it." He walked to the edge of the room and leaned out into the hallway. "Maria!"

"But…" Sylvia's brow creased, her head tipped to the side. "But I want to take Jacob away from you. Why would you do this?"

"Maria!"

"Sí, señor." The older Hispanic woman hurried toward Tate, breathing hard, her forehead knitted in a concerned frown.

"Prepare a room for Ms. Michaels."

Her brows rose into her graying hair. *"Por qué?"*

"She'll be staying here." Tate frowned. "Now, please prepare the room."

"Sí." Maria shot another confused stare at Sylvia and turned away.

"Get this straight…" Tate directed his attention to Sylvia. "I'll be watching you. If you attempt to take Jake before any of this mess is legally settled, I'll kill you."

Sylvia's hand went to her throat, her face blanching. "How do I know you won't try to kill me anyway?"

"All you have is my word."

"I don't know you, Mr. Vincent. Is your word enough to go on?"

"You're asking me to go on your word that Jake is your son." He gave her a challenging look, all the while wondering what he was getting himself into.

"But you should hate me," Sylvia whispered. She didn't think he'd heard until he turned back to her with a pointed gaze.

"I have a philosophy of keeping my friends close, and my enemies closer."

Chapter Five

Sylvia stood at the window of the spacious bedroom, staring out at the dry Texas hill country, her gaze panning the horizon but not seeing a thing. Her ears perked at every sound in the household, hoping to hear the faint noises a baby makes. Her baby. Jacob.

So tuned in to the specific sounds of a child, she didn't hear adult footsteps outside her door.

"These should fit you."

Sylvia spun, her hand going to her throat. "Oh, Lord, you scared me."

The young Hispanic woman Tate had called Rosa, the woman who'd been caring for Jacob in the nursery, stepped into the room, moving with a slight limp. She laid a stack of clothing on the bed, the corner of her lips quirking upward. "These belonged to Mr. Vincent's ex. I found them in a bag of clothing *mi madré* planned to donate to the homeless shelter. That and an old Mexican dress my mother wore." Rosa's lip curled tighter into a sneer.

Sylvia had read everything she could find in the San Antonio public library about the infamous young millionaire and most eligible bachelor of the state of Texas. His wife had walked out on him early in their marriage when Tate wasn't so rich. In fact, he'd been close to losing his ranch and everything he owned when his wife walked out on him. Had she stuck with him "for richer or poorer," she'd have been sitting pretty in this fabulous house that Tate had built onto and modernized to make it anyone's dream home, not wanting for anything. Stupid woman.

Feeling every bit the homeless person, Sylvia had no other choice but to take what was offered, even if it had been the ex-wife's clothing. Another possible strike against her in her struggle to get her child back—a reminder to the great Tate Vincent of what he'd lost in his failed marriage. "Thank you."

"Don't thank me. Mr. Vincent is to thank for allowing you to stay." Rosa's eyes narrowed. "Just so you know, I'm Jake's nanny…and bodyguard. I'm an expert with the 9 mm and I've never missed a target."

A shiver snaked up the back of Sylvia's neck. Jacob's bodyguard could no doubt take her, but Sylvia had no intention of letting Rosa know she was scared. Her back straightened and she tipped her head back, her brows rising. "Are you threatening me?"

Rosa shrugged. "All I'm saying is that the Vincents—that would be Tate and Jake—are like family to me. Hurt either one of them and…" She stared straight into Sylvia's gaze. "Let's just say, a nine-millimeter bullet can make a pretty big mess."

Before Sylvia could respond, the Hispanic woman turned and limped away.

The image she'd left Sylvia with was of herself being gunned down by a crazy woman with a pistol. "And this is the woman he trusts with my son?" Sylvia muttered, her hand sifting through the clothing on the bed.

"Maybe I should check for explosive devices before I wear any of this."

"I see you've met Rosa."

Sylvia squealed and dropped the shirt she'd lifted from the pile, her face burning.

The man who'd been with Tate when he'd found her in the pasture stood with his hat in his hand. "Yes, Rosa can be pretty harsh with her words, but she wouldn't hide explosives in clothing. She's more…" The man paused, his hands turning the hat in his fingers before he stopped and looked up. "She's more in-your-face violent. You'll know when she plans to do harm."

"That's supposed to make me feel better?"

He shrugged. "Don't take her too seriously. She's had a bug up her…" Color rose in the man's cheeks, making them a ruddy brown. "Well, since she took a bullet in Austin." A brief shadow crossed his face, then he smiled, his deeply tanned skin crinkling at the corners of his eyes. "I'm C.W., the foreman. Supper's ready."

Sylvia's stomach growled. She wanted to say that she wasn't hungry. The truth was she hadn't eaten since last night when she'd left the library in San Antonio to drive here. "Thank you."

C.W. waited for Sylvia to pass through the door. "About what Rosie said—"

"Don't call me Rosie. I hate it when you call me Rosie." Rosa's voice called out from another room down the hallway.

C.W. chuckled and winked. "Love to get her goat." All humor left his face. "As for what Rosie—Rosa—said…same goes for me. Tate and Jake mean the world to all of us. If anything happens…"

Although C.W. said the words gently, Sylvia

couldn't mistake the steel behind them. "You have a nine-millimeter bullet with my name on it, right?"

He nodded. "Something like that."

"Point taken." Sylvia sighed. "I'm not here to hurt either one of them. I'm here to get my son back. My son. The child I gave birth to and didn't willingly give up." She planted her fists on her hips and squared off with C.W. "Did you hear that, Rosa?" she called out loud enough for the woman down the hallway to hear.

"Sí." Rosa stepped through a doorway, Jacob perched in her arms, his baby fists waving and a wet smile spreading across his chubby cheeks at the sight of C.W. "Let the courts decide where Jake belongs."

Sylvia's heart melted at the sight of her son.

C.W. met Rosa halfway down the hallway, reaching for the child. "Come here, little man. Come see ol' uncle C.W."

Ready tears sprang to Sylvia's eyes. Jacob was beautiful. He'd grown into a healthy, happy baby. At least she could rest assured he hadn't been abused since coming to the Vincent Ranch. All those months of worry could be left behind. When Jacob had been stolen, Sylvia imagined all kinds of horrors her son could have been subjected to. She'd cried too many tears thinking about it.

The smile on Jacob's face, the happiness he displayed for the people surrounding him let Sylvia know that he'd found a loving family to take care of him until his own mother could find him.

Her arms ached to reach out and hold her son, but she held back, determined to let Tate Vincent know that she was on the up-and-up. She planned to get her son back the legal way. Justice would side with the biological mother.

Sylvia had to believe that, even though, as an investigative reporter, she'd seen too many cases fouled up in court with corrupt judges and equally corrupt attorneys. She marched ahead of Rosa, C.W. and her son, determined to get the ball rolling as soon as she could get a call through to a lawyer she knew in San Antonio. The same one she'd used when she'd filed for divorce from Miguel Tikas a year and a half ago, before she'd known she was pregnant.

With her resolve strengthened, she followed the smell of food toward the kitchen, ever aware of the people at her back.

She passed an open doorway to an office the size of her old apartment. Tate Vincent stood looking out double French doors, his hand pressing a cell phone to his ear. "Tell him I want it done ASAP. The sooner we know something the better off we all are. Tomorrow morning would be best. Have Dr. Richards call to confirm."

Sylvia paused. Now would be a good time to ask Tate if she could use a telephone. Her cell phone had sketchy reception this far out of Austin, the charger lost with the contents of her car.

When Tate Vincent turned toward her, his brows snapped together in a frown. "What are you doing here?"

His abrupt demand raised the hairs on the back of her neck. Before she could answer, Rosa stepped up beside her.

"She's on her way to the dining room." The Hispanic woman jerked her head, indicating Sylvia should keep walking.

C.W. ducked into the office, Jacob perched on his shoulder. "Someone wants to see you."

Even before C.W. got close, Jacob was leaning toward Tate.

Tate held out his hands and plucked Jacob off C.W.'s shoulders. "Come here, Jake."

Rosa hooked Sylvia's arm with an iron grip. "Come with me."

Sylvia's gaze remained on Tate and Jacob until Rosa jerked her past the office with a violent tug.

"Okay, okay, you don't have to get mean. I'm coming." If she could afford to be nasty, Sylvia would have jerked back as hard as she could, hopefully dropping Rosa on her cranky butt. But she couldn't. If she wanted custody of her son, she had to make nice with the people who held Jacob. One in particular, who had enough money to buy a judge of his own.

Deep down, Sylvia realized the difficulties she faced going up against a financial giant like Tate Vincent. The man had unlimited funds at his disposal. He could make the court case last for years with custody of Jacob remaining with him throughout.

Her footsteps faltered and she came to a halt before they reached the kitchen. "I'm too dirty. Besides, I'm not hungry."

"Tough. The boss wants you to eat. So you will eat if I have to force-feed you." Rosa stepped into a formal dining room, Sylvia's arm still in her grip. She whipped Sylvia around and nearly tripped her into a padded seat at the dinner table.

Broad windows lined one wall overlooking a field dotted with horses, tails swishing in the late-evening sun. A perfect setting for dinner. A perfect home for a child to grow up in. A place Sylvia could never hope to own, not as a single mom—an investigative reporter—no less. What kind of life could she offer her son? Nothing like this. But she would give him all the love she had in her heart. That had to count for something.

As she'd been staring out at the hill country, Maria moved in and out of the room carrying trays laden with food. She'd laid out on the smooth wood surface of the long mahogany dining table an array of platters brimming with tortillas, sizzling fajitas, rice, refried beans and fluffy mounds of green guacamole.

Sylvia loved Mexican food, her mouth watering despite herself. The hole in her stomach overrode the worry eating at her insides. If she planned on fighting for her son, she'd better keep her energy up.

Rosa stood over her, her arms crossed over her chest like the tough street cop. "Eat."

Hunger trumped anger and Sylvia lifted a fork, piling spicy chicken into a light flour tortilla. She ate like a starving person, unsure of where or when her next meal would come. If Tate decided to throw her out, she'd have nothing to live on, no money, no food, no home to go to. Basically, she was at his mercy.

Tate Vincent stood in the living room, holding Jake in his arms. The open floor plan allowed him to monitor Sylvia's movements. The blonde shoveled food onto her plate like there was no tomorrow. And maybe the events of the past six months made her feel that way. If her waist measurement was any indication, she hadn't been eating enough food to keep healthy.

While Maria had shown Sylvia to her room, Tate had called his lawyer, asking him to check into the information Sylvia had given him regarding Jake's birth mother. Or, if Sylvia was to be believed, the woman who'd masqueraded as Jake's birth mother.

Tate had pulled Jake's birth certificate from his file of important papers and studied it. Again, he couldn't tell if it was real or not. Even his attorney hadn't picked up that it was a fake. At this point, Tate didn't know who the faker was, Beth Kirksey or Sylvia Michaels. He'd left a call out to Brandon, a buddy of his on the San Antonio police force, to verify whether or not Beth Kirksey had really died and her cause of death, if she had.

Even if Ms. Kirksey was dead, it proved nothing.

Tate's cell phone vibrated in his pants pocket. Juggling Jake on one arm, he checked the caller ID. His buddy from SAPD. His stomach twisted as he pressed the cell phone to his ear. "Yeah."

"Tate. Brandon Walker, here."

"What did you find out?"

"Beth Kirksey died a week ago. She was struck down by a car that jumped the corner she'd been working. The vehicle hit her head-on and left the scene of the accident without rendering assistance."

Tate's arm tightened around Jake until the little guy squirmed. "Any idea who did it?"

"Still looking for the car. A witness reported seeing a black Hummer with chrome grills speeding away from the scene. Not sure it was the one that hit her, but it's our only lead."

"What did you mean 'the corner she was working'?"

"You know. Her corner." Brandon paused and then cleared his throat. "You didn't know? Beth Kirksey goes by the name Bunny. She's one of the local hookers we've hauled in on occasion for prostitution."

The air left Tate's lungs. For a moment or two he

didn't say anything. When the silence stretched on, he swallowed past the lump building in his throat. "Uh, thanks, Brandon."

"Anything else I can do for you, just let me know."

"I might be taking you up on that," Tate said quietly. He clicked the off button and slid the phone into his pocket. Then he hugged Jake so hard, the boy squealed and patted Tate's face.

"Sorry, little man." His eyes burned, but Tate refused to surrender. Not yet. Just because Beth Kirksey was dead didn't mean she wasn't Jake's mother. Tomorrow his family physician was making a house call to collect the DNA samples. Until then, Tate refused to give up hope. Jake was his, damn it!

He carried his little boy into the dining room, intent on telling the trespasser just that.

Rosa stood at Sylvia's shoulder, her arms crossed over her chest.

Tate almost laughed at her stance, sure she'd used the intimidating glare on more than one traffic violator in her job as an Austin cop.

He was surprised Sylvia could eat while Rosa stood over her. But she finished off one fajita and loaded another tortilla with chicken. She must be really hungry.

A twinge of guilt threatened to creep into Tate, which he promptly squashed. After all, this woman threatened the only family he had left. Jake reached out and grabbed Tate's ear and giggled.

Sylvia had raised the tortilla to her mouth to take a bite. Her hand froze, her lips open and ready. When Jake giggled again, her face paled and she turned in her chair. Her face softening as soon as her gaze took in Tate and Jake.

"Oh, baby. Look at you, all grown-up." She choked on the last word, the fajita falling to the plate, forgotten. She wiped her fingers on her napkin and stood next to her chair.

"Don't try anything, lady," Rosa said, taking a step closer, putting her body between Tate and Sylvia.

"It's okay, Rosa," Tate said.

"I'll tell you when it's okay. I'm Jake's bodyguard," she said. "If I think he needs protecting, I'll do it."

Tate chuckled. "Always the protector, aren't you?"

"Damn right. And I can take you, too, if I have to." Without turning her back on Sylvia, Rosa asked over her shoulder, "Want me to take Jake to the kitchen?"

Tate stared at Sylvia, whose eyes swam with unshed tears. "Promise to keep your hands to yourself?"

She dragged in a deep, shaky breath and let it out before she nodded. "I do."

"Then I take it you wouldn't mind if Jake and I join you at the dinner table?"

Sylvia's mouth twisted into a sorry attempt at a smile. "It's your table. I'm the one who doesn't belong."

Tate's jaw tightened, but he refused to rise to her words. "Right." He glanced down at his son. "Jake, do you think you can control your urge to throw your food just this once?"

Jake patted his sticky palm against Tate's face. "Da, da, da."

"I'll take that as a yes." Tate tilted his head toward Jake's bodyguard. "Rosa, could you bring Jake's chair?"

She stared at Sylvia and back at Tate before she responded. *"Sí, señor."*

"Rosa. Stop with the *'señor,'* already." Tate shook

his head. "I pulled your ponytails. We should be able to call each other by our first names, for heaven's sake."

"I work for you now. How will you ever trust me to do my job if I'm all casual?"

"Do you love Jake?"

Rosa's back straightened and she stood as tall as her five-feet-three-inch frame could hold her. "Yes. I do."

"Then I trust you to do the best you can to protect him. Now, would you please get that chair?"

"Yes, sir—" She shrugged, a faint flush creeping into dark-skinned cheeks. "Tate. Yes, Tate." She glared at Sylvia. "Don't do anything dumb."

Sylvia held up both hands in surrender. "I won't."

After Rosa left the room, Tate hooked a chair with his foot and pulled it out at the end of the table beside where Sylvia sat.

"Thanks for trusting me enough to let me stay under the same roof as my son."

"Who said I trusted you?"

"Well, I thought…" Sylvia remained standing, her hands twisting together, her gaze never leaving Jake.

Tate remembered a soldier in the Afghan desert who'd been lost for days without water who had a similar look when handed a canteen of water. That desperately needy look of someone starved for something.

"Do you want to hold him?" He knew the answer before the words left his mouth.

Sylvia nodded once. "More than I want to breathe."

"Sit down and I'll consider it."

As she maneuvered the chair away from the table, a loud pop pierced the silence and glass splintered across the room from a bullet-size hole in the large plate-glass windows.

"Get down!" Tate yelled, dropping to the ground, Jake clutched to his chest.

Sylvia stood frozen, her hands still clinging to the back of the chair.

Another pop splintered the wood on the back of the chair.

Tate reached out and knocked the backs of her knees with his free arm.

Her legs buckled and Sylvia dropped to the ground as another round completely shattered the window, sending shards of glass onto the wood flooring.

Chapter Six

Sylvia lay on the floor, her breath coming in shallow pants, afraid to move should another barrage of bullets come slicing through the air.

Tate shielded Jake with his body as he inched toward where Sylvia lay on the floor. "Are you okay?"

Sylvia nodded, words lodged behind a giant lump of fear in her throat.

"Who the hell would be shooting at us?" Keeping Jacob low, Tate lifted his head above the table.

"Stay down!" C.W. ran past the dining room, a rifle clutched in each hand. Rosa appeared in the entrance to the dining room, holding a high chair. "What the hell?" She dropped the high chair against the smooth Mexican tile of the hallway and grabbed the rifle C.W. threw her way.

"Tate," Rosa squatted, pointing a finger at Tate as he tried to rise high enough to see through the window. "Do as C.W. said. You have to protect Jake."

Tate hesitated, then he dropped below the table, his mouth a straight, thin line, his grip on Jacob tightening. "I've got it covered here. You two find the bastard."

C.W. raced away, but Rosa stood out of range of the

open window. "You sure you don't need me here, Tate?" She nodded her head toward Sylvia. "Could be a setup."

Tate stared across the floor at Sylvia.

She kept her gaze level. "Why would I have someone shoot at me?"

Rosa snorted. "Could be he was a lousy shot. Maybe the shooter was aiming for Tate."

Sylvia shook her head, staring straight at Tate. "I wouldn't put Jacob in danger. You have to believe me."

"Go on, Rosa," Tate said, his gaze still on Sylvia. "And be careful."

Rosa frowned. "Same to ya, boss." She turned, weapon in hand, and ran down the hallway as fast as she could, one leg stiff, emphasizing her limp.

"What the hell's going on?" Tate asked, setting Jacob on the floor in front of him, keeping his profile and Jacob's as low to the floor as possible.

Guilt ate at Sylvia as she watched Jacob pull himself up on the legs of the chair next to him. "I shouldn't have come."

"I wish the hell you hadn't, but now that you're here, is there more to this story you haven't told me?"

Sylvia plucked at the splinters of wood from the chair, pulling them from the Persian rug beneath the table to keep Jacob from getting his hands on them. "When I was searching and questioning people in Mexico about Jake's disappearance, someone shot at me. I thought it was a random drive-by, drug war shooting. Then when I moved my search to San Antonio, I kept getting that feeling that someone was following me."

She looked up at Tate. "If I'd known they would put Jacob in danger, I…" A look at Jacob, using the chair legs to pull himself up to a standing position, made her throat ache. "Believe me, I don't want any harm to come to my son."

The child stared across at her, a smile lighting his face. He reached out with a chubby fist. "Da, da, da."

"I don't know what to believe anymore." Tate kept a hand looped around Jacob's belly, steadying the wobbly baby.

Jacob leaned against the hand, reaching out to Sylvia in an attempt to move in her direction. A frown drew his light blond brows together, his baby blue eyes growing stormy.

Laughter bubbled up in Sylvia's chest, despite the danger, despite the fight she'd have on her hands proving that this was her son. For deep in her heart, she knew. "He always did have a fierce frown. Even as an infant." She rose to a crouch and inched toward her baby. "You don't know how hard I prayed for this day. Hi, little man." She reached out, her gaze alternating between Jacob and Tate, afraid that the multimillionaire would stop her from touching the baby.

Careful to keep her head below the tabletop and from view of the shattered window, she moved closer and sat cross-legged on the floor in front of Jacob, wincing at the sharp stab of pain in her injured leg.

Tate's jaw tightened, but he didn't draw the baby back. Instead, he loosened his hold around Jacob's belly and let the boy sway in Sylvia's direction.

The little guy giggled and took a step, holding on to the leg of the chair with one hand, his other hand reaching toward her.

A swell of joy filled Sylvia's chest as Jacob let go of the chair leg and fell into her arms.

The scent of baby shampoo wafted beneath her nose,

the fine blond hairs tickling her chin as he pressed his hands against her chest.

Tate regretted letting Sylvia hold Jake as soon as the baby landed in her arms. The resemblance was so strong, it hit Tate like a punch to the gut. Both had light golden, straight blond hair, both had the baby blue eyes and pale skin. The tilt of Jake's nose was the exact duplicate of his mother's—

Tate fisted his hands. The DNA testing had not yet been done. Until then, his claim to Jake was legal and binding. The family physician would be out the following morning to draw blood samples from both Jake and this stranger who *claimed* to be his mother. In the meantime, he'd keep a close eye on the interloper and an even closer eye on his son.

Sylvia stared down at the baby looking up at her, her eyes suspiciously bright. "Oh, Jacob, you're such a big boy." She looked up at Tate with wonder shining in her eyes. "You call him Jake."

Tate nodded, his teeth grinding against each other. The way the woman held his son looked natural, touching, too sweet. "I named him after my father."

"I named him after my father, too." She brushed her cheek against Jake's, closing her eyes and inhaling. "He smells like baby shampoo and green beans." Her eyes opened and she smiled across the baby. "He was just starting to eat rice cereal when he was—" She gulped, a tear slipping from the corner of her eye.

Tate scooted closer, keeping his profile low. Without thinking, his hand came up and, with the pad of his thumb, he brushed the tear from her cheek.

"I'd almost given up hope," she whispered, leaning into his open palm.

As soon as her cheek touched his hand, an electric jolt rammed through his body. Tate jerked his arm back.

Sylvia's eyes widened and she stared into his gaze. "I'm sorry. I didn't mean to…" Her gaze sank to the baby in front of her. "It's just that I've been searching so long." Her voice dropped to a whisper. "Alone."

If he hadn't been as close as he was, he'd never have heard the last word. "Sylvia, where's your child's father? Why isn't he helping?"

Sylvia's lips twisted. "I don't think he ever wanted Jacob. We separated when I was only a month pregnant. Miguel just wanted to make my life difficult. He took more pleasure in blaming me for everything that went wrong—Jacob's disappearance…our divorce."

"Bastard." Tate couldn't imagine a father giving up on his own child. Not on Jake. The hardness in his chest softened as he touched Jake's blond hair, the strands softer than silk.

A sigh escaped Sylvia's lips. "He did help me with the Mexican authorities. But crime is out of control in Mexico. More and more kidnappings are being reported, inundating the system. I spent an entire week wading through red tape with the American Embassy and the Mexican police. They did nothing. And the longer they took, I just knew, Jacob would be taken farther and farther away."

The thought of his son being taken away to God knew where made Tate's chest hurt. His hand pressed against his sternum as he asked, "How'd you trace Jake here all the way from Mexico?"

"I advertised a reward for my son's return." She caressed Jacob's cheek. "I went through at least a thousand leads before a man slipped into my hotel room one night and practically scared me to death. He told me about a human trafficking ring stealing babies in Mexico and sending them to San Antonio, Texas, where they were put up for adoption…to the highest bidder." Her brows narrowed, her tone hardening. "They were auctioning babies."

An image of Sylvia alone in her hotel room with a dangerous stranger appeared in Tate's mind and he didn't like it. Her delicate features didn't hide her tenacious spirit, but how would she have resisted if a man wanted to harm her? "Did he threaten you?"

"No. Actually, he looked more scared than I felt."

"You trusted this man's word?"

"I couldn't discount any information. I had to follow it whether or not it was a dead end. When someone shot at me on the street right after I'd met with the informant, my gut told me this was one lead I needed to follow up on."

"What about the other leads?"

"All of them were desperate attempts to claim the reward. Nothing substantial." The hollow look in her eyes told the story.

If Tate were in the same situation, every dead end would rip another piece from his heart. He could imagine how it had been for Sylvia. He fought to remain neutral, to not get sucked into her tale. After all, she could be lying to him, hoping to collect on any sign of weakness. "How did you know this guy was telling the truth?"

"I'm a freelance reporter. I did a piece on gangs in San Antonio two years ago. I got in touch with some of my contacts and had them do some asking around." Her face paled. "They said the prostitutes had mentioned something about babies being sold. I had to follow the lead."

"That's when you found out about Beth Kirksey?"

"I flew to San Antonio and questioned several of the ladies. Eventually I heard about a hooker named Bunny, aka Beth Kirksey. Apparently she had a baby and put it up for adoption as soon as it was born."

A pinch of relief filled Tate. "There you go. I adopted that baby. Beth Kirksey was Jake's mother."

"Except Beth's baby was adopted at birth two weeks before you adopted Jake. I tracked down the adoptive parents. She sold that one for twenty thousand dollars." Sylvia's lips thinned. "My baby was four months old. That was six months ago." She stared down at Jacob. "How old is Jake?"

Tate hesitated. Then he heaved a sigh. "Ten months yesterday."

Sylvia's gaze returned to claim Tate's.

He was saved from further conjecture by the arrival of Rosa. "C.W. hopped on a horse. Whoever shot at you is probably long gone. I heard the sound of an engine as we hit the door on the way out." As if seeing Sylvia for the first time, Rosa glared. "What's she doing with Jake?"

Tate stood, lifting Jake up into his arms, away from Sylvia. "Call the sheriff about the shooting. I want whoever did it caught."

"Will do." Rosa glanced from Tate to Sylvia and back. "You sure she didn't set you up?"

"No, I'm not certain. But we'll have to take her at face value for now."

"I don't like it, Señor Vincent," Rosa said.

"Tate," he insisted.

"Tate." Rosa's glare could have burned a hole in Sylvia.

Tate almost laughed out loud, but the gravity of what had just happened sobered him. "Go on, Rosa. Make that call."

She left the room, throwing barbed glances back at Sylvia, daring the interloper to make a move. Any move. Rosa would take her down, bum leg or not.

Tate looked over the top of Jake's pale blond head, his lips pressing together. He couldn't afford to get softhearted with Sylvia Michaels. Jake represented his world. The only family he had left. He refused to give up on the boy.

He extended a hand to Sylvia. "I'm not saying I buy any of what you just told me. I sent for my family doctor. He'll be here tomorrow to draw blood or swab cheeks, whatever he has to do to collect DNA samples."

He expected her to look scared, maybe uncertain about his announcement. Instead of looking shaken at his declaration, she smiled at the boy in Tate's arms. "Good. The sooner we have proof, the sooner I get my son back."

His arm tightened around Jake. "Don't count on it. Jake's mine until the courts convince me otherwise. In the meantime, I'm keeping an eye on you." He nodded toward the shattered window. "You might be a fake, but those bullets weren't. If anything happens to my son and I find out you had something to do with it, well, let's just say we have ways of dealing justice here in Texas."

Chapter Seven

Boots clattered up the wooden porch, breaking the strained silence stretching between Sylvia and Tate.

"Tate? You two okay?" C.W. burst into the room, his deeply tanned skin red and shining with sweat.

"Yeah, C.W. We're good." Tate hefted Jake to his other arm. "What did you find?"

Sylvia's glance darted to the shattered window. Nothing moved in the field beyond the house. But then, she hadn't seen anything move before the shooting began.

C.W. dragged his cowboy hat off his head and slapped it against his jeans, dust flying off in a powdery cloud. "I grabbed Frisco and followed the tracks of a four-wheeler to the edge of your property along the highway. He had the jump on me by a few minutes. I never caught him."

"Did you get a look at the shooter?" Tate asked.

C.W. shook his head. "No. All I had was the tracks to go on. They led up to a break in the fence close to the highway. Someone cut the barbed wire. Anyway, the ATV had disappeared. There were truck-tire marks in the dust and rubber skid marks on the pavement. Whoever lit out of here didn't mind losing a layer of treads."

"Damn—" The millionaire caught himself short of cursing with Jake in his arms.

"Hey! No swearing around Jake." Rosa reappeared around a corner. "I called the sheriff. He'll be back here in under fifteen." She reached for Jacob. "Let me take the little guy to his room."

Tate's brows furrowed, but he let his nanny/bodyguard take charge of the boy. "Move Jake's crib to a room without windows. I don't want anyone taking potshots at the house and hitting him."

"I'll set up his bed in your closet."

Sylvia frowned. "A closet? Isn't that extreme, locking a child in the closet?"

Rosa chuckled. "Some people have smaller bedrooms than Mr. Vincent's closet."

"Tate." The man shook his head. "Stop calling me Mr. Vincent. You're making me feel old. However, putting Jake in my closet is an excellent idea, Rosie."

Rosa frowned. "It's Rosa to you, Mr. Vincent." She gathered the boy in her arms and headed toward the nursery.

C.W. busted out laughing, immediately sobering. "Sorry, Tate. She's a handful, that one."

Tate shook his head. "Sometimes I wonder why I hired her."

"Because she knows this place as well as you do." C.W. nodded in the direction Rosa went with Jake. "And she's the best person for the job of protecting Jake."

"Darn right, I am." Rosa's voice carried down the hallway.

Tate turned to C.W. "Let me know when the sheriff arrives."

"Will do. I'll get the boys on the job repairing the cut fence."

"Thanks." Tate walked away, stopped and turned back. "Tell them to carry some protection."

C.W. saluted Tate with the tips of two fingers. "Roger that."

Tate disappeared into his office, closing the door behind him.

"Well, hell's bells." Sylvia threw her hands into the air. "You'd think getting shot at was an everyday occurrence with the infamous Mr. Tate Vincent."

C.W. twirled his hat in his hand, his lips twisting into a wry grin. "Used to be in Afghanistan."

"Weren't you and Vincent on active duty together during Operation Enduring Freedom?"

C.W.'s smile faded. "Yeah, so what?"

"Has he always been this cryptic?"

The smile returned. "No, he was much worse. That's Vincent for you. Now, if you don't mind, I've got work to do."

"Don't let me hold you up." She turned around, not exactly sure what to do with herself. "I'm just surprised the great Tate Vincent doesn't have a guard posted on me at all times."

"Guess he figures you're not much of a threat to him."

She snorted. "Nice to know."

"Says a lot. Considering his father was stabbed by a trespasser. He later died of complications from the wounds."

Sylvia's heart clenched in her chest. "I'd read something about that."

"Almost turned into a bum rap for Tate."

Sylvia nodded, recalling the front pages of the San Antonio newspaper blaming Tate for the stabbing. "The person closest is often the first person suspected in domestic violence," she whispered softly. Unscrupulous reporters sensationalized the story, making the public believe Tate had either stabbed his own father or paid someone to do it for him.

"Media tried to crucify him saying that he wanted his hands on the land sooner, so he paid someone to kill his father," C.W. said. He looked over his shoulder. "Not that Tate would want me to be telling tales, but I thought you should know why he's so suspicious."

It had only been eight months ago. Right before Sylvia's trip to Mexico. The police report, the news headlines. Not until she'd returned to San Antonio did she learn of the final outcome. And only then when she'd been searching for information about the man who'd potentially adopted her son.

The newspapers and television had a field day with the dark and brooding Tate Vincent, convicting him before he had a chance to defend himself. And he hadn't defended himself. The man who'd stabbed his father had been caught, but no one could link him to the only surviving Vincent. "His father's death had nothing to do with me or my son."

"Maybe so or maybe not." C.W. settled his hat on his head. He stared around at the shambles of a dining room. "Maria will have grub in the kitchen."

Despite the fact she'd only downed one fajita, Sylvia wasn't hungry anymore. She'd been shot at. Worse, Jake had been close enough to be hit. Claiming her son may have had more lethal consequences than letting him live his life in the lap of Vincent luxury.

TATE STEPPED OUT ON the deck, the warm night air a welcome respite from the cool air-conditioning of his office. He'd checked on Jake, settled comfortably in his crib in the large walk-in closet adjacent to the master suite. Rosa would sleep in the connecting room. The woman claiming to be Jake's mother had the bedroom at the end of the hallway, far enough away Tate felt confident she wouldn't be a threat to Jake.

Wrapped in the heat of the night, Tate kept to the shadows beneath the rafters. The relative silence of the hill country enveloped him. Crickets chirped, frogs croaked and cicadas hummed raucously.

Tate's lips twitched. That was hill-country silence, laced with nature's song. When he stayed in Austin or Houston, he missed the white noise of the countryside, the blare of sirens and horns nothing to compare with the gentle background sounds of the open range.

A board creaked.

Tate stiffened and then relaxed as a waft of cigarette smoke drifted his way.

He leaned against the limestone wall. "I thought you were going home."

Kacee pushed away from the rough-hewn cedar post, her high heels clicking against the dry planks of the deck. She still wore the business suit she'd had on earlier. "I did."

Tate shook his head. "When did you get back?"

"While you were in the shower. I heard you'd been shot at. Sounds like your little trespasser brought trouble with her."

Tate stared out at the night sky, stars twinkling brightly, as if not a care in the universe. How long had it been since he'd hung like a star in the heavens, no worries, no cares? He shrugged. Not since he was a teen. "At least no one was hurt. Any news from Dr. Richards?"

"He called to confirm that he'd be here first thing in the morning."

"What about Double Diamond Ranch? Are they going to sell?"

She took another drag from her cigarette and tossed the glowing remainder over the rail.

Tate made a mental note of where it landed. As dry as it had been, a smoldering cigarette butt could cause the loss of thousands of acres of grasslands. He'd warned Kacee at least a hundred times. What would it take to get it through her hard head?

"Do we always have to talk business?" Kacee leaned close to him, blowing out the fragrant menthol smoke laced with another cloying aroma. Wine. Probably merlot. Kacee liked to drink a glass every night. Helped her to unwind.

She probably needed at least half a bottle as tightly as she was strung. For a woman who could handle the toughest boardroom discussions and keep cool under all the pressure, she did have her crutches. Merlot and the occasional cigarette, habits she'd had long before he'd hired her. Habits no amount of cajoling convinced her to quit.

Her arm hooked through his and she reached up and brushed away the lock of hair hanging down over his forehead. "Look at the moon. Do you ever get tired of looking at the moon? Even in the dirtiest, stinkiest places, the mood shines pure and true. You can always count on it. It'll never let you down."

"Yeah. That's true enough. What brought that on? It's not like you to wax poetic on me."

She shrugged. "Let's just say I'm tired of beating around the bush."

"How so? You never hold your punches, Kacee. If you have something to say, say it."

Leaning into him, she rubbed her cheek against his sleeve. "Sometimes you can't see the nose at the end of your face, Tate Vincent."

Uncomfortable with how close she was, he extricated his arm out of her hold and led her to the swing, hung from the rafters at the end of the porch. "Just how much wine have you had to drink, Kacee? You might want to sit before you fall."

She wiggled free of his hands and walked to the rail, ever composed as the business executive she was. "I haven't been overindulging, if that's what you mean." Kacee spun, swaying slightly. "And I can see more clearly than I've ever seen in the past." Her eyes narrowed, their gray depths darker than the shadows beneath the eaves. "Haven't I always been there for you?"

Tate's brows rose. "Of course. That's why I pay you the big bucks."

She stomped her foot, her brow wrinkling into a fierce frown. "No, I mean when you wanted to buy all those stocks, didn't I get the scoop on that company in Detroit? Wasn't I there to help you make an informed decision?"

"Yes." Too tired to play games, Tate bit down on his tongue. It wasn't like Kacee to talk aimlessly. Something must be bothering her a lot to make her lose focus, more than the wine.

"Wasn't I there when your father took ill? Didn't

I help you find an adoption agency that ultimately brought Jake into your life before your father's passing?"

"You did all that."

"I'm good for you, Tate Vincent. We make a great team."

"Agreed. You're the best executive assistant a person could have."

"That's it?" She threw her hands in the air. "After all I've sacrificed for you. That's it?"

"I appreciate all you've done for me. Didn't I give you a whopping bonus at the end of the year? Didn't I pay for your new car?" Beyond patient, Tate couldn't keep from speaking out. "What's your point, Kacee?"

"God, you're clueless." She stared at him for a long, agonizing moment, then turned her back to him, hugging her arms around her middle. "There is no point."

Tate hesitated before he awkwardly touched her shoulder. "I'm sorry, Kacee. If you thought there was more between us than boss and employee, there is. But it only goes as far as friendship."

She shrugged off his hand. "Thanks. I've got enough friends." Her back stiffened, drawing her up to her full five foot nine inches. "Is there anything I can get you before you turn in? A stock quote, business analysis, staple remover? *Sir?*"

Refusing to rise to Kacee's sarcasm, Tate took the high ground with a level tone. "No, I'm good for the night. Be careful on your drive back into town."

"I'd planned on staying here tonight."

Tate shook his head even before she'd finished her sentence. "You should stay in town. With people taking potshots at the house, I'd rather those who have alternate housing take advantage of it."

"But—"

"Just do it." Patience worn thin, Tate's words came out abrupt, brooking no argument.

"Okay, okay. You don't have to bite my head off."

"Sorry."

"Don't worry about it. I'm used to it." She walked down to the bottom step of the porch before she turned and looked back up at him. "Don't let her get under your skin, Tate. She's bad news."

"What are you talking about?"

"Sylvia Michaels. She's trouble, I tell you. Don't trust her. Most likely she's lying through her teeth to get something out of the Vincent fortune."

"Don't worry about me. I can take care of myself."

"I know you can. But sometimes you need a little reminder. At times you can be downright gullible."

"That's why I have you." Kacee had street smarts, raised by a single mother on the wrong side of the tracks. She'd been tough, savvy and determined to pull herself out of the slums. That's why Tate had hired her. He'd recognized her tenaciousness and knew she'd serve well, advancing his plans for Vincent Enterprises. But sometimes her past flared up when she pushed the envelope of ethics. "Go home, Kacee."

She pinned Tate with a gaze that lasted uncomfortably long. He refused to look away, refused to give her even a shred of encouragement. They were boss and employee, nothing more. At least on his end of the relationship.

Finally, she looked away and headed off across the yard to her Lexus.

Tate stepped off the porch and went in search of the discarded cigarette butt, Kacee's words rolling over and over in his mind. Why would his executive assistant think he'd let a stray get under his skin? He'd warded off more women than a man had a right to consider. Being one of the most eligible bachelors in the state of Texas didn't help. Women of all shapes, ages and sizes threw themselves in his path in hopes of a fairy-tale happily ever after with the rich playboy.

Why should Sylvia Michaels present any kind of a threat to him? The woman had come to take Jake away from him. That was enough reason for him to hate her and he'd fight her with his last breath to keep his son. Any woman threatening to take Jake away was trouble, as far as he was concerned.

Never mind that she'd half convinced him that she truly was the mother of his adopted son. Birthmark aside, her spun-gold hair and light blue eyes were the exact replica of Jake's.

The scent of burning tobacco reminded him of what he was searching for. A cigarette butt, not answers to one of life's most challenging questions—who was the real mother of his son?

Tate pushed into the bushes surrounding the porch and bent to retrieve the still-burning cigarette. As he ground the glowing end into the dirt, the deck boards above him creaked. He froze, lifting his gaze to the latest night walker.

Golden-blond hair caught the moonlight as Sylvia Michaels tiptoed across the wood planks to the steps leading out into the yard. When her feet touched dirt, she made a sharp turn, aimed directly for where he crouched in the bushes.

What was she up to?

Curious, Tate remained hidden.

Sylvia stopped beside him, pulled a cell phone from her jeans pocket and slid it open. She punched a single number and held the phone to her ear. "Tony?" She laughed, her breath hitching.

The sound of her laughter made something wrench inside him and Tate held his breath hoping for more.

"I found him. I found Jacob." She brushed her free hand beneath her eyes. "He's okay, and as far as I can tell, they've taken good care of him." She paused, staring out at the stars. "I'm not sure they believe me, but they have to. I've found Jacob." Tears flowed freely now, dropping into the dust beside Tate's feet.

His heart squeezed in his chest, making it hard for him to breathe. By all appearances, Sylvia Michaels was everything she said she was—a mother whose child had been stolen from her. A mother who'd tracked that child over thousands of miles to find him. If the DNA results came back and proved her claim, how could Tate stand in the way of her waltzing out the door with the only family he had left? About to stand and make his presence known, he shifted.

"Look, Tony, I need to know if you've found out any more about the man Beth Kirksey got Jacob from." She listened for a moment. "Nothing? I want to know as soon as you hear anything. And Tony, I need another favor. Can you check on a Kacee LeBlanc, C. W. Middleton and Rosa Garcia? I don't know how long my phone will last. I've lost my charger. I'll contact you in twenty-four hours. I need to know what I'm up against when I try to get my son out of here. No, I won't do anything stupid. But I *will* take my son home," she said, her voice hard-edged.

After she slid the phone closed, she stared out at the stars again, letting her head fall back, her long silky tresses flowing down her back to her smooth, rounded bottom.

Feeling depressingly like a Peeping Tom, Tate realized his window of opportunity to make his presence known had come and gone. He'd have to wait her out or look the fool.

The cell phone in his pocket vibrated, making him jump, shaking the bushes.

Sylvia swung around, her hands jerking into a fighting position, her heart banging against her chest. "Who's there?"

Beside her, leaves rattled and Tate Vincent rose from among the hedges. "Me."

Her pulse skipped a few beats and continued hammering in her chest. The man was every bit as handsome as his pictures in the newspapers and on television. Especially in the moonlight with his midnight-black hair tinted smoky blue.

Her knee-jerk reaction was to go on the defensive. "Don't you know it's not polite to sneak up on someone?"

He snorted. "That's my line. Who's the trespasser, anyway?"

She relaxed her stance, a low chuckle rumbling up in her chest, easing the tension only slightly. "Touché."

"You should smile more often. Makes you look younger."

Sylvia frowned. "Thanks...I think." She touched a

hand to her cheek. Was she looking old? Not that it mattered. Not as long as she had her son back.

So the man had a sense of humor. Add that to a hunky exterior and he had the charisma of a heartthrob. And now wasn't a good time to notice the minute details like the square cut of his jaw or the way his mouth stretched into a lazy grin, his dark eyes glinting with the reflection of the moon.

Lines appeared beneath the lock of hair falling over his forehead, his brows dipped downward. "Who were you talking to?"

"A friend." Under no obligation to tell him anything, she didn't feel the need to inform him that her friend was a reformed criminal. Having done his time for identity theft, he now hired himself out as a private investigator, conducting legit and sometimes not-so-legit background checks on individuals. For a price.

He did work for Sylvia gratis because of a tip she'd given him that had saved his teenage son from gang violence and a prison sentence.

"If you want to know anything about the people in my employ…" Tate stepped from bushes and out into the open. "All you had to do was ask."

Sylvia crossed her arms over her chest. "I like to do my own checking."

"That's right. You're a freelance reporter."

She straightened, her chin coming up. "That's right. I have my own contacts." She squared off with him, her shoulders thrown back, her chin held high. "I want my son back and I'll do whatever it takes to get him."

Tate closed the distance between them so fast Sylvia didn't have time to react. "I repeat, until the courts say otherwise, Jake's my son."

The man was too close, casting her into the shadows, blocking the moon and stars with the breadth of his shoulders.

Staring up into his smoldering gaze, with the light from a window glinting off his irises, Sylvia found herself at a loss for words, something she never was. Her pulse throbbed against her temples and her throat dried to the consistency of the parched Texas dust beneath her feet.

"Do you understand?" His voice, low and menacing, had a strange effect on her nerve endings. "Anything happens to my son and I'm holding you personally responsible."

Sylvia gulped to wet the lining of her throat. "He's my son. And I could say the same."

He stared down at her, making her all too aware of the way his chest rose and fell beneath the polo shirt he now wore. The fresh scent of aftershave filled her nostrils, reminding her of her complete lack of sex since she'd divorced Miguel. Only Miguel didn't hold a candle to Tate Vincent. At least four inches taller, Tate's shoulders were broad and muscular, probably from working his ranch like the tabloids liked to report.

Miguel's muscles weren't nearly as defined, nor were they produced from real work. He had his own trainer and weight equipment in his hacienda in Monterrey. But he'd never done a hard day's work like Tate Vincent.

As much as Sylvia hated to admit it, she admired a rich man who wasn't so distanced from his roots that he paid others to do all the dirty work. He'd set a good example for his children. Too bad Jacob wouldn't be one of them.

The last thought made her eyes widen. Never in

a million years would she expect Tate Vincent to be the father her son would know growing up. But the image stuck of Tate teaching Jacob to ride a horse… Tate teaching Jacob to mend a fence or work with his hands… Tate teaching Jake about all the animals and the people who made a ranch viable.

The endless possibilities of life on the Vincent ranch, growing up surrounded by everything money could buy and a man who could teach him things Sylvia couldn't was a childhood dream. She'd never ridden a horse or mended a fence. She couldn't even throw a football. Who would be there to teach Jacob how to be a man?

She inched away from Tate, backing away from her feelings of inadequacy. Jacob was her son. She wouldn't abandon him now that she'd found him. She loved him more than life itself. "I'd better go to bed. Tomorrow promises to be an interesting day. You said the doctor would be out to collect DNA samples?" Now she was babbling, but she couldn't help herself. The man flustered her.

The hard line of his jaw softened. "Yes, you should go to bed." His eyes lost their hardness and his lips tipped upward in the corner. He followed her, matching her retreat, step for step. "Did anyone ever tell you that you have very expressive eyes?"

Too late, he'd moved and the moon shone down into her eyes, probably revealing all of her thoughts. "It's a curse."

"Not really. What were you just thinking?"

Close enough she could feel the warmth of his breath on her skin, he made her body hum to life. "N-nothing."

He reached out, cupping her chin. "Nothing?"

"That's right." Her voice squeaked as she tried

to maintain a grip on her senses, all of which were whipped into a frenzy, overpowered by a man known for his charm by women all over the world. Sylvia kept telling herself that he was playing with her. Nothing he said or did meant anything to him other than an angle to get what he wanted. That's what rich men did. They used the little people for their own gain. Like Miguel had used her then left her for another woman.

"Then why did you look so sad?" His thumb brushed against her cheek. "If you really think Jake's your son, you should be ecstatic."

"I am." Her heart banged against her chest, her vision dimmed, until all of her focus centered on his mouth. "Very excited."

"What is it about you? I don't trust you any farther than I could throw you." He murmured the words, the content of which should have infuriated her.

Instead she fell under his spell, unable to pull free, unable to think a rational thought. "Is this how you made your millions?" she asked, her voice no more than a whisper.

"How's that?" He leaned close, brushing his cheek against her temple. His fingers circled behind her neck, his thumb stroking the tender skin beneath her ear. "You smell good. What's that scent?"

"Soap." Her head tipped backward of its own accord. "Did you make your millions by charming snakes out of a basket or women into your bed? Because you could, you know."

"Is that what you think?" His mouth brushed her temple, dragging along her cheekbone to hover above her trembling lips. "Tell me, is it working?"

All thoughts ceased. Sylvia could barely process the

signals coming in from all of her senses. The man was a flame, she the moth drawn inexorably closer to her demise. And the sad thing was that she could do nothing to stop herself. She swayed closer, her lips sweeping across his in a featherlight brush with temptation.

Somewhere something buzzed. A vibration other than her own pulse slammed against her veins, penetrating her clothing against her hip.

"Damn." Tate stepped away from Sylvia and dug into his pocket, unearthing a cell phone. He stared at the device, reading the caller ID. He flipped the phone open. "What do you want, Kacee?" He hesitated. "I'm sorry, Helen, I thought you might be Kacee. What can I do for you?"

SYLVIA TOOK ANOTHER step back, then another, sucking in a long, much-needed breath to clear her head of the Tate-induced fog. What else could she call it? The man could turn her on. He'd proven that in under thirty seconds. Good Lord. Was she that desperate?

She pressed a hand to her breast and sucked in another breath, the second having no more effect on slowing her pulse or steadying her erratic breathing.

What kind of game was he playing? Was he trying to prove something? That she was an unfit mother? If she wanted the courts to take her seriously, she'd have to prove she was fit. If she wanted to get her son back, she'd have to keep Tate Vincent at a distance.

"Good Lord." With the cell phone pressed to his ear, Tate paced a few steps away and pushed his hand through his dark hair, standing it on end. "Is he going to be all right? Don't even worry about it. I'll manage without him. Tell him to concentrate on getting better."

He listened for a minute. "I'll take care of it myself. If you need anything, don't hesitate to call. Thanks for letting me know." He flipped the phone shut and turned toward her. "I don't know what game you're playing, but don't think you're going to get away with it."

Having just had similar thoughts about his game, Sylvia's back straightened. "What are you talking about?"

"You know perfectly well what I'm talking about." In a flash, he grabbed her arms, his fingers digging into the flesh. "I don't take kindly to people who hurt my friends and family."

"I've done nothing to hurt you or your friends."

"Then how do you explain the shots fired earlier?" he demanded, shaking her.

"They were shooting at me, too!" She pulled at his fingertips, trying to dislodge his iron grip. The fury in his face frightening her more than the pain where his fingers clamped into her arms.

"Are you sure they weren't shooting at me? Were they aiming to kill me or just as a warning to pay whatever price you demand?"

"I don't know. Why don't you ask the shooter?" she shouted back at him.

"You said you'd do what it takes to get your son back. Does that include murder?"

Sylvia gasped. For a long moment, she stared up into Tate's glaring eyes before she answered honestly. "I don't know. All I do know is that I'd do anything necessary to protect my son. I sure as heck wouldn't hire someone to shoot at the man holding him."

Tate shoved her away. "My close friend Dr. Allen Richards, the man who was supposed to collect DNA samples, was run off the road by someone less than an hour ago."

Sylvia stood stock-still, the blood leaving her head, making her dizzy. She forced herself to think. "Will he be all right?"

"Yes, but he won't be here tomorrow as planned."

She let go of the breath she hadn't realized she'd been holding and sagged against his grip. "Thank God."

"That he won't be here?"

"No, that he lived to tell you about it."

Tate released one arm and pressed a finger to her chest. "If I find out that you had anything to do with this, I'll…"

"You'll what?" She refused to show her fear, standing as straight as she could, glaring up at him with all the attitude she could muster while being manhandled. "As far as I know, you could be in on the whole setup, stealing babies and selling them to the highest bidder. How do I know you aren't the kingpin to the entire operation?"

"Watch what you say, woman."

"Why? What will you do, Tate Vincent? What will you do that could be worse than stealing my baby?" She jerked her arm free from his grip and stepped back. "You could have set up the shooting, aiming for me. Get rid of the mother and you're free to keep Jacob. Was that the plan all along? Are you the one trying to kill me?"

Chapter Eight

Before Tate could respond to her accusation, his cell phone buzzed with an incoming text message.

Sylvia turned and left him standing there, Tate too taken aback to follow.

He pulled his phone from his pocket and, through a haze of rage, read Kacee's message. "911. Call me."

Afraid of more bad news concerning his friend Dr. Richards, Tate let Sylvia get away as he punched the speed dial for Kacee.

"Tate! Thank God. Have you heard from Helen Richards?"

"Yes."

"Can you believe what happened to Allen?"

"Kacee, do you have anything else you want to report that I don't already know?"

The screen door creaked open and slammed shut on the house. Sylvia had gone inside. Although she'd left his sight, everything about where he stood radiated her presence. From the moonlight to the smell of dust in the air. Tate couldn't get her out of his head. Nor could he discount the words she'd flung in his face.

He still didn't know whether she'd been responsible for Dr. Richards's accident. She'd been with him when the accident occurred so he couldn't pin blame directly on her, though he wanted to. It would make it much easier for him to hate her if she was responsible for running his friend off the road and for the shooting earlier. She'd driven him over the edge with her taunts and her blue-eyed gaze and her pale skin, so delicate and clear, the glow of her blond hair in the moonlight.

Damn her! Tate punched his fist into the solid cedar post of the porch, the pain jolting him back to his senses. His hand throbbed, his knuckles bruised and bleeding. In retrospect, maybe hitting the post wasn't such a good idea. But it had accomplished one thing. It had helped him to focus on what was important: Jake.

That woman was inside with Jake while Tate stood outside. Whoever had shot at the house could still be around. Whoever had run Dr. Richards off the road could be lying in wait for any one of his staff, including him. If Sylvia Michaels really was determined to get her son back, would she do anything? Even hire a killer? Or would she do the job herself?

"Kacee, I gotta go."

"Tate, I contacted a buddy of mine in private investigations. He's doing a check on your Sylvia Michaels."

"Good. Let me know what he finds."

"I will."

"I'll talk to you tomorrow."

"Tate?"

"What, Kacee?"

"Remember what I said. Trouble with a capital *T*."

His grip tightened on the phone as his lips recalled the feel of Sylvia's against his own. "I already know it."

SYLVIA PAUSED OUTSIDE the door to the room she'd been assigned. What had just happened out there in the bushes? Why had she reacted so strongly to a perfect stranger? She'd almost kissed the man! And the scary thought was that she wanted to do it.

She pressed shaking fingertips to her mouth, the nerve endings in her lips jumping at the touch. He'd smelled of mint and leather, his body generating heat that scorched her senses.

How could she even consider kissing a man who held her life and happiness in his grasp? A man with enough money to buy every judge in the state of Texas?

Tate Vincent was nothing to her. Nothing but the man who'd been duped into adopting her stolen baby. A man she'd have to fight in court to regain custody of her son.

Jacob. Sweet, angelic Jacob.

An ache the size of Texas built in her, filling her chest. She let it push out thoughts of kissing the multimillionaire rancher with the midnight-black hair. She let the ache consume her and remind her what was most important: getting her son back.

More than anything, she wanted to see Jacob before she called it a night and attempted to sleep. As much as had gone on in the past twenty-four hours, she should be exhausted. Too jumpy and appalled by her recent actions, sleep was the furthest thing from her mind.

Finally, she'd found her baby. The flutter of excitement in her belly wouldn't dissipate. Six months of searching and she'd finally found him. And he was beautiful, healthy and appeared to be happy.

She longed to go to him and hold him, touch his face, count his fingers and toes as she had done when she'd first held him in the delivery room of Santa Rosa Hospital in San Antonio. Her son. The child she'd loved with all her heart was in a room down the hall.

Before she realized it, she'd taken several steps toward the room she suspected was the master suite.

"Do it, *chica*. Give me a reason to cut you down."

Sylvia yelped and dodged sideways, slamming her back against the wall to face the woman who'd sneaked up on her.

A smirk lifted one corner of Rosa's dark lips, her brown-black eyes narrowed into slits. "Take one more step and I'll consider it an attack on Jake. That's all the excuse I need to take you out."

Sylvia recognized a deep-seated rage in the woman and wondered again if she was the right person for the job of caregiver and bodyguard to her son. Dragging in a deep, steadying breath, Sylvia pushed herself off the wall and faced Rosa. "I'm not afraid of you," she lied.

Rosa stepped forward until she stood toe-to-toe with Sylvia. "You should be," she whispered in a low, dangerous tone.

"Let it go, Rosie." Tate Vincent stepped into the hallway, his hands on his hips.

The tough Hispanic woman rolled her eyes without taking her gaze off Sylvia. "It's Rosa, not Rosie, Mr. Vincent."

"Really, Rosie, call me Tate. Now go check on Jake and call it a night."

Her gaze narrowed even more at Sylvia. "You sure?"

Tate pushed a hand through his hair. The fine lines beside his eyes etched deeper. "It's been a long day. Go to bed."

Rosa blew a breath out her nose like a raging bull before she backed away from Sylvia.

Sylvia let her muscles relax a little, unclenching her fists at her sides.

"I still think she bears watching, Mr. Vincent," Rosa said.

He shook his head, a hint of a smile tipping the corner of his lips upward.

The exhaustion in his face and the simple gesture of a half smile made Sylvia's stomach turn flips. After the near kiss outside, she hadn't stopped thinking about Tate Vincent and his darned lips. Now she found herself staring at them again.

She closed her eyes and dragged in a deep breath. "You're right. It's been a long day. If you don't mind, I'll call it a night."

"And no midnight wandering," Rosa warned. "I sleep lightly and so does Mr. Vincent."

"Rosa," Tate growled.

"Okay, okay. Keep your shirt on, Tate. I'm going."

Tate Vincent squared off with Sylvia. "It's true. Both of us will be sleeping light and watching out for Jake."

Sylvia crossed her arms over her chest. "You do that. I wouldn't want anything to happen to my son. I will get him back if it's the last thing I do."

Rosa pushed past Sylvia, bumping her intentionally with her shoulder. "Keep it up and it might just be the last thing you *attempt* to do."

When Rosa had cleared the hallway, Tate stayed, staring at Sylvia for a long moment. Finally, he sighed. "Get some rest. Tomorrow, you, me and Jake will take a trip into Austin to get that DNA testing done." Then he followed Rosa to the end of the hallway.

Sylvia took a deep breath and let it out. Maybe Rosa was the right one to keep Jake safe. She had the heart of a lioness and could intimidate the heck out of anyone.

So much for seeing her son before she turned in, the

decision made for her by Tate and Rosa. She'd have more of a chance facing off with a gang than going up against Rosa again.

Suddenly the day's events weighed in, exhaustion destroying her will to continue the fight. For now. Today she'd found her son. Tomorrow would be another day.

She opened the door and stepped inside, closing it behind her. The room she'd been assigned had a luxurious connecting bathroom lined in granite and tumbled marble. She shed her clothing and climbed into the shower, letting the warm cascade soothe her jangled nerves. The water stung the cut on her leg and she winced. She hoped her tetanus shot was up-to-date.

After scrubbing the Texas dust from her body and shampooing her hair, Sylvia stepped from the shower and wrapped herself in a warm, fluffy towel. Already anticipating the pillow, she didn't bother looking through the clothing Rosa had delivered earlier. She padded across the cool hardwood floor to the four-poster bed, pulled the white eyelet coverlet aside and lay down, towel and all. She'd thought she would find it hard to go to sleep, but before she could count ten sheep, her eyes closed, darkness claiming the night.

A NOISE JERKED TATE from a light sleep and he darted out of the bed, headed straight for his closet and Jake.

Rosa stood over the crib in the closet, the door to the connecting room opened wide. "Shh. He's still asleep."

"What was that noise?"

"I don't know. Something outside. Do you want me to check or watch Jake?"

"I'll check. You stay here." He turned to go, pulling

a pair of jeans over his boxers, then slipping his bare feet into cowboy boots.

He ran down the hallway and almost plowed into Sylvia as she emerged from her doorway holding a towel around her naked body and pushing her lush blond hair from her face. "What's going on?"

"I don't know. Stay put and keep out of trouble."

C.W. burst through the back door, shouting, "The barn's on fire! The barn's on fire!" He didn't wait for a response, letting the door slam closed behind him as he ran out into the night.

Tate followed at a dead run, exploding out into the yard to see a wall of flame rising from the roof of the hundred-and-fifty-year-old barn his great-grandfather had built. Horses screamed inside as C.W. flung the double doors open and dove inside.

At least eight horses were stabled in the barn, all screaming, their neighs rising with the crackling flames.

By the time he entered the barn, smoke choked the air, singeing Tate's lungs.

Sassy nearly knocked him over racing for the door, the sorrel mare's eyes crazed, her nostrils flared in the light from the rising flames. C.W. struggled to lead the Vincent prized quarterhorse mare, Fandango, out of her stall. She reared, her hooves flailing in the air, knocking C.W. to the ground.

Tate rushed forward, snatching at the lead rope, leaning all of his weight on it, forcing the horse to stand on all four hooves, bringing the frightened animal under control.

C.W. rolled against the side of the stall and staggered to his feet, coughing. He helped Tate drag the horse out of the stall. Once the beast cleared the barn door, the men released the lead and raced back into the smoke.

A shadowy figure stood in front of one of the stalls, struggling to unlatch the heavy clasps. In the swirling smoke, a wisp of blond hair caught Tate's attention. "Sylvia! What the hell?"

She coughed and shoved at the metal catch. The latch released and the heavy wooden door swung out. Even before the door was fully open, the gelding inside slammed into the wood, throwing Sylvia to the ground.

Tate slapped the horse's flanks, sending him in the direction of the barn opening, before he helped Sylvia to her feet. "Get out of here!" he shouted over the roar of the fire.

"No." Her cheeks flushed from the heat and smudged with smoke, Sylvia climbed to her feet and ran for the next stall door. "You can't let the animals die!"

He raced after her, grabbing her shoulder. "You'll die if you stay in here. Go!" He pushed her in the direction of the door, but she refused to go.

"You're wasting time better spent saving your horses." She coughed, bending low to avoid the worst of the smoke.

The horse behind the stall door kicked the wooden walls and screamed in the billowing smoke. Tate read the engraving on the door.

Diablo.

Sylvia reached for the stall door, grasped the iron latch and shoved it hard, opening it in one move. Tate caught the door before it could knock her down, reaching inside for the horse's lead. The stallion reared, jerking the rope through Tate's hand, burning through the calluses on his palms. He held fast, refusing to let the horse die in the fire or trample Sylvia.

He tugged with all his might, edging the horse inch by hard-won inch out of the stall. At last they were free of the walls. Still, Diablo couldn't see in the smoke-choked building. He danced around in a circle before Tate could lead him toward what he hoped was the barn entrance. At last he got the horse out, slapping his rump hard to hurry him along.

C.W. shouted, "One more in the corner stall. I'll get him!"

"No, you and Sylvia get the hell out of here."

"No can do, boss man." C.W. coughed and started back into the barn.

"That's an order. Get out!" Tate ran back into the burning inferno. Where had Sylvia gone? Was she still beside Diablo's stall, disoriented or overcome by smoke?

Tate's heart raced, his pulse thrumming against his ears, almost drowning out the roar of the fire and the screams of the remaining horse. The building wouldn't last much longer. Soon the roof would cave and every-thing left inside would be consumed by flames.

Where was she? He ducked low and moved toward Diablo's stall where he'd last seen Sylvia. The crazy lady should have stayed in the house. He and C.W. were the only ones who should have even attempted enter-ing the barn.

What if she'd succumbed to the smoke? He might never find her.

He coughed, pulling his shirt up over his mouth, ducking lower until he was on his knees. The scrape of metal against metal made him turn toward the last stall in the building. Surely she hadn't gone deeper.

Tate felt his way along the row of stalls, closing the doors and counting as he went to give him a frame of reference and a clear exit through the murky darkness. When he reached the last stall, he bumped into a lump on the floor.

"Sylvia?"

A cough and then the raspy words came to him through the smoke, "Oh, thank God." She threw herself into his arms. "The horse won't come out."

"I'll get her. You need to get out of here. Now." He pushed the hair out of her face and shoved her closer to the ground. "Crawl. The smoke's getting too dense."

"Which way?" She coughed again.

"Feel your way along the stalls and eventually, you'll make your way to the entrance. Hurry!" He gave her a gentle nudge.

Sylvia stayed put. "What about you?"

"I'll get there before you. With the horse. Now go!"

This time she moved, crawling as fast as she could, her form swallowed by the smoke.

With his shirt up over his nose and mouth, his eyes stinging so badly he couldn't see, Tate waved his hands in front of him until he found the horse backed against the very back of the stall, quivering and crazed.

It took him several precious seconds to locate the lead rope, but once he had it, he didn't waste time getting the horse out of the stall. After several convincing jerks, the horse followed, swinging side to side, twisting Tate around in the process.

Thinking himself in the middle of the barn, Tate wasn't certain of his directions. The horse had twisted around so much he'd lost his bearings. The fire had consumed the loft full of hay and flames licked along the walls of dry lumber.

A loud crack shook the structure and a huge beam crashed through the upper flooring, sending sparks and planks flying.

The horse reared and jerked the rope out of Tate's hand, racing away into the smoke. Another beam fell from the ceiling. Tate threw himself into a stall before the ancient timber slammed into a wall, sending a shower of splinters, sparks and flames in every direction. The stall held the weight for only a second, then the door popped off its hinges and the enclosure caved.

Too late to move out of the way, Tate tucked his head and rolled to the side, but the stall door landed on his legs, trapping him beneath. The horse was on her own now. Tate had bigger problems.

His lungs burned, starving for clean, fresh air. He pushed and shoved at the heavy wood-and-iron door, managing to free one leg. But the smoke was getting to him. Then he saw movement through the smoke.

A small figure stumbled toward him. "Tate!"

"Sylvia?"

She bent low and shoved at the door lying over his leg, making little progress. After a few useless seconds, she groped in the dark until she found a charred two-by-four and shoved it under the door, leveraging the wood structure up and off Tate's legs.

"Give me your hand!" Sylvia shouted, holding out her slim arm, her entire body covered in soot and ash.

He held out his hand to her and let her pull him to his feet. Then they were running for the barn door, all the fury of hell on their heels.

As they cleared the door the entire roof caved, in a

billowing belch of soot and ash. Beams, timbers, splintered boards, sparks and flame shot out in every direction as if a bomb had exploded. The scene was like a flashback of the mortar that had exploded in the middle of the Afghan police compound when Tate and C.W. had served during the war.

Tate scooped Sylvia up in his arms and staggered as far from the smoke and flame as he could. Finally, at a safe distance from the raging inferno, he let her feet drop to the ground. She collapsed to her knees, coughing, and he dropped down beside her, sucking in fresh clean night air as fast as he could between spurts of coughing.

He only gave himself a few moments to rest before he pushed to his feet. When Sylvia tried to rise, he pressed her shoulder. "Rest here. I'll be back."

Exhausted, Tate couldn't stay put, too worried about the rest of his men, now all busy quenching the start-up fires trying to spread to the dry grasses of the pasture. There was nothing they could do now to save the barn, but they couldn't afford to let a grass fire consume the house or the rest of the Vincent Ranch.

Sirens blared in the distance—the volunteer fire department on their way to help douse the flames. Rosa or Maria must have called 9-1-1.

As Tate strode toward the burning hull of what had once been his great-grandfather's barn, a voice cried out from behind him. He turned toward the house.

"Señor Vincent! Señor Vincent! Help! *Madre de Dios!* Help!" Maria, the Vincents' housekeeper, ran across the yard in her bathrobe, her long, gray hair loose and flying about her shoulders.

A cold hand of dread gripped Tate's chest. He found

himself running toward the woman, the roaring in his head nothing to do with the fire raging behind him. He caught Maria by the shoulders and held her steady as she dragged in ragged breaths. "Take a deep breath, Maria, and tell me."

She stared up into his eyes, tears running down her face. *"El niño,"* she said, her voice cracking on a sob. "Señor Vincent, Jake—he is gone!"

Chapter Nine

As soon as Sylvia heard Maria's screams, she'd jumped to her feet, her heart slamming against her rib cage. Something besides the fire had upset the housekeeper and Sylvia suspected it involved Jacob. She reached Tate and Maria in time to hear the older woman's announcement.

Jacob had been taken.

The world crashed in around Sylvia. Her head spun, her heart stopping dead in her chest. "No. He can't be gone." She stumbled backward as if in a trance, her eyes wide, her mind a flurry of events playing one after the other, all centered around the cherubic blond angel she'd so nearly reclaimed. She turned and ran toward the house, refusing to believe he could really be gone.

Behind her she heard Tate yell to his foreman, but she didn't stop. She kept running.

How? How could he be gone? Was he lost? Had Rosa taken him? Surely he was sound asleep in his crib, waiting for morning and sunshine to greet him. He couldn't be gone.

Tate Vincent beat her to the door, pushing through ahead of her. He raced to the master suite and through the gaping door.

Two steps behind him, Sylvia jammed a fist to her mouth to keep from crying out.

The crib stood empty, a light blue blanket tossed aside, a stuffed lamb propped in the corner.

Sylvia closed her eyes, pressing a hand to her breaking heart, reliving the day her son was stolen from his stroller in a busy marketplace in Mexico. She'd been the one to be knocked down, helpless to stop the kidnapper from taking her son and disappearing into the crowd.

Rosa sat crumpled on the floor of the closet beside the crib wearing her pajamas, sobbing. She cradled her head in her hands, blood caked on the side of her cheek. "Tate, I didn't see him coming. I should have been ready, but I didn't see him coming." She stared up at him her eyes swollen and red, an angry gash in the dark brown hair, still oozing blood.

Tate knelt beside her and ran his fingers over her, inspecting her for other injuries. "It's okay. No one saw this coming. I shouldn't have left you to fend for him alone."

"But it's my job. I'm trained to protect." Her head sagged forward, her hands dropping to her lap. "I've failed yet again."

"No, Rosa. You didn't fail. Someone got the better of all of us tonight. The fire was only a diversion. A damned good one, if you ask me. Any broken bones?"

"No."

"You may have a concussion. We have to get you to the hospital."

"No. I have to find Jake." Rosa pushed to her feet, holding on to the edge of the crib.

"No, you don't. If they're still out there, C.W. and the guys will find them." He scooped her into his arms and carried her into the connecting room, laying her softly on the bed.

Maria pushed past Sylvia, crying softly. *"Mija, mi amor."* She carried a bowl of water and a fresh towel. "The EMTs are on their way. I called the sheriff, as well. They are setting up roadblocks." She set the bowl on the table and grabbed Rosa's hand, patting it fretfully. "You had me so scared, *mija.*"

The younger Hispanic woman pushed Maria's hands away. "Stop treating me like a baby. I failed at my job. Again."

"Rosa, we'll discuss this later. I don't want you out of that bed until a medical professional gives you the okay." Tate stared at Sylvia. *"You.* Come with me."

"Tate!" Rosa sat up straight, pushing her mother's hands aside again. "Be careful. She could have set this whole thing up."

Sylvia shook her head, backing out of the room as Tate advanced on her. "I had nothing to do with this. I just wanted my son back. I would never put him in danger. You have to believe me."

Tate shut the door behind him, grabbed her wrist and marched her toward his office.

Try as she might, she couldn't shake off his grip. "Let go of me. I tell you I didn't stage this. I'm not a criminal. I'm a mother searching for my son. My son, who is now lost to me again! Good God!" Her vision blurred and she stumbled, dropping to her knees.

Tate jerked her back to her feet, dragging her into his office where he shut the door. "Jake's my son and I want him back." Not until then did he let go of her hand. "What do you want? Money?" He jerked a checkbook out of the top drawer of his desk and opened it, grabbing a pen. "How much?"

Rage flamed through her faster than the fire had spread in the barn. Despite nearly dying in that fire, despite the raspy way her lungs felt from all the smoke she'd inhaled, she felt a surge of adrenaline so strong she had to move.

Sylvia stalked across the room, stood directly in front of Tate and slapped his face as hard as she could.

Her hand stung and she nearly doubled over from the pain.

A bright red handprint marked the spot and twin flags of mottled scarlet stained his high, tanned cheekbones.

"I don't want your damned money," she said, her voice low and gravelly. "I don't want your damned land. I don't want you." She breathed in and breathed out, her chest rising and falling in a measured attempt to calm the anger burning inside. "I only want my son."

"How do I know you didn't set that fire in the barn to distract us?"

"I didn't."

"Rosa's right. Everything was fine until you showed up. How do you explain all that?"

"I don't have to explain myself. I'm here because this is where the trail led to my son."

"I don't believe you. I think you're a lying bit—"

Sylvia's hand swung up to slap him again, only this time he was ready and caught her wrist before it connected.

"Don't do that again."

"Don't accuse me of something I didn't do."

He stared at her long and hard, his grip bruising her wrist.

She didn't flinch—didn't blink—just stared back, holding her ground, the truth her only ally.

Finally, he loosened his grip on her wrist and pulled it down by her side, still not releasing her. "I'm not sure who to believe."

"That's *your* problem." She wiggled her hand, trying to break free. "Let me go. I have to find my son. The longer we wait, the farther away the kidnapper gets. I love my son even if you don't."

He twisted her arm behind her, dragging her against him, crushing her chest into his. "I love Jake more than life itself. He's my reason for living."

His move left her breathless, the feel of his body against hers more shocking than his accusations. "Okay, so you love him. What next?"

"We find him."

"Then what are you doing now?"

"Making a mistake," he said, staring down at her, his smoldering dark eyes burning into hers.

"Then don't."

"For some damned reason, I can't help myself." He lowered his lips to within a breath of hers. "Even when I'm angry at you, you make me crazy, and I don't even know who you are."

Her gaze shifted from his eyes to the lips poised above hers. "Don't do it," she whispered.

"Do what?"

"Do this." She leaned up, pressing her lips to his, which started an avalanche of repercussions neither expected.

He let go of her wrist, his fingers tangling in her hair, dragging her head backward, opening her mouth to his.

His tongue thrust in, claiming hers. He tasted of mint and smoke, his sooty hands now grasping the sides of her face.

She gave as good as she got, hungry for him, despite all he represented. For now, they stood on a level playing field. Each had lost the child they loved.

After only a second, maybe two, Tate clasped her face between both hands and broke off the kiss. "We have to leave now or we may never find Jake."

Sylvia stared up into his eyes, nodding. "This should never have happened."

"It won't happen again." His words said one thing, the hands still caressing the sides of her face said something else entirely. His thumb rubbed at her cheek. "You're all smoky."

"So are you."

"Thanks for helping save my horses." Those words were the closest she could expect to an apology. Tate Vincent probably wasn't used to having to apologize for anything.

Her lips still tingling from his kiss, Sylvia whispered in a smoke-roughened voice, "Thanks for saving my life."

His hand dropped to his side and he nodded toward the door. "I'll give you ten minutes to shower and get ready, then we're hitting the road."

Sylvia frowned. "Where to?"

"San Antonio."

IN LESS THAN FIVE minutes, Tate had showered, dressed in jeans, a blue chambray shirt and a pair of cowboy boots that weren't covered in soot and ash.

He packed an overnight bag and a couple changes of clothing and stepped out into the hallway.

Sylvia stood there in a filmy white Mexican dress Maria had given her, decorated in bright red, orange and pink embroidered flowers, with a wide, bright red belt cinching the excess material in at the waist. She wore a pair of flat thin-strapped sandals on her delicate feet. Her wet hair hung down the middle of her back in a long, thick, braided rope. She looked like a little girl playing dress up. But the swell of her breasts beneath the elastic neckline of the dress made a man look twice.

Tate was no different. He'd come up with everything but a bra for her and the tips of her nipples stood at attention, the soft brown areolas showing through the thick cotton.

His stare must have rested there too long.

Sylvia's arms crossed over her chest, a frown twisting her brows together. "Ready?"

He cleared his throat and pulled his gaze back to her eyes. "Let's go."

Rosa stood in the doorway to her bedroom, pressing a hand to her head, wincing. "Keep in touch, boss man. As soon as I can stand without swaying, I'm right behind you."

"Not without the doctor's permission. I have enough to worry about without worrying about you, too."

Her frown deepened.

"Help C.W. figure out what happened here, then we can discuss your next move."

"Yes, sir."

He strode to her and took her arms. "You did more than was expected of you. And I'm not even paying you hazardous-duty pay."

Rosa smiled crookedly. "Who would have thought taking care of an infant would be hazardous duty?"

"You should know better around here."

"Yeah. I remember following around behind you as a kid. Everywhere you went, trouble followed. I don't know why us being adults would make it any different." She nodded toward the door. "Get going. I want the little guy back as much as you do."

Tate didn't remind Rosa that even if they found Jake he might not be coming home with them. He might be going home with Sylvia. If she truly was the boy's mother.

First things first.

Find Jake.

C.W. had pulled Tate's truck around to the front of the house and parked it there. He was climbing out as Tate and Sylvia stepped out on the porch. "Again, I saw signs of an ATV, but they were smart and got out before anyone could catch them. Same MO. ATV to a cut fence, loaded into a truck and gone. They were prepared."

"And we weren't." Tate shook his head. "I expected a full-on attack. Never thought they'd create a diversion. We're dealing with someone with a few brains."

C.W. nodded toward Tate's bag. "Going somewhere?"

"San Antonio."

"I'm coming with you," C.W. stated, a stubborn look on his face.

Tate shook his head. "You can't. I need someone I can trust here. I'm not convinced Rosa's in any shape to hold down the fort yet. She suffered a concussion and refuses to go to the hospital."

"As thickheaded as she is, I'm surprised they didn't have to hit her a couple times. Guess we're lucky they didn't." C.W. stared at the windows behind Tate as if he could see inside to the woman in question. Although he joked, the tightness of his lips gave lie to his humor. He cared about Rosa. More than either of them would admit.

"Give her at least a day under a doctor's supervision and you can join us in San Antonio. She'll want to follow sooner. Sit on her if you have to."

"Will do." His brows drew together. "Tate, I don't like you going off by yourself. We look out for each other. We've been doing that since Afghanistan."

"C.W.," Tate said, his tone low and steady, "I need you here for now. Rosa needs you here. We need to make sense of the barn burning and see what evidence they find from the break-in and kidnapping. They might even call here demanding a ransom. I need you and Rosa to handle this end of it for now."

C.W.'s jaw tightened, his fists clenching and releasing. He was still covered in ash and soot from the fire. The rest of the ranch hands worked alongside the volunteer firefighters to keep the fire from spreading. The EMTs treated the wounded and one had been in to see to Rosa.

"I'm not needed here," Tate said. "Jake needs me."

"I can help." C.W. gave one last try.

"Sylvia has contacts in San Antonio. We'll find him."

"What about backup?"

"I promise, I'll keep in touch."

"Don't go in guns a-blazing. You aren't John Wayne and this isn't a movie script."

Tate chuckled. C.W. had used the same words on an operation they'd conducted in Afghanistan, right before they'd busted into a home filled with stolen weapons and rebel fighters. They'd been lucky that night. They hadn't lost a single man. Because they'd all looked out for each other.

"I know the value of teamwork, C.W. I'm counting on you to get things squared away pretty quickly and join me as soon as you can."

C.W. nodded. His mouth pressed into a thin line. He glared at Sylvia. "Don't mess with my man Tate."

She planted her hands on her hips and glared back at C.W. "You know, I'm just a little tired of everyone thinking I'm the bad guy here." Then she sighed, her shoulders sagging. "Rest assured, Tate's calling all the shots for now."

"Keep it that way and you'll stay alive." C.W. glanced toward the still-smoldering barn. "I better get back to it. The fire chief said he smelled gasoline. I'm not surprised."

Tate hooked Sylvia's elbow and led her toward his truck. "Come on, we have to find Jake. I have a feeling the guys we're dealing with will make it difficult."

"You think?" Sylvia said, her voice dripping with sarcasm. "I've spent the past six months searching for my son. Let me tell ya, it hasn't been a cakewalk."

As Sylvia climbed into the truck, she sucked in a deep breath and exhaled slowly, refusing to let depression hit her hard enough to bring her down. After finally finding Jacob, to have him stolen again was more than she could handle. The culmination of six months' work had gone up in smoke.

She sat beside Tate in the cab of the pickup, staring straight ahead, wondering where to begin.

"We'll find him." Tate's voice filled the darkness, warming the cold places in Sylvia's heart.

"Do you finally believe me?"

For a long moment, silence reigned.

Sylvia stole a glance at Tate's profile, his square jaw and strong chin a sharp contrast to the fullness of his lips. His eyes stared straight ahead at the road illuminated by the truck's headlights, giving away nothing of the thoughts churning in his head. Only the muscle twitching in the side of his face gave any indication that tonight's fiasco had any impact on him. Sylvia waited quietly, determined that he answer her question one way or the other. As long as he told the truth.

At last he faced her briefly, returning his focus to the road ahead. "I think I've believed you from the start. I just didn't want to admit that I could lose Jake."

She let go of the breath she'd been holding. For a long moment she remained silent, the relief that someone believed her almost overwhelming. For so long she'd struggled to get anyone to take her seriously. She'd fought the battle alone with only the few contacts she'd made during her investigation into gang warfare in San Antonio. Had the kidnappers gone anywhere else besides San Antonio, Jacob could have been lost to her forever.

The hollowness in her gut came with physical pain. "We have to get Jacob back." As soon as she said the words aloud, it dawned on her that she'd used the word *we*. Jacob was her son. When the DNA results came in, Tate Vincent would have no claim to the child. She cast a glance at Tate.

His hands gripped the steering wheel so tightly his knuckles turned white. His jaw could have been carved in granite. "We will get Jake back."

"And then what?" She couldn't help it. She had to know his intentions.

"We'll take it one step at a time."

Sylvia had to be satisfied with that. They had to concentrate on what was most important at the moment. And that was getting to Jacob before something dreadful happened to him. She refused to think anyone would hurt a harmless baby. She'd had to believe that all along or she'd have been a basket case.

"Who in San Antonio did you talk to that gave you the information about Beth Kirksey?" Tate asked, all business now.

With a deep breath, Sylvia shoved thoughts of a confused Jacob crying in the night from her mind and slipped back into the role of investigative reporter, the only role she'd known for the past six months. "I went undercover dressed as a hooker and walked the streets downtown, asking questions."

Tate frowned over at her. "Wasn't that dangerous?"

"Yeah. I had to hide a few times from pimps, but I knew I was on the right track. I just had to ask the right questions.

"I started telling the prostitutes I was pregnant and did they know of an adoption agency or a couple who would pay for my baby. That's when I found Velvet, a friend of Bunny's."

"Do you think you can find this Velvet woman again?"

"Yeah. But she might not talk to me."

"Why?"

"It was after I talked to her that Bunny was killed in a hit-and-run accident."

"How were you able to track Jake if Bunny...Beth wasn't talking?"

"I went to the courthouse and looked through the adoption records and birth certificates. That's when I found you."

"Do you think Velvet would know the men Beth worked with?"

"I don't know. But I'm guessing that she and Beth had the same pimp. He'd be the one who might know who to contact for selling a baby."

"Why do you say that?"

"Most of the prostitutes are under the protection of a pimp." Sylvia snorted softly. "And I use the word 'protection' loosely. It's more like they're under the *control* of a pimp. Anything they want to do has to go through the pimp to be approved. If Beth wanted to sell her baby, I'd bet good money she went through her pimp to do it."

"Sounds like you know your stuff. How did you survive in their territory?"

"I kept thinking about Jacob. Between dodging pimps, undercover cops and amorous johns, I had my work cut out for me."

"Didn't the prostitutes suspect you?" He looked over at her. "I mean, if you weren't taking on clients, how did you convince them you were the real deal?"

Sylvia smiled in the darkness. "I had my own 'clients' pick me up and take me away for several hours, then I'd have them drop me off again on the same street corner."

"You took money for sex?"

Her lips twisted into a wry grin and she shot a "get real" look at Tate. "No. I wasn't that desperate for money then. I called in a few favors and also paid money for a ride from some of my contacts to and from a restaurant."

Tate's lips curled upward. "Clever."

They sat in silence, watching the miles slide away. Sylvia didn't realize she'd fallen asleep until she awoke to the bright streetlights shining down through her window.

She stretched and yawned. "Where are we?"

"San Antonio."

A glance at the clock on the dash left her disappointed. "It's too late to hit the streets. Most of the ladies will be either occupied or home for the rest of what's left of the night."

The darkness of night faded into a battleship-gray predawn light.

"Let's find a room to sleep for a while." Tate ran a hand through his hair. "I'm beat."

"Make it off the beaten path. Out here on the edge of town would be best."

"Done." He pulled into the nearest economy hotel and slid out of the truck. "I'll be back."

Sylvia breathed a sigh that he hadn't insisted on her coming in. She had drained her savings, and the lack of paying work and her recent loss of anything left of value in the car fire had left her penniless. A man like Tate Vincent with all that wealth at his disposal wouldn't understand how low she'd sunk.

Speak of the devil, he exited the motel with an envelope, probably containing a room key card. He climbed in and drove the vehicle around the back of the building and parked.

Sylvia braced herself for what was to come.

"Come on. I could use a couple hours of sleep."

"You do that." It was one thing to accept a room in his house, another for him to pay for a motel room for her. "I'm not sleepy," she lied.

"Yeah. That's why you slept for the last hour."

"That's right. I feel refreshed." She pushed her hair behind her ears and opened her eyes wider, faking being alert and ready to go when every muscle and nerve in her body begged for another four hours of shut-eye.

"I hope you're a better liar when we meet up with the ladies of the night later on this evening." He climbed down from the truck and walked around to the passenger side to open her door. "Out."

"No, really. I don't need sleep. I once went three days without sleep when working a piece on the effects of sleep deprivation."

"Yeah, and I'll bet you didn't have a barn burn down on top of you back then." He held out his hand. "Come on. I'm dead on my feet."

"You go. I'll stand guard on your truck to make sure no one takes it."

"No way. You're sleeping in the room, in a bed. It'll be daylight soon and this truck can get awfully damned hot once the sun beats down on it."

"I'll roll a window down. I'll be just fine."

His jaw tightened. "You're staying in the room." He reached for her hand.

She evaded. "No, I'm not."

"Why?"

With her arms crossed over her chest, she stayed put in the truck seat. "Because."

Tate sucked in a deep breath and let it out. "That's not a reason."

"I don't have to explain myself to you."

"Fine. Have it your way." He turned to leave her.

Sylvia startled when he spun around, reached in and grabbed her, slinging her over his shoulder like a bag of potatoes.

Sylvia landed with an *oomph,* all the breath knocked out of her for a split second. Then she sucked in air and squealed, "Put me down, you Neanderthal!"

"Shh! Be quiet or you'll wake everyone up."

"I don't need you to carry me into the room. I was perfectly happy to sleep in the truck."

"Not an option. And ha! You said sleep. I knew you weren't as wide-awake as you claimed."

"I am now." She pounded his back.

Tate marched toward a room on the back corner, shifting her weight so that he could use one hand to slide the key card into the lock. The light on the lock blinked green and he pushed the door open, carrying her inside.

"I can't stay in here."

He dropped her onto the king-size bed, his hair mussed, but he wasn't breathing hard at all. "Again, I ask why?"

Flustered from being that close to him in a very intimate position, Sylvia couldn't think fast enough to come up with a lie. "I can't afford it."

Tate's black brows scrunched together. "Can't afford it? Did I ask you to pay for the room?"

"No. But I will. As soon as I can." Whenever that might be. She'd have to get some real paying jobs and quickly. As soon as she found Jacob and got him back. But every day she searched cost money, something she was fresh out of. Never in her life had she relied on charity, not even after her parents died.

The magnitude of her predicament overwhelmed her. "I can't take your charity."

"Charity? You think this is charity?" Tate threw his hands in the air. "All this fuss because of a motel room?" He dropped onto the bed beside her and flopped back, his booted feet hanging off the end of the mattress. "I'm so tired I can't even think straight. Having you in this room is not a matter of charity. I want to keep an eye on you and this was the only way I knew how."

Sylvia sat up and glared down at him. "Is that it? You still don't trust me? I thought you believed me. Was that all a lie?"

Tate groaned. "I'm too tired to argue. You're welcome to continue if you want. Sleep in the truck, sleep on the bed, anywhere you want. Just let me get a few minutes rest." He lay with his eyes closed, a hand draped over his face.

Indignation melted away as she studied the lines around his mouth and the dull color of his skin. He did look tired and she'd done nothing but argue with him for the past fifteen minutes.

Guilt made her suck it up and stay put when she wanted to go back out to the truck. Being in a room with Tate Vincent could be dangerous. Especially when the only substantial piece of furniture was a bed.

When he didn't stir to take off his boots, Sylvia relaxed a little.

She didn't know if she was mad or relieved that it wasn't a case of charity but one of lack of trust. Just when she thought she had Tate Vincent all figured out, he opened his mouth and surprised her all over again.

His chest moved up and down in a slow, steady rhythm. Had he fallen asleep that fast? She leaned close to look beneath his arm to see if his eyes were open.

Closed.

By all appearances, Tate Vincent was fast asleep.

If she wanted, she could leave him now and strike out on her own to find Jacob. She'd been doing it for so long, it made sense. Besides, Tate might slow her down. This was her chance.

Sylvia stared at him another minute and made her decision. The boots had to come off.

Chapter Ten

Tate woke to muted light peeking around the edges of the heavy curtain. He didn't recognize his surroundings. It took a full fifteen seconds before all the events of the past twenty-four hours flooded in. The appearance of the blond-haired, blue-eyed beauty claiming to be Jake's mother, the car fire, the shooting and the barn fire.

No wonder he'd slept so soundly. It was a wonder he didn't sleep until Sunday. Movement against his side brought him fully alert. A slim, pale hand slid across his chest, resting over his heart. The woman at the root of all things gone wrong in his life over the last day lay snuggled against him, a bare leg slung over his, her white Mexican dress rumpled halfway up her thigh, exposing an amazing amount of pale skin.

His groin tightened, his hand reaching for hers. A groan rose up in his throat at the feel of her skin against his. How could a woman who appeared so slim and delicate carry the burden she'd carried for the past six months? Alone?

As much as he wanted to hate her for threatening to take Jake away from him, Tate couldn't. Instead he wanted to protect her, to right all the wrongs and return her son to her, even if it meant he'd lose Jake forever.

His fingers stroked hers. Her head lay in the crook of his arm, her breath warm against his shirt. What would it feel like to lie naked with her? Would the rest of her body be as soft and smooth?

The fly on his jeans grew uncomfortably tighter. He should be ashamed of the lusty thoughts he was having toward a woman he'd only met the day before. A woman who could have orchestrated this entire situation to get him alone and make him... What? Aroused?

"Mmm..." Her soft hum did nothing to still his rapidly increasing pulse. Her arm smoothed down over his chest, inching lower until it bumped against the rising seam of his jeans.

The groan he'd suppressed rose again in his throat and he couldn't contain it.

Sylvia's baby blues opened, her full, thick lashes fluttering until she stared up into his face and blinked sleepily. "What...?" Her leg stiffened against his.

"Shh. Be still."

"But..."

"You were tired. I make a good pillow and you've only been asleep for a couple hours. Now, go back to sleep."

Her lashes drifted closed. "But I don't know you."

"Then we're even."

"We shouldn't be this—" she yawned into his shirt "—close." But she didn't move her leg from his nor did she shift her arm higher. Her hand lay within an inch of Tate's growing erection.

He wondered how long he could lie still and hold his breath. Because that was the only way he could keep her there in his arms without making a move. What shocked him most was that he wanted her there. Her soft curves and braless breasts fit against him perfectly.

With more effort than he thought he could muster, he tried to relax and go back to sleep, but he couldn't. His hand slid down to cover hers, stroking it as it moved lower.

Oh, Lord help him. She touched him there, lighting his entire body on fire. No way he could lay still and not react to her nearness. Her skin alone ignited a flame in his loins, making him want to strip off his clothes and bury himself inside her.

Her hand closed around the ridge, smoothing over it, pressing into the denim.

"Are you awake? Do you have any idea what you're doing to me?" he whispered, begging her to quit at the same time wishing she wouldn't.

After a long, lung-arresting moment, she answered, her breathy voice blowing warm air against his sensitized neck. "I'm awake."

The long, naked limb draped over his thigh tightened, bringing her closer until the warmth at the apex of her thighs straddled his trapped leg. Her dress rode higher until he could see that she wasn't wearing panties, the bare, white skin of her rounded bottom teasing him from beneath the dress. Apparently, underwear had been forgotten when Rosa brought clothes for Sylvia to wear. Not that he minded.

Far from it. But he might regret it later. He found it incredibly hard to see or think past the hand on his crotch.

"Do you know what you're doing?" he repeated through his clenched teeth.

"No, I don't know what I'm doing." She laughed into his neck. "But it's becoming more obvious as we go." She smoothed her fingers lower to cup him.

He grabbed her hand and held it still. "I don't expect payment for the room, if that's what this is." His words were steely, more harsh than he'd wanted to sound, but he had to say it.

Sylvia's body stiffened. "It's not," she said, her voice tight.

"Then why?"

"I told you, I don't know. Why did we kiss in the garden? Why have I been lying here half-awake, imagining the possibilities for the past thirty minutes?" She sighed and squeezed him gently. "I don't know. Because it feels right?"

As the pressure increased on him he sucked in a deep breath and let it out. Then he flipped her over on her back and pinned her to the mattress, straddling her hips, holding her hands high above her head.

"Don't mess with me, Sylvia Michaels. I don't take kindly to being led on."

Her eyes wide, her lips soft and full, she stared back at him. "I'm not making any promises. I've been in a failed marriage. I'm not looking for happily ever after."

"Then what are you looking for?" he demanded, the answer more important to him than he'd ever admit.

"I don't know." She stared up at him, tears trembling on the ends of her lashes. "I don't know. I'm just tired of being alone." A single tear slid down the side of her cheek.

Had she lied to him, had she screamed at him to make love to her, he might have taken a step back and let her go. But the one tear and the admission that she didn't know what she wanted from him made him want her more. Damn her!

His mouth claimed hers, his hand loosening its grip on hers, cupped her cheek, holding her steady as he drank from her lips. She reached between them to flick the buttons open on his jeans, circling him with her fingertips, easing him out of the denim.

Tate groaned into her mouth, his tongue circling hers, thrusting deep inside.

In two fluid movements, Tate ripped the belt from Sylvia's waist and the dress up over her head. She lay naked against the sheets, her silky blond hair fanned out against the pillow. She worked the buttons on his shirt while he slipped the jeans down over his hips. "Hey, how did my boots get off?"

Naked, he lay on the bed beside her, and trailed a hand over her collarbone and down over one pale, rosy-brown nipple.

Sylvia shrugged. "I'm not all into that 'cowboys sleeping with their boots on' thing."

"Me, either. Thanks." His lips followed his fingers. He nipped at the nipple closest to him and teased it into a tight peak.

Sylvia squirmed, her fingers digging into his hair. It had been more than a year since she'd made love, the last man her ex-husband. His idea of foreplay was getting her naked in thirty seconds.

"Like that?" Tate asked against her breast.

"Mmm, yes."

He treated the other nipple to the same until both stood at attention, the hardened nubs glistening. Then he moved back up to kiss her, tonguing the line of her lips until she opened to let him in.

"I like the way you taste."

She laughed. "Do you always talk this much when you're…you know…?"

"Making love?" He nuzzled her neck, his hand drifting down between her breasts toward her belly button. "No. Usually more."

She laughed, her breath catching as he lowered his hand to the juncture of her thighs. How she wanted him to touch her there. Probably more than she wanted to take her next breath.

But his hand paused, the delicious stroking ceasing. He lifted his head and stared down into her eyes. "Do you want more? Or should I stop here?"

She would have laughed if she had enough air in her lungs to make the sound. She sucked in a shaky breath and whispered, "Are you kidding me?"

He shook his head. "I don't make love lightly. And I don't take advantage of women." His voice dropped deeper. "And if she consents, I don't leave her unsatisfied."

Ready to squirm and beg for more, Sylvia's knees drew up and her heels dug into the mattress. She covered his hand with hers and moved it lower. "Does this answer your question?"

He held his hand still, shaking his head. "No. Say it, Sylvia. Tell me what you want."

"Can't you tell?" She stroked his fingers through the moist folds. "What do you want from me?"

"I want to hear you tell me what you want. Hasn't anyone ever asked you?"

She shook her head, the lust and desire swelling deeper. Beyond what she should be feeling for a man she'd only just met. The one she'd told that she wasn't interested in commitment. "I want you to make love to me. I want to feel you inside me. I want you to touch me here." She pressed his fingers inside her channel, swirling them around in the moisture he'd inspired. "I want *you,* Tate Vincent."

He smiled and pressed a kiss to her forehead. "Was that so hard?"

She laughed. "Yes!"

He smoothed a lock of hair out of her eyes and touched a gentle kiss to the tip of her nose. Then his lips descended onto hers.

Miguel had started out a conscientious lover, attempting to do things that brought her to orgasm, but never had he asked her what she liked. He'd always assumed she'd like what he was doing. She'd faked more than once to get through it without making him feel like he'd failed.

Making love to Tate Vincent wasn't just about satisfying him. Just like the way he lived his life, he asked questions and worked hard to determine exactly what it would take to succeed. Even when it came to making love.

And oh, did he have the right technique to bring her with him.

His fingers played magic against her folds, stroking and coaxing her into a heightened state of arousal, flicking against the ultrasensitive nub. Her heels dug into the mattress, lifting her higher, her hand pressing him deeper. When she catapulted over the edge, he moved over her, still stroking her with his hand as he settled his legs between hers.

"Wait!" she gasped. "What about protection?" Even

in the moment, she couldn't risk getting pregnant. Not when they were ultimately destined to part.

He held his breath for a moment. "See what you do to me? I almost forgot." While she lay against the sheets in the pulsing aftermath, Tate dove for his jeans, yanking the wallet from the back pocket. He pulled out a foil packet and tore it with his teeth.

"Let me." She took the packet from his fingers and removed the condom from the moist interior, sliding it down over his engorged member. The effort stirred her, making her want more of what he'd started. She lay back, guiding him into her, clasping his buttocks in her hands.

He started out slow, steady, slipping in and out in a gentle rhythm.

Sylvia didn't want slow and steady, she wanted fast and furious. She tightened her hands on his butt and slammed him into her, setting the pace with quick, urgent moves. Her breathing grew more ragged, her body as slick with sweat as his. When he came, he pushed into her, burying himself deep inside, throbbing against her.

She wrapped her legs around his waist and held him there, loving the way he filled her, stretching her so tightly with his girth. A woman could get used to making love to Tate Vincent.

The thought instantly sobered her.

She had no claim on the man. She'd been through one bad marriage and had no intention of doing that again. Not that he'd asked. Nor would he. What would a multimillionaire see in a destitute single mom other than perhaps her legal claim on the baby he loved? Was that it? Was this his way of keeping Jake in the family?

Sylvia lay still, Tate still fitting snugly inside her. Though she wanted to run screaming from the motel room, she couldn't bring herself to break the connection. Sure that once she did, it would be for good. There would be no second chances with Tate Vincent. Not when so much was at stake.

She needed him only as far as she needed anyone who could help get her son back. Beyond that, they had nothing in common, no future. Once she had Jacob, they'd go their separate ways.

But for now, he felt so good, so right inside her.

Tears welled in her eyes. She'd lost so many people she'd loved. Her parents in a car crash right before her wedding to Miguel. Miguel to his mistresses. And now Jacob. Her son...her only reason for living had disappeared.

She didn't trust herself to love another human being. Not when the stakes were so high. And she had no right to love Tate Vincent. He was way out of her league. Not to mention, she'd barely known him for twenty-four hours.

What would she do when the time came to part ways? She'd cried enough tears to fill Canyon Lake. She had no intention of crying more.

Then why did a tear slip from the corner of her eye?

She brushed it away and moved closer to the warmth of Tate's naked body. A smart woman would get up, get dressed and walk out of the motel room.

Lately, she hadn't been so smart.

And Tate's warmth wrapped her in a security she hadn't felt in a long time. She pressed closer.

His arm tightened around her, his leg draping over hers. "What next?" he whispered into her hair.

Her hand trailed over his chest. "The ladies won't be out until dark. I have no idea how to contact them otherwise."

"Then get some sleep. I have a feeling tonight will be a long night."

Despite the tumble of thoughts churning in her head, Sylvia yawned, her eyes drifting closed. "Okay. But only for a minute."

Tate tugged a blanket up over their naked bodies, settling Sylvia into the crook of his arm. They still maintained that intimate connection and Sylvia didn't want to let go. Not yet. Maybe later.

Tate must have drifted off. When he woke, the clock on the nightstand flashed a bright green two o'clock in the afternoon. They'd slept a long time. His lungs still ached from all the smoke he'd inhaled, but his head was clear and he knew what had to be done.

They had to find Velvet and her pimp.

Sylvia lay against him, her pale, smooth cheeks rosy from the warmth they generated beneath the blankets. Her long lashes fanned out below her eyes. Blond hair spilled over his shoulder and across the white pillowcases. He hated to wake her. If the situation had been any different, he'd lie there all the rest of the day and into the next night exploring her body and getting to know her better.

He wanted to know this determined young mother. Not just because she claimed to be Jake's mother, but because of all she'd done, all she'd been through on her own. Hopefully there would be time for that later.

Carefully, he slipped his arm from beneath her head and eased out of the bed. Gathering his jeans, he headed for a shower…a cold one. He was ready for a repeat performance from the early-morning lovemaking, but he'd bet money Sylvia would wake up wondering what the hell she'd done. The woman would need some space to digest their actions.

In the shower, he let the water pour down over his heated body. With the stream running down over his face, he didn't hear the door open, nor did he know he wasn't alone until arms circled around him, a slim, naked body pressing against his back.

"Do you always take cold showers in the morning?"

Tate smiled and adjusted the heat on the faucet before he turned in Sylvia's arms. She was one in a million. "Only when I'm trying to make an effort not to scare my partner." He tipped her head up and stared down into eyes so blue he could see the sky in them. "Any regrets?"

"Only one."

His brow tipped upward.

"This place doesn't have conditioner for my hair." She leaned into his chest, her cheeks pink and shiny wet. "Let's not make this a big deal, okay? Whatever happens, happens. No ties, no regrets." She looked up into his eyes, a small frown creasing her forehead. "Deal?"

Tate wasn't so sure about this so-called deal, but he didn't want to chase her off yet. Apparently, this relationship would take some work, if he planned on it being long-term. And she'd made it clear she didn't want long-term.

She'd handed him what every guy dreamed of: a license to enjoy and move on when he wanted. What Sylvia didn't know was that Tate didn't do one-night stands. He didn't take sleeping with a woman lightly and he might just want a long-term relationship.

Sylvia lathered her hands with soap, then ran them over his body, starting at his chest, working her fingers through the smattering of curly hairs, tweaking his hard brown nipples. Her fingers made him nuts. But when they made their way down…

He groaned, his own hands tangling in her long, wet hair, kneading the back of her neck, thumbing the sensitive area beneath her ears.

When she reached his groin, there was no going back. The hard-on he left bed with had gotten stronger. If he didn't have her soon, he'd explode like a teenager.

He relieved her of the soap and started his own attack on her body, sliding suds over her breasts. He let the shower stream over his shoulder to drip off the ends of her nipples. When the soap cleared, he took one of her nipples into his mouth and sucked hard, teasing the tip with his tongue until it hardened into a peak. She had beautiful breasts.

Sylvia arched into him, her leg circling his thigh.

Tate cupped the back of her buttocks and lifted her, wrapping her legs around his waist, easing her down over his erection.

Her quickly indrawn breath was followed by a long, low moan. "God, that feels so good."

"Now who's talking?" he said through gritted teeth as he fought to keep from spilling into her immediately.

"Shut up and move, cowboy." She circled her arms around his neck and lifted herself up his body, then eased down over him again.

"Too slow," he said. Then he turned her back to the shower wall, leveraging her so that he could drive in and out of her, again and again.

She rode him, her head tilted back, her eyes closed,

water sliding down her body, her own juices making him slip in and out easily. The pressure built, the heat in the bathroom creating a fog around them, wrapping them in a world of their own.

"Oh, Tate, now. There!" She came down over him, her legs tightening around him as he pumped into her one last time, holding back with every ounce of control he could muster. Then he lifted her off him just in time before he came. He held her close, his body throbbing, the water from the shower cooling him, bringing him back to earth.

Sylvia leaned her forehead into his shoulder and whispered, "Wow."

"Yeah." Tate rubbed a hand down her back and over her smooth, rounded butt. "Wow."

"Thanks." She leaned up on her toes and pressed a kiss to his chin. "And just remember, no strings, no regrets." Then she stepped out of the shower and closed the curtain behind her.

Tate groaned. Just as Kacee had predicted, Sylvia Michaels was trouble. Just how much trouble was yet to be seen.

Chapter Eleven

"What's the plan for the day?" Dressed in his jeans, shirt and cowboy boots, Tate stood with his hand on the doorknob, looking more damned handsome than a man had a right to look.

Sylvia cinched the belt around her waist, drawing the voluminous Mexican dress in to fit her figure. She struggled to wrap her mind around the fact that she'd made love with multimillionaire Tate Vincent. Not once, which she could have written off as a lapse in judgment, but twice.

Now she could barely face him without blushing. The way they'd scaled the shower walls was…incredible. She should feel ashamed. But she didn't. Making love to a good-looking stranger had taken her mind off all the possible scenarios Jacob could be enduring. Not to mention she'd made it perfectly clear she didn't expect anything and had insisted on no regrets.

She'd do well to take her own advice on the regrets. Pushing her shoulders back, she forced herself to face Tate, his brown-black gaze melting her resolve with just a glance. "I want to touch base with a few of my contacts, and then tonight I'll walk South Presa Street and see if I can find Velvet."

"I'm not sure I like the idea of you walking the streets like a hooker."

She smiled. "I know what to do."

"I don't know what bothers me more, that you know what to do or that you'll be doing it." His lips twisted into a wickedly stunning half smile. "It's dangerous. Especially now that someone is gunning for you."

No, you're dangerous, Sylvia wanted to say. That smile could send any sane woman over the edge and into his bed. "You don't know that they were shooting at me. They could have been shooting at you." She didn't mention that they might have been gunning for Jacob. And since he'd been stolen, it was more of a possibility than she cared to consider.

The little bit of a smile vanished, replaced by a deep frown, drawing his dark brows together. "I'm coming with you."

"I'm counting on it." She pressed a finger to his chest. "You can be my pimp. We have to make it look as real as possible. Velvet won't buy into it if I'm just hanging out on the corner."

The return of his smile made her heart skip a beat and the butterflies in her stomach take flight. "I like that." The smile faded. "But I don't like the idea of other men groping you."

"Only you?" She grinned. "Don't worry. I have a can of pepper spray…" Sylvia sighed. "I *had* one in my car."

"And the car is toast. I'll get you another one."

"I'll pay you back when this is all over."

"You don't have to pay me back."

She glared at him. "Yes, I do."

He ignored her and continued on. "You'll need clothes to fit the part. I'll cover you on that, as well."

"No."

"You can pay me back. I know, I know."

"As long as you understand. I have just the place to shop for the right stuff." A sly grin stole across her face. "Trust me."

Tate opened the door for her. "I'm not going to like this, am I?"

They spent the next hour in a thrift shop, combing through the shortest skirts, highest heels and skimpiest tops to find the perfect hooker outfit.

While Sylvia sifted through old, new and slightly worn hand-me-downs of questionable taste, Tate stood with his back to the wall, his arms crossed over his chest. Unwilling to try it on for him, she selected what she needed and set it on the counter. She did try on a pair of jeans and regular shirt, something she didn't associate with being in bed with Tate, like the Mexican dress.

Fully transformed in jeans, a simple, white-cotton blouse and a pair of loafers, she stepped out of the dressing room and joined Tate at the counter. The hooker clothes, plus the outfit she had on and a baseball cap cost less than twenty dollars. On the back of the receipt she wrote IOU and signed her name, handing the receipt to Tate.

That she didn't have money of her own made her stomach knot. If it was the last thing she did, she'd pay Tate Vincent back for every dime she owed him. "I don't like being in debt to anyone."

"What's important is that we find Jake. We'll settle up when we do."

Sylvia prided herself on her independence. Miguel had always wanted to provide, to the point he didn't want her making any money of her own. To him, it was an affront to his manhood. To her, he'd stolen her independence.

For the first two years of their marriage, Sylvia had placed her career on hold. Until she'd caught Miguel with his mistress. In their bed. Then she'd realized that she had nothing of her own. No income, no job, no parents to fall back on. She'd stuck with the marriage until she'd sold enough articles to fund an apartment and her attorney fees. When the divorce was final, she swore she'd never be in a situation again where she couldn't walk away from it and stand on her own feet.

A relationship should be one where each person came into it because of love and mutual respect and stayed for the same reasons, not because they had no other means to support themselves.

As they settled into Tate's truck, Sylvia drew in a deep breath. "I need you to drop me off on Market Street and go away for a bit."

"What?" Tate had pulled away from the thrift shop and was driving toward downtown. He stopped at a red light and turned to her. "Why?"

"Remember I said I had contacts?"

"Yeah."

"My contacts like me to come alone."

Tate's palm hit the steering wheel. "I don't like it."

His concern warmed her insides. How long had it been since someone expressed concern over her well-being? Too long. Yet, she knew she had to do this on her own. "I'll be back, I promise. It's broad daylight. He won't do anything in daylight."

"I don't care—"

"It's the only way I can talk to him." She pulled her

hair back, secured it with an elastic band and shoved it into a San Antonio Spurs ball cap.

"Can't you call?"

"No." She placed a hand on his arm. "Please. I know what I'm doing." She didn't tell him that the street she'd be going to was in one of the most notorious neighborhoods in the city, nor did she tell him that her contact was one of the meanest, baddest gang leaders around. Tate would never let her go if he knew. Every time she'd gone to talk to Juan Vargas, she took her life into her own hands. But she'd learned to never show fear and deal straight with him and she'd be all right.

Tate shook his head. "We should go to the police and let them know what you know."

"These people aren't going to be anywhere on the police radar. They've been in operation for at least six months without being caught. Probably longer." The light changed. "It's green. Turn right and let me off at the next corner."

His hands tightened on the steering wheel until his knuckles turned white. "You can't do this."

When he drove by the spot she'd indicated, Sylvia knew she'd have to make her own move. She waited for another stoplight. When Tate pulled to a stop, she yanked open the door and jumped out.

"Damn it, Sylvia! Get back in this truck!"

"I have my cell phone. I'll call you when I need you to pick me up. If all else fails, meet me at the Alamo in an hour." Then she ran down a one-way street that Tate couldn't turn on and disappeared into an alley.

He'd be mad, but she had to do it this way. Juan wouldn't let her close if he knew she had company with her. Wearing the ball cap low over her brow, she hurried

down a side street, away from the fancier businesses
and retail shops lining the riverwalk and angled toward
the older, seedier residences. Even with the bright Texas
sun beating down on her, a chill stole its way across
her skin.

The last time she'd been in this neighborhood she'd
done the gang violence piece. That story had been in
all the Texas newspapers and she'd capitalized on the
information to sell it to a magazine. She'd been able to
pay off her attorney with the proceeds and had enough
left to buy a bed for her apartment. She'd been five
months pregnant with Jacob at the time.

Juan had let her slide on a lot of his gang protocol
because of her condition, his girlfriend having just delivered a baby girl.

Sylvia wasn't pregnant now. Would Juan be as be-
nevolent? Had he read her articles in the paper or the
magazine copy detailing the statistics of gang violence
and the behind-the-scenes descriptions of how some of
the kids came to join gangs? Was he angry at how she'd
described what drove them to do the things they did and
the consequences of their associations?

The last time she'd been in San Antonio looking for
Jacob, she hadn't bothered to look Juan up. Now she had
to rely on all of her contacts, good and bad, in order to
find Jacob. Given what had happened to Beth Kirksey,
Velvet might not be as forthcoming.

A group of young men wearing baggy jeans, chains
hanging from their pockets and T-shirts with scorpions
silk-screened across the back loitered in front of a run-
down store advertising cigarettes and alcohol.

Sylvia didn't make eye contact, crossing the street
to avoid any confrontation with them.

Another block over and one to the left and she'd be at the house where she'd originally met Juan Vargas. God, she hoped he still lived there. She cut through a yard and hurried down a back alley, littered with trash cans and empty beer and liquor bottles.

A burst of laughter made her look back. As she turned to slip through a gap between two houses, she cast a glance behind her. The group of men she'd by-passed had followed her.

Great. Maybe Tate had the right idea. Going to the police seemed like a much better idea than getting gang-raped in a back alley.

As soon as she rounded the corner of the house, Sylvia broke into a run. One block up on the left was the house she'd been aiming for.

Please, let Juan still live there. Please, let him be home.

The laughter increased and feet pounded on the sidewalk behind her.

Sylvia ran for all she was worth, her breathing ragged, fear choking her lungs. She reached the house well before the gang of men came into sight again and pounded on the door. "Please, I must speak with Juan Vargas. Let me in!"

The door remained closed, the windows dark and vacant. The men rounded the corner at a run, laughing and making wolf calls. When they spied her, they slowed, each taking on a cocky swagger.

"Hey, *chica,* want some of this?" One of the young men with a Mohawk haircut pumped his hips at her.

"No, he's a dick. You want a real man." He grabbed his crotch and leered.

Sylvia knocked again, this time in full view of the

men. She tried to look casual, not like she was scared, which she was.

"Ain't no one home, little girl. Looks like it's just you, me and *mi amigos*." The leader of the group, a short, stocky, bald Hispanic man with a scar slashed across his cheek and dragon tattoos covering his arms, neck and the back of his head, pushed through the others.

Sylvia stood with her back to the door. She squared her shoulders and, mustering every ounce of courage, faced off with the gang, forcing a nonchalant smirk to her lips. Inside, she wanted to cower, shake and run screaming. "Oh, grow up. I'm not here to provide your entertainment. I'm looking for my friend, Juan Vargas." She hoped the name would inspire fear.

Not a chance.

The leader crossed his arms over his chest. "Señor Vargas is your friend?" He snorted. "Right, and I had dinner with the president last night. If you were a friend of Juan Vargas, you'd know he doesn't live here anymore."

Sylvia's heart sank into her thrift-shop shoes. It was time for desperate measures. "Oh, yeah, then who do you think that is coming down the street now?"

As one, all the young men turned to look behind them.

Sylvia had only this one shot at escape and she took it. She leaped from the porch of the run-down house and ran as fast as she could.

She figured she only had a few steps lead on the men so she had to make it to a busier street and quickly. Never had she been more glad to be in good physical shape. The daily jogging she did paid off. But the men behind her were young, wiry and fast. Faster than she was.

Pounding footsteps sounded behind her, closing in on her rapidly.

She darted between two houses, leaped over a pile of auto parts and vaulted a short chain-link fence. Her heart pounded in her ears, and she couldn't get enough air to fill her lungs, but she had to keep going. If she stopped, it might be the end. These guys might not just want to play with her, they might kill her when they were done. Sylvia couldn't risk that. Not when Jacob was in danger.

If only she could stay ahead of the men long enough to get back to the busier thoroughfares, to the streets lined with tourists and security cops.

She darted from between two houses, looking behind her as she ran out into the street. A car honked and brakes squealed as the tattooed man caught her arm and yanked her to a stop.

Sylvia screamed, twisted and fought with all her might. Her foot caught one man in the groin and another in the side of the face. Both growled and lunged at her.

Arms covered in inked dragons wrapped around her and lifted her off her feet. One of the other men yanked off her cap and her hair spilled out.

"*Muy linda.* Look at what we have here." With one hand effortlessly clamping her arms to her side, tattoo man lifted a long lock of hair and ran it through his fingers. "Nice."

Sylvia couldn't believe what was happening or that she'd been stupid enough to get herself in this situation. "You won't get away with it." Good God, it was broad daylight.

He leaned close, his nicotine-tainted breath blowing against her cheek. "And who's going to stop me?"

"I will," a deep, heavily accented voice sounded behind them.

"Señor Vargas." The man Sylvia had kicked in the face backed away several steps, a hand clamped to his bruised cheek, his eyes wide. He slapped the guy next to him and nodded toward the big man advancing on them, surrounded by two even bigger, barrel-chested men with snarls on their faces.

The arms clamped around Sylvia let go so suddenly she fell to the ground, the gravel on the street cutting into her palms.

When she looked up, she almost laughed hysterically at the sight of a black sedan parked in the middle of the street. Standing with his feet planted wide and his arms crossed over his chest was the man she remembered from her reporting days.

With a jerk of his head, Juan motioned for the two men beside him to step forward.

One on each side of Sylvia, they lifted her as if she weighed nothing.

Vargas's brow rose at the tattooed man. "Ah, Manuel, aren't you on probation? Don't you have community service to perform or something?"

Manuel stood his ground, the other five young thugs crowding in behind him, flipping open knives.

"This is my woman. I hear you've messed with her in any way, I'll cut you down. *Entendido?*"

"She's in our territory. She's fair game."

"Maybe you don't hear so well?" Juan said.

One of the men holding on to Sylvia's arm let go and advanced on Manuel.

The guys behind him moved up to form a single line, all with knives drawn, including a long, wicked blade that appeared in Manuel's hands.

Without so much as a blink, the larger man's hand whipped out, knocked the blade from Manuel's hand. He grabbed the empty hand, twisting Manuel around, jamming his arm up between his shoulder blades.

Manuel yelped, standing on his toes to alleviate the pressure. "I'll kill you, Vargas."

Vargas spit on the ground at Manuel's feet. "You aren't man enough to try." Then he turned away as if unafraid of the remaining gang members.

The man holding Sylvia marched her to the back door of the black sedan, pushing her inside.

Vargas slid in the other side and the doors closed. One of the big bodyguards climbed behind the wheel and pulled the car forward.

The man holding Manuel jerked the arm up higher, then shoved Manuel into his ranks of hoodlums. The tattooed man stumbled, righted himself and spun to face Vargas's bodyguard.

The bodyguard straightened his skin-tight black T-shirt and climbed into the sedan as if he was just stepping out for a Sunday drive.

As they drove away, Sylvia glanced out the rear window.

Manuel rubbed his arm, glaring at the car. The others gathered around, shaking their knives in the air.

"What brings you to my old neighborhood, Señorita Michaels?"

When Sylvia faced Juan, she wondered whether she'd left the frying pan for the fire.

TATE CIRCLED THE STREET twice and expanded the grid, searching for Sylvia. The more he drove the madder he got and the more he worried. He knew the gang activity in San Antonio wasn't so bad during the daylight hours, but as he drove through some of the more derelict streets, his worry intensified.

He checked his watch. Fifteen minutes had passed. If he hadn't found her by now, he doubted he would. Damn her!

With no other options than to wait for her at the Alamo, he drove to the River Center Mall and parked in the parking deck. With time to spare, he walked the short distance to the Alamo and paced outside the ancient mission building, imagining all that could go wrong with Sylvia's plan.

Among the scenarios that came to mind was the one that she'd ditched him to set out on her own. Without her network of contacts and information sources he didn't have much to go on. But he did have friends in important places. You don't become a millionaire without people to help pave the way.

He flipped open his cell phone and dialed Kacee.

"'Bout time you checked in." She answered on the first ring. "Where are you?"

"San Antonio."

A horn honked in the background and Kacee cursed. "Why haven't you called me?"

"Had a lot on my mind. Where are you?"

"On I-35. Traffic's awful, as usual. Look, Tate, I'm sorry about Jake and the barn. I've been making calls left and right. The FBI are on it and Sheriff Thompson has promised full cooperation. The insurance adjuster is waiting for the full report from the fire marshal. His preliminary findings indicate that someone set the fire."

Tate's back teeth ground together. He'd figured as much. Still, it made his blood pressure rise to hear his fears confirmed. The barn burning had been a diversion for the real crime. Stealing Jake. "I need Zach's number."

"Hang on."

Tate waited while Kacee, no doubt, juggled her BlackBerry while negotiating traffic to find the number requested.

"Ready?" She gave him the number and Tate committed it to memory. "Why are you calling him?"

"I want the name of Beth Kirksey's attorney and the adoption agency."

"I can get all that for you."

"I'll do it myself. Most likely they're here in San Antonio."

"Anything I can do?" Kacee asked. "I can be there in an hour."

"You'd be speeding." He had enough on his mind with Sylvia. Having Kacee riding shotgun would only make it harder. He needed space to think. "Tell C.W. to stay put. I need him at the ranch in case the kidnappers demand a ransom."

"I'll tell him. And Tate…if they do?"

"We'll cross that bridge when we get to it. Later, Kacee."

"Tate, I should be there. There's a lot I can offer."

"I know, but I don't want you involved. I have a feeling this could get more dangerous."

"More than it already has?"

"Exactly. We'll talk later." He hit the off button and dialed Zach Stanford's number.

"Tate! Great to hear from you. How's Jake?"

Zach's casual greeting hit Tate harder than Kacee's condolences. Once again the magnitude of what had happened made the knot in his gut tighten painfully. "Jake's gone."

"What?"

Tate brought Zach up to date. "I need the addresses of the attorney and adoption agency Beth Kirksey used ASAP."

"Will do. Give me two minutes and I'll call you right back."

Tate hung up and surveyed Alamo Plaza. Tourists milled about, reading plaques, taking pictures in front of the old mission church and laughed as if they had no cares in the world. The whole time, Tate's stomach roiled and he could barely suppress the anger building inside.

His cell phone rang and he jerked it open. "Yeah."

Zach listed the street addresses of the attorney and the adoption agency as well as their phone numbers. "Anything else I can do for you?"

"Not yet."

"Keep me informed. I'm sorry this had to happen. They were legit as far as I could tell."

"I'm not blaming you, Zach. These people covered all the bases. Now we just have to catch them and find Jake."

After he hung up, he dialed an old friend he'd met in the military. Special Agent Paul Fletcher, currently assigned to the FBI Field Division in San Antonio. Why Tate hadn't called him earlier, he didn't know.

"You've reached the phone of Special Agent Fletcher. I'm currently out of the office. If you have an emergency, contact Agent Bradley." Fletcher's message gave Tate the number for Agent Bradley.

The Austin branch office had sent an FBI agent in response to the kidnapping. Should Tate call Fletcher's backup or not? He didn't want to cause problems between the two offices and slow the investigation.

After waiting another minute with still no sign of Sylvia, Tate placed the call.

"Agent Bradley," a female voice answered.

Tate almost hung up. He knew Fletcher and respected his work. What did he know about this female agent, Bradley? What did it matter, he needed help and maybe Agent Bradley was his man…er, woman.

"Agent Bradley, this is Tate Vincent. I have a situation I hope you can help me with."

"Tate Vincent? As in the multimillionaire, Tate Vincent?"

Tate ran a hand through his hair, perspiration building with his impatience. "Yes."

"Paul talks about you all the time. What can I do for you?"

Tate wished Paul had been there to answer his call, but he needed an agent who knew the area and the different criminal factions. "Is there any possibility we could meet?"

"As a matter of fact, my afternoon meeting canceled. Where are you?"

"Standing in front of the Alamo. Can you be here in the next fifteen minutes?"

"I'll be there in ten."

Tate walked the length of the Alamo, along the walls

of the ancient convent garden and across the front of the remains of the long barracks. Still no Sylvia or Agent Bradley. He checked his watch. It had only been five minutes since he'd called Bradley and twenty minutes since Sylvia hopped out of his truck.

Five more minutes dragged by and a woman wearing tailored black trousers, black cowboy boots and a white blouse walked across the Alamo Plaza headed directly for him. Young, but not too young, she wore her straight, long, brown hair pulled back in a neat ponytail and a pair of sunglasses hid her eyes. "Tate Vincent?" She held out her hand. "Special Agent Melissa Bradley. What can I do for you?"

Tate shook her hand, surprised at the firm grip and no-nonsense way she got right to business. "My adopted son was kidnapped last night, and I'd hoped you could help me find him."

She frowned. "Sir, have you reported the kidnapping?"

"Yes. He was kidnapped from my ranch in the hill country outside of Austin. The FBI sent an agent from Austin to investigate. But I have reason to believe the kidnapper might be in San Antonio or close by. That's why I'm here."

She removed a notepad and pen from her back pocket. "I'll contact the special agent in charge of the case and see what I can do."

"There's more." He explained how Sylvia played into the events of the previous day. "I'm not sure she's who she says she is, or if my son is her son. But I had a friend of mine on the SAPD check into Ms. Michaels's story. Beth Kirksey is dead. That much is true."

"So you're waiting for this Michaels woman to return now? When did she say?"

"Thirty minutes. That was thirty-five minutes ago."

"Did you consider she might not come back? Do you think she might be in on this whole kidnapping gig?"

"I'm not the one responsible for the kidnapping," a feminine voice said from behind Tate.

He turned, a huge weight lifting from him when he saw her.

Sylvia, her shirt ripped and hair mussed, walked up to Tate and Melissa, her lips pressed in a thin line, her gaze shooting daggers at Tate. "I didn't kidnap my son. But I have a name."

Chapter Twelve

After spending the past thirty minutes wondering if she'd live to see another day, Sylvia hadn't counted on finding Tate discussing her with another woman. Flashbacks of Miguel lying in her bed with his latest love affair made Sylvia's fingers curl into her palms. "Who are you?" she asked, her voice a bit more harsh than she'd intended.

The pretty woman with the light brown hair held out her hand and smiled. "FBI Special Agent Bradley. You can call me Mel."

Despite her gut reaction to seeing the man she'd just slept with talking to another woman, Sylvia couldn't find it in herself to be out-and-out rude. With her son still missing, she needed all the allies she could get. She shook the woman's hand. "Sylvia Michaels."

"Mr. Vincent filled me in on what's gone on in the past twenty-four hours. I'll see if I can pull some strings and get the case assigned to the San Antonio office. I know one of our guys was following a lead on a suspected child abduction ring."

Sylvia's heart skipped a beat, hope swelling in her chest. "You think it might be the same?"

"I don't know, but it's worth a shot."

She placed a hand on the woman's arm. "Jake has been missing since around two this morning. The more time passes, the farther away he could be taken."

"I'll make sure an Amber Alert was issued and get the department out on the streets checking all their contacts." Melissa faced Sylvia. "You say you have a name? What is it?"

Hesitant to get too many people involved and thus alert the man who could have her child, Sylvia glanced from Melissa to Tate and back.

"Mel comes with a recommendation." Tate hooked an arm around Sylvia's waist. "If you have information, it would be safe with her."

"If you know where this guy is, I don't want a swarm of Feds swooping down on him. He might...dispose of Jacob before anyone gets close."

Mel held up her hand like a Boy Scout. "I swear, we'll be discreet."

"My contact mentioned the name El Corredor."

Juan had been very concerned about the child abduction ring. His own baby daughter was a prime target for retribution among the gangs. Although he had a tough reputation as a killer and a member of the Mexican mafia, Juan Vargas took his responsibilities as a father seriously and he loved his little daughter enough to tell Sylvia all he knew.

Mel jotted down the name. "I'm going to head back to the office and do some coordinating. I've got your number." She nodded at Tate. "I'll call when I find out something."

As soon as Mel was out of sight, Tate grabbed Sylvia's arms. "Don't ever do that again."

His hands squeezed hard on a bruise she'd acquired from Manuel and she winced. "Ouch."

Tate pushed her short sleeve up and spied the bruise. "Want to tell me what really happened?"

She shrugged his hands off her arms. "No."

Tate closed his eyes, drew in a deep breath and let it out slowly. When he opened his eyes again, he glared down at Sylvia. Oh, yeah, Tate Vincent was ticked off.

Sylvia stepped back. "I had to do it. I needed information and going alone was the only way to get it."

"Who did this to you?" He closed the gap between them and touched her arm, brushing his thumb over the bruise.

"Not the man I went to see."

He reached for her chin and lifted her face until she stared directly into his eyes.

"I know you've been on your own for a while, but you don't have to be anymore. I'm just as concerned about Jake as you are. Let me help."

She laughed shakily. "When you put it that way." Tension drained from her and she leaned into him, resting her face against his chest. It felt good to rely on someone else for a while. Someone as solid and good as Tate Vincent. Not that she'd get used to it. She couldn't. But for the moment...

His hands smoothed over her hair and down her back to rest at her waist. "Did you learn anything other than the name?"

"No." Sylvia pushed away from Tate; despite the heat of the day rising off the concrete, a chill swept over her. "I waited while my contact made calls to several of his people. No one had anything definite. Only the name 'El Corredor.' He did say that I was on the right track to ask the prostitutes. They will know how to get in contact with someone who could hook them up to sell a baby."

"I think we should let the FBI take it from here."

Sylvia shook her head, her fists knotting. "I can't stand by and do nothing. Jacob was so close. I touched him." She looked up at him through watery eyes. "I can't search for another six months. I don't think he has that much time."

"And if I don't help you, you'll go on your own, right?"

She nodded. "I have to."

"Okay, we have until dark. I have the addresses of the adoption agency and Beth's attorney. We should check them out. I gave the names and addresses to Special Agent Bradley. But maybe we can get there before Mel."

Sylvia rolled her shoulders. The lack of sleep and constant worry had her tied in knots. She shoved fatigue aside. "Let's go."

Tate led the way back to the parking garage located at one end of the River Center Mall. Once inside the truck, Sylvia's cell phone rang.

The name "Tony" displayed on the caller ID. Even as it rang, the low battery indicator blinked.

"Tony, make it fast. My battery is about to die," she said into the phone.

"Did you know Rosa Garcia was a highly decorated cop in Austin?"

"I knew."

"She was medically retired after she received a gunshot wound to the leg. No dirt."

Somehow, Sylvia expected this. Rosa's bark was definitely worse than her bite and she had Jake's and Tate's best interests at heart when she'd been nasty to Sylvia.

"Anything else?"

"C. W. Middleton did time in the military, deployed to Afghanistan three times before getting out. Works for Tate Vincent."

Sylvia avoided looking at Tate. He might not like that she was checking up on his employees. "Anything else?"

"Still checking into Kacee LeBlanc. No police record, but still looking. There's a brother who's done time for drug possession and armed robbery."

"Yeah?"

"I'll let you know more when I know more."

"Thanks, Tony. I owe you."

"You don't owe me nothin'. Just be careful."

Sylvia hung up.

"Who was that?"

"Another one of my contacts."

"Anything?"

She shrugged. "I had him check on a few of your employees."

Tate shot a glance at him. "Which ones?"

"C.W., Rosa and Kacee."

"And?"

"C.W. and Rosa check out."

"They should. I'd bet my life on them."

"I'm sure you did a background check on Kacee before you hired her, didn't you?"

"I did." His gaze narrowed, his finger tightening on the wheel. "And I'm not sure I like where you're going with this."

"Did you know that she has a brother who did time for armed robbery and possession?"

"She told me about her brother in prison. She was

very up-front about it. Kacee grew up in a rough neighborhood here in San Antonio. When I interviewed her she laid it all out."

"And you didn't have a problem with a member of her family having served time?"

"I believe in giving people a chance. Besides, it was her brother's crime, not hers."

"Point taken. Do you think it's a bit coincidental that she's from San Antonio and the baby theft ring is here?"

"What are you getting at?"

"I don't know. I'm just thinking we should look at all angles." She sat in silence, mulling over Kacee's family life.

Would the executive assistant to a millionaire put her career and life in jeopardy to get involved with a human trafficking operation?

Sylvia shook her head. "Where are we going first?"

"The adoption agency."

Tate entered the address into his truck's GPS unit. As he drove through the streets, he thought about all that had happened.

The employees Sylvia had mentioned all had a stake in Jake's adoption. C.W. was Jake's godfather. Tate had hired Rosa first to guard over his dying father. When he'd been informed by the adoption service that a baby boy had come available, she'd become the nanny. Nothing in her demeanor indicated any animosity toward the child. In fact, Jake thought the world of her and by all indications, she returned the affection.

As for C.W., what would he gain from Jake's disappearance? C.W. would lay down his life for his friend and Tate would do likewise. As a godfather, he'd sworn he would raise, love and protect Jake as if he were his own.

Kacee had been with Tate for the past three years. She'd been everything to him from secretary, partner and right hand in all his business dealings. She didn't need him for anything, but she still worked for him even after she'd learned all there was to know about Vincent Enterprises.

His assistant had gone so far as to find an adoption agency that specialized in expediency. She'd been just as eager for him to fulfill his father's dying wish as he had been. She'd even offered to be a surrogate mother to his child.

He'd thought that dedication above and beyond, but she'd laughed it off as just part of her commitment to Vincent Enterprises and the boss.

Could she have had anything to do with Jake's disappearance? Tate shook his head. No. He trusted Kacee as much as he trusted Rosa and C.W.

The GPS indicated one more turn and they'd arrive at their destination. "This is it."

Sylvia leaned forward, craning her neck as they passed the address and pulled into the parking space at the side of the building. "Doesn't look as if there are any lights on."

"Not a good sign." Tate turned off the engine and stared at the building in front of him. "This is the place. There were two other cars in the parking lot when I came with Kacee to interview."

"Where did you meet to sign the adoption papers?"

"At my attorney's office in Austin."

"Is that where they handed over Jacob?"

"Yes. Come on." He climbed out of the truck and waited for Sylvia to join him on the sidewalk.

How could things have changed so drastically in the six months since he adopted Jake?

Sylvia tried the front door. "Locked."

Tate peered through a crack in the blinds. "Empty. No people, no furniture." He looked around. "Someone around here should know when they cleared out."

Sylvia touched his arm and pointed to a beauty salon directly across the street. She looked both ways and crossed, entering the building, a bell ringing over the door.

The strong odor of chemicals stung Tate's nose.

"I'll be with you in a minute," a thin woman with bleached-blond hair called out from the back of the shop where she sprayed water over a woman's hair. She shut off the water, wrapped the customer's hair in a clean white towel and helped her rise from the chair. "What can I do for you two? Haircut? Shampoo?"

Sylvia hooked her arm through Tate's and smiled up at him before she addressed the cosmetologist. "My husband and I were just wondering what happened to the adoption agency that used to be across the street. Have they moved somewhere else?"

The blonde frowned, touching a finger to her chin. "Let's see. Had to be about two months ago. I remember because I had to park in the alley. They had a truck blocking the street for most of the day."

"Any idea where they moved to?"

"I think they went bankrupt. The landlord had to have them evicted." She smiled up at Tate, batting her heavily lined eyelids. "Sure I can't give you a manicure or something?"

Tate noted the way Sylvia's mouth tightened at the woman's blatant flirting. He almost smiled, but didn't. They weren't any closer to finding Jake. "No, thank you." He tugged on Sylvia's arm. "Come on, honey. We'll have to find another agency."

Once outside, they hurried for the truck and climbed in.

"Bankrupt, huh? Now what?"

"The attorney."

As Tate pulled out into the street, a dark vehicle raced by. What sounded like an engine backfire blasted the air.

The back window of his pickup exploded, glass flying toward the front.

"Stay down!" Tate punched the accelerator with his foot and raced after the vehicle. "Remember this number."

As he gained on the black car, he shouted out the license plate number. Sylvia repeated it, lifting her head to look ahead.

"Stay down!"

A hand came out the driver's window of the vehicle in front of him with what looked like a gun.

Tate swerved, reaching out to hold Sylvia's head low.

Another bang sounded and the front windshield shattered.

Sharp pain sliced through Tate's left shoulder. He jammed his foot on the brake and skidded to a sideways halt.

The other vehicle shot forward and out of sight.

"Give me your cell phone!" Sylvia held out her hand.

Tate fished in his front pocket and handed her the phone. Not until too late did he realize it had blood on it.

"Oh, my God, you've been hit." Sylvia practically crawled across the console to inspect the wound.

"It's just a flesh wound."

She shot a frown at him. "Just what I don't need, macho bull crap."

"I'm serious." His arms came up around her, settling her in his lap. "Careful with the knees. The flesh wound I can handle. I don't need more damage to other body parts." He chuckled, liking the feel of her sitting in his lap.

Sylvia's lips twisted into a wry smile. "Okay, it's a flesh wound or you wouldn't be so…eh…flexible." She ripped the tail off her shirt and wadded it into a pad, stuffing it beneath his shirt and pressing hard. "You need to see a doctor."

"You're doing a fine job."

"Infection can kill you if the bullet doesn't."

"Spoken like a true professional. Are you sure you're just a journalist?"

She shook her head and relaxed. "I don't know whether you're joking to keep me from freaking out or if you're delirious."

His smile faded as he stared into her pale, beautiful face. He wanted to kiss the wrinkle from her forehead; he wanted to kiss the worry from her eyes. Hell, he wanted to kiss her in a lot of places. With his truck parked at an awkward angle against the curb, traffic backing up behind him on the narrow street and an interesting woman in his lap, Tate did the only thing he could think to do.

He kissed her.

A horn blared behind them and Sylvia didn't care.

Not until a man knocked on the driver's-side window did she come up for air and a sanity check.

"Hey, you two all right in there?" A white-haired man in faded jeans and a short-sleeved cotton shirt leaned close to the window, peering in.

Tate hit the down button on the armrest and the window slid open. "Yes, we're all right. Had a little trouble, but my partner here is patching me up."

The man gave him a doubtful look that made Sylvia bite down hard on a chuckle.

"Are you sure? That's a lot of blood." He pointed at the spot where Sylvia held her hand to Tate's shoulder. "I could call an ambulance. I got one of those cell phones in my car."

"Not necessary." Tate's hand slipped up Sylvia's thigh to her buttocks. "My partner is a nurse."

"I'll make sure he gets the medical treatment he needs, sir," Sylvia said, fighting back a nervous giggle.

That seemed to satisfy the old guy. "Gotta watch out around here. Been a lot of drive-by shootings." The man's gaze darted around as if another shooter might come along at any moment.

"We noticed." Tate cast a glance at Sylvia. "Thank you for checking on us, but I assure you, we're fine."

The old man climbed back in his vehicle and pulled around the truck, giving them one final long look before leaving.

Sylvia checked beneath the makeshift bandage. The blood flow had slowed. She eased over the console and settled into the seat beside him. "Want me to drive?"

"I've got it."

"Then let's get to the hospital."

"Not until after we check the address of the attorney." Tate bumped over the curb and back into the street, driving with one hand on the steering wheel, the other laying still against the armrest.

"No. Unless you think that was a random drive-by, someone either followed us or knew where we were going. It's too dangerous."

"If we're in danger, what do you think Jake's chances are?" Tate's question made Sylvia sit back against the seat and stare through the windshield with the bullet hole in it, air rushing in from the shattered back glass.

Jacob.

Dear, sweet Lord, let Jacob be okay.

Much as she wanted to let the powers that be handle everything, she knew they were busy people. Hadn't she run into roadblock after roadblock with the authorities? Hadn't it taken six months for her to get where she was today? "Which way to this attorney's office?"

Across town and outside loop 410, Tate pulled the truck into a small row of office buildings, stopping in front of one marked Hastings, Attorney at Law. "This is the place. Richard Hastings was Beth Kirksey's attorney. He didn't come to the adoption proceedings, but he worked up the papers for Beth and the agency."

The windows were shaded with wooden blinds and the door was a solid mahogany. Sylvia reached for the knob, but the door was already open.

Tate grabbed her and pushed her behind him. "Stay here." He ducked low and slipped inside.

Sylvia waited for two full seconds and couldn't stand the pressure. Following his lead, she ducked low and eased through the door, moving to the side just as Tate had.

Inside, the room was dark, only a lamp in the back

office glowed. Coming from afternoon sunlight to a dark interior, it took Sylvia a few moments for her vision to adjust to the limited lighting.

Tate wasn't anywhere to be seen, but she heard movement in the office with the glowing light.

"Sylvia," Tate called out.

"I'm here." She moved toward the sound of his voice.

"You still have my cell phone, don't you?"

"Yes." She fished in her pocket as she moved forward.

"Call Agent Bradley and tell her not to bother to interview Mr. Hastings."

"Why?" As she stepped into the attorney's office, a coppery scent filled her nostrils.

Tate knelt beside the desk.

A pair of shoes was all she could see on the floor behind the desk. Toes up.

Her stomach lurched.

Tate glanced up, his lips tight and gray. "He's dead."

Chapter Thirteen

Sylvia stood on the corner of South Presa and East Nueva streets, desperately trying not to fall out of the impossibly high stiletto heels while keeping an eye out for the black-haired prostitute named Velvet. She'd been standing there since shortly before dark, afraid she'd miss her if she waited too late. After finding Beth Kirksey's attorney dead in his office due to apparent blunt-force trauma to the head, she and Tate spent the next two hours making statements. Sylvia had very little time to change and get in place before sunset.

The last time she'd seen Velvet was on this very corner. She'd had to walk the length of Presa and Alamo streets to find anyone who might know anything about putting babies up for adoption—for a price. With Jacob's life hanging in the balance, Sylvia hoped the search for Velvet wouldn't take as long this time around.

A glance at a recessed doorway half a block down and across the street reassured her that Tate was where he'd promised he'd be, hidden in the shadows.

As usual, a multitude of tourists and employees who worked in the downtown shopping mall and along the riverwalk passed by, stopping at the corners to wait for traffic.

Already her feet hurt and she wondered if she'd be able to run if the need arose. As far as she knew, Tate hadn't told anyone of their plans. No one would recognize her in the clothes and short red wig Tate had purchased. Squeezed into a bright pink tube top barely covering her breasts, a short, black leather skirt and the waitress-red stilettos, she looked the part. She even chewed a stick of gum to help calm her nerves.

"Hey, baby, wanna come ride me tonight?" A lanky young man with a shaved head and pimply skin walked up to her.

She crossed her arms over her chest, still self-conscious about the amount of cleavage showing. With a toss of her short red tresses, she stared down her nose at him, giving him her best drop-dead look. "You couldn't afford me, even if I wanted you to. And trust me, I don't."

"Don't you give out free samples?"

"Cough up the cash or beat it before my pimp stomps your butt." She stood her ground, aware of movement out of the corner of her eye.

Tate had left the semidarkness of his hiding place, headed her way.

Sylvia held her hand up just slightly to stop him.

The young man in front of her snorted. "Yeah, whatever. You're not worth it. Why pay when I can get it free from my girlfriend?"

"Lucky girl."

The man left and Sylvia concentrated on the other women hanging out on the street corners. After thirty minutes standing on the concrete sidewalk and flirting with men who slowed to ask how much, Sylvia was ready to find another location for the stakeout.

Kitty-corner from where she stood, a dark sedan

dropped a woman off, turned down a side street and parked illegally within sight.

The woman stood with her back to the traffic, straightening her clothing and patting her long, black hair into place before she faced the street.

Velvet.

With her first inclination to dash across the street, Sylvia nearly fell off her heels, stopping her headlong rush. From past experience, she knew that if she wanted information from Velvet, she had to work for it.

A silver Lexus slowed to a stop for a red light in front of Velvet, the driver called out to her. The raven-haired prostitute leaned into the window, smiling and flirting with the occupant, displaying a significant amount of flesh from her low-cut, skin-tight, ribbed-knit shirt.

Trying to appear as if she was already going that direction, Sylvia crossed the street with a group of pedestrians. Now she stood directly across from where Velvet still leaned into the car.

Please don't get in. Please.

The light changed and a car behind the Lexus honked.

Velvet stepped away from the vehicle and waved at the occupant.

Breathing a sigh of relief, Sylvia sauntered across the crosswalk with a mob of one-striper airmen fresh out of basic training and still in uniform.

"Maybe if we all pitch in we can get Robles one of them." One young man with a fine layer of strawberry-blond peach fuzz across his scalp grinned and nudged his buddy in the gut.

"He wouldn't know what to do with her. Why waste your money on him?" his buddy replied.

"Excuse me, ma'am. How much?" The strawberry-blond airman blushed all the way out to his ears. "I can't believe I just asked that. It's a first."

"Better be careful, Drukowski. Next thing you know, you won't be a virgin and you'll be getting a tattoo."

Sylvia winked at the airman. "Get the tattoo, honey."

As she stepped up onto the curb, Velvet gave her a narrow-eyed look. The same look she'd given her the first time she'd spoken to the woman. Only Sylvia had been wearing a brunette wig last time. Would she remember her?

Without looking in Tate's direction, Sylvia had to make it appear as though she was just changing corners, not aiming directly for Velvet. She came to a halt a little more than a yard from the prostitute, strutting the best she could like she knew what she was doing.

"Beat it. This is my territory." Velvet gave a sexy smile to a man driving by with his window down, then shot Sylvia an icy glare.

With a shrug and a smack of her gum, Sylvia said, "It's a free country."

The man whistled, his navy blue Camry creeping by. The cars behind him honked and he sped up.

Velvet glanced behind her at the sedan parked on the side road. The one that had delivered her to the corner. "Look, you're going to make Raul mad. He doesn't like anyone messing with his girls."

Sylvia wanted information and she wasn't going anywhere until she got it. But she couldn't just leap into it without scaring Velvet. "Actually, I was hoping you could help me."

Velvet's eyes narrowed and she stared hard at Sylvia. "Hell, I remember you. Last time I helped you, my friend Bunny died."

Sylvia nodded. "That's right, but I didn't kill her. I didn't even get to talk to her."

Velvet turned away with a snort. "You got her killed by asking too many questions."

"I can't help it. I'm desperate. I...I'm expecting a baby and I need to get rid of it."

With her back still to Sylvia, Velvet waved at a passing car. "Get an abortion."

"I can't do that. I want to put it up for adoption. You know, where the family pays all my expenses until the baby's born." Sylvia struck a pose, still talking away from Velvet, but loud enough the prostitute couldn't help but hear.

"Can't help you." Velvet pushed her hair back over her shoulder and plumped her breasts.

"Bunny did it that way. She got money for her baby. That's all I want, a little help and to get rid of this kid. I never got to talk to Bunny to find out how she got rid of her kid."

Velvet glanced her way, brows raised. "And because of you asking questions, Bunny's dead. You do the math."

"Please." Sylvia moved closer and touched Velvet's arm, all the desperation to save Jacob welling up inside her. "I can't afford to have this baby by myself."

Velvet shook off Sylvia's hand. "Your problem, not mine."

"Velvet, baby, got a problem?" A barrel-chested man with dark hair, even darker eyes and tattoos running up each arm into his shirt sleeves flicked a glowing cigarette butt at Sylvia's feet.

So wrapped up in her conversation with Velvet, Sylvia had forgotten to keep an eye out for the pimp. She assumed this thug with the mean look in his eyes was Velvet's procurer, solicitor, *alcahuete*.

"She was bothering me, Raul," Velvet said. "I didn't ask her to come."

Playing the role of a naive prostitute without a pimp of her own, Sylvia laid a hand on the man's arm. "Maybe you can help me."

His glance roved over her from head to foot. "Maybe. You got no *alcahuete* of your own?"

"No. Mine dumped me when he found out I was pregnant."

Raul brushed her arm off his. "Not interested in someone who's dumb enough to get herself knocked up."

"Look, all I want is to have this baby, give it up for adoption and get back to work."

"Can't help you." Raul hooked Velvet's arm in his grip. "Come on, let's get out of here."

"But I haven't found my mark," Velvet protested.

"We'll find another street." Raul's glance panned the area as if he expected to see someone watching them.

Out of the corner of her vision, Tate, his hands in his jeans pockets, head down, looking like any other man in jeans and a black T-shirt, crossed the street.

Velvet hurried along beside Raul, her high heels slowing her down.

Sylvia ran along behind the man, her feet hurting, making it hard for her to keep up.

Raul and Velvet reached the sedan before she did.

"Please, Raul, I need to know how Bunny did it. Who'd she go to when she was pregnant?"

"I don't know what you're talking about." He fumbled in his pocket for the keys, punched the unlock button and jerked the door open.

Before he could get in, a flash of movement raced by Sylvia.

Tate grabbed Raul's arm, twisted it up and behind him, slamming the pimp's chest into the car door.

"What the hell!" Raul grunted.

Velvet stood by wringing her hands. "Leave him alone."

"Who did Bunny sell her baby to?" Tate slammed the man into the car again.

"I don't know."

"I think you do. I think you sent her to him." Tate leaned close and snarled beside Raul's face. "Give us a name and where he can be found and we'll leave you alone."

"*Madre de Dios,* that hurts," Raul cried, his face contorted.

"Tell me, and I'll make it stop hurting."

"He'll kill me," Raul whimpered.

Tate's voice lowered to an ominous growl. "I'll kill you if you don't tell me."

The anger and steely grit in Tate's tone sent chills down Sylvia's spine.

Raul laughed hysterically. "You won't kill me. You don't have the guts."

"Wanna test that theory?" Tate dragged the man's arm up his back even higher until the man squealed.

"*Madre de Dios!* I'll tell you. I'll tell you!"

Velvet backed away from Raul and the car, her gaze darting left and right.

Before she could make a run for it, Sylvia blocked

her path. "You're not going anywhere until we find out where Bunny sold her baby."

"His name is El Corredor." Raul's eyes, wide and wild, darted around the side street, searching every shadow.

"Where can we find him?" Tate persisted.

"You don't find him. He finds you," Velvet said, her tone flat, her face pale beneath the heavy makeup.

"How?" Tate bent the pimp's arm up higher until he was standing on his toes to relieve the pressure.

"Call him," Raul gasped. "The number is in my cell phone under E.C. Call him and he'll arrange a meeting place."

"Get his cell and keys and give them to Pinky here," Tate nodded toward Velvet.

She grabbed the keys off the ground where Raul had dropped them and then dug in Raul's pocket, fishing out a slick black phone. With a little more force than was necessary, she handed them both to Sylvia. "Can I go now?"

Tate loosened his grip on Raul enough that the man could get his feet flat on the ground. "Not yet."

Sylvia scrolled down through the phone's contact list until she found E.C. and hit the call button.

"*Si.*"

Shock struck her dumb. She hadn't expected to get El Corredor on the first ring. "I have a baby I need to put up for adoption," she blurted out. "How much can you get for me?"

"Where's Raul?"

"He's tied up right now. He told me to call you."

"Let me talk to Raul or this conversation is over."

Sylvia covered the mouthpiece, leaned over and whispered into Tate's ear. "He wants to talk to Raul."

Tate yanked Raul's arm up a little. "Tell him whatever it takes to get him to meet with my girl. Can't afford my girls keeping their stinkin' kids." He grabbed the phone from Sylvia, his voice dropping to a low, dangerous whisper. "Just in case you wondered, I speak fluent Spanish, so don't get stupid on me." Tate held the phone to the man's ear.

"Raul here." He listened for a moment, his gaze capturing Sylvia's. "Yeah, she says she's pregnant." He shrugged. "I don't know, maybe three or four months."

Sylvia held up four fingers.

"Four months," Raul said into the phone. "Yeah, she looks like she's the real deal." The man frowned. "I don't know, ask her when you meet her. Okay…okay… Tower of the Americas in fifteen."

Tate didn't give him a moment to say anything else. He took the phone in his free hand, punched the end button and slipped it into his pocket.

"I did what you wanted," Raul said. "Let me go."

"No." With one hand holding the man's arm up behind his back, Tate grabbed Raul's collar and walked him to the back of the car.

Sylvia unlocked the trunk and lifted the lid.

With a hard shove, Tate dumped Raul in the back with the spare tire.

"Hey! I did everything you asked." Raul grabbed the sides of the trunk and tried to leverage himself out.

"Yeah, but I can't risk you alerting El Corredor that we're coming. Move your hands or lose them."

Raul ducked, jerking his hands back as Tate slammed the trunk shut.

"You can't leave me here. He'll find me." Raul's muffled voice sounded from inside the trunk. "Velvet, get me out of here! Get me out of here, or else."

Sylvia took Velvet's hands. "I'm sorry. I didn't know any other way to do this. Once I've met with El Corredor, I'll drop the keys back by here."

Velvet shrugged. "Whatever." Then she walked to the corner and went back to work as though it was any other workday selling sex for money.

Tate grabbed Sylvia's hand and hurried her away from the car on the deserted side street and toward the Tower of the Americas. "Ready to call in the Feds?"

"No. We have to find Jacob tonight. I'm afraid of what they might do to him."

Tate rounded a corner half a block from the tower and pulled Sylvia into the shadow of a recessed doorway. He gathered her into his arms and held her. "You were amazing out there."

She leaned into his shirt, smelling the fresh scent of soap and man. How she wished all of this danger and deception would end so that she and Jacob could go on living a normal life. On the down side, once it was over, she might never see Tate again.

Her arms went around his waist and she held on tight. For the moment she could pretend he was hers. For a moment she could rely on his strength to see her through the hard times. But only for a moment.

"Let me wait for El Corredor." He smoothed a hand down her back and then tipped her chin up to look down into her eyes. "You stay here."

She stared up into his face, loving how dark he looked in the shadows, how fathomless his eyes were, his voice the only thing grounding her. "I can't. He might not show if I don't go out there. I'm the bait."

"Exactly. I don't like it. Someone killed Bunny to keep her from talking. It could be this El Corredor."

"If I thought there was another way, I'd jump on it. But to get him to come out in the open, he needs to think he's got another woman to use, another baby that can make him money." Sylvia smiled up at him. "I've been at this for a long time. I know how to take care of myself."

Tate's mouth thinned into a straight line. "But you don't have to do it alone this time. Let me help."

"Thanks." She took in a deep breath and let it out, her hands resting on his chest, loving the feel of his solid strength. "You've already helped and you can help again, just by being close by." She lifted his hand and checked his watch. "We should get a move on. I'd like to get there before he does so that he doesn't see you."

"I think we should let the Feds handle this before we get in any deeper."

"We're already in too deep, and time's not on our side. Based on Beth's death and all the attempts on our lives, someone doesn't want others to find out who is responsible for the baby-selling business." She gulped back fear. "And they're willing to kill anyone they see as a threat."

Tate's heart skipped a beat, his chest tightening. Jake was just a baby; he'd done nothing to any of the people responsible for his kidnapping. The child deserved a happy life, with his mother.

Sylvia reached up and touched his cheek. "I'll be okay. Promise."

Chapter Fourteen

Tate captured her hand in his, staring down into light blue eyes he could barely discern in the darkness. "I'm going to hold you to that promise." Somehow this brave woman in front of him had grown on him in the past twenty-four hours. He didn't want anything to happen to her, any more than he wanted anything to happen to Jake. Even if it meant she'd ultimately end up with his son. Sylvia Michaels had been through enough.

With time ticking away and a block to cover, Tate let the world wait around him. He captured her face in his hands and bent to kiss her.

What started as a tender union of lips, exploded into a hot, passionate tangle of tongues. His arms circled her, bringing her as close as he could get her without being naked. Her hands circled his neck, clinging to him as he ravaged her mouth, pushing past her teeth with his tongue, thrusting deep, tasting her as if there would be no tomorrow.

And for both of them, that just might be the case. If anything happened to her on this assignment, Tate would take El Corredor down...or die trying.

They split up in the dark, Sylvia moving ahead to the Tower of the Americas. Tate waited one full minute, keeping her in sight while he checked the SIG Sauer he'd taken from his truck. He gave silent thanks to Kacee for all her nagging. She'd been the one to make sure he'd practiced with it and had it licensed.

Having lived on a ranch all his life, Tate knew his way around rifles and shotguns and the occasional pistol. But Kacee had more than a healthy grasp of the pros and cons of each type of pistol. She claimed her brother taught her everything he knew.

Tate frowned. Kacee hadn't told him that her brother was out. He made a mental note to ask her about it.

He glanced at his watch. One minute. Tate crossed the street, moving among shadows. He half walked, half jogged to keep Sylvia in sight.

She turned down the wide sidewalk leading toward the Tower of the Americas; the tower dwarfed the buildings surrounding it. For a moment, Tate lost sight of her.

His hands fisted and the muscles tightened in preparation for whatever might result from this meeting. When he reached the corner she'd disappeared around, he crossed the street to the side she'd been on and paused.

With a deep breath, he sneaked a peek around the corner.

Sylvia stood on the big concrete plaza in front of the tourist attraction, now closed for the night. Alone and small next to the towering structure, she looked entirely too vulnerable.

From a dark corner, a man emerged, wearing a black jacket, zipped up despite the residual heat from the hot Texas sun radiating off the concrete. A small-brimmed hat provided just enough of a shield to the light that Tate couldn't make out the man's face. But his hands were in his pockets and one of them poked out farther than the other.

A gun?

Blood froze in Tate's veins. What could he do? If he let the man know he was there, he could place Sylvia in more danger than she already was.

Tate tucked his SIG Sauer into his pocket and crept around the plaza to a position behind the man, checking for others as he went.

With her back to the shadows, Sylvia didn't see El Corredor at first. She turned three hundred and sixty degrees, then her body stiffened and her hands dropped to her sides. She and El Corredor were far enough away that Tate could hear their conversation only as a murmur.

He shouldn't have let her go out there alone. The image of Beth Kirksey flashed in his mind. She'd been a down-and-out prostitute, probably desperate for money to fund her next fix. But she hadn't deserved to die.

Sylvia didn't deserve to die. Tate had just straightened to step out of the shadows when a movement behind him told him he wasn't alone.

He spun as a fist came out of nowhere, connecting with his jaw.

The force of the impact toppled Tate onto the pavement. His jaw burning, he rolled and leaped to his feet. The guy was on him before he could raise his hands to protect himself.

A flying foot landed in his gut, blasting the wind out of his lungs. He staggered backward, trying to inhale and failing miserably. The edges of his world faded, but Tate clung to consciousness, knowing he was Sylvia's only hope of staying alive.

His chest eased and he sucked in a breath, raised his arms in time to deflect the next kick, tilted and let loose with a side kick his tae kwon do instructor would have been proud of.

He dropped into a fighting crouch and blocked the next punch with his uninjured forearm, landing one of his own punches in the man's solar plexus and a quick jab to his kidney.

The man grunted, staggered back a step and came at him like a charging bull, nostrils flared, fists swinging.

Alert now, Tate blocked an uppercut, dodged a right cross and used the man's momentum to jerk him forward, sending a knee to the man's crotch.

The attacker went down, a low agonized groan the only thing rising from the pavement.

Tate kicked him in the kidney and waited for him to get up.

The guy rolled, clutching his privates, unable to move from the fetal position.

A scream drew his attention to where Sylvia had been in the middle of the plaza.

Only she wasn't there anymore. And neither was El Corredor.

Tate had been so busy saving his own skin that he'd failed Sylvia. Which way had they gone?

A bright red stiletto lay on the far side of the plaza near a wide sidewalk headed toward the exit of Hemisphere Park.

Tate ran, his breathing ragged, his heart beating erratically. They could veer off at any point and Sylvia would be gone. He nearly missed the second stiletto, almost tripping over it.

They couldn't be far, but Sylvia was running out of clothing to leave as a trail for him to follow.

A faint squeal sounded from ahead.

Tate could see the street ahead, where a car pulled up to the curb and El Corredor struggled to shove Sylvia into it.

If he hadn't been so worried about her, he'd have laughed. Sylvia gave the man hell, biting, kicking and scratching. Her fight bought enough time that Tate hoped he could close the gap. He ran full-out, eating up the yards one stride at a time.

"Get in the car, or I'll shoot you," the man said, the gun he'd carried in his pocket now out and in plain sight.

Tate didn't slow down because of the gun. He knew that if Sylvia got in that car, she didn't have a chance. El Corredor would take her somewhere Tate wouldn't be able to find and kill her.

Without thinking, he plowed into the man, jerking his arm upward.

The weapon discharged in the air. The two men slammed against the car, trapping Sylvia beneath them.

Tate held on to the man's wrist, banging it against the roof of the sedan. The man's hat slipped from his head and fell to the ground, exposing dark brown hair.

Sylvia did the best she could to pound against El Corredor's back, her arms too pinned to be of much use.

Throwing his weight to the right, Tate dragged the man with him, freeing Sylvia, but getting himself pinned between the attacker and the car.

Sylvia dropped to the ground and scooted out of range. But not for long.

Tate couldn't see what she was doing until the man

wielding the gun jolted against him and Sylvia's head appeared above theirs.

She'd leaped onto the baby trafficker's back and proceeded to pull hard on his hair screaming, "Let him go!"

She wrapped her legs around the guy and refused to let go.

"Get the hell off!" With a woman on his back, a man holding his gun hand high, the man couldn't maintain his balance long.

His feet backed against the curb and he fell, the gun flying from his fingers.

Sylvia jumped free, landing on her hands and knees on the sidewalk a few feet from the man. She scrambled for the weapon.

The baby trafficker rolled to his stomach and reached for her.

Tate dove for El Corredor, straddling him and pinning him to the ground.

As she reached for the gun, the man Tate had been fighting back by the tower appeared and stepped on the weapon, pointing one of his own at Sylvia's head. "Touch it and I'll blow your brains out."

Tate jerked El Corredor's head back by his hair, pulled his gun from his waist band, and stuck it to El Corredor's head. "Hurt her and I'll blow your boss away."

Sylvia stared across the concrete at Tate, her eyes wide, her hands raised in surrender.

The man beneath him lay still for a long moment.

"Well, what's it going to be?" Tate tugged a little harder on the man's hair. "Looks like we have a bit of a standoff here."

"Let her go," El Corredor called out.

The other man didn't move.

"*Mierda!* Let her go!" He rattled off something in Spanish that Tate could barely hear, but he got the gist.

"No, you won't be taking care of her later. If I catch you anywhere near her, I swear I'll kill you," Tate promised. "Now have your amigo throw down his gun."

"Do as he said," El Corredor grunted.

The man frowned, hesitated for what seemed like an eternity, his gun still pointed at Sylvia. Then he tossed the weapon to the ground, out of reach.

Sylvia leaped to her feet and ran to stand behind where Tate had El Corredor pinned to the ground.

"My cell phone is in my back pocket. Call Special Agent Bradley." Tate climbed to his feet, his hand still holding the gun to the man's head.

As Sylvia dug into his back pocket to pull out the cell phone, Tate didn't notice El Corredor kick out until his foot caught Tate's ankle and knocked him off balance.

The henchman dove for his weapon.

Tate straightened in time to fire off a round at the man before he could grab his gun. The bullet ricocheted off the concrete next to the handle.

The tattooed man tripped and hit the ground. He rolled to his feet and took off across the concrete, heading for the safety of a building.

Taking advantage of the distraction, El Corredor dove into the car and slammed the door behind him.

Tate grabbed the door handle, but the door was locked.

The engine revved to life and the car lurched, climbing the curb before spinning out onto the street, leaving a trail of burned rubber half a block long.

Tate stood in the middle of the road, his gun pointed at the retreating vehicle, but he'd already lost his opportunity. They'd lost El Corredor and with him, their only link to the location of the stolen babies.

Sylvia stood beside him, her shoulders slumped, tears poised on the edges of her eyelids. "Now what? We still don't know where Jacob is."

"We'll find him. Let's get back to Velvet and Raul and see if they know anything."

Sylvia walked several steps, turned and walked back. "We have to find Jacob. Now that El Corredor knows we're looking, he'll be even more motivated to do away with the…" Sylvia's voice broke. "Evidence."

"We'll find him."

"How?"

"Let's get to the truck. If Raul's still in the trunk, I'd bet my shirt Velvet is nearby."

"You don't think he's found a way out yet?" Sylvia shook her head.

"If he has, he'd be hiding if he thought El Corredor was after him."

Tate had already thought the same, but he didn't want to make her more depressed than she already was. "You're a fighter, Sylvia. Don't give up now."

She leaned into his shirt, her fingers clutching the material. "Yeah, I have to be strong. But sometimes it's so darned hard."

He held her, stroking her hair down her back, the red wig lost somewhere between here and the Tower of the Americas. He preferred the silky tresses of her hair as it ran through his fingers. "We'll find Jake," he said, his lips against her temple. She smelled of strawberry shampoo, a scent he would forever remember as part of her.

She let him hold her for a minute more, then she pushed away, sucked in a deep breath, her shoulders stiffening. "Okay, then. Let's find Raul and Velvet. I'll bet my pink tube top they know more than they told us."

Tate hoped they did. For Jake's sake.

Sylvia accomplished the walk back to the River Center Mall parking lot barefoot and in silence. By the time she climbed into the damaged pickup truck, her entire body felt as limp as a noodle and beyond exhausted. But she refused to give up. Jacob was out there somewhere and she'd find him.

Tate pulled out onto Alamo Street headed south. He crossed to North Presa and continued moving slowly, pausing at the street corners.

Sylvia craned her neck, searching for Velvet. She had to be there somewhere.

Just when she'd given up hope, she spied the raven-haired woman climbing out of a shiny Acura, straightening her miniskirt.

She waved at the driver and stepped up on the curb.

"Stop!" Sylvia yelled. Even before Tate could pull to the side of the road, Sylvia had her seat belt off and was halfway out of the truck, dropping down on the street. Dodging cars, she crossed to the other side.

Drivers skidded to a halt, horns honking, but Sylvia didn't care as long as she made it across the street and caught the only person who might possibly know how to find her child.

Velvet looked up at the commotion on the street, her brows rising. When she spotted Sylvia, she turned and ran.

No. She couldn't get away. Not with so much at stake. Sylvia ran after her. Barefoot, she easily caught the woman who still wore her signature stilettos. Her breath coming in sobbing gasps, she grabbed the only thing she could reach—Velvet's dark mass of curls—yanking her to a stop.

"Leave me alone, you witch!" Velvet kicked out at Sylvia, her sharp-pointed shoes connecting with Sylvia's shin.

Sylvia yelped but held tight to the wad of hair. "Where do they keep them? Tell me!"

"I don't know what you're talking about." Velvet swung her claws at Sylvia, catching her arm and ripping into her skin. "Let me go."

"Not until you tell me where they keep the babies." She swung around, the force of her movement slinging Velvet off her high-heeled shoes. She fell to the ground.

Sylvia sat on her, pinning her hands beside her head. "My son is one of the babies they stole. I want him back, do you hear me?"

Velvet's eyes widened. "Your son?"

"Yes, my son. They stole him from me last night." Despite her determination to remain angry, Sylvia couldn't stop the flow of tears. "I have to find him. I think they might try to kill him."

All of the fight left Velvet and she lay against the sidewalk looking up at Sylvia. "I'm so sorry. I really don't know where they are. You have to believe me." A tear fell from the corner of her eye, taking with it a trail of eyeliner. "I'd tell you if I did."

The anger left Sylvia, replaced by a hollow, empty feeling of hopelessness. She wanted to beat the answer out of Velvet, but knew it would do no good.

Velvet's sad eyes brimming with tears told it all. She didn't know.

Sylvia climbed to her feet and held out her hand. Velvet took it and allowed Sylvia to help her to her feet. "Here's the key to Raul's car." Sylvia handed her the keys.

"I have to go. Raul will be looking for me." Velvet glanced around. "If I find out anything, how can I let you know?"

Sylvia gave her the number to her cell phone. "I don't have a charger and my battery is low, but I'll check my messages remotely if necessary. Anything you learn… anything…just call me." She held on to Velvet's hands longer than necessary, as if by letting go, she released her last hope of finding Jacob.

"I will. I promise." Velvet grabbed her bright red clutch from where she'd dropped it on the ground, dug out a rhinestone-encrusted cell phone and keyed the number in. After she dropped the phone back into her clutch, she squeezed Sylvia's hand. "Have faith. You'll find him." Then she left Sylvia standing on the sidewalk on Presa Street.

Tate pulled up beside her, having circled around the block with no place to stop and get out.

Sylvia climbed into the truck and slumped into the seat.

"What happened? Did she get away?"

"No. I let her go."

"But she might know where Jake is."

Sylvia shook her head. "No, she doesn't."

"She could be lying."

"No. If she'd known, she would have told me."

"I wish you'd let me ask the questions."

"Why? I would have beat the answers out of her if I thought she had them." Sylvia leaned her head back and rubbed her eyes. "She doesn't know. The only person who knows wouldn't tell us now if his life depended on it."

Tate eased into the traffic and headed for the interstate. Once on it, he floored the accelerator, bringing the truck up to seventy in under ten seconds. "What now?"

"What can we do?"

"We need to tell Melissa what we know and let her handle it."

"I don't think we have any other choice. Short of knocking on every door in the city of San Antonio, we don't have a clue where to start. For all we know, Jacob isn't even in San Antonio." She dropped her hand to her lap and stared down at her fingers. "Poor baby must be terrified."

Tate reached out and took her hand, holding it in his big warm fingers. "Have faith. We'll find him."

She gave a short, mirthless laugh. "That's what Velvet said. I've been looking for so long, I'm beginning to lose faith."

"You found him once, you'll find him again."

"Thanks." Sylvia lifted Tate's hand and pressed it to her cheek, the warmth in the cool interior of the truck seeping into her cold skin. "Right now I could sleep for a hundred years."

Tate pulled off the interstate at the next exit and got a room at a motel.

Sylvia didn't argue when he only got one room; she didn't care anymore. Jacob was lost. Her heart was breaking and she couldn't fight any longer.

"Come on, sweetheart." Tate helped her from the truck, grabbed his gym bag and led the way into the room.

Once inside, he tossed the gym bag to the floor and stood looking at her. "Get a shower. You'll feel better."

"I don't have the energy to move." Sylvia sat on the edge of the bed and buried her face in her hands. "I'm so tired."

"Here." He slipped his hand into hers and dragged her back to her feet. "Let me help." He pulled at the hem of the tube top, dragging it up and over her head. Without a bra, her bare breasts sprang free, the air-conditioning pebbling her nipples.

Despite her lethargy, Sylvia felt a tug low in her belly and warmth spread slowly upward.

Tate turned her around and worked the button on the black, faux-leather skirt. Then the zipper slid down. His hands slipped inside the edges of the skirt and wrapped around her hips. They rounded her belly and sank lower still, cupping the apex of her thighs.

Sylvia leaned back against Tate, absorbing his warmth, letting his strength seep into her.

With slow, deliberate movements, he slid the skirt off, his hands following over her hips, buttocks, down her thighs to her calves, massaging the tense muscles.

The soft pressure of lips pressed to the inside of her thigh.

She shifted, parting her legs, her hands smoothing down over her naked tummy to the mound of hair.

While Tate trailed kisses from the back of her thigh to the swell of her buttocks, Sylvia slid a finger inside her folds, touching that sensitive nub.

Tate rose behind her, his jeans coarse against her

naked skin, the hard ridge behind his fly tempting her beyond redemption.

With a deep, tortured breath, she turned in his arms, her breasts rubbing against the cotton fabric of his shirt, deliciously soft.

"For now, make me forget," she whispered. Her hands circled the back of his neck, pulling his face close enough she could kiss him.

He held back. "Only for a moment." Then his lips claimed hers, his tongue pushing past her teeth to twist and taste hers.

Her fingers moved feverishly, tugging at the black T-shirt, lifting it up and over his head. She needed him to be naked, to feel his skin against hers, to chase away the demons, the doubt, the worry.

Before his shirt hit the floor, she had the button of his jeans open, her hand sliding the zipper downward.

His member sprang free—long, hard and proud.

Sylvia took him in her hand, reveling in the steely strength and the velvety smoothness. Wanting him more than she cared to breathe, she guided him to her.

"No." He pulled free of her touch.

Sylvia looked up into his eyes, unable to process his withdrawal.

He smiled. "Not yet." He bent and lifted her, gently laying her on the comforter, her knees draped over the edge of the bed, her feet dangling toward the floor.

He shed his jeans and stepped between her thighs. Leaning over her, he took one pebbled nipple between his lips, his hands cupping her breasts, massaging them between his fingers.

Inch by excruciating inch, he worked his way down

her torso, nibbling, tasting and tempting her to scream with frustration.

When he dropped to his knees, his hands guiding her legs over his shoulders, Tate had her body on fire, aching with the need to consummate their union. She wanted him to drive into her, hard and fast. Tomorrow be damned.

His mouth found her entrance, tracing the dewy dampness upward to her folds, tonguing her until her back arched off the mattress.

Tension built to a sharp crescendo, every nerve centered on one place. Sylvia moaned, the pleasure so intense she thought she might die. Then she plunged over the edge, succumbing to ecstasy, her body jerking with the force.

Only then did Tate rise to his feet, and thrust into her, burying himself, his shaft fully sheathed in her heat. He pumped in and out, his hands steadying her hips.

He filled her, completed her like no one had ever done.

On his final plunge, Sylvia planted her heels and raised her hips, meeting his powerful thrust.

Head thrown back, his chest swelled out, Tate held her hips against him, his member throbbing, pulsing inside of her.

Several breath-stopping minutes passed and the tension drained from Sylvia.

Tate slid her up onto the bed and lay down beside her, gathering her into his arms. They lay together, their limbs intertwined until Tate's belly rumbled.

Sylvia kissed his lips. "You need food and I need a shower."

"I thought you were too tired."

"I was." She kissed him again, loving the stubble of his beard, the scent of male and the hardness of his muscles against her breasts. "Can we call out for pizza?"

"They're probably all closed for the night. I'll go see what I can find close by."

"Good. That'll give me time to shower." She rose from the bed, only mildly modest. After what he'd done to her...after what they'd done together, modesty shouldn't be a factor. But Sylvia had promised no strings.

As Tate lay stretched across the bed, his body a magnificent specimen of the male anatomy, Sylvia felt a stab of regret that she'd made that darned promise. She gathered her clothing and headed for the bathroom.

Tate rose from the bed, slipped into his jeans and boots. With his shirt in hand, he paused at the door. "I'll be back in just a few minutes. Don't open the door for anyone but me."

"I won't." She hurried into the bathroom, shutting the door behind her.

THE DOOR TO THE MOTEL room opened on squeaking hinges and closed with a solid clunk.

Sylvia leaned against the bathroom door, the smoothly painted wood cool against her naked backside.

Tate had felt so incredibly good inside. He'd been the perfect lover, gently attending to her desires first. Damn. She'd miss him when the time came to leave.

She pulled the shower curtain back, adjusted the water and climbed in, letting the warm spray wash over her.

If only she could wash Tate Vincent out of her system as easily as she washed shampoo out of her hair.

As she stepped from the shower, her cell phone buzzed from the back pocket of her jeans.

Sylvia dug the phone out, her hand shaking. Could it be someone with news of Jacob? Her low-battery indicator blinked.

She punched the talk button and pressed the receiver to her ear, her breath lodged in her lungs. "Hello?" She prayed her battery would last just a little longer.

A voice, barely above a whisper spoke into her ear. "It's Velvet. I know where they have your son."

Chapter Fifteen

Tate juggled a bag of groceries in his hand, digging in his back pocket for the key card.

Sylvia should be out of the shower by now. He'd contacted Melissa while he'd been driving around looking for a twenty-four-hour convenience store. She'd been sleeping, but as soon as she knew who it was, she'd come wide-awake, taking down the information he gave her and asking questions of her own.

She informed Tate that they had an undercover agent working the gang issues. She'd get a message to him to dig around, see if he could discover where they hid the stolen or purchased babies. "Be careful," she'd warned. "The Crips play for keeps. They aren't afraid to kill first, ask questions later."

The key card slid into the door and the light flashed green. Tate pushed through.

The comforter lay just as tumbled as it had when they'd made love. The door to the bathroom stood slightly ajar. "Sylvia?"

Behind him the door swung shut, the lock engaged, echoing off the walls of the tiny room.

What felt like a cold fist squeezed the air out of Tate's lungs.

He dropped the bag of groceries on the dresser and ran for the bathroom, hitting the door so hard, it bounced off the wall. "Sylvia!"

Steam still fogged the mirror. The clothes she'd taken into the bathroom were gone. The shower stood empty except for the drops of water clinging to the smooth porcelain.

Sylvia was gone.

Tate froze for a moment, no thoughts scrambling in his head, nothing, just emptiness. Then a thousand images crowded in on him. His father riding the fence line; his father lying on the dusty ground, his chest laid open with a knife wound; the first day he'd held Jake, the smile on the golden-haired child's face, the blue eyes staring up at him. Just like his mother's.

Sylvia, whose pale blue eyes mirrored Jake's, whose long blond hair sifted like silk threads through his fingers, whose body completed his.

Gone.

Tate yanked his phone from his back pocket and punched the number Sylvia had given him. The phone rang ten times before a canned greeting answered that the cellular customer was not available.

Was she not answering, or was it that she couldn't answer? She didn't have a way to charge her battery— the phone could have died.

Who could he turn to?

His cell phone rang and he almost dropped it on the bathroom tile.

Kacee LeBlanc displayed on the caller ID.

Tate answered. "Kacee, I need your help."

"What's happening?"

"Sylvia is gone."

"Gone? How? Where?"

Tate pushed a hand through his hair and turned to face the empty room, the essence of their lovemaking still lingering in the air. "I don't know where she is, I just know I have to find her."

"Hold on, big guy. Everything will be okay. Since you can't find Jake, she's probably skipped out of town. Without the kid, she has nothing to leverage over you."

Tate held the phone away, staring down at it as if it were alien. He placed the receiver to his ear and demanded, "What are you talking about?"

"You know, she was probably going to blackmail you into paying to keep Jake."

"You have no idea what you're talking about. You don't know anything about her."

"And you've only known her for twenty-four hours. What exactly do you know about Sylvia Michaels? Nothing other than the lies she's filled your head with. She's not the mother of your son, Tate. How could you believe her? You were there when Beth Kirksey signed over her child to you."

Tate's teeth ground together. When Kacee got an idea between her teeth, short of yanking it out, teeth and all, she wasn't letting go of it easily. "Just get here."

"And where might *here* be?"

He gave her the name of the motel, then paused. "No, never mind. Call me when you're in San Antonio. We can set up a meeting location."

"Can we meet in ten minutes?"

"It's more than an hour from your place."

"Tate, I'm in San Antonio. That's why I called."

"What the hell are you doing here?"

"Nice that you care," she said, her voice dripping

with sarcasm. "I thought I'd pay a visit to a sick friend and while I was at it check in and make sure you don't go off the deep end." She laughed once without a shred of humor in the tone. "Sounds like you might have already. Besides, C.W. was worried about you."

"I can take care of myself."

"Yeah? Then why haven't you answered your phone for the past couple of hours?"

He sucked in a deep breath and let it out. "Again, I can take care of myself."

"Maybe you don't get it, but you're worth millions, Tate Vincent. Anyone with half a brain that recognizes you would be tempted to take you for a ride, maybe hold you hostage to get at all those millions."

"Just meet me here in ten minutes."

"Will do."

As Tate pulled his phone away from his ear, Kacee spoke. "Oh, and Tate?"

"What?"

"Don't fall for her cute little act. That's all it is… an act."

Tate grabbed the groceries, the gym bag he'd tossed on the floor earlier and left the room. Staying there served no purpose and knowing what they'd done in that bed only made him even more angry. He'd wait in the truck before he spent another minute in that room.

His loins ached with the residual reminder of how she'd felt beneath him. With a little more force than was necessary, he threw the gym bag into the backseat of his truck and set the grocery bag down. Then he walked to the lobby and pushed through the glass doors.

The clerk behind the counter smiled a welcome. "May I help you, sir?"

"Did you see a woman leave the parking lot a few minutes ago? Or maybe a car come and go?"

"As matter of fact, I did. A blonde got into a car with someone and they left, just five minutes ago."

"Of her own free will?" Tate asked.

The young man shrugged. "Beats me. She didn't have someone shove her in, if that's what you're asking. She'd been waiting for a minute or two. Pretty blonde." His lips twisted into a grin. "That's why I was watching."

Tate wanted to slam his fist into a wall. "Thanks." He performed an about-face and exited the lobby. So she'd left with someone else. Someone she'd been waiting for. No note, no call, nothing. Damn her!

Kacee's silver Lexus purred into the drive-through in front of the motel and she jumped out. "God, Tate, you don't know how glad I am to see you." She wrapped her arms around his waist and hugged him. "Don't worry, this, too, will pass. You'll be all right."

"Yeah, but will Jake?" He rested his hands on her waist for a moment, then pushed her to arm's length. "That little guy doesn't know what's going on. He's got to be scared out of his mind."

Kacee leaned back and stared up into Tate's face, shaking her head. "He's gotten under your skin, hasn't he?"

"Damn right, he has."

"I don't know why you didn't just settle down and have a kid of your own." She pushed out of his reach and walked a few steps. "There are plenty of women who'd love to have your baby."

Except one. Sylvia had made it clear that she didn't want a commitment from him. No strings, no promises.

What if he wanted strings, what if he wanted more children? What if he wanted Sylvia in his life? Maybe go on a real date, get to know her better than just sex. Although the sex had been...well, damned good.

She'd taken the decision out of his hands. For all he knew, she might have known all along where Jake was. She could have lied like Kacee said. Perhaps have set up the kidnapping, maybe even started the fire in the barn. His mind raced with the depth of her supposed duplicity, all of which he couldn't verify without talking to the woman. Damn it! Where was she?

Kacee touched his arm, her face creased into a frown. "You aren't falling for that woman, are you?"

Tate shook his head. "Like you said, I don't know her." But he *wanted* to get to know her.

"You are!" She stepped back. "What are you thinking?"

He pushed a hand through his hair. "I don't know *what* I'm thinking. I swear she's Jake's mother. He looks just like her."

"And he looked just like Beth Kirksey."

"No. Not after seeing Sylvia and Jake together. He has a birthmark just like hers."

"It could be a tattoo."

"I saw it. It's real." He'd run his lips across it, exploring her body a little at a time.

"Great. The mighty Vincent is in lust." Kacee crossed her arms over her chest. "What could you possibly see in her?"

All the thoughts of her fooling him vanished, and the fierce look on her face as she attacked El Corredor from behind flashed in Tate's mind. She'd been like a lioness protecting her pride. Loyal, courageous and tenacious. "She's beautiful."

"Well, don't get carried away, Casanova. In case your memory is slipping along with your common sense, the woman's gone." Kacee's mouth pressed into a thin line. "Did you bring me here for a reason? Because if not, I could be tucked in a bed sleeping."

"We need to call the FBI and report Sylvia missing."

"She hasn't been gone for more than twenty-four hours. Was there a sign of struggle?"

"No."

Kacee shook her head. "The police won't even talk to you."

"Then we have to get to Special Agent Bradley."

"Special Agent Bradley? An FBI agent?"

"Yes."

"What happened to the guy from Austin who was supposed to be investigating the kidnapping?"

"The case has been transferred." He walked to his truck and opened the door. "I need to touch base with her. She might have a lead on the location where the stolen babies are being taken."

Kacee's brows rose. "Really? You think this is more than just a kidnapping of millionaire Tate Vincent's baby for ransom? You bought into all that stuff that Michaels woman told you?"

"Yeah." He glanced at Kacee, his brow furrowing. "You know, on second thought, I'd rather you went back to the ranch. I can speak with the agent on my own. You don't need to be involved with this mess."

"Nice of you to be concerned. I want to be here. I feel somewhat responsible, since I found the adoption agency for you." She leaned into his arm and touched his cheek. "I knew how much you wanted a child to carry on the Vincent name."

He captured her hand and held it. "Don't fight me on this, Kacee. Go home." He let go and stepped back, putting distance between them.

She bit down on her lip, her brows drawing together. He'd seen that look when she'd been ready to launch into an argument.

He held up his hand. "Please, Kacee. Go."

"Is there any chance…you and me…?" She pointed to him and back to herself.

Tate had known for a while that Kacee wanted more than a boss-employee relationship. He'd never given her reason to believe he wanted the same. She was a good assistant, one he could hardly do without. "No, Kacee. The most we'll ever be is friends."

Without another word, Kacee spun on her heel and climbed into her car. Before she pulled away, she slid the window down. "If you need me tonight, I'll be at a friend's house."

Something Sylvia had mentioned came to Tate. "Kacee?"

She glanced through the window at him. "Yeah."

"When did your brother get out of jail?"

Her eyes narrowed slightly. "Why do you ask?"

Tate found it interesting that she avoided his question. "Just curious. Is that the friend you're staying with?"

She hesitated. "No, it isn't. I'm not on speaking terms with my brother. Is there a problem?"

His gut tightened, instinct kicking in. He could tell she held back. "No, no. I just wonder why you never told me your brother was out of jail."

"How did you find out?"

"I don't remember. Someone told me in passing," he lied. "Maybe Zach."

Her eyes narrowed even more. "I'll head back to the office tomorrow." She raised the window halfway and then lowered it again. "Tate?"

Tate walked over to her.

She reached out and caught his hand. "You'll regret this, Tate. Mark my words. That woman isn't the one for you."

Tate nodded. "Maybe not. But I have to find her."

"WHERE IS JACOB?" Sylvia asked as Velvet accelerated onto Loop 410, the inside loop surrounding the center of San Antonio. "Where is my son? And why is it necessary for me to drive around with you?" The longer she remained away from the motel room, the more likely Tate would worry.

"I think someone followed me. I can't stay in one place too long." The prostitute shot a glance to her rearview mirror and another to the side mirror. "Raul doesn't like it when I disappear."

Sylvia clenched her fists to keep from reaching out and shaking the information out of the woman. "What did you find out?"

"I was talking with Candy. She had a baby not long ago and gave it up for adoption." Velvet looked across the console at Sylvia. "She used the same agency as Beth."

"The agency is closed. I've already checked."

Velvet nodded. "I know. Candy talked about El Corredor and how he'd taken her out to the hill country to a private clinic where she could have her baby. She said they had a nursery there with a number of babies, but she didn't see that many mothers. Just nurses or care-givers feeding the babies."

Sylvia's heart leaped. "A private clinic? Where?"

"She wasn't exactly sure. El Corredor had her blind-folded before taking her there and bringing her back."

Another roadblock. Sylvia sat back in her seat, all her excitement fading. "How can I search the entire hill country? How will I ever find it?"

"She didn't know exactly where it was, but she did see the name of the linen service that delivered to it. She thought maybe that would help."

"Who delivered?"

"Allied Cleaning Services."

"Sounds like a chain."

"No. I checked. They only have an office in Com-fort."

Sylvia dared to hope. "Anything else?"

"No. That was all she saw or heard."

"I need a car," Sylvia thought out loud. "I need to get out to Comfort."

"I can drop you at a car rental place."

Sylvia shook her head. "That won't do. I'm broke. I've spent every last penny searching for my son. I have nothing left. Could you drop me back at the motel?"

"No. It's too dangerous. I can let you out at the next gas station and you can call your guy from there."

Velvet pulled off the highway and behind a gas station-convenience store, parking in the shadows.

"Thank you for everything, Velvet. I'm sorry I gave you such a hard time." On impulse, Sylvia leaned across and hugged Velvet.

When she sat back and reached for the door handle,

Velvet's hand stopped her. With her other hand, she dug into her cleavage and pulled out a wad of bills. "Here, take this. It'll get you where you need to go."

Sylvia held up her hands. This woman had sold her body for that cash, the hardest-earned paycheck Sylvia could imagine. "I can't take your money."

She took Sylvia's hand and pressed the money into it, folding her fingers around it. "Find your baby. Take him home and be a good mother to him."

"Why are you doing this? I thought you hated me."

Velvet pushed a long strand of black hair behind her ear and stared off into the night. "Let's just say I've made mistakes. Mistakes I've regretted."

Sylvia stuffed the cash into her pocket and climbed out of the car. She leaned back in. "Thanks, Velvet. I'll pay you back. I promise."

"Just get there in time, will ya?"

Sylvia shut the car door and Velvet sped off. Sylvia pulled her cell phone from her back pocket and pressed the on button. Nothing. She'd keyed Tate's number into her cell phone, but she didn't know it by heart. Without a battery to boot the phone, she didn't have a way to contact him.

She rounded the corner of the convenience store and walked in. She had to pay the guy behind the counter five bucks to convince him to let her use his phone and a phone book.

With time ticking away, Sylvia dialed the number for the motel and asked for their room number. Tate should be back by now. She hadn't had time to leave a note. He'd be mad that she'd left.

The phone rang ten times before Sylvia gave up. Her next call was for a taxi.

When she finally made it back to the motel, an hour had passed. The first thing she noticed was that Tate's truck wasn't there. She used the key card Tate had left with her, letting herself into the room.

Everything was as she'd left it except Tate's gym bag was gone. If the bed hadn't been mussed, she'd swear he'd never been there. With no way to contact him, she didn't have any other choice but to do this on her own. She climbed into the waiting taxi. "Take me to a place where I can rent a car with cash."

Five minutes later, he'd dropped her off at a car rental place near the airport. Without a credit card, she had to bribe the clerk with an additional hundred dollars to get him to sign over a car to her. Knowing how hard Velvet had worked for that cash made Sylvia sick. But she handed it over, grabbed the set of keys and ran for the car.

The sun would be up in a couple of hours. If she wanted to catch the delivery drivers for the cleaning service, she'd have to get there early. If her memory served her well, it would take thirty to forty minutes to get out to Comfort and a few more minutes to find the business.

Afraid to hope, afraid to get excited, Sylvia drove out of the rental car lot, careful not to draw attention to herself. She couldn't afford to get pulled over by a cop. Jacob needed her and she now had a clue as to where he was.

She angled the car for the on ramp to the bypass and pressed her foot to the floor. "I'm coming, Jacob. Hold on, baby."

Chapter Sixteen

"When was the last time you saw her?" Melissa sat across the conference table in the war room of the San Antonio branch of the FBI, a cup of coffee getting cold next to her.

"Over an hour ago." Tate fought to sit still on the cracked-leather conference room chair. "Did you find out anything? Does your inside guy know how to contact El Corredor?"

"He's working on it as we speak. Not that I think he'll get anywhere, as late as it is. Plus your activities tonight might have spooked El Corredor." She leaned toward him. "I did enter Velvet's pimp into the system and came up with some names of gang members he hangs with. I also have some pictures our undercover guy made with a concealed camera. Maybe you can identify the men you ran up against."

Melissa opened her laptop. She brought up a photo and turned the screen toward Tate. "Any of these familiar?"

The photo was grainy, but Tate thought two of the men looked familiar. "That's him. That's the guy they call El Corredor. The other is his bodyguard."

"How about in the next picture?"

The next shot had three men gathered around a street corner in the business district of downtown San Antonio. The light wasn't all that good and Tate had a harder time picking out someone he recognized. He pointed at a man with what looked like a tattoo on his arm. "That's the bodyguard again. And the man with his back to the camera could be El Corredor." He leaned closer. A man with reddish-brown hair stared straight at the camera. "I think I've seen that guy before, but I can't place him."

Melissa zoomed in on the man. "He's one of the guys I needed to talk with you about." She stared across the table at him. "Our agent said this man is Danny LeBlanc. I believe he's related to one of your employees."

Tate's brows furrowed for a moment then cleared. "Would it be Kacee LeBlanc's brother?"

"Yeah. He's in violation of his parole for hanging out with these gang members."

"Do you know where to find him?"

"Based on his parole records, we have the address of the apartment he's supposed to be living in."

"Let's go." Tate stood, pushing back his chair so hard it toppled over backward.

"Wait a minute, Tate. You're not an agent. You're not even a law enforcement official. I can't take you with me."

"Why the hell not?"

"We don't know if he's involved with the whole baby-selling business. Our undercover agent is working it as we speak. Let him do his job."

"I can't stand by and do nothing." Tate moved toward the door of the conference room.

Melissa caught his arm. "Give us time to do our jobs."

He didn't turn to face her, his mind already ahead of him. "Sylvia and Jake may not have time." He shook off her hand and walked out, weaving through the maze of desks and emerging from the building into the gray of predawn.

Kacee's brother was a gang member? Did she know this?

He got out his cell phone and almost hit the speed dial for Kacee when he thought better of it. If Kacee was staying the rest of the night with her brother, she'd be at his apartment. If her brother really was involved with the thugs who'd tried to kill them tonight, he wouldn't want Tate asking questions.

Tate clicked several buttons on his cell phone and brought up the internet site he used to track the cell phones of the people he employed. He keyed in Kacee's phone number and waited. A map of San Antonio came up with a blinking dot where Kacee's phone was located.

Tate ran for his truck. If he wanted information out of Kacee's brother, he'd better get to him before the FBI agent did. Added to his concern was Kacee. She might be in danger, too.

Meanwhile, the clock was ticking and Sylvia and Jake might be running out of time.

SYLVIA PARKED A block from the cleaners and crept into the building unnoticed. A large delivery van had backed up to a loading dock and two men loaded carts of linens into the back.

Considering how small the town was, the one van probably served all the company's customers. If Sylvia wanted to get into a secret compound, what better way than as a delivery?

When the workers went back inside for another load, Sylvia made her move. She dove into the back of the van and hid behind a rolling cart filled with clean sheets and tablecloths.

Her heart thundered against her ears as she strained to hear movement outside.

"This is the last one," a worker said. A thump jolted the metal floor of the van. The squeak of wheels headed her way had Sylvia ducking low, tugging the corner of a freshly laundered towel over her head. She could just see the tips of black work boots.

Afraid to breathe, afraid to move and alert the worker to her presence, Sylvia waited an eternity for the boots to move. Finally, they left, a metal door slid shut and her world went dark.

The engine revved and the truck lumbered over the rough roads on the way to each of its deliveries. First obstacle overcome, Sylvia managed to fill her lungs and plan for her next move.

After several stops in town, Sylvia began to wonder if there was another truck that had left earlier. There were only two large roll-away carts. If the van was going to make a delivery to the compound, it had to be soon. Hiding between the two carts was no longer an option.

Sylvia stood and moved the sheets, tablecloths and towels around in the cart and carefully climbed over the edge. One by one, she refolded the sheets and stacked them on top of her body and head, completely covering herself.

When the truck jerked to a halt and the engine shut

off, Sylvia's heart raced. She prayed she'd gotten on the right van and prayed even harder that Jacob would be in the compound, alive and safe.

The back door slid upward, light spilling through the opening, barely penetrating the cocoon she'd wrapped herself in.

Buried in the cart, she froze, afraid the sheets would shift and expose her.

"Must have extra guests out here. They sent extra linens this time," the worker said as he rolled the cart across the floor of the van.

"No more than usual," another voice said next to cart. "I'll check the invoice once I get inside. Just leave the second one there. I'll come back and get it."

"Will do."

The cart jolted and then rolled easily across a smooth surface.

Now that she was inside the compound, Sylvia hoped that they wouldn't unload the cart immediately, so she could escape undetected.

When the cart quit rolling, Sylvia lay still for several minutes, listening.

The only voices she could detect sounded as if they moved away from her along with the footsteps.

She moved the sheets aside just a bit and peered out of her hiding place. So far, so good.

She inched her head up over the top of the bin and looked around at what appeared to be a really big closet filled with bedsheets, towels and tablecloths in neat stacks on shelves against one wall. The other walls were stacked with scrubs, white jackets, surgical garb of varying sizes, toilet paper, paper towels, cleaning supplies and disinfectants.

She heard voices getting louder.

Sylvia climbed out of the cart and dropped behind it. She hurried toward a door that stood open at the far end of the room, ducking behind it as two women dressed in green scrubs entered.

"What's the big push to get all the babies ready to go?"

"I don't know. I think they're transferring them to another location."

"I hope that doesn't mean they're closing this facility. I can't afford to lose this job."

"Me, either. Hate to drive all the way to San Antonio for work."

"Still, all this hush-hush is silly. In this day and age, a woman has the right to give a baby up for adoption without feeling persecuted."

"Yeah, makes you wonder about it all. What with the barbed-wire fences and guards at the gate."

"Shh...here comes Barb. She doesn't like us talking. She jumped down the throat of the new girl when she pulled out her personal cell phone on duty. Thought she'd have a conniption fit."

"That's one of the first things they warned us at orientation—no cell phones inside the gates." The woman grabbed baby blankets from a shelf and handed them to the other. "Here, you better get going."

She took a stack of crib sheets for herself and both women left the room in silence.

A larger, older woman entered. Sylvia guessed this was Barb.

The woman pulled a set of keys away from her waist on a retractable cable and unlocked a sturdy metal cabinet, removed a plastic package of what looked like syringes and a couple of clear glass vials. She left, her rubber-soled shoes squeaking on the yellowing linoleum tiles.

Left alone, Sylvia grabbed green scrubs from a stack on the shelf nearest her and pulled them on over her clothes. She tucked her hair up in a surgical cap and peeked around the door.

The hallway, smelling of disinfectant, stood empty. Sylvia moved quickly, glancing into open doorways. The rooms appeared like dorm rooms, with built-in dressers, a twin-size bed and plain utilitarian nightstand. Bare bones, like a low-cost hospital or a nursing home.

In one room she passed, a young woman was lying on the bed, her belly large and swollen, her face haggard. She was asleep, her arms beside her, lined with needle marks.

Sylvia's heart bled for the girl. Pregnant and addicted. The poor baby would probably be delivered addicted, as well. The world was a harsh enough environment for a baby to live in.

At the end of the hallway, Sylvia glanced around the corner to the right. A couple of women in scrubs wheeled newborns in small carts from a room marked Nursery, walking away from her.

To the left, babies' cries carried through the walls. A door opened and the crying grew louder. One of the women Sylvia had seen in the storage room turned her way.

Sylvia ducked back down the hallway she'd come from and into an empty room.

As she waited for the woman's footsteps to pass by, she listened to the noise through the wall.

These babies didn't sound like newborns. They had heartier lungs, like those of older children.

Hope leaped in her chest. Somehow, she had to get inside that room. Jacob could be there.

When the footsteps faded, Sylvia hurried out into the hall and turned the corner toward the room where the babies were crying.

"Hey!" a woman yelled. "Who locked the exit door?" A door at the end of the hallway behind her rattled. "Anyone know who locked this door?"

Women emerged from doorways lining the corridor, some in scrubs, some in nightgowns, sporting enormous pregnant bellies.

Another staff member joined the woman at the locked doorway and attempted to push the double doors open, but they remained jammed shut.

"Let me try the one at the other end of the hall," another staff member called out and turned toward where Sylvia stood.

She marched toward the other end of the passage. When she passed Sylvia, she frowned. "Are you new around here?"

Sylvia nodded, remembering that she wore scrubs like the majority of the staff.

The woman didn't stop, but said over her shoulder, "Give me a hand, then."

Sylvia fell into step behind her, passing the room where the babies still cried.

When she reached the double doors at the end of the corridor, the staff member pushed on the lever. It depressed as it should, but the door didn't open.

"It's jammed. Help me push on it."

Sylvia leaned against the door at the same time as the other woman. The door refused to budge.

"That's odd. This is an emergency exit, locked from the inside. It shouldn't be locked from the outside."

Standing next to the woman, Sylvia prayed she didn't question her more on her employment. All she wanted was to get into the room with the crying babies and find Jacob.

"Smoke! I smell smoke!" The very pregnant woman with the track marks on her arms, ran out into the main hall, screaming.

Fire alarms went off and soon the halls were filled with young women, nurses and clinic staff.

"We can't open any of the doors. They're all blocked!" a young nurse cried out.

"Call the fire department!" Barb, the head nurse, yelled.

A woman leaned over a desk and picked up the telephone. "No signal."

"Someone have a cell phone?"

"No, we aren't allowed to have cell phones here."

Gray tendrils of smoke seeped through the walls, rising in the air.

Sylvia's heart raced, her lungs still scratchy from her last bout of arson. No longer caring whether or not she was found out, she pushed through the doorway into the room with the crying babies, at the same time as two women ran out.

Playpens lined the walls, each with a small child, either standing or sitting inside. All were crying. There had to be at least ten babies in the room.

None of them had light blond hair and blue eyes. Sylvia checked every playpen thoroughly, searching beneath blankets for the one child she'd never given up on. When she reached the last playpen, it was empty. A bottle lay on the mat inside, empty. Where was the child?

A stuffed toy lay on the floor. Sylvia leaned over the playpen. A golden-haired child sat there, shaking a ragged plush toy. "Jacob?" He looked up at her and shook the toy again, giggling.

"Jacob!" She jerked the playpen from the wall and grabbed the baby into her arms. "Oh, God, Jacob." Tears ran down her face.

He patted her cheeks with the toy, his brows drawing together. "Da, da, da."

"Oh, baby, yes. We'll get out of here and you can see your daddy." Sylvia coughed, suddenly aware of the screams from the hallway and the increase of smoke in the baby room. If she could open a window, maybe the smoke would clear. Hopefully they had the fire under control by now.

Based on the amount of noise in the hallway, she didn't think that was a possibility.

Sylvia's gaze darted around the room, noticing for the first time a lack of windows. For that matter, none of the dorm rooms she'd passed had windows.

A woman burst through the doorway. "We have to get these babies out of here. The entire building is on fire!"

Sylvia grabbed another child from a playpen, balancing one on each hip, and she raced out into the hall crowded with staff and pregnant women.

The nurses and patients huddled close to the floors where the smoke wasn't so bad, sobbing. "We can't get out. We're trapped," one patient cried.

Carrying the babies on her hips, Sylvia hurried down

the hallway, checking room after room for a window.
There weren't any. Flames ate their way in from the
outside, burning through the siding and framework.
Someone had built the place like a fortress.

Or a tomb.

TATE FOUND KACEE'S CAR parked in the parking lot of
a run-down apartment building. He couldn't possibly
knock on every door to find the right one. It would give
Danny time to figure it out and run.

Climbing down from his truck, Tate found a position behind a bush close to the middle of the building. Staircases on either side led to the parking lot. If
Danny lived on the bottom floor, he'd just have to run
faster than him.

In position and ready, he dialed Kacee's number.

"Tate? Why are you still up? Did you find the Michaels woman?"

"Where are you right now?"

"Why?" she asked.

"Just want to make sure you got to your friend's
apartment safely."

"I am."

"This friend male or female?"

Kacee laughed. "So now you're interested?"

"Not for the reasons you'd think."

A long pause ensued, then Kacee sighed. "What are
you talking about, Tate?"

"Did I tell you that I had all the business phones
placed on a GPS scanning system in case we lost one?"

A crackling sound came to Tate through the receiver,
and muffled voices he couldn't understand. Kacee had
her hand over the speaker.

"Where are you, Tate?"

"Close by. Mind if I come meet your friend?"

"It's really late. Besides, she stepped out a minute ago."

"I thought you said she was sick?"

A door opened and a man slipped out of a second-floor apartment and raced for the staircase.

"Okay, then, I'll see you back at the office." He clicked the off button and slipped the phone in his pocket.

Keeping low and behind the vehicles in the parking lot, Tate raced across the pavement, arriving at the base of the stairs as the man reached the bottom.

Tate hit him like a linebacker, catching him in the gut and knocking him flat on his back.

The man struggled, his arms and legs flailing out to the sides, but Tate had him pinned.

"Danny LeBlanc, right?"

The man stilled. "You got the wrong guy."

Tate leaned back, and a beam from a nearby streetlight crossed over the man's face. The face he hadn't been able to place until now. Kacee had a photo of a younger version of this guy in her wallet. She'd dropped it one day when she'd been rifling through her purse for a pen.

"Where are they?"

"Where are who?"

"Where does El Corredor keep the babies?"

"I don't know what you're talking about."

Tate pulled his gun out of the back of his jeans and held it to the man's temple. "I don't feel like arguing."

Danny snorted. "You won't shoot."

"Try me." Tate's anger and fear consumed him. He

could barely see the man in front of him for the red shadowing his vision. "All you are is one more obstacle in the way of getting my son back."

"Stop!" Kacee rushed down the steps, hair flying, her blouse untucked and makeup smeared. "Don't hurt him."

"Stay where you are or I'll shoot him," Tate warned.

"Go ahead." Danny laughed. "Shoot me."

"No!" Kacee ran down a couple more steps, tripped and plowed into Tate, knocking him off his feet and flat on his back. His wrist hit the ground, and the SIG Sauer flew from his fingertips and slid beneath a car.

"Danny isn't to blame. Don't hurt him." Kacee clutched at Danny's shirt, pulling him against her chest. "I made him find Jake to begin with, and then I made him take Jake away."

"Shut up, Kacee." Danny rolled to the side, placing Kacee between him and Tate.

"It's all my fault," she blubbered, her voice catching on her sobs. "I started the fire so that Danny would have a chance to steal Jake."

"Why?" Tate inched his way back toward the car where his gun lay.

"Don't you see? I love you," she cried, her eyes filled with tears.

"I told you to shut up." Danny's arm circled Kacee's neck and he squeezed hard, cutting off her air.

Tate dove under the car, grabbed the gun and rolled to his feet, aiming at the man's head. "Let her go, Danny."

"No, I can't." He squeezed harder.

Kacee kicked and flailed, her eyes wide, pleading, her face turning a sickly shade of blue.

"Put the gun down or I'll kill her." Danny tightened his hold on her neck.

If he hesitated any longer, Kacee would die. Tate laid the gun down on the pavement.

"Kick it to the side," Danny demanded.

Tate kicked the weapon out of reach.

"You rich guys want it all and have the money to pay for it. You can even buy children no one else wants." He stood, bringing Kacee up with him, her feet dangling off the ground.

"Put Kacee down, Danny. She's not the one you want to hurt."

"Selling kids to the rich people beats hell out of growing up abandoned, living out of Dumpsters and fighting for everything you have."

Kacee's struggles weakened, her body going limp.

Tate threw himself at the pair, knocking them to the ground.

Danny's head cracked against the stairs and he lay motionless. Kacee rolled to the side, at first still, then her chest heaved and she sucked in a deep breath. She coughed and drew in more air. When the color returned to her face, she crawled over to her brother. "Danny? Oh, Danny." She laid her cheek against his chest. "You're going to be okay, I promise. I'll get us out of this mess."

Blood pooled on the concrete sidewalk beneath Danny's head. Tate felt his neck for a pulse. It was weak.

Kacee sobbed against her brother's chest. "You killed him." She pushed up and threw herself at Tate, scratching and clawing. "You killed him!" she repeated.

"He was killing you, Kacee. If I hadn't stopped him, you'd be dead. Besides, this idiot's not dead."

"He didn't mean it. He's all the family I have. He didn't mean it."

"Kacee, he's alive, will you listen to me?" Tate pulled her into his arms and held her until the sobs subsided. Then he pushed her to arm's length and brushed the hair out of her face. "I'll get him some help, but you have to tell me where they are. Where are the babies El Corredor steals?"

"I don't know." She shook her head, staring down at the brother she so obviously loved.

"You have to know. You're the only one left who can tell me. Please, Kacee, tell me." He shook her gently, but firmly. "Tell me now."

"Out near Comfort." She tried to pull away. "Leave me alone. You never wanted me. No one ever wanted us." Kacee lay down beside Danny's body, moaning.

Tate lifted her up enough to face him. "Where in Comfort?"

She stared up at him, her eyes swimming. "That's all I know."

Tate stood and yanked his cell phone from his pocket. He punched the speed dial number for Agent Bradley.

"Bradley speaking."

"Comfort. They keep the babies somewhere out near Comfort."

"I was just about to call you. I got word from my undercover agent. He said that El Corredor left an hour ago, saying he had to take care of evidence. He followed him to a compound out near Comfort, but it's fenced and under armed guard. I'm on my way to the airport. Meet me there and you can ride with me in the chopper."

"I'll be there in five." He clicked the off button. "I'm

calling the paramedics. Stay with him until they get here."

"I'm not going anywhere. He didn't leave me when our mother did." She held Danny's hand in hers. "I won't leave him. He's my brother."

Tate climbed into his truck, pressing 9-1-1 as he drove out of the parking lot.

When he reached the airport, he called Melissa's cell phone and stayed on with her until he found the helicopter pad.

Within minutes, the bird took off, headed toward the hill country northwest of San Antonio.

Melissa handed him a headset, settling hers over her ears.

As they passed over the small German town of Boerne, Tate leaned forward. A plume of smoke rose from one of the rolling hills ahead.

"We have a fire ahead," the pilot informed them.

"Just got a text from our man on the ground." Melissa leaned over the pilot's shoulder, scanning the horizon. "Looks like the compound is on fire. We have backup on the way, but they might not get there in time. Hurry!"

The helicopter swooped in over the barbed-wire fences, the heat from the flames buffeting the blades, making it difficult to land.

Guard towers stood empty and deserted. Surrounded by a wall of smoke and flame, they were hardly visible.

As soon as Tate dropped down out of the helicopter, he smelled the acrid scent of gasoline. Someone had set the fire. The question foremost in his mind made his stomach roil. Were there people still inside?

Flames crackled and roared, drowning out almost every other noise. But as soon as the helicopter lifted off and away from the burning building, screams could be heard.

His heart stopped for two whole beats before it slammed against his chest, blasting blood and adrenaline through his veins.

Two vehicles pulled out from behind the building. A black Hummer and a silver Suburban.

Tate, Melissa and two other agents stood in the path between the vehicles and the gate leading out of the compound. All four of them had weapons drawn.

"Wait until they're within range!" Melissa called out.

As the vehicles drew near, a man leaned out of the Hummer wielding a submachine gun.

Tate and the agents dropped to the ground and opened fire.

The front windshield shattered and the driver swerved to the right. The second vehicle sped up.

Tate unloaded his clip, aiming for the driver of the Suburban. The agents peppered the vehicle, some aiming for the tires. The Suburban kept coming. At the last minute, the driver's head jerked back, a bullet through the windshield finally stopping him. The vehicle swerved sharply and flipped, tumbling straight for Tate.

Tate dove to the side and rolled out of the way, the whoosh of air, shattering glass and the thunder of a ton of metal pounded the ground where he'd been. The Suburban crashed against the limestone fence and burst into flame.

Screams from inside the building grew louder.

"Leave them!" Melissa shouted, running for the building, dropping her empty clip and reloading as she ran.

Tate tossed his empty pistol to the ground and raced

to catch up. Hands pounded the metal emergency exit from the inside, their voices desperate and frightened. A chain wrapped around the handles barred anyone from entering or leaving.

"Stand back!" Mel placed her Glock against the lock, turned her face away and pulled the trigger. The hasp exploded and Tate jerked the chains free.

When he opened the door, smoke billowed out. Women rushed past him, some pregnant, others carrying babies. They dove for the fresh clean air, coughing and gasping. Melissa and her agents helped those who couldn't make it on their own and rushed back in to help more.

Tate ran past one woman after another. No sign of Sylvia or Jake. This was not happening. He couldn't lose Jake, the boy he loved as his own. He wanted a chance to get to know Sylvia, the courageous woman who'd come to mean more than he'd ever thought possible in such a short amount of time.

Smoke choked his throat and lungs, but he pressed on, pulling his shirt up over his mouth. His eyes burned as he worked his way into the clinic.

"Sylvia!" he yelled into the roiling smoke. "Sylvia!"

"Here! We're in here!"

Tate rounded a corner, running crouched over to stay below the rising smoke.

"In here!" Sylvia cried again.

Tate burst through a door, tripped over a pile of baby blankets and ground to a halt.

Sylvia had a playpen full of babies a few feet from the door. "I couldn't leave them."

In her arms, Jake clung to her, his face streaked with tears. When he saw Tate, he held out his arms.

"Oh, Jake. Baby, come to Daddy." Tate gathered the child into his arms and hugged him tight, a lump rising in his throat. He pulled Sylvia against him with his other arm and kissed her forehead, unable to speak.

She clung to his shirt, tears wetting the fabric, never more happy to see someone. "Thank God you found us." She smiled up at him, blinking back the tears, smoke stinging her eyes, burning her lungs.

"You scared the crud out of me." He kissed her forehead and touched his lips to hers.

She kissed him back, liking the feel of him against her, until the smoke coughed it out of her. "I blocked the door to keep the smoke from coming in, but we have to get out now or we won't make it." Sylvia pushed away from him, her eyes wide as she spied the rising flames licking at the hallway walls.

Tate glanced at the playpen full of babies all around Jake's age. "We can't carry all the babies out one at a time."

"Then you get one side of the playpen and I'll get the other. We can drag it out with all of them in it."

Tate set Jake in the pen. The little guy screamed, coughed and sat down, sobbing.

Sylvia's heart broke for him, but she couldn't take time to get him out and make it back for the rest. And she'd be damned if she left even one of them. Flames leaped in the hallway. Flames they'd have to run through in order to get the babies out. She squared her shoulders, pulled her shirt up over her mouth and shouted above the roar of the encroaching fire. "I've wet the blankets. Toss them over the babies." Sylvia lifted the wet blankets she'd used to seal the cracks around the door frame and threw them over the crying babies. Tate scrambled to get the rest thrown over the kids.

Each adult grabbed the sides of the playpen and they half lifted, half carried the pen through the double-wide doorway and out into the hallway.

Flames climbed the walls, eating at the wallpaper, making it curl up. Smoke as black as night choked the air.

"Get down!" Tate yelled and coughed, dropping to his knees.

Sylvia dropped low, but she couldn't get enough leverage on her knees. Eight babies and the playpen were heavy and tough going in the smoky hallway.

Her lungs burned, every inch a challenge, but she had to make it, had to get the babies out of this nightmare.

With renewed effort, she got behind the playpen, braced her feet on the base and shoved as hard as she could. With Tate pulling at the front and her pushing from behind, they made it to the end of the hallway.

Two men and a woman materialized through the smoke.

Tate yelled to them, "Grab the playpen and get it out of here."

The four of them lifted the playpen and ran out of the building.

With the babies safely out of the building, Sylvia was exhausted. She leaned against the wall, her feet splayed out in front of her. Unable to lift a finger, the effort of pushing the playpen and inhaling all that smoke had sapped every last ounce of energy. She was cooked.

She closed her eyes and lay on the tile, the heat of the fire behind her growing more intense. But she couldn't move. None of her muscles cooperated. Jacob was okay. That was all that mattered.

Blackness surrounded her, filling her lungs, dragging her away into a dark abyss. Then she was floating through the smoke, the heat dissipating, the wall she'd leaned against not quite as hard, but steely strong.

Breathing became easier and she inhaled a lungful of clean fresh air, which sent her into a coughing fit she thought would never end.

Someone pressed a mask over her face. "Breathe, Sylvia, breathe."

She stopped struggling, inhaled deeply and opened her eyes.

Tate stood over her, the sunlight bright and hopeful behind him. He held an oxygen mask over her face. She pushed it aside. "Jake?"

"He's okay." Melissa Bradley appeared beside Tate with Jake in her arms. "He wants his daddy." She handed him to Tate.

Sirens blared as fire engines and emergency vehicles rolled into the compound. Emergency personnel dropped out of them, running toward the people lying on the grass.

"Did everyone get out?" Sylvia asked, amazed at how hoarse she sounded.

"You were the last one." Tate sat on the grass beside her, Jake in his arms. "Everyone's out, and all the children are accounted for."

Jake leaned over, determined to sit in the grass with the adults.

Tate set him down and the little boy immediately began plucking at blades of grass, giggling. His face dirty with soot, his nose running and generally a mess, he was the most beautiful creature on earth to Sylvia. Her heart filled so full she thought it might burst.

Sylvia smiled, her gaze still on her son. "Thank you for saving us." She tried to push into a sitting position, but Tate held her back.

"Stay here until the medics have a chance to check you out."

"But I'm fine except for a little smoke inhalation."

"A little?" Tate cupped her chin, his brown-black eyes bloodshot from all the smoke. "Please."

"Okay." She lay against the grass, staring up at Tate. "Did you find out who set the fire?"

"El Corredor and some of his pals." Tate nodded toward the fence where a vehicle lay on its side. Another stood in the middle of the compound, windows shattered. The local sheriff's department and what looked like FBI agents removed bodies from inside both of them, laying them out on the ground. "They won't be trafficking babies anymore."

Sylvia closed her eyes. "You've been busy."

"You scared a few years off my life." He lifted her hand and pressed it to his cheek. "When I saw the fire…"

"*I* scared *you?*" She laughed, another fit of coughing racked her lungs. "Well, we all made it through and the babies are safe. What now?"

Jake used Tate's sleeve and pulled himself into a standing position, giggling and slapping at Tate's arm. "Da, da, da."

Tate smiled down at him. "That's right, buddy. You don't look the worse for your experience. Ready to go home, little man?" As if he just remembered, Tate's gaze shot to Sylvia. "That's if you two would stay with me until we can figure this whole thing out."

"Do you still believe I'm not Jacob's mother?"

Tate lips twisted. "Any woman who'd go through what you did would have to be the baby's mother." Tate lifted Jake in his arms and stared into the baby's blue eyes. "Besides, he looks like you."

"I can't take your charity."

"Then let me hire you."

"For what?"

"As my executive assistant."

"But you already have one."

Tate's mouth pressed into a straight line. "Not anymore." He explained Kacee and Danny's role in Jake's abduction.

"I almost feel sorry for her. To love the man you work for and him not return the feeling…" Sylvia looked away. "I don't know about this position."

"Do you have a job?"

"No."

"I'm offering you work. I pay well, and one of the perks is a place to live for both you and Jake."

Jake climbed into Tate's lap and lay down, working at the button on the man's shirt as his eyes drifted shut.

Her son loved this man he'd grown to know as his father. How could she take him away?

"Mind if I take Jake for a minute?" Melissa reappeared and took Jake from Tate's lap. "The EMTs want to give him a once-over."

The silence she left behind was as thick as the smoke inside the building.

Sylvia valued her independence and wanted to make

her life work on her own. Relying on a man had only gotten her into trouble.

If she went to work for Tate, would she be falling into the same trap? "I can't work for you. I'd feel like a charity case. Besides, I want to pursue my freelance writing. It's what I do best."

"Then let me help until you get on your feet."

Sylvia chewed her lip. She needed to build up her portfolio and contacts again. She'd be starting from nothing. No photos, no database of articles she'd written, not even a home to bring Jacob to. What kind of life could she provide for her son?

Then again, to work with Tate and not be anything more than an employee? After what they'd been through, all that they'd shared in the past two days... to be so close and not touch him would just about kill her. "I've never been an executive assistant," she said, afraid to voice all of her other reservations when all she'd done since she'd met Tate was keep him at emotional arm's length.

Until the smoke and fire threatened to kill her, she hadn't realized that she wanted more than a no-commitment relationship. She wanted more from Tate Vincent than a romp in the sack, although that had been good. Real good.

She could actually picture herself with him for the long haul. The grow-old and rock-on-the-porch togetherness she'd never felt with her first husband. "I need to think about this."

"Come live with me until you get on your feet." He took her hand and pulled her into his arms. "Do it for Jake. Do it for me. I want to get to know you, Sylvia Michaels."

She smiled, her lips trembling. "Only because of Jacob."

He frowned. "No, not just because of Jake."

"But you're Tate Vincent, multimillionaire and most eligible bachelor in the state of Texas. What do I have to offer in a relationship?"

"Don't you see?" He kissed her forehead. "When it comes down to it, I'm only a man." A work-roughened hand smoothed the hair out of her face and tucked it behind her ear. "And you're one of the bravest women I know."

"How will I know you want me around for me and not just to keep Jacob?" she whispered.

"Do you have any idea how beautiful you are?" He kissed the tip of her nose.

Sylvia laughed, raising a hand to her sooty hair. "I'm a mess."

"The most beautiful mess I've ever seen." His mouth descended and claimed hers, his tongue pushing past her lips to find hers, stroking her, thrusting deep.

Sylvia had never experienced a kiss so tender and yet so filled with passion. She could die in his arms right there and know that he was the best thing to ever happen to her.

When he ended the kiss, he leaned his forehead against hers. "Sylvia, I'm not perfect. I've been in one bad marriage, but I haven't given up on it altogether."

"I thought I had," she said and pressed a finger to his lips, tracing the sensuous line. "But you make me feel… hopeful."

"I want the time to get to know you. I want to date you and woo you like a man should with the woman he's falling in love with."

Her heart fluttered. She forgot to breathe. Tate had mentioned the *L* word. Warmth spread through her body in a rush. She tried to tell herself to be calm, review the facts. Make an informed decision from the mind, not the heart.

If she left with Jacob now, she'd never see Tate again. Never know the feel of his arms holding her. Never know if they had a chance to make a life together work. Her rational thoughts told her to grab for happiness. Her heart echoed the sentiment with a thundering pulse.

"Sylvia, will you give me a chance to get to know you? Do you think you can live with me?"

Sylvia's lips trembled as she reached up to cup his chin. "I do." As soon as the two words popped out of her mouth, she gasped, her face burning. "I mean, I accept your proposal…er, offer." She took a deep breath to gather her jumbled thoughts. "But only until I can afford to support myself. And I promise to pay you back for everything."

"Whatever you want."

"I want to come into a relationship with you as an equal." She laughed. "Well, maybe not in millions of dollars, but knowing that I come into the relationship because I want to, not because I have no other choice." She touched the side of his face. "Don't you see?"

"Actually," he said, touching his lips to hers, "I do see. And it makes me want you even more. I think I'm in love and I want the chance to prove it to you."

"And I want the chance to show you that I can love you with or without your riches."

He kissed her, holding her close.

Finally she pushed him away from her. "As far as

a date? How does a Friday-night movie sound? I'll let you choose."

Tate's eyes lit up and his face split into a grin as big as the state of Texas. He hugged her to him and laughed out loud. "Sounds about as close to heaven as we can get."

* * * * *

HOSTAGE TO
THUNDER HORSE

This book is dedicated to my new grandson,
whose arrival into this world was the
best incentive to get this book written.
Happy birthday, Cade!

Chapter One

He'd gained ground in the last hour, bearing down on her, the relentless adversary wearing at her reserves of energy. The cold seeped through her thick gloves and boots, down to her bones.

Alexi Katya Ivanov revved the snowmobile's engine, thankful that the stolen machine had a full tank of fuel. Regret burned a hole in her gut. Somehow she'd find the owners and repay them for the use of their snowmobile. She'd never in her life stolen anything. In this case, necessity had forced her hand. Steal or die.

She'd ditched her car several hours after crossing the border into North Dakota, and she was tired of wincing every time a law enforcement vehicle passed by. But she didn't know where to go. She'd only lived in Minneapolis since she'd been in the States. Instinct told her to get as far away from the scene of the crime as she could get.

Throughout the night, she'd pushed farther and faster, praying that she wouldn't be pulled over for speeding. Not until Fargo did she realize that the headlights following her hadn't wavered since she'd left Minneapolis. Butterflies wreaked havoc in her belly—whether they were paranoia or intuition, she didn't care. Her gut told her that whoever had framed her as a terrorist had also set a tracking device on the body of her car. How else had he found her and kept up with her through the maze of streets in the big cities?

She'd stopped once and taken precious time to search the exterior, but the snow-covered ground kept her from a thorough investigation of the undercarriage. Thus her need to ditch the car and find alternate means of transportation. Out in the middle of Nowhere, North Dakota, rental cars were scarce, if not impossible to find, not to mention they required a credit card to secure. She hadn't used a credit card since... Katya twisted the handle, gunning the engine. She refused to shed another tear. The bite of the icy wind was not nearly as painful as the ache in her heart. Her beloved father was dead. An accident, according to the news, but she'd gotten the truth from one of his trusted advisors back in Trejikistan. He'd been gunned down by an assassin while driving to their estate in the country.

Immediately after hearing the news of her father's death, Katya had been attacked in front of her apartment building. If not for the security guard she'd befriended, Katya would be dead. The same guard had hidden her from the attacker and let her know that the police had been to her apartment, claiming she'd been identified as a suspected terrorist. They'd found weapons and bomb-making materials there. Things that hadn't been there when she'd left to go to church earlier that day, hoping to find some solace over her father's death. The guard hadn't believed her capable of terrorism. Thank God.

On the run since then, she'd avoided crowded places, sure that someone would recognize her from the pictures plastered all over the local and statewide television.

She'd taken her car, switched the license plate with that of some unsuspecting person and driven out of Minneapolis as fast as she could.

Something slammed into the snowmobile, shaking her back into the present. A glance behind her confirmed her worst suspicions. The man following her had a gun aimed at her. For as far as the eye could see, there was nothing but gently rolling, wide-open terrain without trees, rocks or buildings to hide behind. The best she could hope for was to stay far enough ahead of the gunman to duck behind another hill. As her snowmobile topped a rise, another shot tore into the back of the vehicle.

Ducking low, she gunned the engine and flew over the top of the hill.

The ground fell away from beneath her as the snowmobile plunged down a steep incline.

Katya held on, rocks and gravel yanking the skids back and forth during the descent into a rugged river-carved canyon. With each jarring bump, her teeth rattled in her head. Her hands cramped with the effort to steer the machine to the bottom. No snow graced the barren rocks, giving the snowmobile's skids little to grab on to. The rubber tracks flung gravel and rocks out behind her.

Katya couldn't worry about bullets from the man following her. It was all she could do to live through the ride.

With a bone-wrenching thump, Katya reached the riverbank. She couldn't believe she'd made it. She wanted nothing more than to throw herself on the ground and hug the earth.

Bullets pinged off the rocks beside her, forcing her

back into survival mode. She raced the snowmobile along the riverbank, aiming for the bluff that would block the bullets. The machine ran rough, the tracks slipping on the icy surface, getting less traction than needed.

With the shooter perched on the hillside, Katya was a prime target to be picked off. If only she could make it to the bend, her attacker would have to stop shooting long enough to follow.

Hunched low in her seat, she urged the hard-used machine across the snow and gravel. A hundred yards from the bend in the river and the reassuring solid rock of the canyon wall, it chugged to a halt.

Katya hit the start switch. Nothing happened. Bullets spit snow and gravel up around her. Katya flung herself from the seat to the rocky ground, crouching below the snowmobile. A bullet pierced the cushioned seat, blowing straight through and nicking the glove on her hand.

At the shooter's angle, the snowmobile didn't give Katya much protection. If she wanted to stay alive long enough to see another day, she'd have to make a dash for the canyon wall, where she hoped to find a place to hide among the boulders.

As if on cue, the snow thickened and the wind blasted it across the sky. She couldn't see the top of the canyon wall. And if she couldn't see all the way to the top, whoever was up there wouldn't be able to see her. Sucking in a deep breath, Katya took off, running upstream toward the bluffs.

The wind blew against her, making her progress slow, despite her all-out effort to reach cover. But once she was around the bend, the force of the wind slackened. Katya hid among the rocks, bending double to catch her breath.

Her ride down the canyon wall had been nothing short of miraculous. Would the shooter make a similar attempt? Katya doubted anyone in his right mind would. Which meant he'd have to dismount and leave his machine at the top in order to come down and find her.

Without the snowmobile, she didn't know how she'd find her way back to civilization, but she could only solve one major problem at a time. Her temporary respite from being a target was only that. Temporary. In order to stay alive, she had to keep moving.

As she wove her way through the boulders and rocks, the wind picked up, the snow lashing against her cheeks, bitter cold penetrating the layers of GORE-TEX and thermal underwear beneath. Her feet grew numb and her hands stiff. At this rate, a bullet was the least of her worries.

The cold would kill her first.

MADDOX THUNDER HORSE topped the rise and stared down into Mustang Canyon to the narrow ribbon of icy-cold river running through the rugged terrain. He'd tracked Little Joe's band of mares to the valley below, worried about Sweet Jessie's newborn foal. Full-grown wild horses normally survived the harsh North Dakota winters without problems. But a newborn might not be so lucky. Temperatures had plunged fast, dropping from the low forties to the teens in the past three hours. With night creeping in and the snow piling up, Maddox couldn't look for much longer or he might be caught in the first blizzard of the season.

The handheld radio clipped just inside his jacket gave a static burst. "Maddox?"

Maddox fumbled to unzip the jacket just enough to grab the radio and press the Talk button. "Whatcha got, Tuck?"

"I got nothing here in South Canyon. How about you?"

"Nothing."

"It's past time we headed back. The weatherman missed the mark on this one. *Wankatanka* grows angrier by the minute." Tuck attributed every change in weather to the Great Spirit.

The Bismarck weather report had called for snow flurries, not a full-blown blizzard. But Maddox had tasted the pending storm in the air. He understood this land and the weather like his ancestors, the equally rugged Lakota tribe who'd forged a life on the Plains long before the white man came. He'd felt the heaviness in the air, the weight of the clouds hanging over the canyons. Maddox knew if they were to find the horses, they'd have to hurry.

"See ya back at the ranch." Maddox clipped his radio to the inside of his jacket and zipped it back in place. Gathering his reins, he half turned his horse when movement near the river below caught his attention. With the snow falling steadily and the wind picking up, he had almost missed it. Maddox dug out his binoculars and pressed them against his eyes, focusing on the narrow valley below. Were Little Joe and his band of mares hunkering down in the canyon until the storm blew over?

Bear, the stallion he'd rescued five winters before, shifted beneath him from hoof to hoof, his nostrils flar-

ing as if sensing the storm's building fury. Bear didn't
like getting caught in snowstorms any more than Maddox did. The horse had almost frozen to death that winter Maddox and his fiancée, Susan, had been trapped in
a raging blizzard. Bear had made it back alive. Susan
hadn't.

Maddox peered through the blowing snowflakes to
the bend in the river. His gaze followed the line of the
waterway as it snaked through the canyon.

As a member of the Thunder Horse family, Maddox had grown up living, breathing and protecting the
land he and his ancestors were privileged enough to
own. Over six thousand acres of canyon and grassland
comprised the Thunder Horse Ranch where the Thunder Horse brothers raised cattle, buffalo and horses.
They farmed what little tillable soil there was to provide
hay and feed for the animals through the six months of
wicked North Dakota winter. For the most part, the rest
of the land remained as it was when his people roamed
as nomads, following the great buffalo herds.

Maddox loved the solitude and isolation of the Badlands. He'd only been away during his college days and
a four-year tour of duty in the military. The entire time
away from Thunder Horse Ranch he longed to be home
again. The Plains called to him like a siren to a sailor,
or more like a wolf to his own territory.

Now it would take an extreme change in circumstance to budge him from the place he loved, no matter
what sad memories plagued him in the harsh landscape.
Time healed wounds, but time never diminished his
love for this land.

As his gaze skimmed the banks of the river, he
passed over a flash of apple red. Orange-red and blood

red he'd expect, like the colors of Painted Rock Canyon, but not bright, apple red. He eased the binoculars to the right, backing over the spot. Squinting through the lenses, he tried adjusting the view to zoom in. A white bump near the river's edge caught the blowing snow, creating a natural barrier that quickly collected more of the flakes. On the end of the drift, a red triangle stood out, but not for long. The snow thickened, dusting the red, burying it in a blanket of white.

Poised on the edge of a plateau, Maddox weighed his options. He hadn't found the mares and he still had an hour's ride back to the ranch house. If he dropped off the edge of the plateau to investigate the snowdrift and the red item buried in white powder beside it, he could add another hour to his journey home. In so doing, he risked getting stuck out in the weather and possibly freezing to death.

Instinct pulled at him, drawing him closer to the edge of the canyon, urging him to investigate. He rarely ignored his instinct, following his gut no matter how foolhardy it seemed. His army buddies called it uncanny, but it had saved his life on more than one occasion in Afghanistan.

No matter how cold and dangerous the weather got, if he didn't go down and investigate, curiosity and worry would eat away at him. He might not get the opportunity to return to investigate for days, maybe months, depending on the depth of the snow and how long the ground remained frozen.

With gloved fingers, Maddox tugged the zipper on his parka up higher, arranging the fur-lined collar around his face to block out the stinging snow now blowing in sideways.

He nudged Bear toward the edge of the plateau.

As they neared the dropoff, Bear danced backward, rearing and turning.

Maddox smoothed a hand along Bear's neck, speaking to him in a soothing tone, soft and steady over the roar of the prairie wind. "Easy, *Mato cikala*." Little Bear.

Bear reared up and whinnied, his frightened call whipped away in the increasing wind. Then he dropped to all four hooves and let Maddox guide him down the steep slope into the valley below. With the wind and snow limiting his vision, Maddox eased the horse past boulders and rocky outcroppings devoid of vegetation until the ground leveled out on the narrow valley floor. He urged the horse into a canter, eager to check out the mysterious red object and get the heck back to the ranch and the warm fire sure to be blazing in the stone fireplace.

His gaze fixed on the lump on the ground, Maddox pulled Bear to a halt and slipped out of the saddle. His boots landed a foot deep in fresh powder, stirring the white stuff up into the air to swirl around his eyes.

As he neared the snowdrift, the red object took shape. It was the corner of a scarf.

His heart skipped a couple beats and then slammed into action, pumping blood and adrenaline through his veins, warming his body like nothing else could.

He bent to brush away the snow from the lump on the ground, his fingers coming into contact with denim and a parka. His hands worked faster, a wash of unbidden panic threatening his ability to breathe. The more snow he brushed away, the more he realized that what had created the snowdrift was, in fact, a woman, wrapped in a fur-lined parka, denim jeans and snow boots. Her face, protected somewhat from the wind, had a light dusting of snowflakes across deathly pale cheeks, sooty brows and lashes.

Maddox grabbed his glove between his teeth and pulled it off, digging beneath the parka's collar to find the woman's neck. He prayed to the Great Spirit for a pulse.

An image of Susan lying in his arms, hunkered beneath a flimsy tarp, while gale-force winds pounded the life out of the Badlands, flashed through his mind. This woman couldn't be dead. He wouldn't let her die. Not again. Not like Susan.

With wind lashing at his back and the snow growing so thick he could barely see, he didn't feel a pulse. He moved his fingers along her neck and bent his cheek to her nose. At last, a faint pulse brushed against his fingertips and a shallow breath warmed his cheek.

Relief overwhelmed him, bringing moisture to his stinging eyes. He blinked several times as he tightened the parka's hood around the woman's face and lifted her into his arms.

Too late to make it back to the ranch, he had to find a place to hole up until the storm passed. Being out in the open during a blizzard was a recipe for certain death. As he carried the woman toward his horse, he made a mental list of what he'd packed in his saddlebag.

This far into the winter season, he'd come prepared for the worst. Sleeping bag, tarp, two days of rations and a canteen. Trying to get the woman back to the ranch wasn't an option. Just getting out of the canyon would take well over an hour. Two people on one horse climbing the steep slopes was risky enough in clear weather.

He couldn't expose the unconscious woman to the freezing wind. He had to get her warmed up soon or she'd die of exposure.

Maddox remembered playing along this riverbank one summer with his father and brothers. They swam in the icy water and explored the rock formations along the banks. If his memory served him well, there was a cave along the east bank in the river bend. He remembered because of the drawings of buffalo painted along the walls. He carried the woman along the river's edge, clucking his tongue for Bear to follow.

The stallion didn't look too pleased, tossing his head toward home as if to say he was ready to go back now.

The wind pushed Maddox from behind and for the most part he shielded the woman with his body. He crossed the river at a shallow spot, careful to step on the rocks and not into the frigid water. He couldn't get wet, couldn't afford to succumb to the cold.

The blizzard increased in intensity until he was trudging through a foot and a half of snow in near-whiteout conditions. Maddox stuck close to the rocky bluffs rising upward to the east, afraid if he stepped too far from the painted cliffs, he'd lose his way. Bear occasionally nudged him from behind, the stallion reassuring him that he was still there.

After several minutes stumbling around in the snow, Maddox thought he'd gone too far and might have missed the narrow slit in the wall of the bluff. A lull in the wind settled the snow around him, revealing a dark slash in the otherwise solid rock wall.

The entry gaped just wide enough for him to carry the woman through. Once the ceiling opened up and he could hear his breathing echo off the cavern walls, he inched forward into the darkness until he found the far wall. There he scuffed his boot across the floor to clear any rocks or debris before he laid her down in the cavern.

With little time to spare, he hurried back out into the storm to lead Bear out of the growing fury of the blizzard. As darkness surrounded them, Bear tugged against the reins, at first unwilling to enter the tight confines, his big body bumping against the crevice walls. When the cave opened up inside, the horse stopped struggling.

Running his hand along the horse's neck and saddle, Maddox focused his attention on survival—both his and the stranger's. If the woman had a chance of living, she had to be warmed up quickly. Although protected from the blizzard's fury, the cold would still kill them if he didn't do something fast. Once he came to the lump behind the saddle, he stripped off his gloves, blowing warm air onto his numb fingers.

Leaving the saddle on the horse for warmth, Maddox worked the leather straps holding the sleeping bag in place. Once free, he laid it at his feet on the cave floor. Next, he loosened the saddlebag straps and pulled it over the horse's back. Inside the left pouch, he kept a flashlight. His chilled fingers shook as he fumbled to switch it on.

Light filled the small cavern. The walls crowded in on him more so than he remembered from when he was a child. About half the size of the Medora amphitheater, the cave would serve its purpose—to shield them from the biting wind and bitter cold of the storm.

Without wood to build a roaring fire, they would

have to rely on the sleeping bag and each other's body warmth—hers being questionable at the moment.

Maddox set the flashlight on a rock outcropping, untied the strings around the sleeping bag and unzipped the zipper. He placed the open sleeping bag next to the woman. He had to get her out of the bulky winter clothing and boots and inside the sleeping bag.

Time wasn't on his side. He didn't know how long the woman had been unconscious or whether she had frostbite. Maddox stripped his coat off and the heavy sweatshirt beneath, wadding it up to form a pillow. Then he tugged his jeans off and the long underwear until he stood naked, regretting his lack of boxer shorts. The frigid air bit his skin, raising gooseflesh everywhere.

He went to work undressing the stranger, removing layer after layer. When he tugged off her jeans, she moaned.

That was a good sign. She wasn't completely comatose. Hope burned in his chest as he swiftly finished the job of undressing her down to her bra, panties and the pendant she wore around her throat. Nowhere in her pockets could he find any form of identification. He shoved all their clothing to the bottom of the bag, then laid the woman on the quilted flannel interior.

Tucked inside the sleeping bag, she didn't shake the way most cold people did. Her body had given up trying to keep her warm. The lethargy of sleep had numbed her mind to the acceptance of a peaceful death.

Maddox's body fought to live, his teeth chattering in the cool of the cave's interior. He refused to let the sleep of death claim her, as it had Susan.

Before he lost all his body warmth, he slid into the sleeping bag beside the woman and zipped the edges together. Although the bag was made for one large person, he was able to close both of them inside with a little room to spare. He wrapped his arms around her body, rubbing his hands up and down her cold arms and tucking her feet between his calves to warm them.

Cold. She was so cold.

Susan's face swam before him, her lips blue, her tawny blond hair buffeted by the wind, the only movement on her lifeless form. For a moment his world stood still as he stared down into the quiet countenance, the blank stare of his dead fiancée intruding into his thoughts.

But that was years ago. This woman wasn't Susan. For the first time since he'd found her, he studied the woman, blocking out the sad memories. In the shadowy glow of the flashlight, he leaned back enough to stare at the woman so near death he was afraid he might already be too late.

Dark hair, as black as his own, splayed across his gray sweatshirt pillow in large loose waves. Sooty, narrow brows winged outward in sharp contrast to her pale, almost translucent skin. Her hair dipped to a shallow peak at the center of her forehead and her lashes lay like fans across her cheeks. A pointed chin, perky nose and delicate ears completed her perfection.

As close as he was, Maddox caught a whiff of a subtle yet exotic perfume. His breath caught in his throat. This stranger didn't have Susan's girl-next-door fresh looks, yet her ethereal beauty was so profound it sucked the wind right out of his lungs, his groin tightening in automatic response to her skin against his. He hadn't been drawn to any woman since Susan's death.

He hadn't let himself be, his burden of guilt weighing heavily.

The woman in the sleeping bag with him was a stranger. A beautiful, exotic stranger with skin the color of a porcelain doll and hair softer and silkier than anything he'd ever run his hands through.

He forced himself to focus on anything other than her physical attributes, shifting to all the unknowns, the mystery and reasons he shouldn't trust her. He didn't know her, she hadn't carried a driver's license or passport. He didn't know her background.

Who the hell was she? Would she live to tell him?

Chapter Two

Kat snuggled closer to the warmth in front of her, nestling her face into the hard yet smooth surface. Her nose twitched and she slid her hand between her and the warmth-providing pillow, to brush her hair out of her face.

She couldn't move far with what felt like a tree branch draped across her back, holding her close and adding to the warmth. What was keeping her from moving? She opened her eyes to discover the source of her imprisonment.

Darkness so intense she couldn't see a scrap of light made her close her eyes and open them again. Was she dead? Panic shot through her like a lightning bolt. Had she gone blind? She shoved against the hard surface beneath her hands. The band around her waist shifted, tightening.

She pushed up on her hands, straining against the band. "Help." Her voice echoed as if in one of the large cathedrals of her homeland. "Where am I?" She fought to contain her terror. She had managed to stay alive based on sheer tenacity and by relying on her intelligence for the past two days. She couldn't give up now. But why was it so incredibly dark? Where was she?

"Shh." A deep baritone rumbled in the darkness, the surface beneath her hands vibrating. Then she was rolled to her side. She recognized the band around her middle now as an arm as thick as a small tree trunk.

Her heart slammed against her ribs. Had he caught up with her? Was she his prisoner? "Who are you? Where am I? Am I blind?" Her hip brushed against what could only be a man's... "Oh my god, you're not wearing any clothes!" She pounded against his chest, her feet banging against his shins.

"Slow down." The voice rumbled again, bouncing off the walls of the room they were in. "I'm not going to rape you, woman. Let me turn on the light."

With his one arm still holding her around her middle, he reached above his head. Cold air slipped across her skin, sending wave after wave of chills over Katya. She shook so hard her teeth rattled against each other.

Metal clinked against stone, then a click, and light bounced off what looked like rock walls.

Relief filled her as her eyes adjusted to the muted lighting. She wasn't blind. Light beamed across the room, dispelling the terrifying darkness. Then as quickly as the relief filled her it fled. She couldn't move, trapped against the man's chest and cocooned in a bag. Panic threatened to overwhelm her, but she fought it, taking deep, steadying breaths.

The man's other arm slipped back into the interior of the bag, pulling the gap closed, blocking the chilled air from leaking inside.

Despite her terror at being held captive, she didn't want to die of exposure. Until she learned more about the man she lay next to, she'd do well to appreciate the warmth and gather her strength if she had to fight for her life.

"How do you feel?" the man asked.

"Cold. Incredibly cold. And frankly, a little scared."

"You should be scared, but not of me. You almost died of exposure. You'll probably feel cold for a long time."

Her teeth chattered as she tried to form questions. "What happened? Why are we in this bag together?"

"I found you under a snowdrift by the river and brought you here to warm you. I only had one bag, so you had to share with me."

Her face burned. She stared around at the rock walls surrounding her. "Where are we?"

"In a cave."

"In what country?"

The man frowned. "The U.S., of course."

No *of course* about it. She'd been racing across the country for two days, never on a straight route, always varying her direction, hoping to shake the man following her. If the man currently holding her captive was one of the people after her, they could be practically anywhere. She took a deep breath before asking her next questions. "Who are *you?* Who do you work for?"

"Uh-uh." He shook his head. "You've been asking all the questions. It's my turn. Who are you?" His deep, resonant voice filled the inside of the cave with its ruggedness.

Katya hesitated. His avoidance of her question didn't set her mind at ease. She didn't know who she was dealing with and trusted no one with her identity. Especially after what had happened in Minneapolis. She'd been on the road ever since, until she'd been forced to ditch her car and steal a snowmobile. "Am I still in the Badlands?"

"Yes, ma'am. The Badlands of North Dakota, to be exact."

"My name is Kat," she said tentatively. At least she wasn't lying. Kat was only part of her name, but people she'd gone to school with in Minneapolis had used it as her nickname. "Kat Evans." Evans was an out-and-out lie. Hard lessons had taught her not to give out truth until she knew where she stood. Especially with the colossal accusation of terrorism hanging over her. Homeland Security, Customs and Border Protection, the FBI and every law enforcement agency would be on the lookout for her.

She squirmed against his body, extremely aware of her bare skin rubbing against his bare skin. He was completely naked and she was practically naked herself, except for her bra and panties. "Oh, my!" She tried to scoot away from him, hampered by the close confines of the bag they both occupied. A waft of icy air scraped across her body and she found herself pressing against his skin to re-create the warmth she'd felt a moment before.

"Sorry. You weren't awake for me to ask permission. In these temps, skin to skin is best to bring up body temperature the fastest. Yours was bordering on death."

After straining for a minute to keep from leaning into his chest, she gave up and let her cheek rest against the hard muscles of his smooth chest. "Well, then, I guess I should thank you for saving my life."

He chuckled. "Please, don't strain yourself with your gratitude."

With nowhere else to put her hands, she rested them

against his chest, her fingers smoothing over the hard planes, liking his laughter and the contours of his muscles way too much. "Point made. I am grateful you did not leave me out there to die." She settled into the warmth of his arms, awkward about their nakedness, but too cold to climb out of the bag.

"You're welcome." He rested his chin on the top of her hair, a position both comforting and intimate. "Nothing like waking up in the dark with a stranger, huh?"

"Precisely."

"What were you doing out by the river on foot?"

She swallowed, hating that she had to lie to the man who'd saved her from freezing to death, but she had no other choice. "I was out snowmobiling and my snowmobile broke down."

The man stiffened. "What about the others in your party? Most tours stick together."

"I got separated. I drove around for a couple hours... trying to find them. That is when my machine quit on me." Her words came out in a rush as the lie grew bigger. What if he didn't believe her? What if he was the man who'd been after her and he was just fishing for more information? She couldn't let on that she was Katya Ivanov, just in case he really didn't know. Surely the entire United States had been alerted to a possible terrorist at large.

"I didn't see a snowmobile." His voice had hardened, as though he didn't really believe or trust her.

"I followed the river to see if I could find help. I suppose the snowmobile is a mile or so downstream from where you found me." She had hoped to hide it among the boulders, but had to abandon the heavy machine where it had come to a grinding and permanent halt, in order to save herself from a shooter's aim.

"The closest town to us is Medora and I don't recall anyone there offering snowmobile tours."

"It was a special tour out of…" she grasped for the name of a larger town in North Dakota. "Bismarck!" she said in a rush. How much bigger could the lie grow? And would she be able to remember all the details?

"Still, most tours wouldn't leave a rider behind."

"I am sure the weather cut them short on searching for me. I will bet they notified the authorities as soon as they got back. Assuming they did not get stranded too." Kat couldn't look into his eyes. Lying didn't come naturally to her, one reason she could never be a good politician. The question was: did this man believe any of the lies she had just dished out?

"So really, who are you?" he asked, answering her question. "Kat Evans isn't right. You speak English too proper to have been born in America, and I detect an accent."

She stiffened against him. Like it or not, she couldn't tell him the truth. Not until she unraveled the mess her life had become. "I am from…Russia. And as long as we're stuck in this bag, can we leave it at Kat Evans?"

"Why? Are you wanted for murder or peddling drugs to children?"

"No. Nothing like that. I would just rather not talk about it."

"Running from an abusive husband? In which case, I'd offer a separate sleeping bag, but I don't have one."

"No. No husband." She stared across the cave's interior, wishing he would stop asking. "Is that a horse over there?"

"Consider him our chaperone. Bear is very good at keeping secrets. The stories he could tell, but won't, would shock you."

Katya laughed, although a little breathlessly. "I feel much safer, knowing he is here guarding my virtue." And he gave her a good diversion from the stranger's questions and naked body.

"Damn right." The man nodded toward Bear. "Don't tell her about the mare you stole from that stallion, boy. She wouldn't understand."

"I get it. You are trying to make me relax."

"You're brilliant as well as beautiful." His hand brushed against her hip. "Is it working?"

Katya's breath caught in her throat. The way his work-roughened fingers slid across her tender skin, aroused new sensations, making her body more alert, more sensitized to his nearness. "Somewhat," she lied, again. "I have never lain naked with a stranger before."

"That makes two of us. I usually get to know the women I sleep with *before* we climb into a sleeping bag together." His voice lost all hint of humor. "Short of freezing to death in a blizzard, we didn't have much choice."

A shiver wracked her body and she pressed closer to him, absorbing his warmth, her skin tingling everywhere it touched his. "Good choice." She inhaled the earthy scent of leather and male, noting the smoothness of his chest—not a hair on it. His nearness sparked a charge of electric current in her that made her want to explore more of his incredibly sexy body.

When was the last time she'd felt this drawn to a man? Never. The closest she had come was when she had been in lust with a politician's son back when she was nineteen. A time when all was right with her world and her country.

With her future a black hole of uncertainty and danger, how could she be this attracted to a stranger?

In the rock-solid confines of the cave, with the warm glow of a flashlight chasing away the severe darkness, Katya felt safe for the first time since she'd been on the run. Safe enough to think of something or someone other than simple survival.

With her body heating rapidly, Katya fought for something to break the tension and silence. "Is the weather still bad outside?"

"Listen…" He held his breath and cocked his head to one side. "*Wankatanka,* the Great Spirit, is angry."

Katya listened, concentrating on the silence. At first she heard nothing, then a thin, lonely wail whistled through the cavern, carried on a blast of frigid air that had found its way into their cocoon. Katya tugged at the edges of the bag, pulling it tighter around her shoulders, her face pressing close to the man's chest. "I suppose it's still bad out there." She snuggled closer, the lonely sound of the wind emphasizing the chill still present in her body. His warmth enveloped her and made her feel safe and nervous at the same time. "You still haven't told me your name."

"Maddox." His hand spread across her hip, his arm tightening, drawing her closer to his heat. "Maddox Thunder Horse. You're trespassing on the Thunder Horse Ranch."

"Maddox." She tipped her head up to stare into eyes as black as the cave when it had been the darkest. "Pleasure to meet you. Please accept my sincere apologies for the trespass." Her lips curled upward on the corners. "Thunder Horse is a different kind of last name."

"I'm a member of the Lakota Nation. My father's people were known for their strong horses."

"You are a Native American? Is the ranch on a reservation?"

"No. My father's father purchased the ranch from a retiring rancher fifty years ago. Since then, the Thunder Horses have added to the acreage."

As he spoke, his hand smoothed back and forth over her hip, climbing up to her waist and back to her hip, cupping her bottom.

The more he touched her, the hotter she got, her breath coming in short gasps as if she could not quite catch it. With nothing but her bra and panties between her and the large man holding her in his arms, all manner of wicked thoughts filled Katya's head. Her father would be appalled. "Do you have to do that?"

"What?"

"What you are doing with your hand?"

He jerked his hand away. "I was warming the cold skin. But if you're warm already, I can stop."

Immediately, Katya regretted saying anything. The heat his hand generated warmed her in many more ways than she could have imagined. "No. It felt nice. And I am very cold." And alone.

She could hear the echoes of her father preaching to her. Someone of her breeding should never find herself alone and naked with a man not her husband.

Sadness gripped her anew. The father who had driven her crazy with his archaic ideas of decorum could no longer dictate her life. Nor could he hold her in his arms and tell her everything would be all right.

Boris Ivanov had been murdered two weeks ago, his limousine ambushed by a lone shooter taking him out in a single shot. The news reported his death as an automobile crash. Katya's inside sources told her otherwise.

A tear slid from the corner of her eye and dropped to the smooth skin of Maddox's chest.

He looked down at her, a frown drawing black brows together. His arm settled around her, his hand resting on her hip, his feet touching hers in the bottom of the bag. "What's wrong? Are you in any pain?"

He rubbed his foot along her calf, the warmth helping dispel the chill of her father's death. She shook her head. "No."

"I checked you over for frostbite. You looked okay a few hours ago."

She sniffed, disturbed in a very visceral, but not unpleasant way at the thought of Maddox inspecting her body while she lay semi-comatose. As his foot stroked her calf, she stilled her father's voice in her head, urging her to draw away. She liked the feel of his feet on her legs and especially his hand on her hip. A little too much for having just met the man. "I'm fine. Really."

"Then why the tears?"

"No reason." She sniffed again. "It's just—" sniff "—my father was mur—died." Katya sucked in a shaky breath and blew it out, attempting to pull away from the man's chest to keep from letting more tears drop onto his naked skin. Hadn't her father taught her better? Never let the public see you express untidy emotion. He had classified tears as unnecessarily messy. "I'm sorry. Ivan—" She bit down hard on her bottom lip and started again, struggling at lying to this man. "Evanses do not cry."

Maddox pulled her back in the crook of his arm. "I'm sorry about your father. I lost mine not too long ago."

Katya settled her cheek against his chest again and tilted her head up to study his face.

"I wish I could have said goodbye."

"Me, too."

High cheekbones, a rock-hard chin, dark skin and longish black hair gave away his heritage. The man could easily step into the past, hunting buffalo and living off the land. Again, his earthiness reassured her in the confines of the cave. He appeared to be in his element, completely capable of surviving in the harsh environment. Unlike her.

Having been raised surrounded by bodyguards, servants and political dignitaries, she had always relied on her social skills to survive. In the Badlands of North Dakota, social skills were less in demand and more of a hindrance. If she wanted to survive, she had better do as Maddox Thunder Horse said.

"How much longer do you think the storm will last?" she asked.

"Weather in the Badlands has a life of its own." He tucked the corners of the bag around them more securely. "Rest. At least, it'll pass time."

Although tired, Katya didn't feel even slightly sleepy. "I guess you are correct. Nothing else to do." Except feel his lovely body against hers. She never would have thought lying with a man could feel so good. With her nerves on edge, she could be awake for a very long time. Awake and aware.

He reached out of the bag toward the flashlight.

Her attention riveted on the light, Katya gulped. "What are you doing?"

"Conserving the batteries." He flipped the switch, plunging them into the inky blackness of complete and utter darkness. Katya's sense of sight consisted of the residual glow of the flashlight, fading as darkness settled around her.

Her body shook, her teeth chattering. Her fingers dug into his skin, the sensation of falling into an abyss making her hold on for dear life.

Maddox eased her fingernails out of his hide and laced his fingers with hers. "Don't tell me…" She could feel his head shaking back and forth over her head. "You're afraid of the dark."

"Sorry. It is a curse. Something that has plagued me since I was very small."

"I can turn the light back on, but the batteries will eventually fade, and we might have trouble finding our way back out of the cave."

"Do not concern yourself about me. I will be fine." Trying to keep her teeth from chattering, Katya aimed for nonchalance, failing miserably.

Maddox's other arm tightened around her and he pulled her snugly against him. "Close your eyes and listen."

"What?"

"Just do as I say."

Katya squeezed her eyes shut, blocking out the cave's endless darkness. Now it was just her own darkness she had to overcome.

"Let me tell you a story my grandfather, James Thunder Horse, used to tell us as children." Maddox's voice hummed off the rocks, creating a warmth of spirit no heater or fire could generate. He spoke of a bear lost in the hills, trying to find his way home. Of a sly fox who led the bear farther away from home and a wise old wolf whose ferocity and courage helped the bear discover those virtues in himself. Ultimately, the bear found his way home, depending on the generosity of the wolf, and the assistance of the stars and the sun.

Katya's eyes remained closed throughout the story. Instead of relaxing, her body stiffened with increasing desire, each muscle and nerve intensely aware of Maddox, responding to the rhythm of his voice, the vibrations of his chest in a way she could not have imagined in the palace back home. "You have a gift." A gift possessed by no man she had ever met.

"It helps when you're lying naked with a stranger."

Katya could feel the strength in his body, the tautness of his muscles beneath her fingertips. She had never been this intimate with a man. Confined as they were in a cave, miles from everyone. Alone.

Even when she had explored sex with a classmate in the small school she had attended, she had not felt this close, as though their bodies melded into one.

Her hand slid across the hard planes of his chest, memorizing the texture and shape with her mind, imagining what it would feel like to love a man like this. To let him make love to her.

The heat in the sleeping bag intensified and her hand slipped lower. Would he be as hard all over? Her hand followed the ridges of his abdomen, sliding over the indentation of his belly button.

When her fingertips bumped into the steely velvet of his erection, a big hand caught her wrist, holding it in a vise grip.

"Don't start something you can't or won't finish," he said, his voice strained.

"I have never been with a man in a sleeping bag."

"Then maybe now's not the time to start."

"I must apologize. I cannot seem to help myself. You do something to me."

"You don't know me, and I don't know who you really are."

"What do you want to know? I am a woman. I am unmarried. I do not have any diseases and I am twenty-seven, old enough to make my own decisions." Perhaps she said the words to appease his conscience, but more likely the words came out to quiet her father's voice in her head. Either way, the words were for her more than him, and she recognized them for what they were. Permission to let go.

"Sex between a man and a woman takes two to decide."

He was right. Playing with Maddox Thunder Horse could be like playing with fire. But she wanted the heat he could provide, both outside and in.

Since her mother's death when she was only sixteen, she had been the perfect daughter to her father, playing hostess to foreign diplomats, always doing and saying the right things, never stepping outside the bounds of etiquette. "For once in my life I want to make a decision for myself. For me alone. Not for my father. Not for the people around me." She twisted her fingers around to lace them with his. "I know what I want." Then another thought sobered her. "Do you not find me attractive?"

He sucked in a breath and guided her hand to that part of him standing at stiff attention. "You tell me." His grip tightened on her. "If this is a tease, forget it."

Her hand closed around him. "I am stuck in a cave with a man I find very attractive and who obviously finds me not completely hideous. It is quite dark. We are cold and I am not teasing." She stroked her hand down his length, loving the contrast of velvet and steel. "Make love to me."

For a long moment Maddox hesitated. "This has to be wrong." His hand closed over hers, tightening her grip around him. Then he let go to slide upward to cup a full, rounded breast.

Katya's back arched, pressing her breast into his hand, hungry for his touch, for the feel of his lips against her skin.

Trailing his fingers over her breast to cup her chin, he drew her to him, bringing their lips within a hair's width of each other.

The warmth of his breath brushed across her lips and her mouth parted, a sharp draw of longing tugging at her core.

"I might regret this later, but for now…" His lips captured hers, grinding against her teeth, the force of his claim branding her with a desire so intense it stole her breath away. He moved against her, his sex rigid, pressing into her belly.

She shimmied out of her panties, while he unhooked the clasp on her bra. When she lay as naked as Maddox, Katya's legs fell open, letting him slide between her thighs. He eased her onto her back, settling down over her. Then he thrust into her long and hard, filling her, stretching her deliciously.

Their bodies melded into one, the heat they generated making their skin slick with sweat.

And she wanted more.

She raised her knees, her hands gripping his buttocks, driving him faster, harder and deeper into her, until she lost all sense of time and place. They came together as two separate people, but now they were as one in body and spirit, riding a wave of sensation so intense Katya almost forgot how to breathe. As she plunged over the edge of reason, she let go of her worries and clung to the present and his body.

Eventually, sleep claimed her, wrapping her in warmth and security. She was assured of her safety, if only as long as she remained in his arms.

Minutes, hours, days could have passed before she returned to earth, the floor hard against her back, an icy draft cooling her damp skin.

In a half-sleep state, she listened for sounds of the storm outside. Silence filled the dark interior. No wailing screamed in through the cave's rocky entrance.

With consciousness, reason and memories returned. A few hours ago she had woken up with a stranger, sharing his body's warmth, both of them practically naked.

Katya moved, her knee sliding down Maddox's leg, her bare thigh rubbing against his leg. She sucked in a gasp and her naked breasts pressed into his equally naked chest.

She had responsibilities. Her country needed her. Her people expected so much of her. And she'd just thrown it all to the wind to make love to a stranger.

What had she done? Would he understand when she had to leave? For leave she must, just as soon as she could contact her government for help. Katya chewed on her lip, her brow furrowing. Having ditched her car, and lost her identification and credit cards back on the snowmobile somewhere along the river, getting help would definitely be a challenge.

Chapter Three

Maddox lay beside the woman, guilt gnawing at him. He'd made love to a stranger not quite two years since the death of his fiancée. Susan, who'd grown up in the Badlands, who knew the dangers of living on the prairie, who loved the land and wild horses as much as he did. His perfect match in every way. And in every way so different from the woman lying in his arms.

Susan's sun-kissed tawny hair reminded him of wheat and late-summer prairie grasses, wispy and straight, always blowing in the wind. Her eyes as gray as a storm-filled sky. Her long, lanky body strong and adept at riding the range alongside him.

Kat was nothing like Susan. Her hair lay in a mass of long, loose, black curls, emphasizing her pale skin and eyes as light as his were dark. Her diminutive body, though small, had curves that fit perfectly in his palm, a fact that brought on yet more twinges of guilt. How could he compare them? Susan had been his life, his soul mate, the woman he'd planned to spend the rest of his life with. Only her life had ended and he'd resigned himself to continuing on alone.

Yet this dark-haired beauty, with hands so soft they couldn't have worked a hard day's labor her entire life, lay naked against him. The smell of her skin, the softness of her body, still made him hard as a rock.

Maddox stiffened, his hands dropping to his sides, his fingers burning as though on fire from touching her. He jerked the sleeping bag's zipper down, a frigid blast of arctic air biting at his naked flesh. He reached for the flashlight and switched it on.

Kat blinked, her eyes widening as the cool air hit her skin and pebbled the tips of her breasts. "What's the matter?"

"Nothing." Before he changed his mind and claimed her, Maddox climbed out of the bag, reaching back inside for his clothing lodged at the bottom.

In the freezing interior of the cave, he dressed quickly, fully aware of Kat's gaze watching him, and thankful for the effect of the frigid temps on his libido.

Kat pulled the bag up to her nose, her dark eyes rounded, each breath a puff of steam. "Did I do something to make you mad?" She laughed. "I apologize. I have never been this forward with a man. I'm not usually left alone with one long enough." Her eyes widened and she clamped her lips shut.

Maddox slipped into his insulated trousers, buttoning the fly. "Dress inside the bag. We leave as soon as it's daylight."

"Leave?" She shrank deeper into the bag, a tremor shaking her cocoon.

"Yes. Leave." Her big eyes reminded him of a scared colt, and he almost softened. Instead, he turned on his heels and edged through the crevice out into the bittercold wind.

The sun hovered below the horizon, giving the landscape a steely, washed-out, gray-blue glow. Clouds clogged the sky in a blanket of charcoal-smeared waves of dirty white, churned by the ever-present wind.

Maddox braced himself before leaving the relative shelter of the tumbled boulders to stare up the hillside at the icy terrain. They'd have to climb the rugged sides of the canyon wall to reach the plateau. From there it was an hour's trek on horseback to the ranch house.

As bitter cold and windy as it was, he preferred to get back to the ranch rather than spending another night in the sleeping bag with Kat Evans—or whoever she really was. The sooner he got back, the sooner he could relinquish his responsibility for the woman.

Maddox unclipped the radio from his jacket and flipped the on switch. "Tuck, you out there?" As he waited for any response, he knew he'd get none. The handheld radios had a short range. More than likely, Tuck had made it back to the ranch and was wondering what had happened to Maddox. He hoped they hadn't sent out a search party. With the skies as heavy as they were, they could be in for another onslaught of the white stuff.

Maddox closed his eyes and drew in a deep breath, the frigid air stinging his lungs. He could taste the coming snow, feel it in his blood, chilling him to the bone. It would arrive soon. Too soon for comfort.

Something touched his arm, jerking him out of his trance and back to the canyon floor. He spun, braced for attack.

Kat stood with her arms crossed, the red scarf wrapped around her nose and mouth and her jacket hood pulled up over her hair. Buried in all those layers, her pale face peeked around the edges of clothing, her eyes as wide as icy-blue saucers. "I am r-ready," she said, her voice muffled by the wool scarf.

"Then we leave." He reentered the cave, making quick work of rolling up the sleeping bag. Flashlight in hand, he led the stallion through the entrance and out into the windy gray of predawn.

Kat waited at the cave entrance, stamping her boots in the snow, rubbing her hands along her arms, her gaze darting from side to side as if she feared venturing out for more reasons than the cold wind. "Are you sure we shouldn't stay here?"

One look at Kat and the memories of the night before hit Maddox like a sucker punch to the groin. "We move." He didn't ask permission or warn her. With little effort, he grabbed her around the waist and swung her up into the saddle.

Kat squealed and held on to the saddle horn as Bear reared and danced to the side.

She sat the horse well, despite his nervous dance, as though she'd ridden before. A woman with soft hands who could ride.

Maddox tucked that little bit of insight away in the back of his mind. He'd get to the bottom of Kat Evans when they were safe from the weather. With gentle hands, he pulled on the reins, running gloved fingers over the horse's nose, speaking to him in Lakota, calming him.

Then he set out at a quick pace, leading the horse along the base of the bluffs, searching for a suitable path to climb out of the canyon.

"Aren't you going to ride with me?" Kat called out, hunkered down as low as she could get in the saddle to escape the full force of the driving wind. Her voice barely carried over the roar of wind bouncing off stony cliffs.

"Not until we're out of the canyon." Finally, a break in the sheer rock wall revealed a narrow path zigzagging up the side of the canyon, probably left by elk or bighorn sheep. Maddox climbed the hill, the horse close behind him. Kat clung to the saddle horn as they rose from the riverbed up the treacherous trail.

Several times Maddox's boots slipped on loose rocks, sending a tumble of gravel and stones toward the horse. Bear sidestepped and almost lost his footing. Kat's hand flailed out for balance, her face even more pale and pinched than when they'd started up the incline.

Maddox found that the less he looked at her, the better he felt. Only when he had to did he turn to make sure that she hadn't lost her grip and fallen from the horse.

Kat's fingers and cheekbones burned with the cold. Not long after they left the cave, she started shivering and could not seem to stop. She could not afford to waste all her energy, not when she had to use all her strength just to hang on.

She cast a look over her shoulder to the canyon floor, wondering where the man who had been following her had gone. Had he headed back when the storm struck? Or had he holed up as she had? In which case, he would be out looking for her again.

A shiver shook her so hard her teeth rattled. If not for Maddox, she would have died out there, saving the man following her the trouble of killing her.

Where would that leave her country? Without a ruler, without anyone to lead them into democracy, her people would fall back into chaos and warlords would take over. She needed to find out who was behind her father's death. No matter what the news reports said, that car crash had begun with a bullet. A deliberate attack by a skilled assassin.

Whoever was after her did not plan on holding her hand and escorting her back to her country. He had taken several shots at her before she had lost him. Skimming through streams and across barren rocks had taken their toll on her snowmobile, but had bought her much-needed time to escape in an otherwise snow-covered landscape.

She had taken a huge risk crossing Minnesota and North Dakota in a car. The open farm fields and grass-lands left little cover and concealment. But she kept moving just to escape the law and the predator tailing her. Only he had been persistent and tracked her every move. She was tired of running, tired of always look-ing over her shoulder, completely cut off from everyone who could possibly help.

As they climbed higher, the terrain became increas-ingly more treacherous and their footing more precari-ous. The more Kat looked back at the canyon floor, the dizzier she got. The canyon wall inclined at more than a forty-five-degree angle, the path they followed less than six inches wide in most places. How she longed to be on foot, rather than perched high on a horse's back, even that much farther from the ground.

Nausea fought with vertigo, making her head spin. Kat squeezed her eyes shut and clung to the saddle horn. Because the stirrups were so long, her feet did not quite reach the footrests, giving her no way to balance her weight on the big animal. With her hands quickly freezing and the possibility of a frightening fall making her hold tighter, she thought the ride to the canyon's rim would never end.

With one mighty lunge, the horse nearly unseated her, clearing the edge of the canyon and arriving on the plateau above.

Kat opened her eyes, the wind whipping her scarf across her face. For as far as she could see, semi-barren rolling hills stretched before her.

Behind her, the canyon cut a long, jagged swath out of the prairie walls blown free of snow, glowing a ruddy red in the increasing light from the muted sun. Every breath of the wickedly cold air stung her lungs and bored through her thick clothing. Chills shuddered across her body and she huddled lower in the saddle, praying for the journey to end, preferably in a hot tub. She groaned. How she would love to sink neck deep into a warm bath and stay there until her skin shriveled.

All the while she had been perched atop the giant stallion, Maddox had been climbing the hill. He had to be tired by now. Was he as cold as she was? Did he wish to be done with this trek—and her?

Several hundred feet from the rim of the canyon, Maddox stopped to catch his breath and speak to the horse in a language Katya did not understand. She assumed he spoke the language of the Lakota Nation.

In the light, she could finally see him. Dark skin, black eyes and straight, thick black hair falling to his shoulders. He tugged his fur-lined parka up around his face and turned to face her.

With the ease of one born to ride, he placed one foot into the stirrup and swung up onto the horse's back, landing behind the saddle.

His arm wrapped around her waist and he lifted her,

easing himself into the seat beneath her, settling her onto his thighs.

Immediately she could feel his warmth through her clothing. Just blocking the wind on one side made a difference. She sank back against him, glad for his presence and the balance he provided on the moving beast.

He did not say anything and with the wind so strong it could steal her breath away, Kat did not speak, either.

For several miles, they rode in silence, curled into each other.

The gentle rocking motion of the horse, plus the constant cold, lulled Kat into a dull, half-sleep state. Snow turned to sleet, the tiny hard pellets slung sideways by the approaching storm.

"Don't go to sleep, Kat Evans," a voice said over the roar of the wind.

"Why?" she leaned against him, her eyelids dropping over snow-stung eyes. "I am exceedingly tired."

"If you fall asleep, who will I talk to?"

She snorted softly. "You were not talking." She turned her face into his jacket. "I am so cold."

"We'll be there in less than half an hour."

"I need to sleep."

"Talk to me, Kat," he said, his chest rumbling against her back.

"About what?" she muttered, her eyes closed. She had to keep her secrets, but she didn't have to stay awake, did she?

"How did you get into the canyon? We're miles from the closest highway or public lands."

In her sleepy haze she could not think straight. How much could she reveal? Did she care? She gave a half-hearted attempt at laughter and opted for mostly truth.

"I did not see the canyon. I drove my snowmobile over the edge. It did not stop until it reached the bottom beside the riverbed."

Funny how leaning against Maddox, with the soft swaying of the horse beneath her, lulled her into thinking the horrible tumble down the bluff was nothing but a bad dream. Except for a few bruises, she had survived, only to fall victim to the extreme cold and mind-numbing lethargy.

Other than her hands and feet, she was fairly warm in Maddox's capable arms. They did not build men this rugged where she was from. Her brows furrowed. Or she had never met any men who had been built this sturdy. Her father had kept her surrounded by bodyguards and state officials everywhere she went in Trejikistan.

Maddox shifted her weight, pulling her closer against him. "Why were you snowmobiling out this far? Why not closer to Bismarck?"

"Cars cannot follow." She yawned and settled back against him, her eyelids closing for the final count. "Unfortunately other snowmobiles can."

"Isn't that the idea with a snowmobile tour?" Maddox's words were carried away on the wind as Katya slipped into a numbing sleep.

Maddox stopped the horse periodically to tuck Katya's hands into his jacket and adjust her position to keep her from getting too cold in any one place. As he rode Bear through the storm, he went over Kat's words again and again. They didn't make any sense. Had she been out on a snowmobile tour and gotten lost? And what did she mean that cars couldn't follow but snowmobiles could? Had she been running away from something? Was someone following her?

Maddox vowed to get to the bottom of it all when they finally made it back to the ranch. The one-hour ride from the canyon rim stretched into two as the storm settled in around them.

Sleet turned to snow, blowing in sideways, making it difficult for him to see more than two feet ahead of them. At one point, he took shelter in a ravine, the wind and sleet too harsh for them to be out on the open plains.

Too cold to remain exposed much longer, he ventured out again, hoping Bear knew the way. Maddox couldn't make out any landmarks and the storm only grew worse, nearing blizzard conditions.

Maddox hoped the horse's sense of direction led them back to the safety of the barn and ranch house and not farther away.

When he'd just about given up hope of getting there, the ranch house materialized through the whiteout conditions.

A dog barked, and a light blinked on next to the front door.

Through the driving snow, his brother and a ranch hand raced out into the blizzard toward the horse and the two people sagging in the saddle.

"Take the woman." Maddox handed Katya down into waiting arms. He didn't like others carrying her away, but the cold had taken more out of him than he originally thought.

He nudged the horse toward the barn. When they reached the barn door, he slipped from the saddle, his legs buckling. If not for the horse standing beside him, Maddox would have gone down in the snow.

Three Thunder Horse ranch hands emerged from the barn. One took the horse's reins and the other two rushed to grab Maddox's arms, draping them over their shoulders. His horse taken care of, Maddox let the men walk him up to the house. Once inside, he settled in a chair near the hearth where a fire blazed with enough warmth to thaw even the coldest parts of his body.

His mother, Amelia Thunder Horse, crouched on the floor in front of him and tugged his boots off his feet and the socks with it. "Thank the Lord you made it back. We were so worried. Who is the woman you brought with you? Where did you find her?"

Too tired to answer her, Maddox stood. "I'll answer all your questions later. Where is she?"

"In the guest bedroom."

Maddox stumbled down the hallway, shedding his jacket. When he reached the guestroom, Mrs. Janek, the housekeeper, had just finished tucking Kat into the bed, the blankets drawn up to her chin. The older woman clucked her tongue. "She's out. I hope she'll be all right. Do you want me to call the doctor?"

"No. I'll see to her." Maddox stood next to the bed, staring down at the woman who'd called herself Kat. In his gut, he knew she hadn't told him the entire truth. Despite that, he couldn't help the overwhelming need to protect her that came over him.

Tired beyond endurance, he pulled the covers aside and lay in the bed beside her, gathering her into his arms as he'd done in the cave.

"Maddox?" His mother hovered in the door of the guestroom. "Is she okay?" She twisted her fingers together, her brows dipped in a worried frown. "Are you okay?"

His eyelids weighed so heavily, he closed them. "I don't know, Mother. Somehow, I don't think I'll ever be okay."

Chapter Four

Lights glittered in the myriad chandeliers hanging from the vast ceiling. Too bright, all merging and blending together as she spun around the room, dancing from partner to partner. In a deep red ball gown, her hair piled high on her head and the world at her feet, Katya smiled, laughed and drank champagne from crystal goblets.

At one point her father danced her around the room. She was a little girl all over again, smiling up at him, proud of the man who ruled Trejikistan and made her feel loved and protected. So relieved to see him healthy and happy, she leaned against him and hugged him tight. "They told me you were dead."

He just laughed and spun her into the arms of her brother, Dmitri, so tall and handsome, his wavy black hair so much like her own. His hands held her, gently guiding her through the steps of the intricate traditional dance of her ancestors. Hands of a doctor, a man meant to do good for the people, with a heart so big he could love every child in their country.

Katya smiled and laughed at him. "Where have you been, Dmitri? We have all been so worried."

Before he could answer, the music ended. Dmitri

tweaked her nose, just as he had since she'd been a small child, and disappeared into the crowd.

Standing alone in the crowd of guests, Katya looked around for her father and brother, suddenly sad, lonely and afraid. The orchestra played a waltz, the music so beautiful it melted Katya's fears and sadness away. As she glanced around the ballroom, the sea of blurred faces parted and one man stood at the center. Unlike the other guests, this man didn't wear a tuxedo or the uniform of a military man. He wore buckskins and moccasins, his long black hair hanging down around his shoulders, a wild gleam in his brown-black eyes.

As if drawn to him by a magical thread, Katya floated across the room toward him, the other guests fading away in a haze of gray. She could see his face so clearly, every line, angle and shadow etched in her memory. When the tall, swarthy Lakota native took her in his arms, he moved with the grace of a lion. At ease in his traditional dress, he waltzed her around the room, ignoring the whispers and comments made by statesmen and their wives, oblivious to the pomp and circumstance strictly adhered to in formal settings.

For once, Katya did not care that she might not fit in, that the man she danced with would draw censure from the exalted guests. Princes, princesses and leaders of foreign countries did not matter to her as long as she remained in the Lakota native's arms. The world didn't exist, except for the two of them.

As the music faded to a halt, the world crowded in. Her father gripped her arm and pulled her away from the Lakota.

"No!" she cried out. "I want to stay with him."

But her father's grip tightened and he led her out

*of the palace and into a waiting limousine where her
brother sat, shaking his head.*

"No! Let me stay. I want to dance," Katya called out.

*The limousine sped into the darkness, the lights from
the palace fading with each passing mile. Katya looked
back, her tears blurring her vision.*

*When she slumped into her seat beside her father and
brother, she could not stop sobbing. "Why?"*

*Suddenly, the vehicle lurched, rammed by another
car speeding along the highway. The limousine spun
around and around, the motion flinging Katya around
the inside. Out of control, it pitched over the edge of
the road and tumbled into a ditch.*

*The door nearest her flew open and Katya fell into
the ditch, facedown, her beautiful gown ruined in the
mud.*

*She lay for a moment, wondering if she had died.
But the sticks poking into her hands and face made her
open her eyes and look around.*

*The limousine lay on its side, riddled with bullet
holes.*

"No!"

MADDOX HAD AWAKENED when Kat first kicked out in her
sleep. He stared down at the woman who'd managed to
end up in his arms yet again.

Her brows dipped together and a tear slipped down
her cheek, even as she slept.

What was he doing? What happened to the plan of
dumping her on someone else as soon as they reached
the ranch house? She wasn't his problem and he didn't
want to be responsible for her.

Deep in a terrible nightmare, she cried out.

And despite his determination not to care, his heart went out to her. She must have gone through a lot, getting lost from her tour and falling into a canyon—not that he completely believed that story. If he hadn't come along when he had... It didn't bear thinking about. He couldn't erase the image of her lying in the snow, her face so pale. He could forgive her lies, but he couldn't forgive himself if she'd died. "Kat, wake up."

"Dmitri, don't go!" she mumbled. "I need you."

His chest tightening, Maddox shook the woman. "Wake up." Who was Dmitri? Kat had told him that she was single. He didn't make love to married women. Or even those promised to another man. Too much about Kat Evans remained a mystery, and Maddox didn't like it when he couldn't get to the bottom of things. An unexpected surge of anger powered through him. "Kat!"

Her eyelids fluttered, then opened. "What? Who?" Her gaze shifted around the room and returned to his. "We are not in the cave." She closed her eyes again and leaned her face against his chest.

A knock on the door drew his attention away from the black-haired beauty lying so naturally in the crook of his arm.

Maddox's mother pushed open the door, balancing a tray in her arms. Amelia Thunder Horse smiled. "You two missed dinner, so I brought it to you. And we have company."

Maddox frowned. "In this weather?"

His mother's smile widened. "You've been asleep for several hours." She set the tray on a table and scooted it close to the bed. "It stopped snowing, and the wind is dying down." Amelia planted fists on her hips and stared directly at Maddox and Kat. "Are you two going to sleep the rest of the night away, or are you going to eat some of this food I slaved over?"

Kat sat up, her eyes wide, her face flushing a rosy red. "I beg your pardon." She slipped out of the bed and stood in the rumpled shirt and jeans she'd arrived at the house in. "Is there someplace I could wash up?" She shoved her mass of black hair away from her face. "I must be a fright."

"Of course." She led Kat to the bathroom. "In here. I'll bring a change of clothes in a minute."

Maddox's stomach rumbled as he sat on the edge of the bed and reached for a fork, painfully aware that he'd gone an entire day without eating. "Who's the company?"

His mother picked up Maddox's discarded shirt, refusing to meet his gaze. "Sheriff Yost."

Without taking the bite of food, Maddox slammed his fork down on the tray, rattling the plates and glasses. "What the hell's he doing here?"

Amelia Thunder Horse shrugged. "Checking on us after last night's storm."

"And is he checking on every other rancher in the county, as well?"

"I didn't ask him." She faced Maddox. "He'd like to talk to you and your visitor."

Maddox's eyes narrowed. "What does he know?"

She shook her head. "No more than any of us."

"How does he know she's even here?"

"Tuck mentioned it. The sheriff probably just wants to notify her family that she's all right."

Kat stepped through the door of the bathroom, her fingers attempting to comb her hair into place. "Whose family?"

"Yours, dear." Amelia smiled and crossed the room. "I'll get a brush and those clothes I promised. You have a lovely accent."

"Mother—" Maddox stood, intending to tell his mother just what he thought of Sheriff Yost, but she cut him off with a stern look.

"Maddox Thunder Horse, you'll speak with the sheriff and you'll be nice." She shot a wry smile at Kat and left the room.

Kat stared across at Maddox, her eyes wide, worried. "I don't have a family for him to notify."

"So you say."

"You don't believe me," she said, her words flat. "Are you going to turn me over to the sheriff?"

"Have you committed a crime?"

"Well…" Her frown deepened.

"Why do I have a feeling that this situation is going to get even more complicated?"

"Because it will." She gave him a weak smile. "I do not have any of my documents on me. I am a foreign national, and I lost my visa and all my identification papers back on the snowmobile in the canyon."

"Convenient."

"I have copies stored in a safe place, if I can just get to them."

"Or you could contact your embassy and have them forward them to you."

She nodded, not really answering or committing to his suggestion. What was it she held back? What was she not telling him?

"Look, whatever trouble you're in, you might as well tell me now. I don't like being blindsided."

"You would not understand," she said, her back stiffening. "You might as well turn me over to the sheriff now. I'll go quietly." She faced off with him, daring him to do just what she suggested.

For a moment he considered it, certain that if he turned her over to the sheriff he'd be rid of her. But after that night in the cave, he couldn't. Maddox drew in a deep breath and let it out in a long slow sigh. "I'm not going to turn you over to the sheriff. At least not this one, and not now." He stepped close to her. "However, be warned. I don't like it when people take advantage of me or my family. And I especially don't like it when someone places my family in danger of any kind." He tipped her chin up and stared down into light blue eyes so shiny he could see himself reflected in their depths. "Do you understand?"

She nodded, her bottom lip trembling.

Maddox groaned and kissed her, his mouth crashing down over hers, drawing her into his world and wrapping her in his protection. With her wide, blue eyes, pale skin and diminutive stature, she looked as fragile as a porcelain doll, but her strength and determination to survive shone through.

As quickly as he initiated the kiss, he broke it off, dragging himself several steps away from her. To be that close only rekindled the heat and desire he had no control over. "Join me when you're ready."

As Maddox left the bedroom, his mother met him in the hallway, her hands full of clothing and a hairbrush. "I'll send her along when she's had a chance to change."

A last glance back into the bedroom made Maddox's jaw tighten.

Kat stood with her hands clasped together, the dark

circles beneath her eyes making her appear waiflike, vulnerable.

Her presence made him hot, cold, protective and tense all at once. If he had any sense whatsoever, he'd hand her over to the sheriff and save himself and his family the grief she was bound to cause. He turned away, wishing he could wash the image of her staring after him from his mind. Angry that he couldn't, Maddox grabbed a sweatshirt from his own bedroom, tugged it over his head and marched into the living room.

His brother Tuck stood in front of the floor-to-ceiling windows, his back to the view of the snowy-white North Dakota hills. The brightness of the snow behind him cast his brother's face into shadows, consuming his expression and making it completely unreadable.

Maddox almost smiled. Knowing Tuck, he'd done it on purpose to unsettle the sheriff neither of them cared for.

The tall, barrel-chested man standing in the middle of the room turned to greet Maddox, his hand held out. "Maddox."

Maddox hesitated, then took the sheriff's grip. "Sheriff."

The sheriff nodded. "Your brother tells me you rescued a woman out in the canyon."

Maddox nodded. "That's correct." He didn't volunteer any more information than was necessary.

"What was she doing out there?"

"Snowmobiling."

"Damn city people." The sheriff shook his head. "They've got no sense when it comes to the winters here."

Maddox didn't respond, just stared at the sheriff, willing him to leave.

The sheriff's eyes narrowed as if sizing up Maddox's mood. "Mind if I meet her? See for myself?"

Maddox crossed his arms over his chest. "Why?"

Yost's brows rose. "To see if she's really alive. Come on, a strange woman found in the canyon in a snowstorm isn't an everyday occurrence."

"Any reason to believe she might be dead?" Maddox shot back at him.

The sheriff's eyes narrowed again. "No, none at all. We just get so many missing persons reports over the wire that I like to follow up on them if I get the chance. Has she notified her family of her whereabouts? I'm sure they must be worried by now."

"We'll take care of it," Maddox replied.

Tuck left the shadows and joined Maddox in the middle of the room, facing the sheriff. "Anything else keeping you from performing your civic duties?"

"I'm just paying a friendly visit." His frown deepening, the sheriff glanced down the hallway where Amelia had gone. "If you don't mind, I'll wait and talk to the woman."

Maddox strode to the window and stared out at the stark landscape. Even before the chill of the air closest to the window penetrated his sweatshirt, goose bumps had risen on Maddox's arms. "Why did you come here?"

"I came to see if you and your family—"

"You mean our *mother*," Maddox interrupted.

The sheriff's lips tightened. "—to see if you and your family weathered the storm."

"We're fine. Mother's fine." Tuck took another step

closer to the sheriff. "Go find some other family to check on."

Rather than leave, the sheriff sat in John Thunder Horse's favorite chair as if he owned it. "It would be rude of me to leave when *Amelia* asked me to stay."

Maddox wanted to tell him to stay away from his mother, even though he'd been the one insisting that she get out and date again. Date, yes, but not this sheriff, a man his father never trusted.

Sheriff Yost was an arrogant ass and he'd done nothing to find their father's murderer. Getting into a fight with the man would prove nothing and land Maddox in jail.

What good would that do? Where would that leave Kat? Not that she'd be his problem for much longer. As soon as she contacted…whoever, she'd be out of there. "Five minutes with the girl and you leave."

Chapter Five

"I always dreamed of having a girl, but it seemed Mr. Thunder Horse was set on giving me an entire tribe of strapping boys." Amelia bustled about the room, her presence a welcome distraction.

Katya was happy for her company, especially since it meant delaying the inevitable meeting with the sheriff. And the more Maddox's mother talked, the less nervous Katya was.

"I worried all night about Maddox, stuck out there in the cold. I should have known better. He's just like his father—tenacious, industrious and a survivor." She came to stop behind Katya. "Well, almost," she said, her voice catching.

Katya turned in the chair and captured Amelia Thunder Horse's hands in her own, the ache of her own loss still burning in her chest. "What happened to your husband, Mrs. Thunder Horse?"

With a half smile and her eyes suspiciously bright, Amelia recalled the accident that took her husband's life. "He fell off his damned horse." She laughed, the sound more of a sob.

"I'm sorry." A tear slipped from the corner of her eye and Katya squeezed Amelia's hands. "I lost my father recently." She stared up at the older woman. "Does the ache ever go away?"

Maddox's mother smoothed a hand over Katya's temple, tucking a long strand of hair behind her ear. "No. But it does start to subside." Amelia's blue eyes swam with tears of her own.

"I hope it does soon."

"It can take years. It's taken Maddox the past two years to get over the death of his fiancée."

A gasp escaped Katya's lips before she could stop it.

"I don't suppose he told you." The older woman stared at her reflection in the mirror. "They were so much alike, both used to the outdoors, both passionate about the wild horses in the canyon, both born and raised in this desolate part of the country. Such a shame."

Katya looked down at her hands in her lap. How did she compete with someone like that? Not that she was competing. The woman was dead, and Katya wasn't staying around to start anything with the handsome Lakota man who'd saved her life. Her main goal was to stay under the radar of the law and live to find out who'd set her up and who was responsible for her father's murder. Most of the pictures circulating in the media were ones where her hair hung down around her face. Usually an asset, her glossy black locks were a dead giveaway if anyone was looking for her. "I believe I'll pull my hair straight back into a ponytail today."

"But you look so lovely with it down."

"Thank you, but it'll be so much easier to manage up."

"I'll be back in a moment with a rubber band." She left the bedroom.

In seconds, she returned and Katya pulled her hair back into a severe knot.

"Only you could get away with this harsh a hairstyle, my dear."

"How so?"

Amelia tucked a stray hair into the knot. "You have the bearing of royalty."

Her heart skipping a beat, Katya forced a laugh. "My brother would laugh. He thinks I am too much of a hoyden."

"Your brother is so wrong. You're a beautiful young lady. I can see why Maddox is so taken with you."

"Oh, please, Mrs. Thunder Horse. We barely know each other."

"Maybe so, but I know my sons and love them very much. I don't like it when someone tries to hurt any one of them."

Katya's lips twisted. "I understand. I won't be staying long enough for that to happen. Your son has done so much for me already. I'd never hurt him."

"I know you wouldn't—intentionally."

"What do you mean?" Katya thought she'd spent enough time in the United States to understand the nuances of American English. But Amelia's words escaped her comprehension. In the short amount of time she'd known Maddox, she couldn't have had that much of an impact on him, nor he on her. Right?

Last night in the cave, she'd made her own decision and had only one regret—that the night hadn't lasted longer.

"Looks like you're all done." Amelia patted her hair. "I can see why my son saved you."

"He'd have saved me if I'd been a seventy-year-old grandmother."

"You're right. That's Maddox for you, always trying to save the world."

Katya laughed. "I can see that in him."

"His problem is usually that he's so busy saving the world, he doesn't remember to save himself." Amelia laid the brush on the dresser beside the pile of clothing she'd loaned Katya. "Are you feeling okay, dear? Your cheeks are flushed."

The older woman laid a palm across Katya's forehead.

Her face burned hotter at the same time Katya realized how much she missed having a woman care about her. Her own mother had passed away right before Katya's sixteenth birthday. For that brief moment, she closed her eyes and pretended this woman was the mother she missed more than ever. Her eyes burned with unshed tears and a lump rose in her throat. Swallowing hard, she leaned away from Amelia's hand and straightened her shoulders. Wishing didn't make things happen. Both her mother and father weren't coming back. Her brother was missing, her country in turmoil and she was alone in the world. She couldn't bring her family back, but she might be able to help the people of her country. "I'm fine, really."

Amelia stared into her face for a long moment, and sighed. "Come on, then. The men will be wondering what's keeping us."

Katya followed Mrs. Thunder Horse down the hallway to the spacious living room with windows reaching from floor to ceiling and a massive stone hearth blazing with a fire. Despite the warmth of the room, a chill feathered across her skin. Maddox and his brother stood near the window, their backs to the room. A man in a law enforcement uniform sat on the sofa. When he spied Maddox's mother, he rose and extended a hand to her. "Ah, Amelia."

Katya only glanced at the sheriff before her gaze sought out Maddox, the man who had saved her from death and lit a burning fire inside her.

His face could have been made of stone, if not for the muscle twitching in his cheek and the way his fists clenched in tight knots. He didn't even look at her, his gaze pinned on his mother and the man kissing her hand.

"Amelia, my dear," the uniformed man said. "Thank you for seeing me on such short notice."

Amelia blushed and pulled her hand free. "Stop it, William. Please have a seat while I get some hot cocoa. Tuck, why don't you help me?"

Tuck shot a glance at Maddox.

When Maddox didn't look his way, he nudged him in the side.

As if noticing others in the room for the first time, Maddox looked at Katya. "Go on. I can take care of things here," he said to his brother, his voice low.

When Amelia and Tuck left, Katya stood in the middle of the room, alone and completely aware of Maddox's barely leashed anger. She prayed that the sheriff hadn't seen the news or gotten notification to be on the lookout for a suspected terrorist. The only photos the police could have would be those from her apartment, all of which had her hair hanging down, framing her face. Katya hoped that by pulling it back, the sheriff wouldn't recognize her. She fought to keep her nerves steady.

"Five minutes, Yost," Maddox ground out between clenched teeth.

Sheriff Yost raised eyebrows at Maddox and smiled at Katya.

She shivered as if a snail had crawled across her skin, leaving a slimy trail.

"Miss…"

"Evans," Katya finished for him.

"I understand you had a snowmobile accident out in the canyon yesterday."

"That is true."

"Were you with a group?"

"Yes, sir."

"Care to elaborate?"

"It was a tour group out of Bismarck." She prayed she was giving the same answers she'd given Maddox.

"Where is the rest of your group, Miss Evans?"

"I don't know. I lost them." She stared directly at the sheriff, squaring her shoulders. "Is there a reason for all these questions? Am I being arrested or something?"

"No, no." The sheriff held up his hands, smiling, although the smile didn't quite reach his eyes. "I'm just doing my civic duty to protect the good citizens of the county by checking on anything out of the ordinary."

Katya nodded. Fair enough. She just wished this inquisition was over. The longer he was there, the greater the chance of him recognizing her.

"Three minutes, Yost," Maddox warned.

"Miss Evans, you have an accent." Sheriff Yost crossed the room and walked around her. "Not from around here, are you?"

"No." Katya didn't look at the sheriff, her gaze seeking Maddox's, her only rock in this island of uncertainty.

"Foreign?"

"Yes."

"Where from?"

"Russia," she lied. If the police had her passport, they'd know she was from Trejikistan.

"Do you have a visa or passport?"

"Not on me."

"Somewhere you can get to it?"

"If you give me a couple days to send for it." A couple days should allow her enough time to get away from here.

"For a stranger in a foreign country, seems a little odd that you aren't carrying legal documents with you."

"I didn't think I'd need them for a snowmobile ride. I didn't plan on being away for more than a day while I was on the tour." Katya couldn't meet Maddox's gaze as she told one lie after another.

"Is there someone who could forward your documents to you?"

"I hope so."

"So do I. If you can't come up with the necessary proof of legal entry into this country, I'll have to notify Homeland Security."

"I can get you those documents," she insisted, trying to keep her voice calm with no sign of the panic rising like bile in her throat. "I just need time."

The sheriff touched a finger to his chin and tipped his head to the side. "Maybe I should place you in holding until that time comes."

"That won't be necessary." Maddox stepped forward

and slipped an arm around Katya's waist. "She can stay here."

Sheriff Yost's lips pressed into a straight line. "I'll have to check with headquarters. They may want me to secure your little houseguest until she can come up with identification papers."

Katya's heart thundered against her chest. She forced herself to remain composed on the outside. "Completely understandable, Sheriff. If the Thunder Horses are willing to host me until my documents arrive, I would be very happy to stay here." Another lie. Katya fought to keep from choking on the lump rising in her throat.

She had to get word back to Trejikistan and seek out some kind of diplomatic immunity until she could figure out what to do. When she had left Minneapolis, all she had was what she took with her to the church. Her purse, a few credit cards and the remaining U.S. currency she had taken out for incidentals the day before. Her credit cards could be traced, so she cut them in pieces and disposed of them. The little money she had was already gone.

Since she had left the Twin Cities, she had not stopped long enough to call her homeland. She would not know who was left—and who to trust—even when she did.

She could try to get in touch with her cousin, Vladimir Ivanov, on his personal cell phone if he had not also been a target of the takeover. Her personal servants back at the palace were only available through palace telephones and they were not secure. She had to try her cousin when she finally had the chance.

Her passport had been in her apartment, probably confiscated by the police to use as evidence to convict her. She could not stay with the Thunder Horses too long, or the sheriff would begin to get suspicious when her papers failed to arrive. If the sheriff kept up with the news, he might be back sooner with a warrant for her arrest.

No doubt the sheriff would check the databases for anything on Kat Evans. If her pursuer was still trying to track her down—if he didn't think she had died in the snowstorm, he might be listening to police scanners in the area. He might suspect that foreigner, Kat Evans, was really Katya Ivanov and come to check her out for himself.

The sheriff gathered his hat and jacket. His eyes narrowed as he looked across at Katya. "I'll hold Maddox Thunder Horse responsible for your whereabouts until I can review your documents. So don't leave."

"Your five minutes are at an end," Maddox cut in. "And so is my patience."

"Careful, Maddox." Yost glared at Katya's rescuer. "This young lady is a stranger. Who's to say you aren't harboring a criminal?"

Katya gasped, her hand clapping over her lips.

"Get out," Maddox demanded.

"Don't push me."

"Or what? You'll kill me, too?"

"Are you accusing me of something, Thunder Horse?" Yost stood, feet braced, his hands rising dangerously close to his holstered pistol.

Maddox didn't answer, his jaw tight and eyes smoldering.

"Here we are." Amelia sailed into the room, followed by Tuck bearing a large tray filled with steaming mugs.

"Ah, Amelia, how kind." Sheriff Yost smiled and reached for one of the mugs.

Maddox got to it before he did, blocking his path. "The sheriff was just leaving."

"So soon?" His mother pouted, settling the tray on the coffee table.

Yost's smile slipped.

Katya expected him to say something to contradict Maddox. Instead, Yost took Amelia's hands in his. "You're as lovely as ever, Amelia. Much as I'd like to stay, I have work to do. Maybe we can get together for lunch in Medora?"

"No," both Maddox and Tuck said in unison.

Their mother gave them both a stern look before smiling at the sheriff. "That would be nice. How's tomorrow?"

"Perfect." He shot an oily smile at both Maddox and Tucker.

Standing beside Katya, Maddox growled.

Sheriff Yost turned to Katya. "Miss Evans, I'll be in touch. Don't go anywhere until we clear up this matter."

"Yes, sir." Katya vowed to leave as soon as she could. If not to keep her identity safely secret, then to keep the Thunder Horses out of her troubles.

Chapter Six

Maddox's muscles remained tense after Sheriff Yost departed. He walked to the window overlooking the front yard, rolling his shoulders in an attempt to release the pent-up anger over the sheriff's visit.

Sheriff Yost's SUV taillights disappeared down the long drive leading toward the county farm road.

"What did he say?" Tuck stepped up beside Maddox and stood at the window with him.

"You heard him. He wants Kat to stay put until he can contact his superiors or until she can cough up her legal papers."

"We should get Dante in on this. As a member of Customs and Border Protection, he should be up on all the passport regulations."

Katya cringed. Another law enforcement official *and* a member of the family? Great. Just what she needed.

Maddox nodded, unaware of the panic rising in Katya. "Isn't he due for a visit?"

"Heard Mom on the phone with him yesterday. He was scheduled to fly over two days ago, but the storm grounded him in Grand Forks."

"The weather's cleared somewhat," Maddox said.

"Right." Tuck turned and strode across the living

room. "I'll call him and see if he's headed this way. If not, at least we can get his take."

"Thanks." Maddox remained at the window, his gaze on the road leading to the homestead. The only indications of the sheriff's visit was the anger burning in Maddox's chest and the tracks left in the newly fallen snow.

Kat crossed the room and stood beside him. "I am sorry. I had no intention of staying or causing you any trouble. I should leave immediately."

"No." The one word came out harsh.

Katya stepped back. "No, what?"

"No, you can't leave." He faced her. "I promised that you would stay here."

Kat's lips tipped upward. "I did not get the impression that you cared for what Sheriff Yost said or did."

"True." Maddox's mouth twitched at the corners and then firmed. "However, for as long as your alien status remains in question, I'm now the responsible party. You stay."

Kat's brows furrowed. Used to bodyguards in her home country, she should have been fine with his determination to protect her. But Maddox wasn't a paid bodyguard. He had been a Good Samaritan in the wrong place at the right time to save her. Now he felt obligated to keep saving her.

Being with her because he wanted to be with her was one thing. Being with her because he was forced into accepting responsibility for her was something entirely different. Kat didn't like it. The more she thought of someone being obligated to watch her like a child, the more the idea grated on the hard-won independence she had been nurturing before her father's death. Staying was not an option. Maddox's stubborn determination to detain her placed her and his family in danger.

What if the man following her tracked her to the Thunder Horse Ranch? Would he attack her here and anyone else who might get in the way?

Then there was the criminal element. If the sheriff matched her face with a wanted poster that might be circulating for a suspected terrorist, the Thunder Horses could be in a lot more trouble for aiding and abetting an alleged dangerous criminal.

Katya closed her eyes and dragged in a deep breath. *Think, Katya, think.* She had to leave. But how could she and not implicate them?

Maddox grabbed her arms. "I don't like that look."

Katya's eyes popped open. "What look?" For a moment she feared he could read her mind and see her plotting her escape. Even more frightening was that he might see the desire ignited by his hold on her arms. His hands squeezed her. Instead of trying to break free, all she could do was recall how his fingers had felt on her naked skin.

"You looked like you were thinking."

She forced a laugh, making light of his comment. "Do not tell me you are one of those men who believe a woman should not have a mind of her own."

"Of course not. But if the woman is dreaming up a cockamamie scheme, I can tell you now, I don't like being surprised." His eyes narrowed. "I'm watching you, so don't do anything we'll both regret."

"Fine," she said. Her brows rose and she stared down at his hands on her arms. "Do you mind?"

He let go as though he hadn't realized he was still

holding her. "What do you need to get your legal documents sent here?"

Katya swallowed her flippant response and settled on, "I need to make a long-distance phone call."

"There's a phone in my office."

"I would rather not impact your long-distance bill." She tipped her head to the side. "Do you have a computer with internet service?"

"Sorry." He shook his head. "We haven't broken down and had the satellite internet service installed yet."

Katya's mouth twisted. "Is there internet service anywhere nearby?"

"Closest is in Medora, a thirty-mile drive."

A surge of hope combined with a sinking in the pit of her belly. "Can you take me there?" She knew what she had to do and it did not make it any easier. If she remembered correctly, Medora was a little town on the interstate highway.

"The library will be closed by now," Maddox said.

Katya had not realized how late it had gotten. At least she had a plan forming. The sooner she executed it, the better. She would contact her homeland via the internet and then hitch a ride as far away from the Thunder Horse Ranch as she could get. Maddox and his family did not need to assume the burden of her problems, nor did they need to be accused as accessories to the crimes someone was trying to frame her for.

"You're doing it again." His hands rose to her arms, only this time he rubbed them gently up and down. "What are you thinking?"

She could not meet his eyes. "How much you and your family have done for me, and how much I appreciate it." She could not tell him goodbye without cluing him in on her plan to escape. At least she could let him know he had done enough. "Thank you." She lifted up on her toes and kissed him.

As soon as her lips touched his, his arms closed around her, drawing her into his embrace. The kiss deepened, his tongue thrusting past her teeth to stroke hers.

Lust and longing burned through her, pressing her body closer. If the kiss could last forever, Katya would be content to let it. Reality had a different plan for her. That plan being to escape and leave Maddox behind. She realized that her plan was only half-baked, as her American classmates would have said. If she wanted to get out of this alive and without spending time in jail, she could not keep running. She had to find out who had set her up. She had to go back to Minneapolis.

A flash of fear streaked through her, making her want to press even closer to Maddox. In the short time she had known him, she had completely relied on his strength and survival skills. Going forward, she would have to do this alone.

Kat broke off the kiss and leaned her forehead against his chest. Their lives were worlds apart. She would have to go home and take on her royal responsibilities, running a country in her father's absence. Until her brother was found alive, she was the next in line for the throne. Katya sighed. As if she didn't have enough to worry about. She backed out of Maddox's reach. "This was never meant to be."

"I know."

Katya's gaze met his, unexpected tears welling in her eyes. She reminded herself that Ivanovs didn't cry.

Before they could spill over and run down her face, she turned away and made a dash for the bedroom she'd shared with Maddox earlier, closing the door between them.

Maddox stared after Kat, his lips tingling, his heart thudding against his rib cage. He hadn't planned on kissing her, but he couldn't help himself. Kissing Kat was as natural as breathing.

The sooner he got her out of his house, off his ranch and out of his life, the sooner he could return to normal.

How he could be drawn to such a woman was beyond him. Susan had been open, honest and straightforward.

Kat had lied to him every step of the way, even down to her name. She was holding back information and he'd better find out what it was before someone got hurt.

Maddox hurried toward the office, intent on calling Pierce, his brother who worked for the FBI, to see if he could dig up anything on Kat Evans or a woman fitting her description. It was a shot in the dark, but a shot worth taking if it led to information on the mysterious woman occupying entirely too much of Maddox's thoughts.

After several rings, his brother answered. "Hello."

"Pierce. Maddox here."

"Hey, brother. How's everything? You guys got hit with a pretty bad storm, didn't you?"

"Yes, we did."

"Have a chance to check on the wild horses to see how they fared?"

"Not yet."

Before Pierce joined the FBI, he'd been just as involved with tracking the wild horses as Maddox. He always asked, as if they were part of the family. To the

Thunder Horses, the horses were a part of their family, their heritage.

"Look, Pierce, I need a favor."

"Name it."

"There's this woman…"

"About time, brother. I know how broke up you were over Susan, but you need to move on. It's been over two years and you aren't getting any younger. I want to be an uncle before I'm too old to enjoy it."

"Pierce, will you shut up for just a minute and let me finish?"

"Don't get your boxers in a wad. Shoot."

"It's not like that." Maddox told him how he'd found Kat and his doubts about her name. "She says she's from Russia—that part I believe. She also said her father recently died. Maybe that will help."

"I'll look into it." Pierce paused then added, "So is she really hot?"

Oh, yeah. With hair the color of midnight, eyes so blue he could fall into them, and a body that, well… "It doesn't matter, she's in some kind of trouble. I need to know what it is before our favorite sheriff finds out."

"Gotcha. She's hot." Pierce laughed. "Give Mom a hug. I'll call as soon as I learn anything."

Maddox hung up and stared out at the sky. Darkness settled in early in the frozen northern states. The clouds had all but disappeared, leaving a crystal-clear blanket of stars scattered across the heavens. Temperatures would drop well below freezing with nothing to keep the warmer air from rising. A chill slithered across Maddox's skin.

He stared out at the night, not seeing any of it, his

mind on the stranger in his house. Who was she, and why did she have this power over him?

KAT LAY IN HER BED, dressed in the warm flannel pajamas Mrs. Thunder Horse had loaned her, wishing she were lying naked in a sleeping bag with Maddox.

She sat up, punched her pillow and flopped back down. The man had a way of monopolizing her thoughts when she should be planning her next move. For the next hour she forced herself to think about how she would get word of her survival to her cousin back in Trejikistan. Trying to board an airplane with every Transportation Security Administration staff and police element searching for her would be an impossibility. Even if she managed to board a flight bound for home, there was no way to guarantee her safety upon arrival.

She didn't have a clue what was going on back home. Access to the computer in Medora was imperative—not only to notify her contacts that she was alive, but also to glean anything she could from the news about her country and the power struggle that was surely occurring there. Knowing her cousin, Vladimir, he would have taken temporary control. Which made it all the more important that she return as soon as possible. Vladimir's approach to ruling the small nation was exactly the opposite of her father's vision of a democratic society with free elections.

Surely Vladimir would not have time to force the country to move backward into an autocratic state. All the more reason for her to contact him and let him know she had every intention of returning to rule the country and continue to implement her father's dreams of democracy for Trejikistan.

The more she thought about home, the more her heart ached. Yes, she loved her country and wanted to do right by her people. She could not abandon them to her cousin, Vladimir. Not after her father had made the promise of free elections the next year when they had everything in place and candidates identified. She hoped Vladimir wouldn't resist her claim and declare himself king.

Katya would rather not rule her country. She had been happy that her brother meant to carry on his father's work after he performed a humanitarian mission in Africa. Just two weeks before he was scheduled to return, his convoy had been ambushed. Some of his team were killed, but they never found her brother's body. Her father had been devastated, and Katya was preparing to go back to Trejikistan when she had received word that her father had been in an accident, as well.

Her mind roiled with all that happened in the past couple of weeks, her heart heavy for her losses. As the hours passed and the night wore on, exhaustion claimed her.

A sound jerked her awake. Or at least she thought it was a sound. She might have been dreaming, but she could not slow the thump of her heart against her chest. Katya's eyes opened wide and she looked around the room. Starlight shone through the gap in the curtain, allowing a narrow blue ray across the room. From her vantage point, nothing moved.

Having been followed and shot at, Katya was not leaving anything to chance. She rolled over in the bed and eased herself to the floor, using the bed as cover and concealment. If someone was in the room, she did not have much of a chance. If the noise was from outside the house, she needed to hide until the source was discovered.

After several long minutes, she ventured to the end of the bed, her gaze darting from the window to the door that connected her room to Maddox's. Should she check out the noise herself or wake Maddox and have him check it out?

Calling herself a coward, Katya chose to alert Maddox. If she investigated the strange sound alone, she had no backup, no way to alert the rest of the family should something happen to her.

Keeping low to the ground, with the bed between her and the window, she crept toward the door. As she reached for the knob, another sound penetrated the thrum of blood banging against her eardrums. Her flight instincts kicked in. She twisted the knob and dove into the room.

"What the hell?" Maddox leaped from the bed and landed in a crouched stance, his fists clenched. He stared down at her, his eyes narrowing. "Kat?"

"Shh…" She pressed a finger to her lips. "I heard something outside."

Maddox grabbed her and pulled her around to the other side of his massive bed. "Stay here."

"No. I can check on it. I just wanted you to know." She tried to get up, but he held her down.

"I know this house better than you do. Promise me you'll stay put." He waited, refusing to move until she complied.

"I promise." She did not like hiding behind the bed when Maddox might be placing himself in danger.

Instead of going to the window, he tiptoed out into

the hallway. He moved so stealthily, Katya couldn't tell which way he had gone.

All she knew was that he could be in danger, and it was all because of her.

Several long minutes passed. Katya could not hear or see anything from where she sat, and the suspense was making her crazy with worry. When she could not stand it any longer, she crept out into the hallway.

A light sprang to life in the living area and low male voices rumbled, one of them belonging to Maddox.

Katya hurried toward the sound. When she emerged into the light, Maddox and Tuck looked at her.

"You promised."

"I did stay for as long as I could. What was the sound?"

Tuck stared at her. "Someone was prowling around outside the house."

Maddox crossed his arms over his chest. "Care to enlighten us on who it might be?"

Katya's eyes widened, her cheeks burning. "How would I know? I did not go outside." What was it the Americans said? The best defense was a good offense. She hoped that was the case. She could use a good defense with Maddox glaring down at her.

How could she talk her way out of this one? She had to get to Medora tomorrow before she could escape the Thunder Horse clan. They didn't need to know any more than they already did. The more they knew, the more likely they'd be arrested for helping her.

Maddox shook his head. "Not buying it. Try the truth."

Chapter Seven

Maddox waited, anger burning inside.

The way Kat's gaze darted from Tuck and back to him didn't give him any confidence that she would tell the truth this time.

"Really." She sighed and stared at her feet. "I do not know who it was."

Anger exploded in him and Maddox grabbed her arms. "No more lies. I want the truth."

She stared up at him, her eyes an icy-blue, glistening with unshed tears. "I am telling you the truth. I do not know who is after me."

Tuck laid a hand on his shoulder. "Let her go, Maddox."

He ignored his brother, shaking his hand off. "I saved your life in that snowstorm, and you repay me by feeding me lie after lie."

"I am deeply sorry." Her gaze dropped to where his hands rested on her arms, squeezing hard. "I have no idea who was outside my window."

"You said you didn't know who was after you."

Kat stilled, refusing to look up from her feet.

"Is that why you were in the canyon? Someone was after you?"

She squared her shoulders and looked across the room, her gaze never making contact with him. "I got lost and fell into the canyon."

Maddox didn't move and didn't say anything. He'd been having romantic thoughts about this woman, something he hadn't done since Susan's death. She'd been lying to him, and he'd been stupid, knowing she lied and not caring.

He cared now. When it came to endangering his family, he didn't take kindly to a stranger's lies.

"Look, whoever it was is gone. Let's get some sleep." Tuck plucked Kat from Maddox's grip. "I'll stand watch over our guest." He turned to lead her away.

Maddox, unwilling to let go of his anger so easily, removed Tuck's hand from around Kat's waist, but didn't replace it with his own "I found her, I'm the one answering to Yost for her. I'll keep watch."

"You get all the fun stuff." Tuck shrugged. "Have it your way. I'm going to bed."

Kat didn't wait for them to settle the argument. She headed for her room.

Maddox let her go, entering his own room. Once inside, Maddox paced the floor. He hated it when he was lied to. Even worse, he hated when he still felt protective of the one who lied. How could she stand there and refuse to tell him the truth, yet still look like the victim?

And what kind of fool was he to continue to play her game? Anger pushed him through the door and into the connecting room.

Kat lay in the bed, the coverlet pulled up to her chin, her ice-blue eyes wide and wary. "What do you want?"

"The truth."

"I've told you the truth. I can't help that you don't believe me."

"You aren't telling me everything."

"I've told you what I can."

He stared at her. Even with the sheet pulled up to her chin, wearing those ridiculous flannel pajamas his mother had given her, she looked sexy.

He strode across the room and flung the blanket back.

Kat yelped and drew her knees up to her chest.

"You're coming with me." Grabbing her hand, he pulled her up and led her to his room.

She yanked her hand free and backed away from the king-sized bed. "I cannot sleep with you."

"Why not? It's not as if you haven't already."

"I know." She twisted a button on the pajama top and backed up another step. "I just can't."

"It's too late to go modest on me. Get in the bed."

"No."

Maddox scooped her in his arms and deposited her in the middle of the mattress. "You're staying where I can keep an eye on you."

She scooted across the bed to the farthest corner, glaring at him. "Barbarian."

"Keep it up, and I'll show you barbarian." He stripped his sweatpants and sweatshirt off and crawled into the bed in his boxer shorts. He rolled over to switch the light off. "I suggest you sleep. And don't try anything."

"Why? Are you going to throw me again?"

"No, but I'm about ready to turn you over to the sheriff."

She sat at the foot of the bed, her arms wrapped around her flannel-clad knees, her eyes wide, glowing in the starlight streaming in through the window. "You would do that?"

"You haven't given me any reason not to."

"Would it help if I told you it is for your own good?"

"No." He turned away, afraid that if he continued to stare at her, he'd do something stupid, like take her in his arms and make love to her. "I suspect you're in a whole lot of trouble and we've only just scratched the surface."

His body ached with the desire he fought to control. Those damn pajamas had a stronger impact on him than seeing her naked.

Kat sat for a while at the end of the bed.

Maddox feigned sleep.

Eventually, she crawled beneath the covers, keeping as far away from him as possible.

He knew she was there. His body recognized every movement. Her scent filled the air and drove him crazy with need.

Tomorrow he had to do something to get her out of his life.

KAT WOKE TO THE SUN streaming through the window, and the other side of the bed empty. She'd done something she hadn't done in a long time. She had silently cried herself to sleep. She sat up and stared across the room into the mirror hanging over the dresser.

Her hair stood on end, the masses of curls a riotous mess. Her blotchy skin and red-rimmed eyes did nothing to instill a sense of confidence in her.

The door to the bedroom opened, and Mrs. Thunder Horse entered, bearing a tray loaded with food. "Good morning." She smiled brightly and laid the tray on the dresser. "I figured that after all the fuss last night, you'd be too tired to join us at the breakfast table."

"Really, Mrs. Thunder Horse, you are not my servant. I could have come to the table."

"I rarely have guests. Please, let me spoil you a little."

"But I am not a guest. I am just one who has been foisted upon you and your family."

"In my view, that makes you a guest, and this is my chance to pull out the good china. I can't believe I slept through everything last night."

"I'm sorry there was such a fuss."

"Why should you be sorry? It's not as though you invited whoever it was to lurk around outside our house."

"Your son seems to think I did. Or at least that I invite trouble."

"Maddox tends to see only the black and white. Gray disturbs him. It's out of his control and he's uncomfortable with things he can't control."

Katya smiled at the woman. "You remind me of my mother. Thank you."

Amelia's cheeks reddened. "Oh, well then. You're quite welcome. How about some food?"

What Katya wanted most was to know where Maddox was, but she did not want to sound anxious or needy. Not when she planned to escape Maddox's protective custody as soon as the opportunity presented itself.

"Maddox is out helping Tuck feed the animals. He said to be ready when he gets back in. He'll run you to town."

And drop her off at the sheriff's office? A shiver of apprehension feathered across the back of her neck. Sheriff Yost would lock her up so tight she would never see the light of day if he knew she was a suspected terrorist. The sooner she left the county, the better off she and the Thunder Horses would be. "Do you have a pen and paper I could use?"

"Certainly." Amelia laid the tray on the bed. "I didn't know what you eat in Russia or what you like to eat in America, so I put a little of everything on your plate."

"I could not possibly eat all of that."

"I don't expect you to. Enjoy. I'll be back with your pen and paper." Amelia sailed out of the room.

Katya picked at the toast and scrambled eggs, her appetite less than healthy. The thought of leaving Maddox did not inspire her to eat. Yet she knew if she wanted to find the man who framed her, she would have to keep her strength up. With that in mind, she forced herself to finish the food and she downed the glass of orange juice.

By the time Amelia returned, she had finished eating and gotten out of bed to dress.

"Here are your clothes, dear. Now, I've got to go finish my grocery list for Maddox to pick up while you two are in town." She paused at the door. "How does baked chicken sound for supper?"

Kat almost cried again. She hated to disappoint the woman, but she had no intention of returning. "Baked chicken sounds wonderful."

Mrs. Thunder Horse beamed. "Good." The older woman left the room, a spring in her step.

She'd be making food for a guest who would not be there if Katya's plans worked out the way she hoped. She quickly dressed in the clothing Amelia had thoughtfully cleaned and returned to her room. Someday she hoped she could return all the favors this family had bestowed upon her during her stay. But for now, survival and proving her innocence took precedence.

She was just zipping her snow boots when Maddox arrived, filling the doorway.

"Ready?"

"I am." She stood, straightening her shoulders.

He didn't say anything, just turned and walked down the hallway.

Katya assumed she was to follow.

Amelia gave Maddox her list and hugged him before he pushed through the door.

She surprised Katya with an equally warm hug, which threatened to bring more tears to her eyes.

A blast of cold wind swirled in, enveloping Katya in its icy clutches. She had not been out in the cold since they'd come in from the storm. The wind chill bit into her exposed skin, sending violent shivers across her entire body. She hurried down the steps and out into the snow-covered drive where Maddox stood next to a large truck with knobby tires.

She rounded the hood to the passenger side and climbed up into the truck. The interior of the truck smelled of hay and leather. The gloves on the seat beside her explained the scent of leather. Beside it was a handheld radio.

Maddox climbed into the driver's seat and started the engine.

Tuck came down the steps of the house with a paper in his hand. "You forgot Mom's list. And I just heard from Dante. He's on his way and will be here in less than an hour."

"Good. Let him know we've headed into town. We'll see him when we get back." Maddox took the list and hit the button to close the power window and block out the blasts of cold wind filling the truck.

Katya huddled in the seat, quietly taking it all in and trying to be as invisible as she could be in the tight confines of the pickup truck.

They made the thirty-mile drive in just under an hour on the snowy roads.

When they arrived in Medora, Maddox parked in the library parking lot and got out.

"I can do this myself," Katya insisted.

"Without a driver's license, they might not let you use the internet." Maddox's dark brows rose. "Got one of those?"

"No."

Maddox led the way into the facility and proceeded to charm the librarian into letting Katya use a computer with internet access without a driver's license or passport.

As she sat in front of the computer screen, Katya wondered how she could tell Maddox to go away so that she could send her message in secrecy. He had been right to be angry with her last night. After saving her life, he should expect her to be forthcoming with the facts. But she did not want him to know anything in case the authorities interrogated him and his family. She had to have time to discover the real culprit.

Just when she opened her mouth to tell Maddox to go get the groceries his mother wanted, a cell phone rang in Maddox's pocket.

Katya jumped. "They get reception out here?"

His lips twisted into a grimace. "Sometimes." He dug in his pocket and pulled out the phone. "Excuse me." Maddox walked toward the front entrance to the library and out into the street, speaking into the receiver.

Katya breathed a sigh of relief and hoped whoever

it was would stay on the line long enough for her to get word to her people. She had spied a gas station not far from the library. A large tractor-trailer rig had been parked there, the driver filling the tank. If she hurried, she might be able to catch a ride with him, assuming he was headed for Minneapolis.

She keyed in the web address of her internet provider and brought up her email. Several of the students in her master's program had sent emails asking her where she was, and when she would have her portion of their group project done. A stab of guilt made her skip past them quickly and click on an email from her former bodyguard.

If she trusted anyone, it was Andrei Sokolov. He had protected her for most of her childhood. Since she had been gone, he had been in a state of semi-retirement, augmenting the team of bodyguards protecting her father. She had been in contact with him, exchanging emails like old friends up until two days ago. The message was short and in her native Russian. "Where are you?"

She quickly typed, "Are you there now?" Katya hit the Send button and glanced over her shoulder toward the glass front door of the library. Maddox stood with his back to her, the cell phone pressed to his ear, hunching his back against the wind.

Please be there, Andrei, please. She rubbed her fingers over the pendant her father had given her, wishing her friend would come online. She needed to communicate with someone from home.

It would be close to nine o'clock in the evening in Trejikistan. Andrei liked to go online and send emails at that time. Hopefully, the turmoil in the country had not changed that. After several long seconds, Katya realized that she'd never have time to wait for his response and still catch a ride with the trucker. She composed a brief message to let Andrei know that she was okay and that she had trouble in the States. She would contact him when she had more information and let her cousin know that she would return to Trejikistan as soon as possible.

She signed off the email, erased the computer's history and shut it down.

Katya stole a glance at the door where Maddox still stood with his back to her. Pulling the paper and pen Amelia had given her from her pocket, she dashed off a quick note of thanks to Maddox and folded the paper. She hurried to the front desk and asked the librarian to give it to Maddox when he came back in.

Then pretending that she needed to use the ladies' room, she walked toward the narrow hallway where the bathrooms were located as well as the rear exit door.

Before she could change her mind, she slipped through the back exit and out into the open. Katya hurried toward the corner of the building and peered around. The space between the library and the next building was empty. She ducked behind the next building and ran to the end. A gust of wind whipped her red scarf up into her face. Temporarily blinded by the scarf, she did not see the person behind her until too late. A gloved hand clamped over her mouth and another lifted her off her feet and ran her toward the open trunk of a car waiting in the gap between the buildings.

Kat kicked and tried to scream, but the wind carried away what little sound made it through the thick gloves. She braced her feet on the car, refusing to let the man shove her inside. Once in, she knew her chances of escaping were slim to none.

The man kicked at the backs of her knees and her legs buckled enough for him to shove her through the opening, slamming the trunk lid over her.

Darkness and the smell of tire rubber and exhaust surrounded her, filling Katya with despair.

Chapter Eight

"Yes, she has black hair and ice-blue eyes," Maddox said into the cell phone, having a hard time hearing his brother, Pierce, over the wail of the wind.

"Pretty?"

"We established that the last time we talked."

"I think you have a problem on your hands, my man."

"Tell me what I don't know." Maddox shifted the phone to the other ear. "What did you find out?"

"One Katya Ivanov, a college student, from a Russian breakaway country called Trejikistan, went missing from her apartment here in Minneapolis two days ago."

"Katya." She hadn't been lying about that part of her name and Ivanov was close to Evans. "So? Why the fuss?"

"Her picture is all over the news in Minnesota, and CNN picked up on it today."

Maddox gripped the phone hard. "What the hell did she do?"

"Bad news, brother."

As if what he'd already learned wasn't bad enough. He steeled himself for more. "What?"

"Authorities suspect her of plotting a terrorist attack based on the weapons and explosives they found in her closet. They have flyers going out to all the law enforcement agencies in Minnesota and all the surrounding states. They want to bring her in for questioning. I have my people digging into her background."

Maddox let out a long breath. "Wow. I guess that's why she didn't want to tell me anything." He shook his head, calling himself every kind of fool. "Great. I was harboring a potential terrorist."

"Not a good place to be, bro. You know I'll have to report it."

"Do that. It's what I get for saving a stranger's life."

"You can't blame yourself. You didn't know."

Maddox snorted. "I knew she was lying."

"But you didn't know about what."

Still, he hadn't followed that gut feeling, instead following lust.

"You have to bring her in."

"Where?" Maddox kept his back to the library, afraid Katya would suspect him of plotting to turn her in. "I can't turn her over to the sheriff. Yost is a sadistic bastard. He'd use this to hurt her and our family."

"If you could keep her away from Yost for the day, I could be there to take her off your hands. I have a buddy with a private pilot's license. He could get me there in as little as five hours."

"Let's do it. She already has someone following her. I'm not sure who it is, but I suspect he chased her into the canyon. I don't know how dangerous he is. You might check and see if it's one of your guys."

"Will do. I'm on my way as soon as I can secure a plane ride. Keep her close."

"Right." Maddox hit the End button, terminating the call. What was Katya doing on the internet? Sending notes to her terrorist buddies? Maddox pushed through the door and hurried across the floor.

"Sir?" As Maddox passed by the front desk, the librarian held out a folded piece of paper. "The young lady you came in with asked me to give you this."

He grabbed the paper, jammed it into his pocket and kept on walking toward the bank of computers. The seat where he'd left Kat was empty, the computer screen blank.

Great. Just great. She'd ducked out on him. Maddox ran through the shelves of books, searching for a back door, finding it in the aisle with the bathrooms. She had to have gone out this way. She hadn't come through the front.

As he ran out the back, he looked left then right. A man struggled at the back of a dark blue car and finally slammed the trunk. Before the lid closed, Maddox could see a flash of red scarf and coal-black curly hair. He heard a female cry for help.

"Kat!" Maddox ran toward the car.

The man jumped into the driver's seat before Maddox could get close enough to stop him.

The car pulled away as Maddox reached it, only giving him enough time to slam his hand against the metal doorframe before the vehicle skidded out into the street and headed south out of town.

Maddox yanked his cell phone from his pocket and punched in the number for Dante. He didn't wait for an answer, sprinting out onto the main road and back to the library where his truck was parked. Dante's number went directly to an answering machine. Damn reception!

He tried his house. Maybe Dante had already arrived there.

After the second ring, Dante answered. "I just landed at the ranch. Where are you and your hot foreign number?"

"Crank up your bird and get over to Medora ASAP!"

"What's going on?"

"Someone just snatched Kat. They're headed south out of town in a dark blue, four-door sedan."

"How do you know he snatched her and she didn't go willingly?"

Maddox climbed in behind the wheel of his truck, flipped the ignition and yanked the gearshift into reverse. "She was thrown in the trunk. Can you hurry? And bring the handheld radio. Cell reception is nil once you leave town."

"On it. I'll bring Tuck with me. We'll see you in a few."

Maddox flung the phone onto the seat next to him and slammed his foot down on the accelerator. The truck shot forward, the back end fishtailing on the ice.

By the time Maddox had his truck on the road, the car carrying Kat was long gone. He hoped and prayed that the kidnapper didn't turn off the main highway onto one of the side roads.

Kat must have slipped out the back door of the library and run into trouble outside. Her attacker couldn't have grabbed her from inside the building without raising a ruckus and alerting the library staff.

Maddox pounded his palm against the steering wheel. How had he let this happen? He'd only been away from her for a few minutes, talking to his brother. Hell, why did he even care?

Kat hadn't planned on sticking around. That had to be why she'd convinced him to come to town. To make contact with her people.

Really. Why did he care? She'd lied to him, tried to ditch him and could be a terrorist. Why was he so concerned that someone had kidnapped her?

An image of her lying naked in his arms, the soft glow of the flashlight shining in her eyes and on her hair came to mind. His groin tightened and his foot pressed the gas pedal to the floor.

She'd reawakened him, reminding him what it was like to allow himself to care again. The least she could do was live long enough to tell him the truth. Had making love to him been a means to an end? Had she only given herself to sucker him into protecting her?

Kat had dragged Maddox from the fog of the emotionless existence he'd buried himself in for the past two years. An existence in which he refused to care about anyone who wasn't family. Maddox now warred with the full spectrum of emotions. Anger, betrayal, fear and...*oh, please, no*...the potential to love again.

Hadn't he been better off emotion-free?

Ten miles outside Medora, Maddox worried that he'd gone in the wrong direction. He hadn't seen the car, even on the long, straight, flat stretches of road. Had the kidnapper gotten that far ahead or had he taken a side road Maddox missed?

Overhead the loud rumble of an aircraft engine and the telltale thumping of rotary blades made Maddox let out the breath he held. The green-and-white CBP helicopter blew past him, following the ribbon of highway.

Several miles ahead, the helicopter slowed and appeared to be hovering or moving very slowly.

The handheld radio buzzed on the seat next to him. He grabbed it and hit the Talk button.

"Hey, it's Tuck. We just passed you and found a dark blue four-door car ahead on the highway." The radio crackled, static blasting in his ear, but Maddox held on to it like a lifeline.

"That's it," he shouted.

"Two miles ahead over the next rise. He's going pretty fast."

"Can you slow him down or stop him?"

"How? You want Dante to land on him? He's already in enough trouble taking the chopper out on non–Border Patrol business."

"Never mind." Maddox pushed his truck past the safe driving speed for icy roads. "Just keep him in sight until I catch up."

"Then what? If we force him off the road, he might crash." The static increased, filling Maddox's ear.

Maddox's chest tightened. No matter how many lies Kat had told him, she didn't deserve to be kidnapped or to die in the trunk of a car.

"We'll figure it out when I get closer." Maddox stuffed the radio into his pocket. As his truck closed in on the helicopter's position, the dark blue sedan came into view.

The man drove like a lunatic with a death wish, spewing snow and ice behind his tires. He slowed and turned off the main road into an area Maddox knew to be filled with ravines and canyons dropping off the sides of the road. If they didn't stop him soon, he could easily slip off the road and crash down a sheer drop.

Dante's helicopter dipped low over the car as Maddox caught up.

The car hit a bump of ice on the poorly maintained road. The wheels jerked to the right, launching the car up a ramp of snow, pitching it over the edge of the road and down into a steep ravine.

Maddox's heart skipped several beats before kicking into an adrenaline-pumping machine. He forced himself to slow gradually on the snow and ice until he could come to a complete and safe halt at the point where the car disappeared off the edge of the road.

Slamming the gearshift into Park, Maddox dropped down out of the truck and ran to the road's edge. Far below in the bottom of a deep crevice, the sedan lay on the passenger side, its front wheels still spinning.

Panic threatened to paralyze Maddox. He pictured Susan lying lifeless in his arms. He couldn't and wouldn't let that happen to Kat. He leaped over the edge and scrambled down the hill toward the mangled vehicle, his breath hung in his throat, his legs shaky and threatening to buckle with each step.

She couldn't be dead. Not Kat. She had too much determination to survive.

A shot rang out, the bullet pinging off the rocks next to Maddox's feet. He threw himself behind a large outcropping of boulders, knowing the trip down the ravine made him an ideal target for someone below. More shots hit the rocks and dirt behind him.

He glanced toward the sky. As if on cue, the helicopter flew over with Tuck leaning out the door, a rifle in his hand, firing at the kidnapper.

The overwhelming rumble of the helicopter was all that Maddox could hear. Soon the chopper eased farther away, following the flow of the ravine down into a small canyon.

With the helicopter noise gone, the sounds of gunfire had ceased. Maddox couldn't see a shooter. He had to assume Tuck's cover fire had chased him off.

Kat could be injured in the trunk, maybe bleeding.

Unable to wait a moment longer, Maddox abandoned the relative safety of the boulder and continued his descent.

As though moving in slow motion, he slipped and slid on snow, ice and rocks, until he landed beside the vehicle.

With the car lying on its side, the undercarriage facing him, Maddox couldn't see inside. No one had shot at him on his trek down the hill, but that didn't mean the guy wasn't hiding, waiting for his chance to nail an easy target.

Maddox eased up the undercarriage of the overturned vehicle and peered down into the interior. Nothing moved. The driver's window was gone, shards of glass scattered all over the seats.

"Kat!" Maddox said, loudly enough so she could hear him, but hopefully not so loud that the shooter could zero in on him.

"Maddox?" Kat's muffled voice sounded from the rear of the vehicle. "I cannot get out. Find the key."

Still up on the side of the car, Maddox felt around the steering column until he found the keys. He yanked them from the ignition, pushed backward and dropped to the ground, glancing around for signs of the shooter.

When he moved around to the back of the car, he groaned. The trunk lay wedged against a huge boulder. Even with the key, he couldn't get the trunk open.

"Hang on, Kat. I'm going to need more help."

"Hurry!"

324   *Hostage to Thunder Horse*

Maddox pulled the handheld radio from his pocket and hit the Talk button, praying the helicopter was in range. "Where are you guys?"

"Following your sedan driver. He disappeared into the canyon."

"Leave him. I need your help here." Maddox explained the position of the car and what he needed to get Kat out.

The helicopter rumbled into sight and hovered over Maddox.

Tuck appeared in the door, leaned out and latched a cable to the skid, dropping the coil of cable down below the helicopter.

Dante eased the helicopter above where Maddox stood, the cable dangling closer and closer until Maddox could grab the hook and direct it toward the undercarriage.

He hooked the cable on the car and waved up at Dante.

Tuck, rifle in hand, scanned the terrain below the helicopter.

Maddox climbed up the hill and to one side of where the car rested. "Hang on, Kat! The ride's going to get bumpy again."

Maddox waved to Tuck. Tuck leaned into the helicopter.

The cable tightened, the helicopter straining against the weight of the vehicle.

Maddox held his breath, hoping that by righting the car it wouldn't slip farther down the ravine.

Metal scraped and groaned and the car teetered, swaying toward the helicopter. Gravity kicked in and the car dropped toward the ground, tugging hard on the cable.

The helicopter dropped a couple feet before it steadied and hovered low enough for the cable to hang loosely.

Maddox unhooked the cable from the undercarriage of the car and waved at Tuck who gathered his end and reeled the cable back up into the chopper.

The helicopter lifted higher into the sky and circled back toward where the attacker had disappeared.

"Kat?" Maddox slipped and slid down the rocky hillside to the back of the car and stopped.

"Surprisingly, I am still here," she said through the metal of the trunk.

Maddox fitted the key in the lock and twisted. Dented and battered, the lid didn't budge. He fit his fingers beneath the edges and lifted hard, throwing his back into freeing Kat.

Metal scraped against metal and the trunk sprang open.

Kat blinked up at him, her face bruised, her hair tangled and matted with blood from a gash on her forehead, but she was as beautiful as ever.

Maddox reached for her, pulling her out of the trunk and into his arms.

Kat clung to him, her body shaking, speaking in a language he couldn't understand, her words coming fast and furious.

He tipped her face up to his and stared down into icy-blue eyes awash in tears. Then his mouth crashed down over hers with the force of his anger, his desperation and his fear. He couldn't stop the flood of emotion he experienced whenever he was around her, and he hated himself for his lack of control.

Her hands circled behind his neck and if it was possible, she drew him closer, kissing him back as if they were the last man and woman on earth.

When he came up for air, Maddox pushed aside the intense relief and allowed his anger to resurface. "When we get back to the ranch, you're going to tell me everything. Do you understand? Especially what the hell you were planning to do with the guns and explosives."

Chapter Nine

Katya sat in a straight-backed chair in the Thunder Horse living room as Amelia cleaned the blood off her forehead using a damp cloth. Tumbling down a hill in the trunk of a car had taken its toll on her and she had the lumps and bruises to show for it.

As Amelia worked her magic, Maddox paced the floor in front of her, finally coming to a halt. "That's good, Mom. She can do the rest later."

Amelia Thunder Horse shot a narrow-eyed glare at her son. "Don't you think she's been through enough?"

Maddox crossed his arms over his chest and shook his head, his lips pressed into a thin line. "We haven't even begun."

Undeterred, Maddox's mother dabbed antibiotic ointment on the gash, plastered a bandage over it and stepped back. "She could have a concussion. She really needs to see a doctor."

Katya shook her head, a blast of fear racing through her veins. "No."

Maddox's mouth twisted. "Care to tell my mother why you don't want to see a doctor?"

The harshness of Maddox's gaze sent a chilling wash of despair over Katya, making her feel colder than if she'd been lying beside the river in a bank of snow. For a brief moment she'd allowed herself to rely on Maddox to protect her. But that was over. She squared her shoulders and lifted her chin the way her father taught her when facing her adversaries. "What do you know?"

"That you've been lying to us all along. Your name is Katya Ivanov, you were a student in Minneapolis and you're a terrorist."

Amelia gasped. "Maddox!"

"What?" Maddox pinned Katya with his stare. "It's true, isn't it?"

Katya winced, at once relieved and concerned that he still didn't know the whole picture. What he did know was bad enough. She drew in a deep breath and let it out. "Part of what you just said is true."

Maddox's eyes blazed and he stalked across the wood floor to stand in front of her, trapping her in the chair. He leaned over her, bracing his hands on the chair's arms. "The part about lying to us? Or the part about being a terrorist?"

Katya leaned back in order to look directly up into Maddox's eyes. She held his gaze, determined to give as good as she got. All the while her heart pounded in her chest, her breath catching in her throat at his nearness. "My name and the part about being a student in Minneapolis."

"What are you talking about, Maddox?" Amelia touched her son's arm. "Katya isn't a terrorist."

"Evidence indicates otherwise." He directed his words at Katya. "Doesn't it?"

Anger bubbled up inside Katya. She had been through hell and she was damn tired of it. "Not everything is as it appears. And if you would give me a chance, I will explain."

"You've had more chances than I can count to explain yourself, to tell the truth, but you didn't."

"I did not want to get you and your family involved in my troubles."

"Hate to tell you, darlin', but we already are." Maddox pushed away from the chair and towered over her. "Since we're about as deeply involved as we can get by harboring a terrorist, maybe you can enlighten us."

Katya stood, placing herself toe-to-toe with Maddox. "I came to the United States to go to school, not to blow it up. The weapons they found in my apartment are not mine. Someone set me up. You have to believe me."

"Why? You've lied to me from the beginning."

"I had to." She looked around the room at the faces of Maddox's family. "When I woke up in that cave, I did not know who you were. I do not know who has been following me or why, but he tried to kill me."

"And you thought I might be him?"

Katya shrugged. "I didn't know. I was unconscious when you found me."

"So you slept with the enemy, just in case?"

Katya's face burned, anger making her pulse race with the need to strike back. Dammit, she was the victim, not the villain. "That is correct. Keep your friends close and your enemies closer." She turned to the others in the room, avoiding Maddox. "I am not a monster bent on destroying your country. I am a student who has been targeted by someone, for what reason I do not know." She had her suspicions, but she was not sharing them until she knew for certain. "Go back to the canyon and find the snowmobile. You will see the proof."

"Proof that I was a fool to believe you in the first place?" Maddox ground out, no pity in his gaze for the woman he'd rescued.

Katya swayed, her head throbbing. "Proof that whoever is after me is shooting real bullets."

Amelia gasped, hurrying over to Katya. "Maddox, you've bullied her enough. Let the child lie down. She's been shot at, almost frozen to death and now she's been in a car wreck. I'm surprised she's still on her feet."

"She still hasn't told us why the weapons were in her apartment." His brows rose. "Why, Kat—Katya— or whoever you are?"

"I do not know! I am a student and a citizen of Trejik- istan, not a terrorist."

Maddox crossed his arms over his chest, his jaw taut, but for a muscle twitching in the side. "Give me one reason why I shouldn't turn you over to the authorities right now?"

"I'll give you one." Tuck grinned. "Yost is the only *authority* in the neighborhood. I wouldn't turn over a rabid dog to that man."

"Tuck!" Amelia admonished. "Sheriff Yost is an of- ficer of the law."

Tuck snorted. "Maybe he should pay more atten- tion to the law."

"Turning her over to Yost will only make it bad on you, Maddox," Maddox's brother, Dante, said. "He won't wait to get the truth."

Tuck shook his head. "The man wouldn't know the truth if it bit him in the—"

"Tuck!" Amelia planted her hands on her hips. "What would your father say?"

Maddox's gaze shifted from Katya to his mother, his expression softening. "A lot more if he were still here."

"But he's not. And we have to carry on." Amelia sighed. "Why are you all so down on Sheriff Yost? He's been nothing but good to me since your father's death."

Tuck crossed to his mother and draped an arm over her shoulders. "We don't trust him, Mom." When she opened her mouth to argue, Tuck held up a hand. "Don't ask why, we just don't."

Dante stood. "Which comes back to our little problem here."

Katya's lips twisted into a grimace. "By 'problem' I assume you mean me."

Maddox nodded, the frown a permanent fixture on his forehead since they'd returned to the Thunder Horse Ranch.

She sighed, her shoulders drooping with the weight of fatigue and defeat. "I did not put those weapons in my apartment. Someone else did. And I do not know why."

Dante stood with his arms crossed over his chest. "The question is what to do with her until we have an answer. I could turn her in to Customs and Border Patrol as an illegal alien."

Maddox didn't respond.

Katya held her breath. If they turned her over to the police or CBP, she might never learn the truth and be punished for a crime she had not committed.

Tuck moved to the window and peered out. "You'd better figure out the solution quick. Our favorite sheriff just drove up."

"He's here to take me to lunch." Amelia hurried toward the door. "Relax. I'll take care of the sheriff. Maddox, you take care of Katya. Go out the back, I'll keep him inside long enough for you both to escape."

While Amelia hurried toward the door, Maddox stared across at Kat. "What's it going to be? Come with me, go with the Border Patrol or go with the sheriff?"

She shrugged. "You have to do what you feel is right. If you are so certain that I am a terrorist, you should turn me over to the law. If it makes it any easier, I'll go now." She took two steps in the direction Amelia had gone before Maddox blocked her path.

"No." He pushed his hand through his long hair and sighed. "I don't know who you are or what your game is, but for now, you'll come with me."

"Where?" she demanded.

"I don't know. But you're my problem until I can figure this mess out. Get your coat and gloves. It'll be cold outside."

Railroaded into agreeing, Katya went for her outdoor gear, gathering her coat, gloves and scarf while Maddox spoke quietly with his brothers.

Katya could hear his mother talking to the sheriff and the sheriff's answering murmur. Her pulse quickened, fear pushing her forward despite how tired she was and how much her head hurt.

When she emerged from the bedroom, Maddox met her, outfitted in a heavy winter coat, carrying gloves and a bag. He marched Katya through the house, urging her to silence with a finger pressed to his lips.

At the back door, she paused. "I'm sorry I brought you and your family into this."

"No more so than I am." He held the door open and a blast of frigid air blew in.

Katya shrugged into her coat and gloves and stepped

out onto the porch. "If you could get me to the interstate, I could leave you and your family in peace."

"You're not going anywhere until we figure out exactly what trouble you're in."

"But you don't have to help me." She stared up into his eyes.

"I'm not. I'm helping myself and my family." His lips thinned into a tight line and he gazed down at her. "If you are a terrorist, we are all guilty of harboring you. I don't plan on my family going to jail because I was fool enough to rescue a stranger."

"You could let me go and claim that I escaped," she offered.

"Or you could be my hostage and I'll turn you over to the police when I know for certain that you are a terrorist."

"And how will you know that?"

"I don't know yet." Maddox pulled the hood of his parka up over his head and slid his hands into the gloves. "For now, you'll stick with me."

She opened her mouth to disagree, but he cut her off with a raised hand.

"No argument." He grabbed her elbow in his hand and ushered her off the porch and across the snow-covered yard toward the barn.

Once inside, he bypassed the horses and headed for the two snowmobiles parked in an empty stall. He laid the bag on the back of one snowmobile, securing it with flexible cords.

Katya shivered. The cool air had nothing to do with the chill spiraling down her spine. The last time she'd been on a snowmobile, she'd almost lost her life. That and the amount of animosity radiating from Maddox made her want to run away as far as she could get. From warm, caring rescuer to tall, cold stranger, filled with nothing but anger and accusations. He was breaking her heart.

How? How could a man—practically a stranger—have such a hold on her emotions? Was it some psychological attraction she felt for him because he had rescued her? It had to be.

It could not be because he was so tall, strong and earthy, the exact opposite of the men she was used to. Or that he accepted the risk of rescuing her, placing his own life in danger. And he had rescued her again when she had been kidnapped.

"Rescuing me is becoming a habit for you, isn't it?" she stated, more to herself than to him.

Maddox shot a glance her way and, without responding, walked to the opposite end of the barn and flung open the back door. A gust of wind whipped through the barn, carrying with it a spray of snow. Then he climbed onto one of the machines and cranked the engine, backed it out of the stall and drove it through the door. "Hop on."

She crossed the interior of the barn, pulling the collar of her jacket up around her neck. "Shouldn't I ride on another?"

"No. I don't trust you on your own." He dismounted and closed the barn door behind her, before resuming his seat on the machine.

"I see." Katya stood, anxiety and something else burning low in her gut. "What if I don't want to ride with you?"

"Tough."

She could not imagine riding behind Maddox, her arms wrapped around him. "And if I refuse?"

"If you refuse to come with me, I'm sure Sheriff Yost would love to add you to the scalps on his belt." His brows raised. "What's it going to be?"

Knowing there was only one answer to his question did not make it any easier for her to give in. She was not known for her easy acceptance of any awkward situation. Her father had called her stubborn. But the choice was clear. She couldn't go with Yost or she would be thrown in jail, no one the wiser for who had actually planted the weapons in her apartment.

If she was to be Maddox's hostage, she had to convince him to help her find the real terrorist—the one who wanted her dead or at least so buried in the penal system that she couldn't get out to go home to Trejiki-stan. If she could not convince Maddox to help her, she had to find a way to escape from him and get back to Minneapolis to get answers to this mess on her own.

Katya slung her leg over the backseat of the snowmobile, keeping as far away as she could from actually touching Maddox. She could not risk letting her guard down with him. He did not trust her and because of that, she could not trust him. With what seemed like an entire country on the lookout for her as a suspected terrorist, she did not see how she would find the real culprit without help. But she would manage, or die trying.

Maddox revved the engine and shot out of the barnyard, careful to keep the barn between him and the ranch house for as long as possible, thus lessening the chance of being seen or heard until they were too far away for the sheriff to give chase in his pickup.

At first Katya refused to hold on to him, but as they

bumped across the drifts of snow, she was nearly un-seated several times and finally grabbed him around the waist, holding on as tightly as she could.

A certain sense of justice filled Maddox, along with a rising need to feel her body against his. She'd been a mystery to him from the first time he'd laid eyes on that damn red scarf blowing in the wind. And nothing she'd said or done had cleared up the mystery surrounding her since. He'd be damned if he let her go until he figured her out. If that meant holding her hostage until she came clean, so be it.

They sped across the expanse of snowy terrain, putting as much distance as possible between them and the sheriff.

"Where are we going?" Kat yelled over the roar of the snowmobile engine.

He didn't answer, letting her guess, as she'd had him guessing since they'd met. That little bit of payback did nothing to settle the thrumming in his veins, the adrenaline kick he couldn't set aside in anticipation of their destination.

An hour later, fingers cold and Kat clinging to him to keep warm, Maddox pulled up to a small log cabin out in the middle of the frozen tundra. He parked the snowmobile behind the cabin in a lean-to built for that very purpose.

"What is this place?" Katya stood, stretching stiffly, tucking her hands beneath her armpits for warmth.

"The family hunting cabin. We come out here during the fall and stay for a week."

"Why here?" She looked back the way they came.

"Hard to find and harder to get to if you don't know where you're going."

The logs were old and weathered a dull gray, the door made of planks held in place by a combination lock. Maddox removed a glove and tumbled the combination, twisting it left then right until it fell open. He removed the lock and opened the door.

The inside was as gray as the outside, only darker. A small table, one rickety chair and a rough-hewn bed made of carved wood posts with rope strung across was the extent of the furniture. A fireplace, lined with river rock, filled one end of the cabin. Next to it was a footlocker, which could be used as a second chair.

Maddox tossed the bundle he'd brought onto the bed. "There's canned food in the footlocker. See what you can find while I bring in the firewood."

When she didn't move, he stared across the floor. "You do know how to cook, don't you?"

"Yes, yes. Of course I do." Katya hurried toward the box on the floor and lifted the lid.

Once outside, Maddox collected logs. Being alone in the cabin with Katya brought back way too many memories of their night in the cave, memories best left in cold storage. The more time he spent alone with her, the less he was able to rein in his libido. The woman was hot, in or out of all the winter clothing. And one bed between them spelled trouble. Thank goodness they wouldn't be there the entire night.

Grateful that his family kept the cabin stocked, Maddox carried a full load of wood inside and laid it by the fireplace.

Still wearing her coat, and blowing steam as she breathed in and out, Katya had opened a can of beans with the manual can opener they kept in the footlocker.

Beside it was the pot they would hang over the fireplace to heat their food.

"See, I'm not completely useless. But I do need to relieve myself. Are there any facilities I can make use of?"

Maddox glanced over at her, attributing her inability to make eye contact to her embarrassment over asking about a bathroom. "There is an outhouse behind the cabin."

Her brows furrowed.

"An outhouse is an outdoor bathroom. It's either that or expose yourself to nature and the biting wind."

"I'll risk the outhouse." Her forehead smoothed. "Thank you for everything, Maddox." With that, she turned and left the cabin.

Something about the way her last statement came across didn't sit right with Maddox. He tossed the kindling he held into the fireplace and straightened. As he did, a distinct rasp of metal on metal was accompanied by a sharp click.

In the back of his mind, Maddox knew it wouldn't be there, yet he looked at the table where he'd laid the combination lock when he'd come into the cabin the first time. The table was empty.

"Katya!" Maddox raced for the door and shoved the bolt to the side. When he pushed on the door, it remained closed. "Dammit, woman, unlock the door!"

"I will not let you be held responsible for my predicament. This way they will know that I tricked you."

Maddox dragged in a deep breath and let it out, counting to ten at the same time. In as calm a voice as he could manage with anger and panic warring within him, he said, "Katya, don't do this. It's almost dark. You'll get lost on the prairie."

"It is a chance I have to take to keep you and your family out of trouble with the law." She paused. "I won't forget you, Maddox. Thank you for helping me when I needed it most. Thank you for...everything."

His heart pounding in his ears, Maddox hit the door, hard. The metal latch held.

"Katya!"

Chapter Ten

The cabin door shook with the force of Maddox slamming against it.

Katya jumped away, afraid the metal latch wouldn't hold under the force of his weight and anger.

Her heart thundering, she raced around the cabin to the lean-to in the rear. She hoped Maddox had left the keys in the ignition of the snowmobile. Without them her attempt to escape would be hopeless. An hour away from the ranch house, she could not possibly make it back to a highway to hitch a ride before nightfall. As it was, darkness descended on North Dakota early in the winter, making it difficult to see in the shadows of the overhang. To add to her dilemma, clouds covered the sky, negating any possibility of starlight to navigate by.

"Katya!" Maddox's angry cries thundered through the solid log walls.

Katya straddled the snowmobile and ran her fingers across the controls, searching in the dark for a key or starter switch.

As her hands closed around the key, a great crash sounded behind her.

With her breath lodged in her throat, Katya turned

the key and the engine revved to life. She jammed the gearshift into Reverse and backed out of the shed.

Once clear, she shifted into Drive. As she twisted the handle, giving the engine a quick burst of fuel, something heavy landed on the back of the machine, arms closing around her waist.

She screamed, her hand letting go of the throttle.

Maddox's arms circled her waist and yanked her off the seat and into a pile of snow.

She landed with a jolt on top of Maddox. He held tight, taking the brunt of the landing.

The snowmobile slid to a stop, the engine humming, but the machine motionless with no gas to power the tracks.

"Let go!" she yelled. "This is the only way to keep you safe."

"No way. Not until I know everything."

"How can you know everything when I don't even know it?" She struggled, kicking and flailing like a turtle on its back, unable to gain purchase.

"Will you be still?" Maddox grunted.

"No! I need to get out of here. I have to find out who is doing this to me."

"Be still, dammit!" He shoved her off him, letting go for just a moment.

Taking her only chance left, Katya leaped to her feet and ran for the snowmobile.

Before she had gone two steps, Maddox tackled her, taking her down in one inglorious heap, face-first in the snow. The wind knocked out of her, she could not move or fight him off. He flipped her over and straddled her hips, pinning her hands over her head in the snow.

"No. More. Running," he said through gritted teeth, glaring down at her.

Katya stared up into his eyes. Completely immobile, captured by her rescuer and powerless to escape. He outweighed her and could easily fend off any attempt she made at fighting him. Defeated, she gave in, hopelessly hostage to the way he made her feel. "I never meant for this to happen."

The lines across his forehead eased, his gaze shifting from her eyes to her lips. "Neither did I." Then he was kissing her, his lips slanting across hers, his tongue pushing past her teeth to twist and taste, thrusting past her defenses.

Determined to remain immune to him, Katya felt her resolve dissolve under his savage onslaught. She couldn't feel the cold snow on her backside for the heat burning within. She couldn't fight him…she didn't want to. This was where she'd wanted to be since their first night together in the cave.

When he lifted his face, she gathered air into her lungs and made one last attempt at reason. "You should not get involved with me."

"I know." He smoothed a tendril of hair out of her face. "And yet I can't help myself." His gaze broke contact with hers and he stared around at the snow as though just becoming aware of his surroundings. "Come on, it's getting cold." He climbed to his feet and extended a hand to her.

She laid her gloved hand in his and he pulled her up against his chest.

With his arm like an iron band around her waist, he stared down into her eyes, his gaze fiercely determined. "Promise me that you won't try to run again?"

"Being with me puts you in danger."

"*Kitala igmu taka,* little lion." His jaw tightened. "Promise."

After the past couple days on the run, alone and without anyone to call for help, Katya couldn't resist Maddox's strength. "I cannot continue to rely on you to protect me. You have your own life, and getting involved with me could ruin it."

"Let me worry about that." His gaze never wavered from hers.

Katya sighed, leaning her forehead into his chest. "I promise."

For a brief moment, his arm tightened, then he moving her away from him. "I'll take care of the snowmobile."

Without his arms around her, the cold crept beneath her jacket, making her shiver. As Maddox climbed aboard the still-humming machine, Katya looked on with a mix of regret and relief. Finding her way across the frozen North Dakota Badlands in the dark had been a foolish idea, one born of desperation and panic.

Maddox spun the snowmobile around and parked it beneath the lean-to, purposely pulling the keys from the ignition and dangling them for her to see before he tucked them into his pocket. He led her to the front of the cabin and stepped inside.

Katya entered the cabin, noting the splintered latch where the lock had been until Maddox busted through. "I am sorry about the lock."

"It can be fixed." He knelt by the fireplace, arranging the kindling and then striking a long wooden match across the stones. Before long a small fire burned, casting an intimate glow in the tiny cabin.

She turned away, forcing herself to think, to reason away the yearning she could not seem to deny. Ever since her mother died, she had taken on the role of hostess for thousands of diplomatic dinners and meetings, all the while longing for the freedom to be herself, to be alone with only one man. A man of her choosing.

A smile curved her lips. Funny how this man had not been of her choosing. The situation had chosen him for her. Yet she could think of no other she would rather be stranded with on a windswept prairie.

Heat spread through the cabin and pulsed throughout her body, carried by a rapidly increasing heartbeat.

How could she keep her distance from Maddox Thunder Horse, the tall, dark Native American hero who'd saved her from death not once, but twice? Despite her determination to keep her distance, Katya glanced toward him.

His back to her, he was staring down into the fire. His presence filled the room, broad shoulders blocking the light cast by the fire, silhouetted with the blaze bright between his spread legs.

He unzipped his jacket and tugged it from his shoulders.

Katya caught her breath as his muscles flexed beneath the stretchy cotton of the long-sleeved shirt he wore. Her fingers tingled at the memory of his smooth, dark chest beneath her hands, the way his skin tasted on her lips. That moist place between her thighs throbbed, achingly aware of his every movement.

When he turned toward her, she could not drag her gaze from his, could not hide what could only be longing shining from her eyes.

Maddox stared across the cabin at Katya. The faint

glow of the fire reflected in her ice-blue eyes and gave her black hair a soft shine, highlighting the waves. Even bundled in her winter coat, the woman held herself like a queen—regal, elegant and yet fragile in the sparse surroundings of the hunting cabin.

Every fiber of Maddox's being cried out to protect this small woman—from the ravages of the weather to the violence of the man determined to abduct her.

When she'd locked him in the cabin, panic catapulted his anger, pushing adrenaline through his veins like pressurized steam. Every possible scenario that could happen to her erupted in his mind, none with a good outcome. First and foremost was Katya lost in the Badlands, only to be found too late to help, her frozen face staring up at him. Her image merged with his memory of Susan.

"What do we do now?" she asked, her voice a hushed whisper in the confines of the tiny cabin.

Maddox could think of a lot of things they could do to pass the time. But he didn't want to scare her or take advantage of her after her tumble in the back of the wrecked car. "You could start by telling me everything you've been hiding from me."

"You already know I've been framed."

"Why?"

"I don't know." Katya turned away.

Maddox closed the distance between them. "I think you do." His arms circled her waist and he drew her back against his front. "Tell me."

At first she remained stiff in his arms. After a long moment, she leaned into him. "My father was…" she hesitated, then continued "…an important political figure in Trejikistan, my homeland, formerly part of Russia. I received word two weeks ago that he was involved in an accident. There was no accident. He was murdered, and I think the people who murdered him are after me."

"But why set you up as a terrorist?"

"So that if they do not manage to kill me, I could never return to Trejikistan and carry on my father's legacy."

"I thought you were just a student."

"I am… I was, until my father's death. I just wanted to have a normal life, to blend in and be a student, not a political figure with an entourage of paparazzi following me around the rest of my life. I wanted to be me." Her voice dropped to a whisper on the last word.

Maddox turned her in his arms.

She gave little resistance, laying her cheek against his shirt, her fingers curling into the fabric. "Just me."

He tilted her chin and looked down into her eyes, amazed at how brave she'd been under the circumstances. No matter how badly he wanted to push her away and believe the worst, he couldn't. He might be the biggest fool ever, but he wanted to believe her story.

"I'm tired of crying," she said, looking up into his face. "And I'm tired of running." Her chin hardened, her lips pressing into a thin line. "If you want to help me—and I am not asking you to—I need to get back to Minneapolis and find out who planted those weapons in my apartment."

"Are you sure you want to go back where you're probably on everyone's watch list?"

"I have to." Her gaze raked his face. "Do you not see? If I do not, the police will crucify me. I am a foreigner. The media will try to convict me without bothering to get their facts straight. I will never be able to go home again." Her hands clenched in the fabric of his shirt. "My father's death will remain an *accident* while a killer runs loose out there. Whoever did this will win."

For a long moment, Maddox stared down into those bottomless blue eyes. "If I agree to help you, will you agree to do it my way?"

Her brows dipped slightly. "You know you will be labeled an accessory to whatever crime they pin on me. Are you willing to take that risk?"

He nodded. "You didn't answer my question."

The frown furrowing her brow lifted. "I will do it your way."

"Good." Maddox still held her in his arms. "That wasn't so hard, was it?"

Katya sighed. "I still do not like that you are involved."

"I made that decision, not you." He brushed a lock of raven-black hair from her forehead. "Get over it."

"I am finding it very difficult to get over it as far as you are concerned." Her eyelids drooped, the long, lush lashes shadowing her pale irises. When her tongue swept across her full dusky-rose lips, Maddox couldn't hold back.

He had to taste her, touch her lips with his own. His fingers rose to cup the back of her head, lacing through the long, luxurious layers of hair. When his mouth descended onto hers, he took her slowly in a deliberate kiss, one meant to explore, discover and learn everything there was to know about this woman in his arms. He knew so little about her, and he longed to know more. From her favorite color to the name of her first pet, to the places on her body that made her crazy with desire.

Maddox's groin tightened and he pulled away. He wanted her so badly he was afraid it would cloud his judgment.

Katya's arms circled his neck and drew him back down to her mouth. "Is this part of doing it your way?" She pressed her lips to his. "Because if it is, I will agree to more of this—no argument."

A chuckle rose up his throat and he kissed her hard, before setting her away from him. "You aren't obligated to kiss me."

Her brows winged upward. "Do you think I kissed you out of obligation?" She unzipped her jacket and let it fall to the floor. "My reactions to you have never been those of one who feels obligated." She closed the short distance between them. "More a sense of the inevitable." She stared up at him. "Do you kiss me out of obligation?"

Maddox snorted. "No." His gaze captured her stormy one, his pulse racing, his hands aching to take her back into his arms, but he refused to make the first move this time. If she wanted what he wanted, she'd have to tell him. Taking her, making love to her in this tiny cabin might be the biggest mistake of his life. This woman could be a master spy, a consummate liar, a terrorist, for all he really knew about her. But if she took him into her arms and kissed him, she would have conquered him completely, undermined his ability to resist.

Katya's gaze retained its hold on his. "My father never let me be with men he deemed unsuitable. He kept a very tight rein on my activities, not that I would disappoint him in any way."

"And your father would deem me unsuitable."

She curled her fingers around the hem of her sweater and pulled it up and over her head, tossing it onto the table. "Probably. You do not provide any political value to the equation. You are not from Trejikistan or one of its neighboring countries." She unzipped the snowpants she'd borrowed from his mother and slid them down her legs. "You do not own a fleet of ships or oil wells." Her fingers tugged the button loose on the jeans she wore beneath, flicking it open.

His breath caught and lodged in his throat as her jeans followed the snowpants to the floor.

"You do not have any major political connections. You would be unworthy of my affiliation." Katya strode across the floor, wearing nothing but a black lace bra, panties and the pendant she fingered now.

Maddox's heart fluttered, the ache intensifying in his groin. "You know how to build a man up, don't you?" She didn't have to say a word to make him hot.

"I did not say that I agreed with my father." She stopped in front of him and ran her fingers down his chest to the button of his snowpants. "I loved my father. But he was, after all, a father looking out for the best interests of his only daughter."

"And you found his scrutiny too confining?"

"Yes." She unzipped the pants and pushed them down his legs.

Maddox stepped out of them and kicked them to the side. "And now that your father can't call the shots?"

Her hands paused on the rivet to his jeans. She closed her eyes and sucked in a ragged breath. "I miss him."

Maddox's hand closed over hers. "Don't do this just because you can."

Katya opened her eyes and stared up at Maddox. "I've been a student in your country for six months. I could have made love to a dozen men by now."

"And have you?"

"No."

"Why me?"

She didn't step away, didn't remove her hand from his jeans. Instead, she stared up into his face. "I don't know. For some reason, you make me feel as though I am living life for the very first time."

That cold lump in his chest he'd given up on when Susan died swelled, filling and expanding to accommodate the blood flowing swiftly through his veins. The rush of emotion was quickly chased by panic. "And you make me feel…again. And frankly that scares the hell out of me."

She raised her hands to his cheeks. "I'm sorry about your fiancée. That must have hurt a lot."

He nodded, unable to voice the amount of pain he'd experienced at the time. His fingers tightened in her hair. "I can't do that again. I won't." His jaw clenched, his teeth grinding away at his memories.

"You don't have to." Her smile softened, her blue eyes swimming in a film of unshed tears. "I cannot stay in your country, anyway. Once I clear up this mess, I have to return to my home."

She'd left him an out. The opportunity to make love with no regrets, no ties, no claim on this woman, or her on him. He didn't have to invest his emotions as he had with Susan.

But what if he wanted to? "Do you have to go back?"

She nodded, her fingers stroking his stubbled chin. "Yes."

He sucked in a deep breath to steady his heartbeat, hoping he could turn it back into stone, although he feared it was too late. "Well, then, we'd better get some sleep." Maddox pulled her arms down from his face and stepped away from her tempting body, clad only in her underwear. It cost him.

Dearly.

"Sleep?" She stared at him, her breasts rising and falling behind the black lace, her arms wrapping around her middle, covering the rising goose bumps.

"Sleep." He nodded to where the sleeping bag lay spread across the ropes strung between the hand-carved bedposts. "You can have the bed."

She glanced at the bag, a shiver wracking her body.

Maddox wanted to take her back in his arms and warm all parts of her body, but he dared not. He couldn't afford to put his arms around her. If he did, he was afraid he'd never let her go. And she'd made it plenty clear to him that she was not sticking around.

One by one, she gathered her clothes.

His pulse thundering in his veins, his body stiff and ready for what he knew he couldn't have, Maddox couldn't watch. He turned his back to her and stirred the logs in the fire, the flames flaring up, sending a shower of sparks across the floor.

She'd done that to him. Stirred the embers in his heart and made him want the flame again. How had he come to this? How had he let himself feel for a woman again? Especially one who came with so much baggage and promised she'd be leaving.

Damn her!

Chapter Eleven

Katya dressed in her jeans and sweater before crawling between the folds of the sleeping bag. She lay facing Maddox, silhouetted in the glow from the fire.

How she wanted to go to him and put her arms around him, bring him back to the bed to make love to her as they had in the cave. But that was before he knew she was an accused terrorist. Before he knew she'd be leaving soon. Before she knew she was falling in love with this tall, dark Native American, whose heart and family were tied to the North Dakota Badlands. Even if she wanted him to follow her back to Trejikistan, she couldn't lct him.

She didn't know what awaited her there. With her country torn apart by warring factions, she would be in constant danger, forever looking over her shoulder. And how did she expect the people of her country to follow her when it had taken every ounce of political pull and diplomacy her father could muster to steer the people toward democracy? And what had it gotten him? He'd been murdered, probably by the very people determined to squelch the democratic movement and return a king to ultimate power.

Who would they choose as the leader? Who would

they put in power if Katya decided to stay in America? If she decided to abandon her country, her people?

She gathered the edges of the sleeping bag around her, the thick fabric unable to dispel the chill suffusing her body. Her life, her moral code, instilled by her father, dictated that she return to her country. Without a ruler to guide them, Trejikistan would become a military state. Whoever orchestrated her father's death would take power and ruin the people's chances of a democracy.

As her father's daughter and until her brother returned, she was next in line to rule Trejikistan. She had to assume her position and responsibility at least until the elections the following spring.

Maddox poked at the fire, his broad shoulders flexing and retracting with each movement.

The temptation to go to him grew stronger with each passing minute. If she hoped to get any sleep whatsoever, she couldn't continue to watch him. Forcing herself to be reasonable, she turned over in the bag, turning her back to Maddox and the alluring glow of the fire. She stared at the dark, bleak walls, so cold from the temperatures outside. Even if she didn't go to sleep, she could rest. She'd need to be ready to go whenever they made their next move.

With the pendant her father gave her clutched between her fingers, her eyelids drooped and she fell into a troubled sleep.

Trapped in a canyon, giant boulders blocking her path, forcing her into a maze she could not find her way out of, Katya ran. Her breathing came in ragged gasps. Behind her a man with cold eyes followed, closing in on her location.

She ducked inside a cave, crouching low to the floor, dragging in enough air to keep from passing out. When would this nightmare end? Surely it was only a dream. Soon she'd awaken in her own bedroom.

Katya closed her eyes and reopened them, hoping for the familiarity of her floral bedspread and the clock radio on her nightstand. Instead she awoke to her apartment filled with machine guns, blocks of plastic explosives and someone banging on the door.

"Police!" someone yelled through the wood paneling. "Open up!"

Katya closed her eyes again, wishing for escape, only to find herself back in the cave, the sound of footsteps running toward her. She had to get away. She couldn't let the murderer capture her—her family depended on her to clear their name. Her people depended on her to save them from a crushing military dictatorship.

Katya leaped to her feet and ran for the cave entrance, ready to stand up to the man chasing her or die trying.

As she emerged from the cave into the night air, hands grabbed her, pulling her against a rock-solid body. "No!" she cried, beating her fists against her captor's chest.

"Wake up, Katya!" Her captor shook her. "Wake up!"

Katya opened her eyes to the soft glow of fire in the fireplace and Maddox's worried gaze. Her struggles ceased, and she fell into his arms, her body shaking, exhausted.

"It's okay. You were only dreaming."

"But it felt so real." She buried her face in his neck,

inhaling denim, leather and Maddox's fresh soap smell. Her fingers clung to his shirt, clutching him close to her.

"You're safe for now," he crooned softly, his lips against her temple, his hand stroking her hair down her back. "You're safe."

"No, I am not." She moved closer, her body curling into his. "I will not be safe until the man chasing me is caught, or I am dead."

"I'm here. I won't let anything happen to you."

"You cannot promise that," she whispered into his neck, afraid to let go, lest she wake up to find he was never there.

"I can and do." Maddox's hand continued to stroke the back of her head, threading his fingers through her hair, trailing them down her back.

Slowly, her muscles relaxed and she let herself breathe again. "I cannot live this way."

"No one could. That's why we're going back to Minneapolis to figure this whole thing out."

"When?"

"Soon." He glanced at the watch on his wrist. "I arranged to meet my brother, Tuck, at the highway in a couple of hours when the coast is clear and the sheriff won't be awake to track us down."

She looked up into his face, loving the way the firelight enhanced the rich dark tones of his skin. "How did you arrange that? Does this cabin have telephone service?"

"No. I did it before we left." He stretched his legs out on the sleeping bag beside her, leaning against the cabin's log walls.

"You planned on helping me all along?" she asked.

"Yes."

His warmth spread throughout her body, chasing away the fear and dread from her dream. "Thank you."

"Don't thank me yet. We don't know what we have in store for us in Minneapolis."

"Still, you're putting your life on hold and in danger to help me." She leaned up and kissed his beard-roughened cheek. "Thank you."

Gratitude had nothing to do with her next kiss. She pressed her lips to his, loving the smooth fullness. The closer she moved, the closer she wanted to be to him.

He broke away, his hands still entangled in her hair, the rigid evidence of his arousal pressing into her thigh. "No. We shouldn't."

"No one knows that more than I do." She leaned forward and kissed him again.

"Someone needs to stop before we go too far."

"Would that be you?" she asked.

"Not this time. If you want this to end now, you'll have to say so. I've been wanting to do this since the cave." He laid her down beside him, nestled in the sleeping bag. Leaning over her, he kissed her so thoroughly he took her breath away.

Katya clung to him, her pulse quickening, her breath tight, short spasms, providing little relief to her oxygen-starved lungs. Her fingers shoved at the shirt he wore, pushing it up and over his head, her hands splaying over the hard planes of his chest, feverishly memorizing every contour. Later, when she made it back to her home country, she would have little more than her memories to keep her warm at night.

Her breath caught in her throat and a sudden welling of tears threatened to take over. Dammit, she was done with crying. She had shed enough tears in the past three days to last a lifetime. With so little time left with Maddox, she wanted nothing more than to seize the moment, experience everything she could before she went home—should she live long enough and bypass the legal system to get back.

Maddox tugged her shirt up over her head and flung it over the bedpost. Her jeans came next, then the scrap of silk underwear and lace bra. The chill air pebbled her skin and made her breasts form pointed peaks.

Maddox stared down at her, drinking in every detail. Her pale skin reflected the warm glow of the firelight, her hair held a sheen similar to moonlight on still water. Her legs parted, her knees falling to the sides, welcoming him.

He stripped off the rest of his clothing and crawled into the sleeping bag with her, covering her body with his, settling between her legs. His erection pressed against her opening, but he refused to dive in like an eager teenager.

Katya had insisted that she couldn't stay. Her words hurt more than Maddox cared to admit.

His revenge would come in the form of sensual torture. He lowered his lips to hers, poised a hair's breadth from the temptation of her kiss. When she leaned up to capture his lips, he pulled away.

Instead, he pressed a kiss to her nose, her forehead, her cheeks and trailed a line of tender caresses along her jawbone, nipping and tonguing the pulse at the base of her throat.

His hands smoothed along the regal line of her neck and downward, skimming across her collarbone, edging ever closer to her breasts.

Her back arched, bringing her breast in contact with his fingers.

He tweaked the rosy-brown nipples to a velvety peak, his fingers massaging until Katya moaned.

"Maddox, please." Her body writhed with each touch, her feet churning the sleeping bag into a tousled heap. Her fingernails scraped his buttocks, digging in, tugging him closer, urging him to fill her.

He resisted, letting his lips follow his fingers to her breasts, taking them into his mouth one at a time, tasting the luscious sweetness.

Katya's legs wrapped around his waist, her heels digging into his back. "Please, Maddox," she begged.

"Patience. I want to bring you with me."

"I am with you. Oh, please. What you are doing is making me completely insane." Her words came out in breathy gasps. Her feet falling to the sleeping bag, her heels digging in, lifting her hips upward.

When he didn't think he could hold out any longer, Maddox slipped lower on the shifting rope bed, his knees digging into the sleeping bag, finding the gaps between the ropes. He levered himself lower, his tongue skittering across Katya's flat belly and lower to the apex of her thighs.

"Please come inside me, please," she begged, her fingers clutching at his hair in spasms.

He wasn't finished. His tongue delved between her folds, lapping at the swollen nub until her bottom rose off the bed and her fingernails pressed into his scalp.

Her body tensed, then a soft gasp whooshed from her lips. She clung to him, breathing hard.

Only then did he shift up her body and slide into

her heated slickness. He thrust deep, riding the wave of his desire.

At last he catapulted over the edge, his body throbbing to a rhythm as ageless as time. Spent, he collapsed over her, drawing her into his arms without severing the intimate connection.

Together they fell into a deep dreamless sleep, arms and legs intertwined, the sleeping bag pulled up around their shoulders as the fire died.

A loud roar and insistent beeping woke Maddox. He jerked away, stabbing at his watch to silence his alarm. It took several seconds for him to realize the sound was coming from outside the cabin. The roaring wasn't the wind but the revving of a snowmobile engine.

Maddox leaped out of the bed and dragged his jeans up over his hips.

"What's happening?" Katya sat up, clutching the bag to her breasts.

"I don't know."

"Maddox!" Tuck's voice called to him through the thickness of the wooden door.

Maddox grabbed his sweater and flung the door open, letting in a blast of arctic air. "Tuck, what are you doing here? Is it time already?" He glanced down at his watch, the icy wind against his exposed skin making him shake so badly he could barely see the digital numbers.

"Get your clothes on. Someone alerted our favorite sheriff that Katya is a wanted woman. He's on his way out to check the hunting cabin."

"How did he know to come here?"

"Heck if I know. I heard it on the police scanner and hightailed it out here as fast as I could." Tuck nodded at Maddox's naked chest and glanced toward the dark interior of the cabin. "Better get her out of here before the sheriff arrives."

"What about the truck?" Maddox asked, tugging his sweater over his head.

"Dante's driving it to our designated location on the highway. He'll take the snowmobile back to the ranch. He didn't dare take the chopper out. As it is, he'll have enough explaining to do with the Border Patrol."

"I am ready when you are." Katya stepped up beside Maddox, zipping her jacket up to her neck.

Maddox could have kissed her already kiss-swollen lips. "Give me a second, and I'll meet you in back by the lean-to." He shut the door, blocking the wind from blowing through the already freezing cabin while he finished dressing in his cold-weather gear.

When he had his boots on and his hood pulled down over his head, he pulled Katya into his arms and kissed her. A quick, brief kiss, but it would have to do until he could kiss her again. And he planned on kissing her a hell of a lot more. So much so that she would change her mind about going back to Trejikistan. With her father dead, what could possibly make her want to return to a country that didn't want her back to begin with?

When Katya walked outside, the full force of the wind hit her, making her step back before she could get her balance. Each time she went out into the cold, it got harder. She'd give anything to sit in a sauna and ease the chill out of her bones. But now was not that time.

Maddox jogged ahead of her and backed the snow-mobile out of the lean-to, dusting the snow off the seat.

Katya climbed on the back and looped her arms around his waist.

Without another word to his brother, Maddox raced off into the night, headed toward the highway where his other brother waited. Tuck's snowmobile kept pace at his right, neither rider using headlights.

Katya glanced behind her at the cabin, a dark shape barely illuminated by the sketchy starlight was intermittently revealed by the skittering of clouds across the heavens.

A light blinked on the horizon past the cabin, a tiny light, barely the size of a distant star—only this wasn't a star.

Katya's heart raced, her hands tightening around Maddox's waist. "We're being followed!" Katya yelled and pointed back at the light.

Weighed down by two people, the snowmobile could not outrun the one following. The best they could hope for was to stay ahead of it and arrive at the truck before it did.

Tuck's snowmobile pulled close and he shouted over the roar of the engine, "We should split up. Maybe he'll follow me."

Maddox nodded. "Don't go and get yourself shot. Mom would never forgive me."

"Don't worry. I'll take a punch for you, but forget the bullets."

Despite his words to the contrary, Katya would bet her life that Tuck would take a bullet for Maddox. The Thunder Horse brothers were a force to be reckoned with and they obviously loved each other, even if they did not say it outright.

Tuck split off and dropped back to intercept the other snowmobile.

Maddox opened his machine up full throttle and raced off across the snow-covered landscape.

The last time Katya had been on a speeding snowmobile, racing away from the bad guy on her tail, she had gone over the edge into a canyon. Between peering around Maddox at what lay ahead and tracking the light of the snowmobile behind them, she could not be still on the backseat.

She wished they did not have to go quite so fast, but slowing down was not an option.

If the man following them was the sheriff, he would throw her in jail, and wait for Homeland Security to come get her and sort things out. And when they did, her quest to clear her name might as well be over. Who would think to look further than a foreigner?

If the person behind them was the man who had tried to kidnap her, she might not see the morning dawn.

Squelching her fear of speed, Katya buried her face in Maddox's back and held on. The bumps and dips were amplified by the speed, slamming them into the earth or making them go airborne off the snowmobile's seat.

Several times Katya nearly lost her hold on Maddox, her body flying into the air, only to crash down when the skids hit the hard-packed snow.

Even while trying to hold on to Maddox, Katya worried about Tuck. Whatever he was doing back there, the light had not wavered once. In fact, it was getting bigger. The vehicle was closing in on them.

Katya glanced ahead. Where was the highway and Dante with the waiting vehicle? Would they make it in time?

Another look behind and the light was closer still. Then Katya saw a shadowy form cross in front of the other snowmobile. Over the roar of the engine, a loud crack ripped through the air.

Starlight glinted off Tuck's snowmobile as he swerved and raced back across the path of the other snowmobile.

Her breath lodged firmly in her throat, Katya could only watch with a dreadful sense of doom as another crack blasted through the air. Tuck's snowmobile veered to the right and slowed to a stop.

Had their pursuer shot him? Was Tuck bleeding to death in the frigid cold? "We have to go back. Tuck's hurt."

"We can't," Maddox insisted. "The truck's ahead. Once we reach it, I'll send Dante back for Tuck."

"It could be too late. He could bleed to death!" Katya pulled at Maddox's sleeve. "You have to go back. You can't leave him there to die!"

Chapter Twelve

Maddox wanted to turn around and go back for his brother, but he'd promised Katya that he'd keep her safe. He couldn't do that by driving back into bullet range of their pursuer.

Ahead the sporadic starlight reflected off something metallic. That something had better be the truck his brother, Dante, was bringing. When they got to the truck, Dante would go back and check on Tuck.

That is, if they made it there before their pursuer planted a bullet in Katya's back. The only saving grace was that the terrain was bumpy, and steady aim would be impossible. But that didn't rule out a lucky shot—or an unlucky one if it hit one of them.

A quick glance over his shoulder kicked up his pulse a notch.

The snowmobile behind them was catching up fast.

A loud bang sounded over the noise of his engine.

Katya's arms tightened around his waist, her face digging into his back.

Maddox would have zigzagged to make it harder for the shooter to use them as target practice, but anything other than a straight line would slow them enough for him to catch up. With the throttle wide open, Maddox pushed the snowmobile to its limits.

A small beam of light flashed out over the snow. Using a handheld flashlight, Dante guided them to the truck.

Like a sprinter racing past the finish line, Maddox didn't slow down until he passed the truck and put the body of the vehicle between him and the shooter.

Dante stood behind the truckbed, a rifle aimed at the oncoming snowmobile. He fired off a shot.

The pursuer swerved, killed the headlight and pulled a tight circle, regrouping now that the odds were stacked against him.

Maddox pulled the snowmobile up to the pickup and leaped off. "Tuck's down back there. Promise me you'll take care of him."

His brother's eyes narrowed, his grip tightening on the rifle. Their pursuer kept his distance, just out of range of Dante's rifle. Which meant he was also out of range to fire a pistol at Maddox and Katya. "I've got this covered. You get her out of here."

"That's the plan." Maddox opened the passenger door and, keeping his body below the outline of the truck, climbed in and cranked the engine to life.

Katya hesitated. "We cannot leave Tuck out there. He could be hurt."

"I'll take care of him," Dante said, his focus remaining on the snowmobile in the distance. "Go!" he barked.

Katya threw herself into the truck, keeping her head below the level of the windows.

Even before the passenger door closed, Maddox shoved the gearshift into Drive and shot down the highway, slipping sideways on the snow-covered, icy road.

Katya looked over the top of the seat. "I think the snowmobile is following us. It is hard to tell. He still has his light off."

"Keep your head down. Until we get to the interstate highway, he has the advantage on these snowy back roads."

The truck skidded and bumped across the treacherous path.

Every few minutes, Katya sneaked a peek out the back windshield. "I can't see him."

Maddox didn't slow or lose focus. With the headlights of the truck reflecting off the snow, their night vision would be less than adequate past the manmade illumination. They had to make several turns to get to the highway. The snowmobile didn't. The shooter could cut across fields and head them off if he knew where Maddox was headed.

Katya sat quietly in the seat beside him, slumped low, her eyes wide, brows furrowed. "I hope your brothers are all right."

"They've been through worse." His words belied his own worry as he fought to keep the truck from sliding off the road and into the ditches.

As they neared the intersection of the county road and the main highway leading to the interstate, Maddox slowed to make the turn.

Serving as his lookout, Katya swiveled in her seat, panning the horizon. "On your left!" She ducked.

The snowmobile roared across the road in front of the truck. Instinctively, Maddox slammed on his brakes.

The truck skidded sideways, not slowing any sooner. A loud pop ripped through the air and the driver's-side window shattered, spraying glass throughout the interior.

"Stay down!" he shouted. Something stung his arm, but Maddox didn't let go of his grip on the steering wheel. He straightened the truck and skidded through the T-intersection, aiming for the interstate, sure that if they could get there, the snowmobile wouldn't be able to keep pace.

On the straight road, Maddox pushed the truck as fast as he could, praying he wouldn't slide off the side. The frigid air blowing in from the shattered window took his breath away. He reached for the heater, twisting the knob to the highest setting to keep them from getting frostbite. Lights reflected off the low-hanging clouds that had moved in from the west—it had to be the small town of Dickinson.

With hope in sight, Maddox increased his speed. As they neared the town, the road had less and less snow until all that was left was the sand and salt used by the highway department.

"I think we lost him," Katya said, looking through the rear window.

Houses and businesses lined the road into the town, and towering lights lit the interstate.

Katya touched Maddox's arm. "If the sheriff knows about me, he will have put out a message to all the law enforcement agencies, especially those along the main routes."

"You're right. Having a busted window won't help, either." Maddox slowed the truck and pulled down a side street, taking a less conspicuous route to the interstate. "We have to ditch the truck."

"How will we get to Minneapolis? Do they have a bus station here?" Katya asked.

"No, they have something better—truckers." Maddox parked two streets away from a well-lit truck stop, behind a large Dumpster.

Maddox dropped down out of the truck and rounded the vehicle to Katya's side. He opened the door and held his hand out to her.

She reached for it, but drew back, her forehead wrinkled. "Maddox, you're bleeding!" Katya slipped out of the truck without his help, her gaze on his arm with the blood-soaked sleeve. "We have to get you to a hospital."

He hadn't realized that he'd been hit. The shattering glass and the wild ride hadn't given him time to think about anything other than getting them to safety. "We don't have time. Besides, it's just a flesh wound." He touched his hand to the wound and fought back a wince. "Let's find a ride." He hooked her arm with his good one and led her toward the truck stop.

As they neared, Katya dug her heels into the pavement. "You cannot go in there. With all the blood, someone will get suspicious. They might call the police."

Maddox frowned. "You're right. But we can't risk you going in. What if they have flyers with your picture on them? If there are any cops in there, you could be caught."

"We'll have to take that chance."

"I'll sneak in and wash up in the bathroom."

"You'll need help."

"Here," Maddox dug in his back pocket and removed his wallet. He handed her a couple of twenties. "Buy a hat to cover your hair and face as much as possible.

Get some bandages and meet me at the bathroom door in five minutes."

Katya nodded, accepting the money, her bottom lip caught between her teeth. "Are you sure you are okay?"

"Yeah. As far as I can tell without looking, the bleeding's stopped. I'll be fine. Just stay away from cops." He leaned close and brushed her cheek with his lips. "See ya in five."

Katya tucked the money into her snowpants pocket and entered the building through a side door. The truck stop had a store on one side and a restaurant on the other.

Through the front window, Katya spotted two county sheriff's cars parked along the curb. Her heart pounded against her chest as she moved through the aisles, keeping her head lowered. She found a rack of knitted hats in soft pastel colors. She chose one in rose and gray, colors so very different from her own hair color. Then she found the row with the first aid items, grabbed a box of gauze and medical tape and hurried to the counter to pay, careful to avoid contact with anyone. From the corner of her eye, she located the bathrooms between the restaurant and the convenience store. Now all she had to do was pay and get to Maddox.

A man asking for cigarettes got to the clerk first. Katya stood behind him, her head down, her gaze fixed on the floor.

As she waited her turn, a pair of brown boots appeared beside her. In her peripheral vision she could tell that the man wore brown trousers, as well. The same color worn by Sheriff Yost.

A quick glance upward confirmed her guess. A sheriff's deputy stood beside her, talking to another man in uniform behind him.

At last the man with the cigarettes paid for his purchase and left.

Katya laid her items on the counter, praying that the lawmen wouldn't question her need for gauze and tape. The men were so deep in conversation, maybe they'd completely ignore her.

The one closest to her was saying something about an APB. "Sheriff Yost issued it a couple hours ago. We're supposed to be on the lookout for some Russian woman suspected of terrorism."

Katya's heart skipped a beat at the man's words. She struggled against the urge to run, before the officers realized the woman they were supposed to be watching out for was right in front of them.

The clerk lifted the knit cap. "Ma'am, the hats on the other rack are half off."

"That's okay," she said, keeping her voice low and as American sounding as she could. She had practiced the American accent, wanting to fit in at school. "I like this one."

"There's one just like it on the other rack. Well, almost. Want me to get it for you?" The clerk stepped away from the register.

"No," Katya said, desperate to pay and leave the deputies behind. "I want this one."

The young man shrugged. "Have it your way. But the others are cheaper." He rang up the purchases and took the twenty she handed to him.

Her heart thumping wildly in her chest, Katya tried to fake a calm she didn't feel.

"Not from around here, are you?" the deputy beside her said.

Katya jumped, but refused to make eye contact with the man talking to her, preferring to fix her gaze on the clerk. "Nope," she said as quietly as she could.

"Where ya from?" he asked.

The man behind him elbowed him. "Give it up, Swenson. She's not interested."

The deputy closest to her turned to his friend, a fierce frown pulling his brows down over his eyes. "Shut up, Roe. Let the lady decide." The deputy faced her again. "Ignore the jerk. Where are you from?"

Remembering a movie she'd seen with her neighbor, she forced a response she hoped sounded genuine. "Jersey," she said, laying on the thick Jersey accent from the movie. Thankfully, the clerk handed her change to her. Relieved beyond reason, Katya was about to make her escape.

The clerk smiled at her and delayed her further with, "Really? What part? I have relatives in New Jersey."

Caught in her own lie, Katya's mind went blank. She couldn't remember the name of a single city in New Jersey.

As she groped for a response, the clerk tipped his head to the side. "Newark, I think. My cousin lives in Newark. You from anywhere close?"

"Newark," she said, gathering her items.

"Need a bag for that?" the clerk asked.

"No, thank you."

"Hey, I'm off in thirty minutes." The young deputy said. "Care to have breakfast with me?"

"Sorry, my husband is waiting," she said and hurried toward the bathrooms and Maddox. Not until she ducked down the hallway and out of sight of the deputies did she draw a breath. Then it was only to have it yanked out of her when a hand grabbed her from behind and tugged her into the men's bathroom and one of the stalls.

Her face burning, Katya stood chest to chest with Maddox. "I cannot be in here. This is the men's bathroom. What if someone comes in?" Katya protested.

"We'll take that chance." He had his jacket and shirt off.

Katya's hands, full of the hat and bandages, pressed into his warm, smooth skin. Her breath caught now for another reason entirely.

"Good, you got bandages." Maddox smiled. "You took longer than five minutes."

"Couldn't be helped." Katya eyed the wound.

He had managed to clean the blood off his jacket and hung it on the back of the stall door. The edges of the cut were cleaned, as well, but fresh blood oozed out.

"Here, hold these." She handed him the hat and box of tape. Ripping two sterile packages of gauze from the remaining box, she folded one into a tight pad and pressed it against the injury, then laid the other over the first. She held out her free hand. "Tape."

He handed her the box of tape. "Are you a nurse back in your country?"

"No, but I had a brother," she said. "He was constantly getting into scrapes."

"What do you mean *had?*" Maddox's forehead creased. "Did he die?"

"No," she answered too quickly. She refused to believe that her brother was dead. If he was, she had no other family but her cousin, Vladimir. In other words, she had no family. "No, he is not dead. We...I do not know where he is."

Maddox's lips turned up in a gentle smile. "You've misplaced your brother?"

"You could say that. I have not heard from him in months. But he is alive." She stretched a band of white tape over the top of the gauze. "He has to be."

"Now we're getting somewhere. You know that I have three brothers. I know that you have at least one. Any other family I should know about?"

"No. It was just me, my brother and my father." Her voice cracked on the last word and she fought to keep from shedding another tear. She ripped off another strip of tape and plastered it to the bottom of the gauze. "There. You were right. It was just a flesh wound. You probably need a tetanus shot to be safe."

"Yes, ma'am. As soon as you're safe." He smiled down at her. "Thanks." Then he kissed her nose.

How she could get all hot and bothered by a man kissing her nose, Katya did not know, but she could not stop the rush of blood to the lower regions of her belly. She pressed closer to him, her hands sliding over his dark-skinned chest. "I do not understand why I cannot keep my hands off you."

"You don't hear me complaining." He captured her fingers in his and drew them up to his lips where he kissed her fingertips. "Much as I like what you're doing to me, we have to get out of here."

"Right." Katya said, dragging her focus back to the more immediate need for transportation. "And there are a couple of sheriff's deputies out there."

The outer door to the bathroom swung open.

Katya stepped up on the edge of the toilet seat and

squatted down so that whoever came in wouldn't see two sets of legs in one stall.

The door next to them opened and closed.

Maddox pressed a finger to his lips, slipped his shirt and jacket on, then slid the lock open on his stall door. Before she could guess at his next move, he grabbed her around the legs and lifted her up.

She swallowed a scream and held on as he carried her through the stall door to the exit.

Once outside the door, he dropped her on her feet. He took the hat from her hands and stretched it down over her hair, tucking the long strands up underneath. "There. Now we have to find a ride."

Maddox led the way through the restaurant, head down, eyes averted to avoid being recognized.

The deputies were sitting in a booth in the far corner, laughing over coffee and breakfast. The one who had hit on Katya looked up, his eyes narrowing at Maddox.

Pretending she didn't see him, Katya moved on to another booth as far away from the deputies as possible.

A group of truckers sat between Katya and the deputies, their loud voices and laughter enough to drown out any conversation Maddox and Katya might attempt.

"Aren't you afraid the deputies will question us?"

"We won't find out where the trucks are going if we don't eavesdrop on the conversations."

Katya sat with her back to the lawmen. Maddox faced them and the truckers. He stared toward Katya while he surreptitiously studied the truckers.

"Haven't seen the wife in a week." An older gentleman with a weathered face and graying hair twisted his coffee cup in his hands.

"Lucky dog." The man with his back to Maddox,

with strawberry-blond hair and freckles running together on his arms and neck, waved at the waitress
with his mug.

"Unlike you dirtbags, I actually like my wife." The
older man sipped his coffee and grimaced. "She makes
a better cup of coffee than this swill."

"You're probably the only man I know who still gives
a crap about his ball and chain." The man in the booth
beside the older gentleman had the gravelly voice and
heavily lined face of a smoker.

The gray-haired trucker shrugged. "She puts up with
me and she's still as pretty as the day I met her."

The waitress swung by with a steaming pot of coffee.

"Where is this wife of yours?" The younger, freckled man set his mug on the table for the waitress to fill.
"Might need to pay her a visit while you're out of town."

The men all laughed.

"She's out of your league, Red."

"How do you know?"

The man in the booth beside the freckled man,
nudged him in the side. "Any woman in her right mind
would be out of your league."

Ignoring the younger men's antics, the gray-haired
man looked over at the smoker. "Where ya headed?"

"Spokane."

"I'm going the other direction." The older man stirred
sugar into his coffee. "I'll be in Chicago by nightfall.
Only have to make a quick stop in Minneapolis."

Katya's gaze connected with Maddox's and he
mouthed the word *Bingo*.

After topping off the truckers' coffee mugs, the waitress stopped beside Katya. "You want a menu, or do
you already know what you want?"

Maddox stood, keeping his torn sleeve out of sight of the deputies in the corner. "We've changed our minds. Come on, darlin'."

The waitress shrugged. "Don't blame you. The food here sucks."

Katya slid out of the booth and preceded Maddox out of the restaurant and into the convenience store.

Without saying a word, Maddox purchased shrink-wrapped breakfast biscuits and a couple bottles of orange juice, all the while keeping a watch on the gray-haired trucker in the restaurant. Whether or not he knew or liked it, the old guy was their ticket to Minneapolis.

As he paid the clerk, Maddox could see the trucker zipping his jacket and pulling on his gloves.

"Come on, we have a bus to catch." Maddox grabbed the plastic bag with their food and hurried toward the door leading out to where the truckers parked the big rigs.

"Bus?" Katya said, running to keep up with Maddox. "I thought you said we were not taking a bus."

"Just some American slang." He smiled and held out his hand. "Come on. Let's get out of sight until our bus driver comes out."

Katya grinned and slipped her gloved fingers in his. Her eyes widened and her smile slipped when she looked past him. She tugged him hard and shoved him behind a large trailer.

"What? Was it something I said?" Maddox leaned over the top of Katya's head as they peered around the corner of the trailer at the county sheriff's car pulling up to the other two parked at the curb.

Sheriff Yost climbed out of the car and scanned the area.

Maddox and Katya ducked back behind the trailer. "We have to get out of here." He looked around the corner again. Their gray-haired potential bus driver stood talking to the sheriff, looking down at the paper in the sheriff's hands.

The older gentleman shook his head and took off across the parking lot toward the tractor-trailer rig where Maddox and Katya were hiding.

Maddox swore under his breath. The only man they'd found going their way had gotten the heads-up from the sheriff. What chance did they have now that he would let them in the truck?

Chapter Thirteen

"Sorry, folks, but this is as far as I can take you. From here, I'm on to Chicago." Chuck Goodman pulled the truck into a huge distribution center in the warehouse district of Minneapolis. He climbed down out of the truck and stretched.

Maddox descended to the pavement and reached up a hand to help Katya out of the tall vehicle. They met Chuck in front of the truck. "Thanks for giving us a ride this far."

"You guys did me the favor by keeping me company. I hope things work out for you two. You seem nice enough."

Maddox held out his hand to the older man and they shook.

Katya bypassed the hand and hugged the man's neck. If not for him, their trip might have ended at the truck stop. "Thank you for taking a chance on us."

"Probably wouldn't have if you weren't such a pretty little thing. Can't imagine you had anything to do with whatever stuff they found in your apartment. And even I've heard of the Thunder Horse Ranch. Makes me proud to know someone is looking out for the wild ponies of the Badlands." He shook Maddox's hand again.

"Your wife is a lucky woman, Chuck. I hope we meet again." Maddox waved and led Katya through the gates and out onto the sidewalk.

They left Chuck at the distribution center and hiked toward a convenience store they'd spied a couple blocks away.

"We can take a taxi or the city bus from there," Katya said.

"I want to make a call first."

"Tuck?" Katya shot a glance at him. "Why didn't you borrow the trucker's cell phone?"

"I didn't want any law enforcement officials tracing anything back to Chuck. He did us a favor giving us a lift."

"Right."

At the convenience store, Maddox purchased a throwaway cell phone for himself and one for Katya. "Just in case," he said.

Katya shoved the phone in her pocket and stared out the window of the store at the gray skies and traffic, praying the news was good from the Thunder Horse Ranch.

Maddox finished his call and joined her. "*Wankatanka* is looking out for Tuck. He's fine."

That little bit of news was such a relief—it lifted some of the weight off Katya's shoulders. She couldn't have lived with herself if something bad happened to any one of the Thunder Horse clan.

"One more thing." Maddox paused, his lips pressed into a thin line. "I told Dante where we'd left the truck."

"And?"

"A man was murdered near the truck stop and his

car was stolen. The sheriff was all over it, blaming us for the murder and the theft."

Katya's stomach clenched. Another crime to add to her growing list. "If they catch me, I will be in jail for the rest of my life."

"You didn't kill anyone, Katya." His hands gripped her shoulders. "Look at me."

Her eyes opened and she stared up into the fathomless depths of his brown-black eyes.

"We'll get you through this."

"How?"

"I don't know. But you have to believe we'll make it through." He pulled her close and held her for a long moment. Then he put her away from him. "Just believe."

Katya stared out the store window, trying not to fall apart. She twisted the chain around her neck, remembering the day her father gave her the necklace—the day she left for school in the United States. He'd wanted her to have something to remember her family back home in Trejikistan. He'd had the thick, white-gold pendant engraved with the family crest. "So that I always know you are safe," he'd said. "And so that you always know where you belong."

And she belonged with her people, now that her father wasn't there to protect them from the potential of an unwanted dictatorship. Katya could only guess at who had attempted the coup. Trejikistan was such a small blip on the American news radar that finding any information about the country's upheaval would be next to impossible. If only she could get to the internet again. When she'd been at the Medora library, she hadn't had time. At the very least she needed to check for her bodyguard's response. Perhaps her brother had made his way back home after hearing of their father's death. *If* he'd gotten word. *If* he was still alive. Katya prayed that her brother was alive.

In the meantime, she had to find out who was trying to frame and kill her.

A taxi pulled up to the curb in front of the store. Maddox circled her waist with his arm. "Ready?"

Ready to walk back into the apartment where all her troubles had begun just a few short days ago? No. Katya's chest tightened and the uncontrollable urge to run hit her, panic setting in. The last time she was there, someone had tried to grab her. Would the man who'd been following them find her here? After all the cross-country trekking, she'd have thought she'd shaken the pursuer.

Like a pit bull terrier with his teeth dug in deep, her nemesis wasn't letting her go that easily.

Katya gave the taxi driver directions to the hair salon where she had her hair done, two blocks from her apartment complex. She pulled the knit hat down low over her forehead, the bulky yarn covering her dark brows. If the entire police force of Minneapolis was searching for her, she'd be discovered in no time.

"How will you find out who set you up?" Maddox broke into her thoughts, his voice low enough so the driver couldn't overhear.

"I'm not sure." She hadn't thought further ahead than arriving at her apartment complex alive. Now that they were this close, she didn't have a clue. "I suppose I could talk to the neighbors."

"Does the apartment have a security system?"

"Yes." Katya sat forward, remembering her father's insistence on staying somewhere that had good security. He'd wanted her to be safe so far away from home. "The apartment complex has a high-end security system. Surely part of it consists of a camera and a digital history of that day."

"If we could get the historical videos, maybe we can find our real terrorist." Maddox grabbed her hands. "Do you know the security guards? Ever talk to them?"

"As a matter of fact, one of them is a friend of mine. Casey Reed. I set him up with my classmate." He was the man who'd helped her escape her attacker and hid her from the police.

"Perfect." Maddox sat back, staring out the window. "Maybe he'll get us in to see the videos."

Katya stared across the backseat at Maddox, her heart swelling in her chest. "Thank you, Maddox."

He turned toward her, his brow furrowing. "For what?"

"For helping me when you really should not." She leaned across the seat and kissed him full on the lips.

The kiss deepened, Maddox's hands circling behind her neck to draw her closer. His tongue thrust between her teeth.

Katya melted against him, wishing the kiss could last forever.

Not until the taxi driver cleared his throat did they break apart. The kiss was everything she could have hoped for and yet it broke her heart into a million pieces. Once she cleared her name, she would be on her way back to Trejikistan. Maddox would be half a world away.

Katya climbed out of the taxi and stood on the sidewalk, her mood as dreary as the Minneapolis winter. She should not have kissed him, knowing they could never be more than acquaintances. The more physical contact she had with Maddox Thunder Horse, the harder it would be to say goodbye.

They took the side roads to the apartment complex, arriving at the rear entrance. "We won't get in without my card key, and that's somewhere back in the canyon with the snowmobile," she said.

"Then we'll go around the front and wait for your friend."

"He works the midnight-to-noon shift. He should be leaving any moment. I have a better idea that won't be so conspicuous." Katya took his hand and, like lovers, leaned into him and guided him a block away from the apartment to a park within view of the front entrance, but shaded by the overhang of trees and bushes.

A metal park bench faced the street and gave them a good vantage point from which to watch for anyone entering or leaving the building.

Katya dropped onto the metal seat and tugged on Maddox's hand. "Sit."

Maddox complied, his glance panning the area. "Aren't you afraid your stalker will make an easy target of you?"

Katya's lips pressed into a line. "I'm hoping he is still back in North Dakota scratching his head." She patted her hat. "And with the disguise, hopefully, he will not know who I am."

"I want to know how he found you at the cabin."

"Maybe he followed the snowmobile tracks."

"I suppose he could have."

A man dressed in a security guard uniform exited the apartment building, walking toward them, head down, hands tucked in his thick winter jacket.

Katya gripped Maddox's hand. "That's Casey."

Maddox stood, pulling Katya to her feet. "Let's get started."

"What if he is spooked by all the publicity about my being a terrorist?" Katya stared up into Maddox's eyes, pretending that she was his lover for anyone passing by. Her heart skipped a few beats when he leaned close.

With his lips close to her ear, he whispered, "We'll just have to convince him that you aren't."

Katya's stomach tumbled, all her nerves bouncing from his gentle breath on her neck.

Maddox straightened and stepped in front of the security guard, blocking his path. "Excuse me, sir, are you Casey Reed?"

Casey stopped abruptly and backed up a step. "Yeah, that's me."

Katya laid a hand on the man's arm. "Casey, I need your help."

The security guard stared down at her hand then into her face, his eyes widening, a grin spreading across his face. "Kat?"

She darted a glance around the street. "Yes, Casey, it's me, Kat."

Casey's gaze swept the area, as well, before returning to Katya. "Holy cow, Kat. Where have you been? The entire Minneapolis police force and the FBI are all looking for you."

"I know."

Casey shook his head. "What happened? Where did all that stuff come from? Tell me all those weapons and explosives weren't really yours. I never believed it, but the media sounds so convincing."

"No, they weren't mine. I have no idea how the weapons got into my apartment. They were planted while I was out that morning."

"I knew it. When they told me all that stuff was yours, I didn't believe them. You're too nice to be a terrorist. That's why I helped you get away."

"I had to leave." Katya recalled the man who had jumped her on her way back to her apartment that fateful morning. "Someone tried to kill me, Casey. I have been running ever since."

Maddox broke into the conversation. "Look, we can't stand out in the open much longer. We need your help to clear her of the charges."

Casey nodded. "What can I do?"

Katya touched a hand to his arm. "You were on duty between eight and noon that morning. Did anyone deliver anything to the building?"

"The cops asked the same question. We had a furniture delivery scheduled for apartment 627 at nine." Casey ran a hand through his hair. "I watched from the monitor. Everything was on the up and up. They brought in a couch and a love seat. No boxes or anything else. That was all that was delivered that morning."

"Did you actually see them take the furniture to 627?"

"Yeah. They delivered at exactly nine o'clock. I remember because Mrs. Carmichael walks her shih tzu every morning at nine o'clock."

Maddox stared across at Katya. "We need to see the videos of the entrances to the building. If that was the only delivery, they had to have gotten the weapons in during that time."

Before Maddox finished speaking, Casey was shaking his head. "The Feds confiscated every video for the last six months you've lived here."

Katya's hopes sank. "All of them?"

"Were the videos on tape or on a hard drive?" Maddox asked.

"Everything is backed up from the hard drive to tape once a month," Casey said. "We'd just completed a backup when the Feds charged in. They took all the tapes."

Maddox stepped forward. "Do you wipe the videos from the hard drive when you back up to tape?"

"You know," Casey scratched his chin. "I believe we do it a week later, just in case one of the tapes is bad on the monthly backup."

Katya pulled in a deep breath and let it out, feeling lighter. "Can we look for that day, just in case the video is still on the hard drive?"

In the corner of her peripheral vision, Katya noted a Minneapolis city police car pulled up to a stop sign two blocks away. "We need to move this discussion inside." She hooked Casey's arm and moved toward the apartment building.

Casey resisted. "I can't take you in there now. My boss is filling in for me while I'm on lunch break. He doesn't expect me back for another fifteen minutes. Besides, he's very strict about who gets inside the control room."

Katya changed direction, leading the two men to a small bistro a block from the complex. "Then let's get you some lunch and we can plan our next move."

Fifteen minutes later, Casey walked out of the bistro, his steps swift, his gaze shooting from side to side.

Katya regretted having to involve Casey. If he were

caught assisting her now, he, too, could be considered an accessory to a potential terrorist wanted by the police and the FBI. And the poor man was scared to death.

For that matter, Katya was scared. Walking into the apartment building set her up for capture. Casey had given her his master key card. While he searched for the video from that day, Katya and Maddox would perform some illegal activities of their own. It was too dangerous to enter her own apartment, but based on Casey's observation, the owners of 627 were out.

Maddox and Katya were going to check out the furniture they'd had delivered and inspect it for any anomalies.

Katya pulled her collar up over her chin and ducked her head as she strode past the cameras at the entrance and in the front lobby.

Casey's boss had left shortly after he returned from lunch, but they didn't need to leave clear evidence of their visit on the videos.

Katya and Maddox took the stairs two at a time up to the sixth floor.

Maddox slowed near the top to wait for Katya. Adrenaline pulsed through his veins at the prospect of breaking and entering someone's apartment. He'd always lived his life by following the rules. This was outside his comfort zone, but it had to be done. They needed to know how the weapons got into Katya's apartment. Maddox was almost certain the furniture delivery was the key.

"Casey said it was a red leather sofa and a matching love seat," Katya reminded him as they paused in the stairwell.

With a nod, Maddox pushed through the stairwell door and hurried down the hallway to apartment 627.

He pressed his ear to the door and listened. Nothing. No sounds of movement, voices or music. After taking a deep breath, he slid the master key card Casey had provided into the door lock and waited for it to give him a green light. The locking mechanism clicked and the light blinked green.

As soon as the door swung open, Maddox and Katya rushed inside, closing the door behind them to keep other tenants from looking in while they poked around.

The red leather sofa sat against the living room wall, the love seat stood with its back to the entrance, framing the living area.

Without saying a word, Maddox and Katya rushed to the furniture and pulled the cushions from the seats. Beneath the cushions both pieces looked like most sofas, with a layer of fabric and padding beneath.

"Grab the other end," Maddox said, grasping the end of the couch. Together, they tipped the couch over. Again, nothing looked like a storage place for weapons.

"How did they do it?" Katya voiced the question in Maddox's mind.

"I don't know."

"Should we check out my apartment? It's the one right below this one."

Maddox shook his head. "If the cops or the FBI are looking for you, they might have someone watching it."

"They would watch the building entrances, too. We succeeded in making it this far…"

For a moment Maddox considered her argument.

"We are in danger no matter where we go," Katya

continued. "Besides, we might find a clue as to how they got the weapons in without detection."

"Okay, but I go first."

"As they say in the American movies…" Katya stuck out her hand for him to shake. "Deal."

"Deal." He took her hand, pulled her to him and kissed her. Then he headed for the stairwell.

On the fifth floor, Maddox scanned the hallway before edging out. "Stay here until I tell you to come," he said to Katya.

Yellow crime-scene tape crisscrossed apartment 527. Maddox carefully removed one end of the wide ribbon, shoved the key in the lock and pushed the door open.

He slipped through the doorway, into the apartment. Tastefully furnished with solid mahogany occasional tables and a soft, cream leather sofa festooned with colorful cushions in shades of burgundy, pumpkin and apple green, the room should have been warm and inviting. But the place was a wreck. Kitchen cabinet doors hung open, dishes and canned goods littered the polished granite counters. In the bedroom, drawers were laid across the dresser top and bed, their contents tossed.

"They took my photograph," a soft voice whispered behind him.

Maddox spun to face Katya. "I thought I told you to stay put."

"Someone was coming up the stairs. I had to move or be discovered."

Although he didn't want to, Maddox accepted her explanation. "See anything out of place, missing or different?"

"Other than the fact they went through all my belongings and made a mess?" She sighed. "I do not know." Katya reached for the drawer containing her panties, her face reddening. "It's hard to accept that people have gone through my personal belongings." She glanced around the bedroom and out toward the living area. "Where are the crates of weapons they say I had?"

"The FBI or ATF must have confiscated them as evidence." He didn't know what he'd expected by sneaking into her apartment, but the effort had netted nothing.

Katya released the undergarment she held and crossed to the nightstand, her fingers brushing its surface. "They even took the photograph of my father and brother." She hugged her arms around her middle. "It was the only one I brought with me to America. I feel as if I have been violated." Her gaze shifted to his, her ice-blue eyes suspiciously bright, the dark smudges beneath them more noticeable.

"To be expected when strangers go through your stuff." Maddox wanted to go to her, wrap her in his arms and drive away the fear and sadness. If he did, he wasn't sure he could let go again or stay alert and focus on keeping them alive.

On the dresser, Maddox found a gold-plated hairbrush and let his finger trace the intricate design on its back. "Is this some kind of coat of arms?"

Katya stiffened. "Why do you ask?"

"It's the same as the one on your pendant. Does it have special meaning?"

"The pendant and the brush were gifts from my father. The symbol is our family crest."

"It looks expensive. This apartment looks expensive." Maddox stared around again with a more critical eye. "What did you say your father did?"

She turned away and headed for the living room.

"He was an important political figure in my country. Should we get out of here before someone comes looking for me?"

Maddox followed her out of the room. "I suspect you're still not telling me the entire truth."

"Oh, it is true. My father was an important political figure in Trejikistan."

His gut told him there was more to it than that. "He wasn't a terrorist, was he?"

Katya rounded on him, the color flaring in her cheeks. "My father was an honorable man, concerned only with his people—the people of Trejikistan. He would never kill innocents or destroy out of hatred. He was good and kind and respected—"

Maddox grabbed her arms and held her still. "Okay, okay. Your father wasn't a terrorist." He stared down into her eyes, a moment before full of sadness, now flashing with the fire of her passion. How he'd love to make love to her and see her eyes flare with another kind of passion.

Despite their need to hurry, to get out of the apartment building before they were caught, Maddox couldn't stop himself from stealing a kiss.

Just one.

His mouth descended on hers, hard and swift.

Still stiff, she resisted his caress.

Maddox softened his assault, teasing the line of her lips with his tongue, urging her to open and let him in.

A little at a time, her shoulders relaxed, and finally, with a soft sigh, she unclenched her teeth.

He swept in, his tongue tasting, thrusting and ravaging her. She spread her hands across his chest, her fingers digging into his shirt. She stood on her toes, leaning into him, their bodies melting together.

He was the first to break away, but only far enough to trail kisses across her cheek, to take her earlobe between his teeth. "You make me ache."

Her gentle laugh made him even hotter. "I do not know whether to apologize or to be flattered."

"Both. I can't think when you're in the same room. Given the situation, that could be dangerous." He moved her away from him, sucking in a deep breath. "Much as I'd like to continue this conversation, we should get down to the control room and see what Casey has found."

"Agreed." She touched her fingers to her swollen lips and ducked past him into the hallway.

They took the stairs back down to the main level and emerged into the hallway near the door to the control room.

Casey opened it before they could knock. "I saw you coming. Come see what I found." He let them in, looked out toward the lobby and then locked the door. "I was able to bring up the day of the raid by the ATF."

The room contained an elaborate array of screens. Each revealed different floors and community spaces in the building, even exterior corners and the lobby.

Maddox's pulse quickened. "Did you figure out how they got the weapons in?"

Casey's lips twisted. "Yes and no."

A surge of impatience made Maddox want to shake the security guard. "What do you mean, *'yes and no'*?" His words came out angrier than he'd intended.

Katya stepped between the two men. "Casey, show us what you have."

The young man sat at a computer keyboard separate from the other video screens, and clicked on a file. "Here. Watch this."

The video played, displaying an almost-empty lobby with the occasional tenant entering or leaving, the image slightly grainy, yet clear enough to make out the faces.

A man entered pushing a dolly with a large box, the size of a love seat. He disappeared from the camera's view onto the elevator.

A few minutes later, he exited the elevator with an empty dolly only to return a few minutes later with another box of a similar size to the first.

"Wasn't the sofa larger than that?" Katya asked.

"Yes." Maddox nodded, his gaze fixed to the screen and what happened next.

"Do you have the security video of the fifth floor about the time he would have gotten off the elevator?"

"I checked. This is the interesting part." Casey clicked another icon displaying the man with the box in the elevator. The man turned his back to the camera, partially out of sight, then a hand came up with a spray can and suddenly the video turned black.

"Where did the picture go?"

"That's the interesting part. I think he used black spray paint. Now listen." Casey increased the volume.

The automated assistant for the elevator sang out, *Fifth floor.* A swishing was then followed by the rumble of a heavy cart bumping over the elevator threshold.

"Fifth, not sixth floor," Katya said.

"And an extra love seat," Casey added. "I was on the phone at that time and didn't catch the additional load."

"Back it up." Maddox leaned forward.

Casey rewound the video to the where the man on the elevator faced the camera.

Maddox poked a finger at the screen. "Stop."

The frame stopped on the man's face, giving a fairly clear picture of him. Blond hair, gray or blue eyes, tall with a muscular build under the gray coveralls of a delivery driver.

"I need you to send a copy of that picture to an email address."

As Casey brought up his email account, Maddox wrote an address on a sticky note pad. "Send it there."

The young security guard keyed in the email address. Just as he maneuvered his mouse and clicked the Send button, Katya gasped.

"Boys, we have company." She pointed at the screen displaying the lobby. Men dressed in blue coveralls emblazoned with the bold yellow letters ATF AGENT entered, carrying scary-looking automatic weapons.

Chapter Fourteen

Katya's heart thundered in her chest like a bass drummer out of control. "Is there another way out of here?" she turned around looking for a back exit, anywhere she could go to escape the law enforcement officials who'd obviously been tipped off by someone.

"No. That's it." Casey nodded toward the door, then his eyes widened and a grin spread across his face. "Wait." He jumped up from his chair and ran across the small control room to the back wall. "If I recall correctly from my orientation, we have an emergency exit somewhere around here, just for the building security force that leads from the back of the control room to the parking garage two floors down." Like a madman, he pushed aside boxes and a copy machine, revealing a small door in the back wall. "I never think about it because we aren't supposed to use it unless it's a real emergency. I, personally, have never actually been down there."

He fumbled with the keys on his massive key chain, fitting one at a time into the door's lock. "Geez, which one of these keys goes to the door? I've never opened the door so I really don't know which one will make it open—*if* I even have the key."

Katya alternated between monitoring the screen and the progress the ATF men were making toward the control room and checking on Casey's progress in the back of the room. "Hurry, Casey. Some of them are headed up the elevator. Two are on their way here."

"I'm going as fast as I can." Casey dropped the ring of keys on the floor and dove to recover. "How close are they now?"

"Outside the door to the control room," Katya said, her voice low. With her insides quaking, she abandoned the screen and ran for the little door.

As she reached the two men standing there, Casey fitted a key in the lock and turned it. The door opened to reveal a metal ladder leading down a tiny shaft into darkness.

"Wow, this is too cool." Casey stared down at the escape route and then stepped aside, motioning for them to proceed. "You two better go."

Katya almost backed away. Dark, narrow ladders into an abyss weren't a normal, everyday occurrence in her life.

Maddox stepped up to the door. "I'll go first." He cupped her cheek. "I'll be there—all you have to do is follow my voice." He pressed his lips to hers in a hasty kiss. "Ready?"

She nodded and waited.

Maddox climbed onto the ladder and lowered himself into the darkness. "Now you, Katya. It's not so bad once you start down."

Katya, her hands shaking, grasped the cold metal rungs and placed her feet on the first step.

A loud banging on the control room door made her jerk and almost lose her hold on the ladder.

"Go," Casey whispered. "I have to shut the door and move the boxes in place before I let the ATF in. Be careful."

"Thanks, Casey. For everything." Katya sucked in a deep breath and lowered herself down the rungs.

Above her, Casey closed the door, shutting out all the light, leaving her in utter darkness.

"It's okay, Katya," Maddox said below her. He touched her foot. "One step at a time, and we'll get out of this."

Katya clung to the ladder, her breathing coming in quick, shallow pants, her fingers in a death grip on the metal rung. "I can't do this."

"Yes, you can." He stroked her calf then guided her foot to the next step. "See? One at a time."

"I am beginning to think this nightmare will never end."

"It will. Keep moving." Maddox coaxed and guided her every step of the way.

After what seemed like forever, dull gray light shone up the shaft from the bottom. Then Maddox was dropping the last few steps into a secluded area in the parking garage. He held his arms up. "You have to jump from the last rung. It's only five feet down. I'll catch you."

Katya climbed as low as she could, then let go, falling the last five feet into Maddox's arms. For a long moment, he held her, smoothing his hands over her hair. She wished she could stay that way forever, in the warmth and security of Maddox Thunder Horse's arms. She looked up into his face. "Do you make it a habit of saving damsels in distress?"

Maddox's expression hardened, his jaw tightening.

"No. Sometimes I'm too late." His arms dropped to his sides and he turned away.

Katya remembered what his mother had said about Maddox's fiancée dying in a blizzard. "You have to let go of the past, Maddox. You did not kill your fiancée— the blizzard did."

"What do you know about it? You weren't there."

"No, and I was not there for my father when he was murdered." Katya touched Maddox's arm. "You do not know how I wished I had been there for him."

He turned on her. "And if you had, you'd be dead, too."

"Exactly. You do not know how many times over the past couple of days I wished I could die and be with him."

"But you didn't."

"I know." Her hand moved up his arm. "Because of you."

"I won't always be there."

"No, but I am thankful for when you are." She pressed her cheek to his chest and hugged him around his middle. "I know you will not always be there. Especially when I go back to my country." She hugged him hard, then pushed away. "But we have to get out of here, or I will never make it back."

Maddox grabbed her hand and stopped her from stepping out of the concrete alcove. "Would that be such a bad thing?"

She gazed back at him, wishing with all her heart that she didn't have to return to Trejikistan. If she had her choice, she would stay with this tall, dark Lakota native on the Plains of North Dakota with his beloved wild horses. What a glorious life that would be. "Yes. I have to return to my country."

Maddox nodded and, still holding her hand, stepped up to the corner of the alcove, peering around the edge.

Nothing moved in the garage, the spaces empty, most of the tenants gone to work for the day.

Maddox tugged her hand, drawing her along the walls, keeping to the shadows. When they reached the exit, Katya yanked Maddox back.

A big, black van stood in the road, against the curb. Several men in the navy blue uniforms of the ATF team stood beside it, talking into handheld radios.

Maddox pointed to a bush close to the exit ramp. He let go of her hand, his gaze on the men by the van, then he ran across the ramp and dove into the bush.

The men at the van continued to talk on their handheld radios, oblivious to Maddox's exit.

Her heart thumping in her chest, Katya focused on the men in the street. When she was sure they were not looking, she followed Maddox, running across the concrete ramp. She dove behind the bushes, crashing into Maddox. He caught her and cushioned her fall, pressing a finger to her lips.

He parted the bushes and stared out.

Katya held her breath. Would this be it? Would the ATF finally catch up with their suspected terrorist?

What appeared to be the man in charge spoke to several men standing in front of him and pointed toward the building, specifically the garage exit.

"Time to move out." Ducking low, Maddox pushed between the bushes and the brick wall of the parking garage until they reached the far corner, leading toward the next building. A small gap between the hedges was all that separated the buildings.

Maddox went first, then Katya.

Someone shouted behind them.

Katya and Maddox didn't look back. They ran down a side street, leaving the apartment complex and the ATF behind.

Maddox didn't stop until they were ten blocks away. He yanked Katya behind a building and they both bent over at the middle, gasping for air.

Katya couldn't get enough oxygen. She dropped to her knees, her head thrown back, pulling in air as fast as her lungs could take it. "What...do...we...do now?"

Maddox straightened, his chest heaving, but closer to normal than Katya felt. "I had Casey send that picture to my brother, Pierce. He's an FBI agent. Maybe he can identify the man."

"In the meantime, what else can I do? I don't have anywhere to go, no one who can clear me." Her lungs hurt, her shins and calves screamed from the effort she'd expended.

"We locate a place to hole up until we hear from Pierce." Maddox looked around. "We should be able to find a motel around here."

"A motel?" she asked, her shoulders drooping. She didn't think she could run another step.

Maddox glanced at her. "We need rest."

Katya nodded, the idea of a pillow and a comfortable bed so very appealing after being on the road all night and chased by a crazed killer and the ATF. "A motel sounds great. Will it be safe?"

"As safe as anything when you consider that the ATF is after you."

She grimaced at Maddox. "You are making me feel *so* much better."

He smiled and held out his hand. "Good, then let's get moving. We aren't out of hot water yet."

She laid her hand in his and let him pull her to her feet and into his arms. "Hot water sounds wonderful. I could use a bath."

Katya guided them to a bus stop with a route to the outskirts of Minneapolis. Keeping her head down, Katya climbed aboard and moved to a backseat where she pressed her hand to her face, pretending to cough. Maddox sat beside her, shielding her from view of the other passengers. He didn't like being in a public place where someone might recognize her.

Maddox found a motel off the beaten path of the interstates and main thoroughfares. While he obtained a key, Katya huddled in the bushes at the far end of the parking lot.

He didn't like leaving her even for a moment, but he couldn't risk a clerk matching her face to the ones plastered all over the television screen behind him.

He'd asked for a room at the end of the building, farthest away from the road, and paid cash. When he unlocked the door, he scanned the parking lot and the street beyond before he motioned for Katya to join him.

Keeping close to the hedges surrounding the parking lot, she moved quickly and quietly until she entered the room.

Maddox shut the door and locked the dead bolt. "Well, now, that wasn't so bad, was it?"

Katya unzipped her heavy winter coat and dropped it onto a chair. She stood with her shoulders sagging, and stripped the hat from her head, her long luscious

locks falling free in a tangled mess around her face.
Her pale face was as pale as when he'd first found her
almost dead by a frozen river. The dark smudges beneath her eyes stood out like bruises. Yet, despite how
tired and worn-out she looked, she was still the most
beautiful woman Maddox had ever seen.

"I'm tired," she laughed, her voice shaky, her lips
trembling.

"I'll bet." He held out his arms and she fell into them.

For a long moment, they stayed that way, holding
each other, the warmth of her body chasing away the
chill in Maddox's. A chill that went back to the day
Susan died in his arms. She was right. He couldn't hold
on to the past, not when the present was kicking his butt.

"You can have the bathroom first."

"Thanks. But I don't think I can move." She sighed
and leaned closer.

"I'd help, but I need to place a call to my brother,
Pierce, and check on Tuck."

Katya stepped away, her arms dropping to her sides.
"That's more important. I'll be quick."

As Katya stepped into the little bathroom, Maddox
pulled the throwaway cell phone from his pocket and
dialed Pierce's number.

"Pierce? Maddox here."

"Where the hell are you?"

"I can't tell you yet. Are you near a computer?"

"I can be. Give me a sec."

A moment later Maddox heard the squeak of what
had to be an office chair.

"Shoot, brother," Pierce said.

"I had an email sent to you. It contains a picture of
a man we think planted the weapons in Katya's room.

He might also be the man who's been following her and who tried to shoot her."

"I'm on it. I'll see what we can do to ID the guy. Can I reach you again at this number?"

"Yes."

"I'll call as soon as I get a hit on your man."

"The sooner the better. We're hiding out from just about every law enforcement agency in the country and this man you're going to be looking to match."

"I know. We even got the heads-up on the girl here at the Bureau. Won't be long before you're on the same dance card. Be safe."

"Will do." Maddox clicked the Off button and sighed. After another call home to make sure Tuck, Dante and his mother were all right, he let some of the tension slide from his shoulders. For the moment they were relatively safe.

The sound of the shower called to Maddox. Knowing that Katya was naked in it made the decision for him.

He stripped off his clothes and entered the bathroom, shoving aside the curtain.

Katya, her face and head beneath the water, rinsing the suds out of her eyes, didn't hear him enter.

God, she had a beautiful body. Maddox stepped into the tub behind her and slid his hands around her waist.

She jumped at first. When she realized who it was, she relaxed, leaning against him. Katya fit him perfectly.

He rubbed soap in his palms and smoothed them over her belly and upward to cup her breasts.

Katya breathed deeply, her chest pushing against his hands. She reached behind her, capturing his buttocks, pressing him closer, his erection nudging against her.

He tweaked her nipples, drawing them to hardened points. Then his fingers trailed through the slippery soap down her torso, over her flat abdomen to the thatch of curls at the apex of her thighs.

Her hand found his shaft behind her and stroked him from tip to stem.

Maddox groaned, his fingers dipping into her folds, matching the rhythm of her strokes, flicking and teasing her until her back arched against him.

He wouldn't last long, not as hot as she made him and as good as her body felt against his. Nothing could top that, except being inside her.

As if reading his thoughts, Katya turned in his arms, one perfect leg trailing up over his calf.

He hooked her thighs in his hands and turned her back to the cool hard tile wall of the shower, balancing her as he lowered her down until he nudged at her opening.

"Please," she said, easing herself down until she took him fully inside.

Maddox's breath caught in his throat. "You feel so good."

"Make love to me, Maddox, like this is the last time."

He froze, his hands holding her legs wrapped around his waist. "No. I'll make love to you like this is the first time." He drove into her. "The first of many." In and out, he thrust, the tension pulsing through his body. Desperation, frustration and anger fueled his passion, pushing him harder and faster.

Katya had come to mean more to him than he ever expected, and he didn't want to lose her—wouldn't lose her. Not after all they had been through together.

When he climaxed, he pulled her close, holding her tight against his body.

Her arms and legs clung to him, her body shaking. They remained this way until their passion and the water cooled.

Maddox set Katya on her feet and they finished rinsing off. He dried her body and she dried his. Maddox carried Katya to the bed, laying her among the sheets, where he kissed every inch of her body. When she tried to return the gesture, he stopped her. "No, I want you to sleep. This is my treat."

Katya lay back, her damp curls splayed out across the pillow, while Maddox explored every inch of her body with his lips. She fell asleep soon after.

Although he could have gone for another round of lovemaking, he knew she was tired and his mind and muscles ached for sleep. Eventually, he crawled beside her and fell into a deep sleep, her body curled against him. Where she belonged.

He couldn't have been asleep for long when his cell phone buzzed on the nightstand beside the bed. Maddox fumbled for the phone, punching at the unfamiliar buttons until he stopped the ringing. "Yeah."

"Maddox, you have a serious problem."

It took him a moment to surface from sleepiness to recognize his brother Pierce's voice. He shoved a hand through his hair and sat up, hoping the movement would jar him more fully awake. "What problem?"

"The man who is after Katya is a professional assassin."

Chapter Fifteen

"What is it?" Katya sat up behind him, pressing her naked breasts against Maddox's back.

He sucked in a deep breath, completely awake, adrenaline firing throughout his system. "Who is he and who would have hired him?"

"Richard Fulton, alias, Rick Masters, alias, Patrick Delaney, and the aliases go on. We suspect him of at least twenty assassinations and those are only the ones we know about. He's at the top of the FBI's Most Wanted list."

"Damn." Maddox sat back, sick to his stomach. "What do we do?"

"You can't keep her safe by yourself," Pierce said. "You need to let me help."

"I can't drag you into this. I've already implicated the rest of the family in Katya's problem—no need to drag you in, as well."

"Just my knowledge of this has me fully involved. Let us help. We have the resources to figure this thing out."

"The ATF hasn't figured it out yet. How can the FBI?"

"I have a vested interest, brother," Pierce's voice

dropped, low and insistent. "I can get my boss to buy in. We bring in the girl, Fulton will follow."

"Use her as bait?"

"No, provide her protection."

"The way this guy has followed us, he'll find her."

"Not where we'll hide her. We can set her up in a safe house with dedicated agents to guard her. Then we can set up a phony safe house and let it slip that she's there. He'll come after her, we'll get our man and Katya will be cleared."

"Sounds like you have this all planned out."

"Either way, Maddox, she's not safe out on her own."

"She has me and she's still alive."

"Fulton is a professional. He always gets his mark. It's only a matter of time."

Maddox held the phone to his ear, but he didn't respond. "Let me think about it. I'll call you back."

"Maddox—" Pierce shouted into the phone as Maddox hit the Off button.

Let someone else protect Katya? Every one of Maddox's brain cells screamed, *No!* But he wasn't alone in this. Katya had a say in what she wanted to do.

"I only caught a little of that." Katya pulled the sheet up over her trembling body, her eyes rounded. "An assassin?" She shook hard, her fingers clenching the sheet to her breasts.

"Richard Fulton." Maddox ran his hand through his hair. "From what Pierce said, the man is a paid assassin and extremely dangerous. He's at the top of the FBI's Most Wanted list."

"What did your brother suggest?"

Maddox stared across at her, his chest tightening.

"He wants to put you in a safe house and use you as bait to catch Fulton."

Katya didn't utter a sound, the only indication that she heard him was a slight widening of her already rounded blue eyes.

"My gut feeling on this is no." Maddox twisted the phone in one hand. "We've managed to stay safe this long, and we can continue doing what we've been doing while the FBI looks into the video we sent."

"How long will it take for them to clear me of suspicion?"

"I don't know."

"I don't have time to wait for a full-fledged investigation." She dropped the sheet and crawled across the bed to Maddox where she kneeled beside him. "I can't expect you to protect me forever."

He frowned and opened his mouth to protest, but she placed a finger over his lips and then replaced it with her mouth. She brushed a kiss across his lips and pressed her cheek to his. "I want to go to the safe house, Maddox. But I want it on the condition that I am freed of charges and sent back to Trejikistan once they capture the assassin."

He slipped his hands around her waist and pulled her onto his lap. "What if I can't let you go?"

"You have to. I am not your responsibility and no matter how this ends, I cannot stay." She reached up and cupped his cheeks with her hands. "I have to go home."

Maddox stared down into her eyes. Anger, fear and something else battled in his heart, making his chest hurt. He captured her hands in his and squeezed them hard. "If that's the way you want it." He stood, lifting her with him to set her on the floor.

As much as he wanted to drag her naked body back to the bed, he didn't. She wanted to leave, and he'd make it possible. As she'd stated from the very beginning, back in the cave on the ranch, *no strings.* "Get dressed. I'll arrange a transfer point with the FBI." Too bad the strings he'd allowed to grow were now choking his heart.

HOURS LATER, KAT STOOD at the window, staring out at the group of cars leaving the small house perched in an isolated location west of Minneapolis. Maddox had left well over an hour ago after he had seen her settled in. He had not wanted to go, but she insisted. Better to cut the ties now. If all went as planned, she would be back in her country within the week.

The four men positioned at every corner remained outside.

"You should be safe here." Pierce Thunder Horse laid a hand on her shoulder. "We've leaked word that you are at the other safe house. We have an entire squad of agents surrounding it, ready to capture Fulton as soon as he makes his move."

Katya didn't respond, her gaze on the now-empty road.

Pierce's lips tipped into a small smile. "Maddox didn't look too happy about leaving you with me. What's up between you two?"

"Nothing," she replied. Her life was back in Trejik-istan. Her people needed her leadership to see them through the next few months in preparation for their first election. Maddox had a family and a ranch to go home to. She had a country to lead into democracy.

"If it makes you feel any better, Maddox looked pretty miserable."

Why did Maddox's brother insist on poking at her wounds? She frowned and captured Pierce's gaze in his reflection in the window. "Why would that make me feel better?"

"He made me promise to take good care of you."

"He would do that for anyone. Maddox is a good man."

"True." Pierce nodded. "But he seems a little hurt that you chose the FBI to look after you rather than him."

"I do not know why. I have only been trouble to him since he saved me out in the canyon."

Pierce chuckled. "Yeah, I heard about some of that from Tuck. I didn't think you'd come to the FBI for help. What changed your mind?"

Katya avoided Pierce's gaze in the window's reflection, preferring to stare out at the dirt road leading to the remote cabin. "Maddox."

"He did? Maddox convinced you to turn yourself over to us?"

"No. I did it for Maddox. I could not continue to lead him on."

"How so?"

"I have to return to Trejikistan." She straightened her shoulders the way her mother had taught her so long ago. *You are royalty. Act like it.* "It is my duty."

"And he didn't want you to go?"

She nodded.

"Did you tell him why you had to return?"

"No." She hadn't wanted anything to change between them. Had he known who she was, he might have been like everyone else and looked at her differently, like a freak or someone who was too fragile to even think for herself.

"Did you tell him about your family?" Pierce persisted.

Katya's heart skipped a beat and she turned to face Maddox's brother. "What do you know about my family?"

"I just got your dossier on my way out the door to pick you up." He held a file in his hands and flipped it open. "Seems your full name is Princess Alexi Katya Ivanov. Daughter of the late Boris Ivanov, king of Trejikistan."

She sucked in a deep breath and let it out slowly. "Did you tell Maddox?"

"I didn't have time to read the dossier until we were on our way out here."

"Don't tell him, please." She knew she had to leave, and she didn't want Maddox's opinion or memories of her to change because of a stupid title that would mean nothing in a few months.

"Why not?"

"I came to America to be me, not Princess Alexi Katya Ivanov. If Maddox chooses to remember me, I would prefer him to remember me as just a girl, a foreign exchange student, not a princess from some faraway land few people in America had even heard of." She took Pierce's hands in hers. "Please, don't tell him."

Pierce stared down into her eyes. "I'm beginning to see why Maddox has fallen in love with you."

Katya shook her head, her hands falling to her sides. "Do not be foolish. We have not known each other long enough for him to fall in love with me."

"He left for home with the most wounded-dog look on his face I've seen in a long time. What else could it be?"

"Not love." Katya turned to stare out the window again.

Pierce started to say something else when his cell phone rang. "Excuse me." He turned and walked into the kitchen of the little cabin.

Katya strained to hear his end of the conversation.

"You bastard, what have you done with my brother?" Pierce's expletive drew Katya into the kitchen, his privacy be damned.

Her pulse thundered in every vein, her heart banging against her chest. Maddox was in trouble.

Pierce paced the length of the small kitchen, the phone pressed to his ear with one hand, the other clenched in a tight fist by his side. "Where do you want to make the transfer?"

Katya's fingers twisted together and she bit down hard on her lip to keep it from trembling. What had happened to Maddox?

Pierce hit the Off button and reared back to throw the phone against the wall.

Katya caught his arm before he could let the device fly. "What happened to Maddox?"

"Fulton has him and wants to make a trade. We're to meet him at a warehouse close to the Port of St. Paul in an hour."

"He wants to trade me for Maddox?"

Pierce looked at her, his mouth set in a firm line. "Yeah. But I can't do that."

Katya nodded, every part of her body growing still.

She knew what had to be done and didn't hesitate. "Yes, you can. We have to make the deal."

MADDOX PRESSED THE accelerator to the floor, pushing the rental car to its limit on the interstate between Minneapolis and Fargo. His little throwaway cell phone hadn't had reception since he left the Twin Cities.

The urge to turn around and go back fought with reason. He couldn't just go back to Minneapolis, find Katya and take her back under his wing. He wanted to force her to stay with him, even after all the danger died down. Thank God he'd insisted on taking her to the safe house himself. At least he knew how to find her.

What if Katya didn't want him to come?

She'd insisted that he leave her with the FBI. They knew better how to protect her. They were trained to man a safe house and provide the security needed to keep her out of Richard Fulton's sights. For all intents and purposes, *she* had rejected *him*. She had told him to leave.

Maddox had traveled nearly an hour away from the safe house before his resolve crumbled. He lifted his cell phone for the fifth time in as many minutes. Still no reception. Resisting the urge to throw the phone, he noticed an off-ramp coming up. On this long stretch of interstate in Minnesota, they were few and far between. His foot slipped off the accelerator and the car veered off the road and onto the ramp. Maybe if he got to higher ground off the ramp he'd get a bar or two of reception.

He drove to the top of the ramp. The longer he was out of cell phone range, the more certain he was that something was wrong. He had to get hold of Pierce, even if it meant turning around and heading back to Minneapolis.

He checked his phone again. Still no bars. That decided it. Without slowing, he barreled through the stop sign and flew across the overpass and onto the interstate, headed back east to Minneapolis. The sooner he was within range of a decent cell tower, the better. Once he talked to Pierce, he'd relax and return to the ranch.

As he neared Minneapolis and the turnoff to the safe house, four bars sprang up on his cell phone screen. Finally! He hit the speed-dial button for his brother and immediately got his answering machine. An hour out and just under an hour back since he'd left Katya and his brother at the safe house. Why he didn't trust them to keep Katya safe, he didn't know. But he couldn't just walk away. Not after the past two days of taking care of her. If something happened...

He tried his brother again. Still no answer.

Damn! Why wasn't he responding? A lump of lead weighed heavily in his gut. Was the safe house outside cell phone reception? Or could it be that Katya was once again in trouble?.

"MADDOX WOULDN'T WANT you to do this." Pierce held the door for Katya to climb into the SUV that would carry her to the warehouses located on the St. Paul side of the Mississippi River.

"Maddox cannot speak for himself. Because of me, he is a hostage of that murdering bastard." Katya stared straight ahead, calm, determined to face whatever lay ahead. Maddox had rescued her several times over the past couple days. If it was the last thing she did, she would make sure he came out of this fiasco alive.

Images of him holding her close in the sleeping bag in the cave kept playing through her mind. The dark Native American with his long, straight black hair had hands that could crush, but were gentle. He had coaxed her away from a frozen death, given her a second chance to redeem her name, her country and her life. The least she could do was negotiate his freedom.

"I have a squad of agents moving into place around the warehouse. If Fulton shows, they'll nab him. Maybe even before you arrive."

She touched Pierce's arm. "No! You cannot let Fulton see them. If he suspects we are not alone, he might hurt Maddox."

"Don't worry. They are under strict instructions not to make a move until they know where Maddox is and have a clear shot at Fulton."

Bullets might fly and one might hit Maddox. "Can we just trade me for Maddox and leave all the bullets in the guns?"

Pierce smiled at her. "You really like the guy, don't you?"

She nodded. "He is a good man. He does not deserve to be caught in the cross fire."

"I agree. But we have to take Fulton out or you'll never be safe."

"I don't care about me."

"Consider that his next victim will not be safe."

"You're right."

Pierce dug a small disc out of his shirt pocket and handed it to her. "Put this in a pocket, somewhere that can't be found. A safe place where you won't lose it."

She turned the disc over. A plain shiny disc, it looked like a large watch battery. "What is it?"

"A gift from me and Maddox. In case things don't go according to plan."

She shrugged and shoved the disc into her pocket.

"No, someplace no one would think to look."

Katya's brows pulled together. "Is this a GPS tracking device?"

Pierce grinned. "Smart as well as beautiful. Yes. That's exactly what it is. Just in case we get separated, we'll be able to find you."

She pulled the disc from her pocket and pulled the neckline of her sweater out enough so she could slide the disc into her bra. "Better?"

"Much." Pierce gulped. "Definitely smart as well as beautiful. Eyes on the road, Thunder Horse," he said beneath his breath.

The sedan in front of them slowed as they neared a T-intersection, crowded by trees and tall mounds of snow that had been pushed off the road.

As the car moved out into the road, a truck barreled at it from the south, slamming into the side of the sedan, sending it careening off the road and into a ditch.

Katya screamed.

The SUV driver slammed on the brakes and Katya hit the seat back in front of her, stunning her.

Before she knew what was happening her door jerked open and she was yanked from the SUV, a gun pointed at her head. "Don't try anything or I'll kill her," a deep male voice demanded.

"You kill her and you're a dead man." Pierce held his gun up in his hand, letting it dangle from the trigger guard. "Let the girl go."

"No can do. She's money."

"What have you done with Maddox?"

Fulton laughed. "Nothing. Not a damn thing. He's probably halfway to North Dakota by now. Move it, Princess, we have an appointment to make." He grabbed her elbow and backed away from the vehicle, the gun pressing into her temple.

Despite the threat to her life, Katya couldn't stop the flood of relief from warming her insides. Maddox was safe. Fulton hadn't captured him.

The metal gun barrel bounced, slamming into her temple as Fulton forced her to walk backwards to the waiting truck with the smashed front end. The assassin slid into the driver's seat, pulling her in next to him, close enough that if anyone tried to shoot at them, they'd hit her as well. "Close the door."

Katya reached for the handle and pulled the door toward her. All the while Fulton kept his head close to hers, using her as a human shield.

He shifted the gun to his left hand and reached for the gearshift with his right. "Don't get any ideas. I can shoot equally well with both hands." With a quick tug, he had it in reverse, backing away from the FBI vehicles until they were out of range. Then he swung the truck around and hit the accelerator, rocketing the vehicle down the highway.

Katya let him take her without a fight. She wanted to get as far away from the agents as possible. Enough people had been hurt in this man's quest to capture her. This way, Maddox's brother, Pierce, would be safe.

"You're a hired assassin, aren't you?" Katya asked.

"Not your business."

"When I'm the target, that makes it my business," she retorted.

Fulton laughed, driving one-handed. "The princess has a mouth on her."

"Who hired you to kill me?"

The man focused on navigating the road ahead. "Who said I was going to kill you?"

"You've shot enough bullets at me to take me out a couple times."

"If I'd wanted to hit you, trust me, I'd have hit you."

"You didn't answer me." She tried to turn her head to look at him, but he held the gun to her temple, pressing so hard she couldn't. "Who hired you?"

"Your future husband."

"What?" She tried again to turn her head. Cold, hard metal dug into her flesh. "What do you mean, my future husband?"

"You're a smart girl. Figure it out." He slowed to negotiate a turn from the county road to a state highway. The truck shot forward, slipping sideways on a patch of ice.

Katya shook her head. "I don't have a future husband."

"You do now, and he was willing to pay big bucks for me to bring you back to Trejikistan to marry him."

"Trejikistan?" She searched her memory for anyone who had ever even hinted at wanting to marry her back in her country. She'd eavesdropped on a conversation between her father and… "Vladimir?"

"Bingo! Give the princess a prize."

"Vladimir wants to marry me? Why?"

"You're failing in my estimation, Princess. And I was beginning to think you were a smart cookie." Her captor shook his head. "The man thinks that by marrying you, he can build his case as the new ruler, now that your father is out of the way."

Katya gasped. "Vladimir is responsible for my father's death?"

"Not for me to say—you'll have to ask him. I don't like to brag about my work." His eyes narrowed, the gun pressing harder into her temple. "You've slipped through my fingers too often lately. Makes me look bad."

Rage boiled up inside her. This man had killed her father. "You murdering bastard. You can rot in hell for all the people you've murdered, and for what? A few dollars?"

"More than a few."

Katya stared at the road ahead, her blood pounding in her veins. She wanted to kill this man who'd taken her father from her, to make him hurt as much as he'd hurt her father and her family. "You're a coward, a lowlife murderer. You'll pay for this. I promise you."

"You need to shut up." He swerved, flinging her head against the window.

Katya blinked back the pain, refusing to show this man an ounce of fear. "How much is he paying you?"

"Enough. More, if I bring you back alive. That's the beauty of it. I get paid either way. Dead or alive."

"If it's all the same to you. I'd prefer to be dead than to marry Vladimir." She grabbed the steering wheel and yanked it to the left.

Richard Fulton jammed his foot on the brakes, let go of the gun and used both hands to regain control of the vehicle. The truck veered off the road and into the ditch filled with mounds of snow.

Katya shoved the door open, jumped out and ran.

"Damn woman. Stop!" Footsteps pounded on the ground behind her.

She didn't look back, pushing harder to reach the road. She had to get away from this killer and warn her country about Vladimir's plan. As she reached the top of the ditch, her feet slipped out from under her on a patch of ice and she went down hard, her head hitting the pavement.

Richard Fulton stood over her, his gun pointed at her head. "I should have killed you back in that canyon."

Blackness consumed her.

Chapter Sixteen

Maddox took the turn, skidding sideways and almost running into an SUV that barreled into the intersection—the SUV that had taken Katya to the safe house. What was it doing out here?

He blocked the road with his rental car and leaped out.

Pierce dropped down from the driver's seat and ran toward Maddox. "Fulton has her."

Maddox ground to a halt, all the air leaving his lungs in a rush as though he'd been sucker punched. "What?"

"Fulton set up an ambush and grabbed Katya before we realized what was happening." Pierce jerked his head toward the other agent who'd been in the SUV with him. "Move the car." He grabbed Maddox's arm. "Ride with us. We have a tracking device on her. He won't get far with her."

"If he doesn't kill her first." Maddox stated, his feet like lead as he forced himself to move toward the vehicle. He couldn't bear to find her dead. He'd been through that once with Susan.

"She's not dead. He'd have killed her on the spot, not taken her hostage. Hell, he'd have killed her a long time ago if he really wanted her dead. He's a paid assassin. They don't miss unless they want to."

Maddox climbed into the passenger seat of the SUV. Pierce climbed in beside him and tossed a device with a screen on it. "Follow the moving dot. That's Katya's tracking device."

"How did he find her? I thought safe houses were supposed to be secret."

"All we can figure is that he might have an insider in the FBI feeding him information."

"He knew where to find us when we were out at the hunting cabin." Maddox stared ahead as they pulled around the rental car and picked up the agent. "He knew where to find us in Medora. He was always there."

"It's as though he has his own tracking device on her."

"Her necklace," Maddox said. "Katya said her father gave it to her so that he'd always know she was safe. He must have had a tracking device embedded in it."

"And Fulton knew it. Someone from Katya's country had to have given him that information." Pierce shook his head. "She would never have been safe as long as she had that necklace on her. We should have taken all of her belongings away before we brought her to the safe house. Sorry, Maddox."

"She wouldn't have given it up easily." It was her last gift from her father. Maddox's teeth ground together at the thought of Katya in Fulton's hands. "The main thing is to get her back before Fulton does something stupid."

"That's the plan. I've mobilized a task force. They have the tracking device up on their screens and will converge on Fulton, wherever he takes her."

"As long as they don't hurt Katya."

"What, and start an international incident?" Pierce shot a look at Maddox. "I put out strict instructions not to harm a hair on her pretty head."

"Good." Maddox sat back, clenching and unclenching his fist. He'd feel a whole lot better when he saw Katya again. Alive. "They're headed for Minneapolis."

"We'll keep a safe distance from them until they come to a halt."

Minutes dragged by. Maddox's hands gripped the tracker, the knuckles growing whiter the longer they trailed the killer. What was happening to Katya? Was she still alive? The only thing they knew for certain was that she was with the killer. Would he never stop? "At what point will you try to force him off the road?"

"We won't. He'll have to stop sooner or later, if for nothing else, fuel. We follow until he does so."

"If we don't run out of gas before he does." Maddox stole a look at the gas gauge.

"Don't worry. We're full and there's a backup tank."

Maddox's attention returned to the tracker. "Wait. I think they've stopped." He leaned closer. Was it true? Yes. The dot on the screen had stopped.

"Where?"

Maddox zoomed in on the tracking device and gave Pierce the address.

"That's near the port. What's he doing there?"

"Wherever he thinks he's going, he's not taking Katya with him." Maddox stared ahead.

Pierce relayed the information to the other agents. They agreed to set up operations two blocks from the tracker location and move in on foot. When he got off the radio, he stared across at Maddox. "You need to stay with the SUV. I can't risk having a civilian involved if shots are fired."

"Like hell."

"Maddox, I need to concentrate on saving Katya. Not you."

"I can't sit back and do nothing."

"You damn sure can."

Maddox clenched his teeth to keep from saying anything else.

"Promise you won't interfere?" Pierce insisted.

Maddox nodded.

Two blocks from Katya's GPS location, the vehicles pulled together. Pierce joined the team and weapons were distributed—everything from SIG Sauer pistols to high-powered rifles only sharpshooters would know how to use correctly.

Darkness had fallen, the streetlights casting beams of light out into the street and shadows consuming all else.

As soon as the team set off, Maddox counted to ten and followed. He had promised not to interfere, but he didn't promise not to follow. Wherever Katya was, he wanted to be.

"GET UP!" FULTON SHOOK HER until her teeth rattled and her eyes opened.

Pain sliced through the back of her head as she stared up at her captor. "Where are we?"

For an answer, he yanked her to her feet and shoved her ahead of him toward a dark building that looked like a warehouse. The place smelled of rank water and diesel fumes.

"Where are we going?" she whispered, so careful not to speak too loudly that her voice echoed in her head. Her feet caught on an old cardboard box and she fell flat on her chest, the wind knocked from her lungs.

"Get up!" Fulton grabbed her by her hair and jerked her to her feet.

She got up quickly, standing on her toes to loosen his pull on her hair. His unrelenting hold brought unwanted tears to her eyes. "Okay, okay. I am coming." She hurried to keep up, all the while feeling for the tracking device she'd stuffed in her bra. She couldn't feel the little metal disc. The more she patted her chest, the more desperate she became. If she didn't have the disc, Pierce and the FBI would never find her. She could be tossed on a ship, or left somewhere to die, while they scratched their heads and wondered where Fulton had taken her.

Fulton yanked on her arm, forcing her ahead of him.

"What is your hurry, anyway?" she asked.

"The sooner I get you on the boat, the sooner I get paid." He reached the end of the alley and crossed a street to another equally dreary warehouse that appeared as though it hadn't been used in a decade. Windows, high on the brick walls, gaped open like faces frozen in horror, the glass broken, shadowy darkness revealing nothing within.

"I'm going on a boat?"

"On a container ship. In a container."

Katya sucked in a deep breath in an attempt to ease the panic rising in her throat. "How much is my cousin paying you?"

"Shut up."

"He doesn't actually have access to any money in Trejikistan without my—or my brother's—permission. Did you know that?"

Fulton came to an abrupt halt and glared down at

her. "You'd better hope he has the money he promised to pay. If not, you'll both die."

She waited until Fulton resumed his breakneck pace, knowing she had scored with her previous comment. Maybe she could get him so distracted that she could escape. "Did you know that my cousin is a habitual liar? He once promised to buy a yacht from an English duke, but after testing it for six months, he backed out of the deal, claiming it was damaged."

"Shut up, woman!" Fulton jerked her to a halt and slammed her up against a brick wall. "Your mouth will get you killed. One more comment, and I'm through messing with you."

Katya clamped her lips closed on her next retort. Fulton was distracted. Now she just had to look for an opportunity to trip him or pull free of his hold on her.

Her father's killer took off again, headed for the back of the vacant warehouse. They had to pass by a stack of broken pallets to get to the back door.

As they came alongside the pallets, Katya faked tripping, falling to her hands and knees.

"I should just shoot you now." He pointed his gun at her head, his breathing harsh and strained like a bull in a rage.

"Maybe you should," Katya taunted, her fingers closing around a single slat with nails protruding from the opposite end.

When he leaned forward to grab for her hair, she stood up, swinging the board at the hand holding the weapon.

The nails jabbed into his wrist. Fulton screamed, flinging the gun to the ground.

"You bit—"

He didn't finish the word before Katya swung back around with the board, this time catching the side of his face. The nails dug into the skin and ripped a long bloody path across his cheek. He screamed again, grabbing for his face.

Katya flung the board at him and ran the other way as fast as she could. If she could only make it to the end of the building and duck down another alley, she might lose him.

Her heart raced and her breathing came in ragged gasps, but she pressed on, moving as fast as her feet would carry her in snow boots.

Feet pounded on the pavement behind her, sharp curses flung at her from the angry man. "When I catch you..."

She reached the corner and spun to the right, running all out. The buildings were too long to give her any cover or concealment. Her only hope was to outrun him. Given his height and athletic ability, that didn't seem likely. He'd brought her to the oldest warehouses imaginable. Most appeared abandoned. She was on her own, with no one to rescue her. If she planned to survive, she'd have to rescue herself.

She amazed herself when she rounded the end of the next building and ducked down a back alley. This one contained a rusty trash Dumpster and old metal barrels. Before Fulton appeared around the corner, Katya hid behind a barrel and searched the trash-strewn ground for something she could use as a weapon. She grabbed a broken beer bottle from the ground and held it in front of her as she peered between the barrels at the man moving toward her.

"You might as well come out," he said. "I'll find you sooner or later."

She kept still, her pulse banging so loudly against her eardrums she was afraid she wouldn't hear him when he made his next move.

"If you escape from me, I'll only go after your boyfriend," he taunted. "Do you want me to kill your boyfriend?"

Katya's breath caught in her throat. She wanted to jump out and stab the murderer in the face. He had killed her father, he had tried to kill her and Tuck, and now he was threatening Maddox. Enough was enough.

She tamped down her raging anger and waited until he stepped in front of the barrel behind which she hid. When he did, she leaped from her hiding place, screaming as loud as she could and thrusting the broken bottle into Fulton's face.

THE FBI TOOK THE direct route toward the blip on the GPS tracking screen. Maddox had seen the screen and had a general idea of the layout of the streets. He hoped to get close enough to Katya to be there if she needed him.

Maddox ran from building to building, working his way closer to the last blip he'd seen on the screen. Fulton had been moving Katya toward the river. Hopefully, he didn't plan to toss her in. Maddox didn't know whether or not Katya could swim. There were a lot of things he didn't know about Katya and, *dammit,* he wanted to find out. All he needed was a little more time with her.

A scream ripped through the night, firing his adrenaline. He ran in the direction of the sound, hoping it hadn't echoed off the buildings from the opposite direction. Running full tilt, he skidded around a corner and into an alley filled with trash, barrels and an abandoned Dumpster.

There among the debris were two shadowy figures struggling in the darkness.

"Katya!"

"Stay back or I'll kill her!" Fulton shouted, twisting his hands in her hair and yanking so hard, her feet left the ground.

Katya yelped and kicked out, landing a boot against his shins. "He isn't armed!" she yelled.

Maddox didn't slow down, didn't stop to think, his entire body in reaction mode to the danger Katya was in. He charged the two like a raging lion, roaring at the top of his lungs.

He hit Fulton on the side, flinging him up into the air. The man slammed into the heavy metal Dumpster, dragging Katya by the hair.

Thrown off balance, she hit the ground next to the assassin, but came up fighting, twisting and kicking.

As distracted by Katya as he was, Fulton didn't see Maddox's second advance until too late.

Maddox balled his fist and rammed it into the killer's face. Bones snapped and blood gushed from Fulton's nose.

Katya pulled free and flung herself out of the way.

The assassin pushed to his feet and lunged at Maddox, hitting him in the gut. The two men fell to the ground, Fulton landing on top of Maddox.

Maddox bucked and fought to get his hands free, but remained pinned to the ground by the trained assassin. No matter how hard he tried, he couldn't shake free.

A loud crack rent the air and Fulton fell to the side, stunned.

Maddox leaped onto him and held him down.

Katya stood over the two men, holding a four-foot-long two-by-four like a warrior, ready to take on an entire army.

Suddenly the alley filled with men carrying weapons. One of them was Pierce.

Momentarily distracted, Maddox wasn't prepared when Fulton rolled to the side and out from under him. The assassin leaped to his feet and ran.

Pierce and every other agent on the FBI assault team raced after him. He didn't get to the end of the warehouse building before Pierce caught up with him and slammed him to the ground in a flying tackle.

Four assault rifles pointed at the fugitive as Pierce yanked the man's hands behind his back and handcuffed him. "You have the right to remain silent..."

As Pierce read the man his rights, Maddox stood and looked around for Katya. More FBI special agents had arrived in the alley and Maddox couldn't find her among them. His heart skipped several beats. Panic made him push through the men standing around until he spotted the dark-haired woman, his chest tightening at the sight of her.

She sat on the pavement, her arms wrapped around her knees, her shoulders shaking. She looked like an abandoned child, her hair tousled, her face streaked with dirt. But she was the most beautiful woman Maddox had ever seen.

He sat beside her and pulled her into his arms. For a long moment, they leaned against each other.

Pressing his lips into her hair, he whispered, "Thanks for rescuing me."

She gave a shaky laugh and looked up into his face. "I should be thanking you."

The dark alley couldn't dim the light in her pale blue eyes. She smiled. "You're my hero."

"And you are mine. He had me until you came at him like a warrior." He smoothed the hair out of her face. "Where'd you learn to fight dirty like that?"

She cupped his face with her hand and leaned forward to brush a kiss across his lips. "I did what I had to." She kissed him again.

This time Maddox didn't let her off so lightly. His arms tightened around her and he deepened the kiss, his tongue pushing past her teeth to toy with hers.

She gave back, pressing into him, her hands circling his neck, bringing him closer. When she broke contact, she whispered against his lips. "I wish we could stay like this."

Maddox chuckled against her lips. "What, in an alley, sitting on the cold hard ground?"

She sighed, nestling into his embrace. "In your arms. It is as close to heaven as I have ever imagined."

Maddox's hands closed on her shoulders and he pushed her far enough away to look down into her face. "Then stay with me. Don't go back to Trejikistan."

Her chin drooped and she pressed her forehead to his chest. "I cannot."

"Can't—or won't?" His tone hardened. When he'd left her with Pierce, he'd known it was one of the biggest mistakes of his life. "Katya, in the short time I've known you, you've become such an amazing part of my life. You reminded me how good it feels to be alive."

He tipped her chin up and gazed down into her eyes. "Stay," he said, his tone low, uncaring if the one word sounded like begging. He'd get down on his knees if he thought it would help.

A single tear rolled from the corner of her eye. "I have to go back. I have to do what has to be done."

Before he could question her further, an ambulance arrived, the sirens blaring and the lights flashing in their eyes.

Emergency medical personnel dropped down from the vehicle.

Pierce appeared before them. "I called the EMTs. Fulton needs attention, and I want them to have a look at you both."

Right behind the ambulance, a news van skidded to a stop, followed by another and another. Soon the alley looked like a celebrity mob scene.

The EMTs insisted on checking out Katya and Maddox. Between the reporters and the EMTs, Katya and Maddox were separated.

Maddox wanted to go to her, to protect her from the onslaught of the media.

A reporter stuck a microphone in Katya's face. "Is it true? You're not a terrorist? The weapons found in your apartment were planted by someone else?"

"Yes," Katya answered, standing on her toes, her gaze panning the crowd until she captured Maddox's.

Maddox mouthed the words, "Are you okay?"

She shrugged, a weak, unconvincing smile curling her lips.

People crowded around her, pressing so close that her eyes rounded, her hands coming up in a protective gesture.

Maddox shoved an EMT aside. "Thanks, but I'll
live." He had to get to Katya.

As he pushed through the media, a reporter yelled
out over the others, "Katya Ivanov, we have it from a
good source that you are actually royalty from Trejikistan, Princess Alexi Katya Ivanov, next in line for the
throne now that your father is dead and your brother is
missing. Is that true?"

Katya gasped, tears welling in her eyes. She looked
toward Maddox and back to the reporter. "No comment." She ducked her head, letting her hair fall over
her face.

Maddox froze in place. Princess? Katya was a princess? How had he not known that? Surely the reporter
had his facts wrong.

"Princess Alexi," another reporter pushed her way
through the crowd gathering around Katya. "Are you
seeking asylum in the United States since your government has been taken over in a military coup?"

Yet another reporter pressed in with his camera and
microphone. "Princess, are you abandoning your country just when the people were on the verge of conducting their first democratic election?"

Maddox remained frozen in place, staring over the
cameras and reporters to the woman trapped in the middle. Who was she? Did he even know?

Katya's head came up and she pushed her shoulders
back. "I am not abandoning my country. As soon as I
can get cleared to travel, I will return to Trejikistan and
lead my people until the elections and the new democratic government is in place."

Pierce muscled his way beside Maddox. "We need
to get her out of here."

When Maddox didn't move, Pierce frowned. "She didn't tell you, did she?"

All Maddox could do was shake his head. The woman he'd made love to, the woman he'd raced across the prairie with on the back of a snowmobile was a princess? "You knew?"

Pierce nodded. "She didn't want you to know. For what it's worth, she thought it would make you treat her differently. Does it change the way you feel about her?"

"Damn right."

"Take some time to digest it, brother. Don't do anything stupid." Pierce left his brother and pushed through the crowd. "Show's over. Leave the lady alone, she's been through enough."

Katya was loaded into an ambulance, Pierce climbing in beside her. Richard Fulton, under heavy FBI guard, left in another ambulance.

Maddox stayed where he was long after the ambulances and the press left the scene.

"Can I drop you off somewhere?" One of the remaining agents touched Maddox on the arm.

Until then, his mind had been somersaulting over everything that had happened in the past few days. When the agent brought him back to the present, his thoughts came together, one thing becoming crystal clear. He wanted to be with Katya. "Can you drop me off at the hospital?"

"Which one?"

"Whichever one they took the princess to." He ran toward the agent's vehicle and jumped in. When the agent didn't get right in, Maddox opened the door and called out. "Are you coming?"

The agent chuckled, sliding into the driver's seat. "Suddenly you're a man on a mission?"

"Damn right." A mission to find his princess.

Chapter Seventeen

"Thank God, you're alive!" Katya cried out in her native language. Propped against pillows in a sterile white hospital bed, she held Pierce's cell phone to her ear, tears of joy sliding down her cheeks.

"Yes, sister. I returned from Africa as soon as I could find transportation out," Dmitri said. "Vladimir had the armed forces mobilized to declare a military dictatorship, claiming the country would fall apart if he didn't take immediate action."

"Oh, Dmitri. What a horrible mess to come home to. I should have been there."

"Not to worry," he assured her. "I was able to avert disaster. As for the elections, everything is back on track."

"I am truly happy that you are alive and well." She dabbed at yet more tears. "Did you find out what really happened to Father?"

Dmitri paused. "Katya, Father was murdered. Cousin Vladimir is in prison. He confessed to hiring an assassin to murder our father."

"I know." Katya twisted her fingers around the pendant containing the tracking device that had almost gotten her killed. She had yet to give it up, and might never if she could find a way to destroy the device her father had implanted inside it to keep her safe. "They captured the assassin here."

"Excellent news."

"It's hard to believe Vladimir would kill his family for a throne," Katya said softly.

"I know." Her brother cleared his throat. "Speaking of news, word has come to us via the paparazzi that you have been busy yourself. What's this about you being a terrorist?"

Katya laughed. "It's a long story that I'll tell you all about when I arrive home. For now, I'm clear of all charges and free to leave whenever I get out of this hospital."

"Hospital? Are you well? Should I come to the United States to rescue you?"

"No. I am fine, just a few scratches and bruises. I promise I'll tell you all about it. If all goes well, I should be home in the next couple of days."

"Why?"

"Why? Don't you need me in Trejikistan?" She sat up, her brows furrowing.

"You are always wanted and needed, but everything is under control here. I do not know what you could add by returning. Father's funeral was today. The elections will take place soon and the monarchy will no longer be needed. If you want to stay in the United States, do so. I know it has always been your dream to lead a 'normal' life. Katya, this is your chance."

His words made her hands shake. "Are you sure?" Could it be that she would be free to lead her life just like anyone else? Free to choose where she could go?

Free of political functions and dull, formal meetings? Free to choose who she wanted to be with?

"Yes, Katya, my dear."

"What about you?" she asked. "What will you do?"

"I will be here until our people are comfortable with their new government. Then…?" He laughed. "Perhaps I will join you."

Katya laughed, too, her heartbeat erratic, joy, elation and hope playing havoc with her ability to think. "I have to go."

"I love you, sister."

"And I love you." She pressed the End button and held the phone to her chest to keep her heart from jumping out.

Pierce Thunder Horse appeared in the doorway. "Good news?"

"The best!" When he reached for the phone, she couldn't help but hug him. "Thank you."

"For what? The use of my phone?"

"Yes!" She hugged herself and closed her eyes, afraid she was still dreaming and she'd wake up. She had to find Maddox. Katya opened her eyes and tossed the sheet off.

"Whoa, what's this?"

"I have to get out of here."

"You can't go anywhere."

"Am I still considered a terrorist suspect?"

"No. Between the videos and Fulton's confession, you're off the hook."

She stood, holding the back of her hospital gown together. "Where are my clothes?"

"In the closet. But don't you think you should wait until the doctor releases you?"

"I can't wait." She ran for the closet, hauling her dirty clothes from the shelf.

Pierce captured her hands, clothes and all. "Could you wait at least until after one more visit?"

"I don't need another doctor to tell me what I already know. I'm fine. And I'll be even better when—"

"Not a doctor. A friend." Pierce turned her toward the door.

Maddox stood with a bouquet of deep red roses in his hand, a strangely shy expression on his face. "Katya." He stepped into the room, his gaze locked on hers.

"Maddox." Katya's breath lodged in her throat, her heart banging against her rib cage. She let Pierce take the clothes from her nerveless fingers and place them back on the shelf as she stood rooted to the floor.

"I see you two have a lot to talk about. I'll just leave you alone." Pierce pushed past Maddox and shut the door behind him.

When he didn't say anything, Katya cleared her throat and tried to tell herself not to get too excited. "What are you doing here? I thought you'd be on your way back to the ranch."

"No. I'm here to see you."

"The doctor did not find anything wrong. I can leave as soon as he signs my release papers."

Maddox took another step toward her, still holding the flowers. "That's what I wanted to talk to you about."

He was close enough for her to see the lines next to his eyes. Maddox looked tired and she wanted to reach out and stroke away the frown tugging his brows downward. "Did you want to talk about the doctor or my leaving?"

"Your leaving."

She swallowed, wondering how she could tell him she was not going back home without throwing herself in his arms and making a complete fool of herself. "About that…"

He closed the distance between them and pressed a finger to her lips. "No. Let me have my say, then you can throw me out if you want."

"But I don't—"

He pressed his finger over her lips again. "Just listen."

She nodded and his hand dropped to his side. "I'm not sure how things work in your country. I don't speak the language and I'm not familiar with your protocol, but I'm willing to learn."

"Why are—"

"Shh, let me finish." He paced the floor, still carrying the bouquet in his hands. "What I'm trying to tell you…no, asking you…ah, hell." He stopped in front of her and held out the roses. "I want to be your bodyguard, or whatever it takes to be close to you. Don't you see? I want to get to know you. How you became a princess, your favorite color, when you lost your first tooth. Everything."

Tears welled up in Katya's eyes. Of all things he could have said, she'd never expected this, and she couldn't force words past the lump in her throat.

Maddox reached out to her, apparently realizing that he still held the roses. "These are for you."

She took the bouquet and held it up to sniff the fragrant petals.

His hands free, he wrapped them around her waist and pulled her close. "Don't you see? Crazy as it seems, I think I'm falling in love with you. Not the princess, not the political figure that could skate circles around my knowledge of protocol, but the passionate woman I first came to know in the cave. The warrior so much like my ancestors who's smart enough to know when to clobber a criminal with a two-by-four." He laughed. "So what do you think? Do you need another bodyguard? Think I could cut it in Trejikistan? I'm willing to go wherever you go."

Katya smiled and cupped his chin with her empty hand. "Maddox, look at me." When she had his attention, she told him her good news, "I'm not leaving."

His eyes widened. "You're not?"

"No. My brother is alive and well in Trejikistan. He'll take over all royal responsibilities. I'm not needed back home."

Maddox closed his eyes, sucked in a deep breath and let it out slowly. When he opened his eyes, a grin spread across his face. "Thank God. I really stink at foreign languages."

"Now that I'm not in line for the throne, I don't think I'll be needing a bodyguard, either."

His grin disappeared. "No?"

"No."

"Would you consider going on a real date with me?"

"To get to know you? Although we have been together pretty much nonstop for the past couple days, I do not know a lot about you." She smiled, her world a brighter place because of Maddox Thunder Horse. "I would be delighted to go on a date with you…on one condition."

His grin returned. "Name it."

"Don't call me Princess."

"Deal."

His dark eyes blazed, and he stood tall, his carriage that of a proud Lakota warrior. Then he bent to kiss her, his lips brushing gently against hers. *"Wankatanka yuha yuwakape miye.* The Great Spirit has blessed me."

* * * * *

SPECIAL EXCERPT FROM

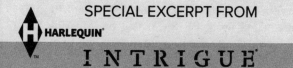

HARLEQUIN

INTRIGUE

Read on for a sneak peek at
BODYGUARD UNDER FIRE
by Harlequin Intrigue author **Elle James,**
available September 2013.

When P J Franks walks back into Chuck Bolton's life, he'll
do whatever it takes to keep her—and their baby girl—
from being the next victims in a line of attacks.

Chuck glanced at PJ standing with her back to him. "How was it?"

"What?"

"Your pregnancy, the delivery? I want to know."

"I did fine. I guess my body is built for bearing children. No health issues and a natural delivery."

He wanted to know more, but he clamped down on his tongue to keep from asking too many personal questions. "I would have been there...."

"I know you would have. If you could have."

"Why didn't you tell me?" He tipped Charlie into the crook of his arm and stared down into her little face.

"You weren't here. You wouldn't have been here even had you known." She stood for a long moment, unmoving. "Your focus needed to be on staying alive. What was the point in telling you?"

His anger stirred again. "The point is, I'm Charlie's father."

"And if there had been complications, what could you have done from Afghanistan?"

Chuck sighed. "Nothing."

A long silence stretched between them.

"I won't try to keep you from seeing Charlie," PJ said.

Chuck stared up at PJ. She'd lied by omission about Charlie. Would she lie about trying to keep him from seeing his daughter?

PJ glanced at him and sighed. Then she held her hand up, spoon and all. "I swear on my mother's grave I won't keep you from Charlie. There. Are you satisfied?"

Chuck liked the strong, determined woman she'd grown into in the year he'd been away, and found himself even more attracted to her than before. "Okay. I trust you." He might trust her about visitation with Charlie, but he wasn't as sure about where they stood, or if he trusted her with his heart. Was attraction enough?

Footsteps pounded on the staircase and then in the hallway outside PJ's apartment door.

PJ turned to Chuck. "Give me Charlie." She held out her hands for the baby.

Chuck handed her over and motioned for her to get behind him. "Go into the bedroom and close the door."

PJ did as she was told, her eyes wide, her face pale. As she closed the bedroom door, someone pounded on the door to the apartment.

"Help! Please, help!" a female voice called out, followed by loud sobs.

Chuck peered through the peephole and then yanked the door open.

The young woman from the resort front desk fell against his chest, her face streaked with tears. "Please help him."

Don't miss
BODYGUARD UNDER FIRE
by Elle James

Available September 2013 from Harlequin® Intrigue®.

WIN *Vegas*

A **TRIP** TO

& **TICKETS**
TO CHAMPIONSHIP
RODEO EVENTS!

Who can resist a cowboy? We sure can't!

You and a friend can win a 3-night,
4-day trip to Vegas to see some real
cowboys in action.

Visit
www.Harlequin.com/VegasSweepstakes
to enter!

See reverse for details.

Sweepstakes closes October 18, 2013.

HARLEQUIN®
INTRIGUE®

HE'S MUCH MORE THAN A COWBOY SPY....

Moses Mann didn't need to be in an interrogation room to be intimidating. Molly Rogers found that out the hard way. Her brother had been accused of smuggling and murder, and now Moses considered her a suspect, as well.

Moses was no ordinary agent poking around Texas border country. And he kept finding new reasons to bring his investigation to Molly's farm. Yet trusting him—especially around her son—came so easily. Even if he was an undercover agent with secrets buried deep in his soul....

MOST ELIGIBLE SPY

BY DANA MARTON

BOOK ONE IN THE HQ: TEXAS SERIES

Available August 20, only from Harlequin® Intrigue®.

HI69715R

HARLEQUIN®

INTRIGUE®

Edge-of-your-seat intrigue, fearless romance.

Use this coupon to
SAVE $1.00
on the purchase of
ANY
Harlequin Intrigue book!

Available wherever books are sold, including most
bookstores, supermarkets, drugstores and discount stores.

SAVE $1.00 ON THE PURCHASE OF **ANY**
HARLEQUIN® INTRIGUE® BOOK.

Coupon expires October 31, 2013. Redeemable at participating retail
outlets in the U.S. and Canada only. Limit one coupon per customer.

CANADIAN RETAILERS: Harlequin Enterprises Limited will pay the face
value of this coupon plus 10.25¢ if submitted by customer for this product
only. Any other use constitutes fraud. Coupon is nonassignable. Void if
taxed, prohibited or restricted by law. Consumer must pay any government taxes. Void if copied. Nielsen Clearing House ("NCH") customers
submit coupons and proof of sales to Harlequin Enterprises Limited,
P.O. Box 3000, Saint John, NB E2L 4L3, Canada. Non-NCH retailer—for
reimbursement submit coupons and proof of sales directly to Harlequin
Enterprises Limited, Retail Marketing Department, 225 Duncan Mill Rd.,
Don Mills, ON M3B 3K9, Canada.

52611009

U.S. RETAILERS:
Harlequin Enterprises Limited will
pay the face value of this coupon
plus 8¢ if submitted by customer
for this product only. Any other
use constitutes fraud. Coupon is
nonassignable. Void if taxed,
prohibited or restricted by law.
Consumer must pay any govern-
ment taxes. Void if copied. For reimbursement submit coupons and proof
of sales directly to Harlequin Enterprises Limited, P.O. Box 880478, El Paso,
TX 88588-0478, U.S.A. Cash value 1/100 cents.

5 65373 00076 2   (8100)0 11869

HICOUPWBLEJ